THE THREE SISTERS BAR AND HOTEL

Also by Katherine Govier

Novels

The Ghost Brush

Three Views of Crystal Water

Creation

The Truth Teller

Angel Walk

Hearts of Flame

Between Men

Going Through the Motions

Random Descent

Short Stories

The Immaculate Conception Photography Gallery

Before and After

Fables of Brunswick Avenue

Travel Anthologies, editor

Solo: Writers on Pilgrimage

Without a Guide: Contemporary Women's Travel Adventures

THE THREE SISTERS BAR AND HOTEL

A Novel

KATHERINE GOVIER

HARPER
AVENUE

For my dad,
George Wheeler Govier,
born in Nanton, Alberta, 1917

The Three Sisters Bar and Hotel

Published by HarperAvenue, an imprint of HarperCollins Publishers Ltd

First edition

HarperCollins Publishers Ltd
2 Bloor Street East, 20th Floor
Toronto, Ontario, Canada
M4W 1A8

www.harpercollins.ca

Library and Archives Canada Cataloguing in Publication
information is available upon request

ISBN 978-1-44343-664-9

Printed and bound in the United States of America
RRD 9 8 7 6 5 4 3 2 1

HEADING OUT

Gateway, June 1911

Isabel stood on the platform. The caboose disappeared around the curve; the mountains closed in. The tallyho driver had loaded their trunks and sat, reins poised. Maxwell handed her father up into the seat. Doctor Professor Charles Hodgson would go directly to the Sanatorium. Tomorrow they would depart by pack train for the backcountry; tonight he would take the waters, in preparation.

"Come along, dear."

"I won't ride with thee, Father," said Isabel. "I believe I'll walk through town and over the bridge."

He returned her gaze, pointedly. "You won't take the baths?"

Doctor Professor Hodgson was keen to indulge, claiming benefits to health: you could take the hot sulphur waters Turkish, Russian or tub style. There were trained nurses. There was also an apothecary attached where a Quaker like him could purchase whisky. For medicinal purposes.

"I am not ill, thank thee."

"It is your last chance for the whole summer. We won't be back this way." The professor turned to his man for support.

Maxwell stood blank-faced with his hands clasped behind his waist. Humphrey was halfway between his father and sister, indecisive.

"I want to stretch my legs, Father. Walk in the fresh air." Isabel was delicate but could be wilful.

"Well then, Maxwell, you'd better go with her. There are men here who can manage the bags."

Humphrey followed her lead, so it was brother and sister and Maxwell the butler who walked down Main Street from the station on a perfect blue-sky day in the Rocky Mountains. Their legs loosened. Their hair blew in the wind. The sun sparked like electricity. Before they had gone far they came to a strange-shaped building, log on the bottom and hip roof on the top, with a big veranda and a rail to which small, patient horses were hitched. The sign above read THE THREE SISTERS HOTEL. They climbed the steps and went in.

The lounge smelled of woodsmoke, whisky and tobacco; after the bright daylight, it was dark, the corduroy walls absorbing light into their chinks. Through the smoke Isabel could see great mounted animal heads, a bear rug by the fire and men seated at tables, their hats pushed back off their foreheads. Maxwell had become invisible except for his eyes and teeth.

Isabel scanned the room, trying to make out faces. A husky, white-haired woman with a lined face, wearing a cowboy hat and a buckskin jacket with beaded fringe, sat at the piano. Her voice was deep and rich, with a twang. Isabel wondered if she was married or if she had come here on her own, who she travelled with. Around her was an aura of independence, in fact orneriness. She was an entirely different creature to the women one met back east.

"You going out on a pack?"

Isabel nodded.

"What are you? A writer? A painter?"

"Oh no! I have no such talent," Isabel said.

"Buck up," said the woman at the piano. "Maybe you'll find one." She began to bang the keys. "*Won't you come home, Bill Bailey? Won't you come home? I cried the whole night long. I'll do the cooking, honey. I'll pay the rent—*"

She sang in a fine contralto. Between songs she spoke over her shoulder, loudly enough for Isabel to hear. The famous English writer Mr. Kipling was in the area. They'd passed him on the trail. He was horrified by the locals. Rough-and-tumble women, dreadful. No doubt he would write about them. He was brave enough on paper, she said, but not in the flesh. "Never got out of the buckboard!" she crowed.

Isabel took a few steps farther into the room. Her eyes roamed until she saw the guide. He was talking to a group of cowboys but was staring at her. She lifted her hand to her cheek: hot. Her father would say it was unbecoming.

The guide was Mr. Wishart. He pushed his way up to her end of the bar and set a glass of Seagram's in front of her.

"Get yourself outside of that." He had an accent—half English, half cowboy. "Would've come to meet the train but Maxwell told me not to."

She nodded. Humphrey waved for a drink too. Maxwell declined.

"All ready and accounted for?" said Mr. Wishart.

Maxwell nodded solemnly. "Doctor Professor Hodgson has gone to the baths. He's asking when we leave."

"We leave when the cook arrives, the food is loaded on the horses and the men are sober."

Isabel smiled into her glass, shyly.

"You know what your father wants?" said Mr. Wishart. "To go in around the Fist up above the chain of lakes to Magic."

Brother and sister both nodded.

"Like I said, I'm prepared to take you. But there's easier ways. Just warning you it's a tough ride in, and also—there's nothing up there," he said.

"Very good," said Maxwell. "We'll count on tomorrow?"

Mr. Wishart turned his back on them and continued with some story about a mountain sheep. Isabel lifted the glass to her lips and tipped it toward her. The fumes brought tears to her eyes.

"How do people drink this stuff, Maxwell?"

"I believe they find it rather pleasant, Miss Hodgson."

Isabel got the whisky down. Humphrey did too, a little more easily, and was about to order another, but Maxwell said they must go. The guide collared her just as they got to the door.

"Come in here to the Map Room and I'll show you the route."

As he steered her behind the bar, she heard a voice say, "You dog, Herbie. I wouldn't put it past you, not one bit. Right under her father's nose . . ."

He opened a door marked LOUNGE. The room was small and dark. He snapped on a desk light. A wooden table was covered with paper. There were wide, flat sheets of white with black hand-drawn lines, and there were folded pale blue sheets shaded with darker blue lines—rivers, she supposed. She stepped closer as he chose one and smoothed it with the flat of his palms. How could you tell a mountain from a valley? The slopes were defined by fine tiny lines, close together. There were white spaces that must have been the tops of mountains. Nothing in between. Just space on the map. There were small spines with cross threads—railroad tracks. What were those things marked in red? Trails, she supposed. There were no roads. Mr. Wishart fished expertly around in the pages, finding one he wanted.

"You see?" He pointed to a blue spot like a thumbprint. "You're going in above Magic Lake. And we're going to walk all around this way—" He showed her a route that took a huge loop to the south. It did look like a long way around, that was certain. "Now if you took the train to Laggan"—he ran his finger along the thin line with the hatchings—"it would be only a day's walk. You see?"

Isabel flushed again and stepped back. "It's no good showing me," she said. "I can't read them at all."

Humphrey leaned over and examined the map closely. The thin blue lines were like the veins on a leaf. He drew his finger along them. "See how they start in the shady bits and run toward each other? See how the blue lines that are composed of other blue lines drain to the valleys, and eastward?"

"I don't," said Isabel.

"I do," said Humphrey. "I understand."

Isabel could see Mr. Wishart clearly now. She had met him only once before, last summer. She had forgotten how singular he was, how alive. His skin was tanned by the sun; he had a wave in his black hair and a jutting chin with a dimple. His blue eyes were charged with energy and intelligence, and mischief. She could hardly turn away from them. He was examining her too.

"Are you glad to be back in the Rockies? Are you turning into a mountain girl?"

"I—"

He gave up on her and turned to her brother.

"Humphrey, if you're interested in maps, have a look at this. You see the early ones are just drawn freehand? And now the government prints them. You see where the boundary is? Gateway is right on the edge. Beyond us that's all park—empty, empty."

"I see, I see. I suppose it is immense. How do you ever find your way?"

"I know my way. I've got trails. Got 'em from the Indians. Map-makers get them from me. See those little lines in peacock-blue ink? Copied from our tracks," said Mr. Wishart.

"We should get along," Maxwell said from the doorway.

Turning around in the small room Isabel realized that it had a second purpose: there was a counter with books, and above it a shelf with a row of hats. All kinds of hats—this brim and that brim. The wide, the skinny, the stiff, the floppy. There was a mirror behind the counter. She glimpsed her face—sharp, white. She caught Mr. Wishart seeing her seeing her own face. Her colour rose again.

"You'd be surprised how often cowboys come in here to find out what they look like after a month on the trail. You see, they forget their own faces."

"They do?" She thought that must be the first step to madness.

"And that's why they drink."

"Is that true, Mr. Wishart?"

He laughed, high and gleeful. "You have to call me Herbie; that's a serious instruction. You know how on the trail there's got to be a boss? I'm the boss. And I say you've got to call me Herbie."

He stood directly in front of her. She lost her reflection in the mirror; he was in her way.

"You want one of these hats? This is the one the ladies wear." He pulled it off the shelf and held it in front of her. "Wide brim they can turn down, chin strap to keep it on." He placed it on her head. "You need one size smaller." He removed it and reached for another. She shook her head no. "You don't want it? But you will. I'll order you one."

She took a step backwards. It would be wrong to accept. Still. "Father will be waiting."

Outside, in the middle of the street, they said goodbye properly with a handshake.

"Be optimistic, show up at nine. We'll see how fast we can drag the packers out of bed. They'll be hungover as all hell."

Part One

Chapter 1
THE ANNOUNCEMENT

Gateway, June 30, 2011

THE MEETING TOOK PLACE over dinner at the Wolf Den. From the patio you could look across the river valley and see mountains shooting up to the south, west and north, while to the east the view stretched back down the valley, winding through the foothills and east to the prairies beyond. There were only a few nights in a Gateway summer when you could sit outside—the rest were too windy or too buggy—and this was one. The orange sun was going down into a puddle of oily water in the parking lot. Above it, a light, warm breeze twisted the poplar leaves so they flashed silver.

Walter and Iona sat under the canvas umbrella, dignified and natty, the tiny perfect elders. He was ninety-three, erect, with a full head of wavy white hair, and wore a blue blazer. Iona had never let herself go grey. She had brown hair and wore a red tailored jacket. The old couple had brought their three daughters, Lynn, Nancy and Ann, back from various points on the continent. Waiting for the drinks to arrive, they made small talk:

"How do you like the new location?"

"The Wolf Den has gone upmarket." Walter's critical eyes scanning, withholding judgment. The building's slanted roof was planted with wild grasses. The train tracks ran only a hundred feet away, with the new bike trail beside them.

The restaurant had been started in the seventies by hippies who had moved uninvited into the little mining town at the entrance to the mountain parks. A few episodes of streaking had outraged the population, but gradually there was a rapprochement: the hippies made good food. A few years ago the Wolf Den had moved off Main Street to this new place on the outskirts.

"I hear they even brought the phones."

Back in the day, and after being inspired by a James Bond movie, the owners had put funky telephones at each table—baby-blue plastic receivers with a push-button dial under the earphone. They were relics now, rather than novelties.

"Oh god, remember those? It used to be such a thrill. You'd sit down and it would ring, some guy across the room wanting to buy you a drink."

Nancy laughed, short and sharp. Gone were the days when strange men called her from across the room in bars. "I can't believe they work."

"I wouldn't recognize the place," said Iona, always a little behind.

"You could say that for the whole town."

"Imagine what Grandpa would say?" He'd seen tourists flock to Gateway, but he'd never have believed all this. Waiters from the Philippines and Australia; oysters from Prince Edward Island.

"He'd have broken out in his crazy hyena laugh."

Walter's martini arrived, and three glasses of wine—Iona didn't drink. The light remarks died out in favour of an expectant silence. Walter took a sip and sat smiling like the Cheshire cat with his hands folded in his lap. Then he said they probably wanted to know why he had asked them to come. He would make his announcement.

"Are you ready for it, girls?" Another sip.

"Yes, we are."

"Your mother and I have bought the old Three Sisters Hotel and put it in your names."

The "girls"—all women now, married, or had been, one with grown children—looked at each other, and back at their parents. The joke had fallen completely flat. Walter continued to smile. Maybe it was not a joke.

"You didn't!"

"Yes, we did."

"You did not."

Yes, they had. Nancy asked why. Why would they do that?

"You've got history here. It's one of the most beautiful places on earth. A paradise. You should have a foothold," said Walter.

"That hotel is not a foothold," said Ann. "It's a sinkhole."

"Is it so we can all be together for summers and Christmas? Because if so"—that was Lynn—"there are easier ways."

"Isn't it a little late for family togetherness?" Ann again.

Walter raised his hands. Was it too late? Maybe for him. But not for them. Perhaps he wanted them to try this family one more time. Wanted them to be close when he was gone. To remember their history. Or perhaps it was simply a gift. One he wanted to make them. Wasn't that all right?

He replaced his hands on the table, flat, side by side, fingers parted. The palms were thick and his engineer's iron ring was tight on his little finger. They were working hands but not as rough as his father's had been. That first Mariner, a miner in Nova Scotia whose name was Joe, had as a widower of thirty scraped enough money together to take the train west. They'd all heard the story. He had four kids. He bought two tickets and sent three of the kids to the bathroom when the conductor came through. When he looked out the train window and saw the ragged east edge of Rundle Mountain lining the valley, they all got off.

Joe Mariner chose the place for the coal in the ground. But there was so much more, a whole other life on the surface, beauty everywhere you looked, paths leading into the deep forests, game to hunt, fish to catch. He made himself a life in Gateway, becoming the mine's explosives expert, remarrying and having two more kids, the last of whom was Walter.

The miners—Welsh, Scots, Polish, Italian, Ukrainian and Finnish—moved up from boxcars to company-built houses. They had vegetable gardens and picked wild strawberries. They loaded the coal into boxcars and the trains took it away. Gateway coal, prized because it burned with very little smoke, creating no cloud to alert the enemy, fired the navy warships through the First World War. But in the twenties there was a strike and the mine closed.

Most families left but the Mariners held on, finding work where they could. With the next war the mine reopened. Walter joined up to fight and came home unscathed. After he went to university free of charge on the Canadian G.I. Bill, he got an offer to come home and manage the Gateway mine—which he accepted, maybe because Iona Wishart, a girl far too pretty to stay around, had come home too. Their girls were born and raised in the town. Walter Mariner was still in charge on Black Friday in 1979, when the company closed the mine for good and the miners made a bonfire of their work clothes. Shortly after, he sold the family home and his father's tiny, dilapidated "miner's house," and bought Iona the seafront cottage outside of Victoria she'd been asking for.

But Gateway wasn't finished. After being overlooked for decades as nothing more than an ugly mining town and the staging place for trips into the park, it was discovered. The valley was beautiful. The river braided under the three-peaked mountain to form creeks and a pond. The town had character: people loved the old railway station with its slanting eaves, the false-fronted Union Hall, the old log cabin that once did double duty as the Mounted Police station and jail. Most of it was intact. The English and the Germans and the eastern Canadians began to buy up property for second homes; the town grew ten times; golf courses were laid out, condos ran along the terraces above the river.

Where Joe Mariner's bungalow had stood rose a glassy duplex. Now on Main Street, two-storey restaurants with cathedral windows aimed into the peaks. But the old Three Sisters Hotel had never changed, hip-roofed, glowering, a fixture, its name in the original font propped up on a shingle on the edge of the roof.

"You've already done it, signed the deal?" Nancy confronted her dad, the organization man, the unsentimental man. The man who lived for progress.

"Yes. That is correct."

"Your grandfather always wished he'd had the money," said Iona.

Nancy sat back, astonished.

"Okay. And you do have the money. I see that. I understand." Lynn, the eldest, spoke carefully, as if to a child or a crazy person. "But—does that mean *we* should buy it? Isn't it—a little *irrational*?"

That was just about the worst thing you could call Walter. But he continued smiling, that Cheshire cat now sitting atop a brick wall, his tail hanging down in front and twitching slowly side to side.

The youngest daughter appealed to her mother. "Mom, what are we going to *do* with it?"

Iona just beamed. Only that day there had been an article with her picture in the *Gateway Trumpet*: daughter of pioneer guide returns to take ownership of the Three Sisters Hotel. This was turning out to be quite a lot of fun.

"I do worry that it's falling apart," she said.

"Well, so are we," said her husband.

Iona waved her hand: she could not agree with that. If she was, as others said out of her hearing, "failing"—an unfortunate word that one could only take as criticism—she was not going to admit it. "Fading" might have been better. Yes, there was fading going on. But it had nothing to do with her. The world was fading, but she was not letting up her watch for one minute.

"I think it will be an adventure for you girls," she said. "Your father is giving you a wonderful gift." In her gaze was a warning: *And you'd best be grateful.*

Because no one, least of all her, was going to stop him. Walter was not a man whose course was changed by others. When he was young his will was never questioned, not by his wife and certainly not by his children. He was bent on making a better life and he knew how to do it. When he grew older his will prevailed because by then he had succeeded and was reaping the rewards of his hard work. And now that he was truly old—even he had to admit there was no other word for ninety-three—he got his way because he *was* old.

Ann, the youngest, slapped the table with her hand. She was angry. So the Three Sisters Hotel—named for the triple-peaked mountain into whose flanks the mines had been drilled—was the gift that could not be refused? But why? Was it an old man's folly, not much more than a play on the name? He had three daughters, so why not give them the hotel? Was it overwhelming love or foolish vanity, a King Lear event? Might he have given them the mountain itself, if he could? Or was he trying to run their lives, as he always used to do? Did he think the three "girls" would just drop everything and move here to run it?

Lynn, the eldest, considered her parents warily. Might they need psychological help?

But Nancy was the middle sister, and as middle, she gauged the temperature of the table, took note of everyone's feelings and wasn't sure about her own.

She didn't hate the place the way her sisters did. Her childhood home was still her life's blood: the bold rush through the valley of wind, snow, the river, the highway and the train, its long vowels growing and ebbing. Gateway didn't have history, it was history—her father was right. That was not too grand a term. Characters of mythic status had walked these streets; pack trains had wound through the passes in living memory.

But the history was larger than the stories of runaway aristocrats, cowboys and miners, and lovelier. The valley was an open book. Indian teepees had stood on the Morley flats. Wild horses had run on Pigeon Mountain. Everywhere were the rocks, the mountains themselves, tossed up, turned inside out: time exposed in its vagaries. A foothold? Yes, she understood: to have a Gateway past was a gift, and they should keep it.

But her love for the town existed *in absentia*. She learned it by leaving. Wasn't that what you did with your hometown? The truth about this valley was that everything and everyone passed through: she, too, the whole family, had moved on. She had a sudden memory of holding her father's hand by the railway crossing as a silk train burst out of the trees and ripped through the town. It went from China to the Queen, in London, at great speed, and never stopped. She had believed it was to protect the silkworms, which were alive and spinning, until her father explained that the rush was all about the cost of insurance.

Ann was arguing with Walter. "*Dad*, for most people it was far from paradise. It was a hard place. If it had comforts, they were hard won."

"And all the more reason then you should not give it up."

How strange it was to hear her father say that now. It seemed to Nancy that he and his wife had held themselves above the town, aspired to be other, and elsewhere. Iona hated curling; she wanted theatre, dance and music. She did not wish to dress "as if she had just come in from a hike." She sent her daughters on the Greyhound bus to ballet lessons in Calgary; the girls left for university and did not come back. When the mine closed, husband and wife retired to the coast, gladly.

And now this. It wasn't the beauty, the park, she thought, that he wanted to tie them to. It was the legend of Gateway, the old story. That legend was complex, and it placed their family in a questionable light. Was Walter ready to embrace it, to repair it, to rewrite the story? Had anyone in the family fully escaped it while they lived here? She guessed that for all of them it had been a relief to leave. This whole gambit—the hotel, the gesture of purchase, the gathering of her father, her mother, her sisters, family down to toddlers—felt unlikely. It was not the kind of thing this family did. It made Nancy nervous. She was tempted to do what she'd done before: bolt. Go someplace where she was unknown. She tipped her wineglass up. The sun was disappearing and it was getting cool. Maybe this was not one of those rare evenings in Gateway when you could eat outside.

"Can it be stopped?" she wondered aloud, gesturing for the waiter to get them a table inside.

Everyone looked at her. No. Too late. It was done. The purchase made, the gift offered, not to be refused. They were talking practicalities: possession date, work permits from the town. Walter was in his element, assigning tasks, suggesting schedules. Iona was as alive as she had been in years, laughing like a young woman, squeezing her husband's hand.

The waiter found them a table inside, in the back looking west along the bike path toward Cascade Mountain. They collected their purses, got Iona up on her walker and paraded through the crowded restaurant, attracting attention. Nancy had just settled her mother in the chair and stowed her walker along the wall when the baby-blue telephone rang at their table.

Everyone laughed.

"You're kidding."

"Answer it."

"No!"

"Answer it or I will."

Nancy answered. "Hello?"

"Hello." The voice was hesitant. Polite. A man but not young. "I don't want to bother you."

"Good, then don't." She looked around. She spotted the caller, standing at the hostess station at the entrance, the blue receiver in his hand. In his other hand was a bicycle helmet.

"I'm sorry. Please accept my apologies. I don't want to disturb you. I was riding by. I couldn't help but see you and your family."

Obviously he wasn't trying to pick her up. She glared at him over the telephone receiver. She did not smile.

"You're Nancy Mariner," he said.

She had not asked him who he was. But he said, "I'm Kaz Otaka."

As if that should mean something to her. "Do I know you?"

"No, I suppose not." He was disappointed. "Here to take on your new acquisition? The Three Sisters Hotel? I read about it."

"Yes. Bit of a surprise. We're—absorbing it."

"Yeah," said Kaz. "Well, people are happy you're going to save it. When the last owner closed up, he expected no regrets from the town. But then there was this upsurge of affection for the place. It has to be preserved, that sort of thing. I guess you're the people to do it."

"I'm sorry. Our dinners are arriving." Nancy put down the phone.

"Who is that guy?" said Ann. "He seems to know you."

"No, he doesn't. He doesn't."

Kaz rode off. The dark couldn't come fast enough for him. He shouldn't have stopped, surprising them that way.

He had been riding back in from a circuit on the Legacy Trail. He liked to do that on a long June evening, looking at Cascade as he went west. It was a wonderful mountain. If this were Japan it would be worshipped, like Fuji-san. Its shape would be famous throughout the land. When the whole of it was sparkling with snow, people would bow to it and sigh. Vantage spots like this would be full of pilgrims. He had reached the foot of it and ridden back eastward with the mountains behind him when he saw, through the tall windows of the Wolf Den, the Mariner family standing around their window table, getting Iona into her seat, and he couldn't help himself.

He was surprising everyone tonight. The family. The bear. Both were beautiful to see, and both left him feeling bereft.

The trail had been full but not of worshippers—of people exercising.

It was a popular trail, but in his view not great. Too bad they had to put it so close to the highway, and right next to the train tracks. The ground was soggy and water from the creek flooded it. Here was a place where you lost elevation for no reason, where the trail swooped down and around before resuming its upward slant. Of course it was made for bikes, and that was different than a trail made for feet, for horses. Its purpose was to help riders maintain momentum.

At the hoodoos he stopped and pulled his Thermos of tea from his backpack, taking pleasure in the feel of the smooth stainless steel. He was fond of this Thermos. Plain and simple form and function. A reminder of home and homely rituals. He undid the cap, poured and sipped. There was one small irritant. Couldn't the makers of Thermos work out a way that he didn't have to feel the rubber rim against his lip?

He lowered the cap. He was just as bad as all the guys he complained about, wanting to upgrade the backcountry, no longer willing to sleep on bunks in dorm rooms, needing hot showers. Getting soft. Maybe he should have just stayed in and had tea at home.

But sunsets still fascinated him, each one changed from the week or even the day before by the sun's slow progress northward in the first half of the year. Now it was about time to move south. These crazed giant rocky heaps you thought you knew took the light at a different angle and became other, again and again.

Mountains: he was hooked on them. Like many in the valley, he made excuses to stay. Face it, there wasn't much work, maintaining trails or making new ones. If Parks had their way they'd close them all down. He could teach, maybe even write a book. Everyone here had a book under way, and if they didn't they had a cause. He could get a cause, he supposed. When he was sitting in the Bagel a girl he recognized came up and asked whether he would support the international cloth-diapering community, who were having a Change-in on Earth Day. Issues, whether they were diapers or water or bison or affordable housing, put him off. He told her he was thinking about moving over the mountains to someplace like Creston, where you could buy a bit of land. Here even the studio he rented, an old garage that he had insulated and heated, cost a fortune.

"You don't mean it," she said. "You'd never leave."

So he was a fixture.

At Lake Minnewanka he had taken the circle away from the highway. He'd intended to sit there a bit but millions of biting midges at the water's edge drove him out. He had started back cruising, quiet. He'd got about partway when he sensed movement at the corner of his vision. He knew what it was and slowed to a stop, so as not to surprise him.

The bear lay across the sleepers on the railroad track. His empty swag of a belly rested on the warm gravel bed underneath and his front legs were propped over one rail, while his back legs spilled over the other. He was that big.

The sun had exposed the raised track while snow still lay in the shades and hollows around it. Wheat and soybeans had dribbled there all winter and were now piled inches deep. Under that were the kernels of wheat with their dusty dryness and rich sun smell.

The big creature lifted his snout and waved it. Kaz knew what he was smelling—creosote and cedar, diesel and exhaust. But he could see the bear had picked up a human stink, his own. They were both still for a moment. Then the bear returned to his meal, running his snout expertly over and under the rusted steel rail, cleaning out the spill. Normally by this time the bears would have retreated upward, away from the tourists, but the snow had stayed late up high, and much of their food supply would still be out of reach, buried in snow piles. This fellow had taken a risk, coming up the berm. There were the trains. And just beyond, the highway.

It lay like an old wound, white as a car flashed along it. In an instant the car was gone, leaving its red tail lights as a goad. But the sound hung in the air: in the stillness Kaz heard it more clearly than he ever had. The big fellow must be wary of it. Yes, he was: he finished his meal and drew back into the darkness as one more vehicle rent the darkening air and, after a slight delay, left its tearing noise to ring up into the untried mountainside. When quiet returned, the bear emerged to move easily down the side of the mound. He stood on a fallen tree, his four feet all close together underneath him like an elephant on a circus ball.

It was too good to miss. Kaz shifted the backpack and pulled out his camera. He got the zoom on him and picked out the collar; it was the Boss. Known to Parks authorities. Been around for years. A beauty, a large male, golden brown grizzly with black legs. When the animal turned around 180 degrees, and then a full 360, Kaz got the hump in profile.

Now the bear had found something to eat. Kaz had no idea what—an animal carcass? His camera formed a shield. He moved in tiny shifts backwards, holding it with both hands, his bike propped at his hip, hoping he looked small and unthreatening. He prayed none of the cars going by on the highway would see the bear and pull off. The space between him and the bear widened until he stood in some last pool of light. He lowered his camera. But he was stuck. Even if he had wanted to ride through he couldn't; the animal was too close. The wind was blowing a little from the west, away from Kaz.

They stayed like that, the two of them. The bear seemed indifferent to the man.

Every year bears were hit on the train tracks, and on the highway. Usually it was cubs. But now and then it was a mature bear, a female who had led her cubs there to feed. Every year cyclists and hikers were attacked by bears they had surprised.

As Kaz stood, the trail was changed. The road and its ripping noise faded away. The bike path—not much more than an exercise track with a good view—became a human vanity, an illusion of human purpose in the world where huge animals bred and travelled.

The shovel face turned toward Kaz. He could see the bear's eyes. They were deep set, a little close together, fanned with thick hair, brown and recognizable: for a few ludicrous seconds Kaz thought this was a human in a fur suit. Those fairy tales of men confined inside beasts. But no, these were simply intelligent eyes, belonging to a fellow creature. The bear was looking quizzically at the camera. Kaz shifted it from his waist to his back. He felt a wash of embarrassment, even shame. The grizzly turned its ruffed head away, lifted his snout, leapt away from the fallen tree and the carcass, and in two stretches of his legs was gone into the bush.

But at that moment, a train entered the valley. It didn't hoot; it screamed. The sound echoed high up against the rocks. It must have confused the Boss because he turned and came back. He was rattled. He considered Kaz and considered the highway. Then he considered the open railroad track. He chose it, jumping onto the rail bed and walking on the rails, away from Kaz and toward the train, on the wooden sleepers between the tracks.

The train was moving fast. Coming straight at him.

The bear kept walking. His shit fell out behind him.

Kaz shouted. He pounded his bike and screamed. He roared and bounced his bike up and down. The Boss kept walking toward the train. But then he seemed to hear; he slowed, turned his head and jumped off the rails, gathered his feet underneath him and was gone into the trees.

Kaz waited a few minutes, and then mounted and rode on, his sweat cooling in the wind. At some point he had to stop. He leaned over his handle bars and wept from the shock of it.

It was after he had composed himself, remounted his bike and ridden into town that he came upon the family. Unwisely he had approached them. It had not been the right time. He was rebuffed.

Now he rode away, into that growing dark. His hands shook on the bike's grips. Was it the bear or the family? It was then he decided, couldn't help but decide, to ride by the old hotel just to see if they'd got in yet.

*

The old couple with their three daughters made their slow way back to the Ramada. Iona bent over her walker, pushing it with peculiar zeal. Walter walked alongside, straight and strong, telling her where the ramp was. Then he said he was going up to bed. "Come along, dear." They got themselves into the elevator and turned, facing out to their three daughters.

"We'll talk more in the morning," said Walter, he who had called the meeting now adjourning it.

Iona did not look tired. She opened her mouth and closed it. Nancy reached in and grabbed the handlebar of the walker. "Why don't you stay with us for a half an hour, Mum," she said. She drew Iona out, the doors closed and Walter was gone. "I think we should go over and take a look, don't you?"

"Oh yes," said Iona.

They loaded her walker in the trunk of Nancy's car, got her seated in the front and drove the half mile to Townside.

The centre of town was low and flat, an island, really, set inside the braided streams of the Bow River. Before the dam was built there had always been flooding. Nonetheless it boasted the old train station, the Mounties' cabin and Main Street, now lined with boutiques and bars. There were two stoplights along its length. By one of them, in darkness, a taxi lingered, its roof light orange: TWO BROTHERS TAXI. You had to smile: local wit. At the intersection of Main and Muskrat was the shingle on top of the veranda roof of the hulking old log building: THE THREE SISTERS HOTEL. They pulled up in front. The old building, painted the traditional forest green, slouched in darkness like a drawing, its outlines suggested feebly by the beige trim. A veranda ran along the front, with a long wooden bench facing the street. In the light of the street lamp, the sign was just legible: THIS BENCH IS FOR THE COMFORT OF OUR SENIORS. The hitching posts with the metal rings were still there.

"It's very well built," their father had said. He should know—he was an engineer. The structure was of stone, log and wood. It had been constructed by a renegade count who hoped its revenue would recoup his gambling debts. His French-ness accounted for its mansard roof, the squared hip of which allowed the count to squeeze in a top floor with garret windows. When he absconded early on, leaving an unsigned will and many claimants to his expended estate, the hotel was sold at auction to a local booster, Foxx. And sold again, several times. Now, again, a Sold sign was tacked up on the second floor. It was theirs.

"Can we get inside?"

"No, it'll be locked. We don't have the key yet."

"Nothing is locked in Gateway."

"It is now."

"I don't really remember this place," said Ann, standing in the empty street and staring up at it.

"Sure you do. Everyone loved it, although no one went there anymore because it was a dump."

"I barely remember Grandmama and Grandpapa."

"That's because you're so much younger."

Ann went around to the back and peered in the windows. Her resistance was leaving her. "So Dad bought it. That is *nuts*. Brilliant, though. I'm getting excited."

Nancy stayed in front with her mother; together they peered in the windows. The public rooms at ground level had housed a big noisy bar. It looked like the stone fireplace was still there. There had been a few stuffed chairs by the fire, and the rest of the room was filled with wooden tables and chairs for the drinkers. And there were certainly drinkers. The smell of whisky and smoke came back to her.

"Mum, did you send me here to bring Grandpa back for dinner?"

"Oh, likely." Iona gave up trying to see through the dark window. "I don't need to see the place," she said in a minute. "I remember. That bar opened when whisky was cheaper than water, as my dad used to say. It survived Prohibition and lasted through the Prescribed Alcohol stage, with neighbours lending a hand. All the pack trains used to set off from here. Off the bar was a small lounge with a big table and chest of narrow drawers where maps were stored. I used to do my homework there."

"That can't have been conducive."

"There was a big kitchen and a dining room with two long boarding-house-style tables. The middle floor had half a dozen regular-sized hotel rooms and the top floor with its sloped ceiling used to be a dormitory for the cowboys. Once a year they'd clear out the bunks from their dormitory and have the Packers' Ball. Everyone went. There was dancing all night to a big band, so the floor bounced and you thought it was going to give way. I never got to dance, though. I was too young."

"Not when you got older?"

"When cars replaced horses, the packers disappeared. Then construction crews that built the roads took over the dormitory."

Iona turned around in her walker and lowered herself onto the seat. "Your dad says I'm not to do this. It isn't safe." She smiled: the prohibition seemed to increase her enjoyment.

"There was always music. That's what kept it going. Oh, it was wild. Used to be fistfights broke out between the nationalities. During the war years."

"I remember in the seventies when the names of the bands were written on the blackboard. There was one called Brain Damage."

Lynn joined them. "There was Local Infraction. Remember them?"

"And the bikers! Remember the bikers in black leather? I'd always see them squint in the daylight as they emerged and headed for their Harleys."

"Always a line of Harleys in front."

They all laughed, suddenly, loud in the quiet.

"Yes, but what are we going to do with it? We're not going to run a bar, surely."

"Why not? My mother did!" Iona said. "You can renovate; you can each have a nice little unit for your family."

Ann called them from the Muskrat Street side. "Hey, look what I found."

There was a plaque, rusted and old. She had to brush off the dirt from the traffic that came too close: the hotel had been there much longer than the cars.

FROM HERE DEPARTED, IN JULY 1911, THE HODGSON
EXPEDITION, SEARCHING FOR FOSSIL EVIDENCE OF
THE ORIGINS OF TRUE COMPLEX ANIMALS.

They stood looking for a moment. Then Lynn spoke. "Let's get you home, Mum. Dad will be worrying."

Chapter 2
THE OUTFIT

Gateway, June 21, 1911

IN THE MORNING THE PACKHORSES were at the rail. Had they been there all night? The outfit consisted of Mr. Wishart, How Long the cook, half a dozen packers and a couple of cowboys called the Tree brothers, ten packponies and as many saddle horses. Wishart had one foot up against a pony's belly and the other stretched out behind him. He bounced like a dancer doing warm-ups. The pony snorted, and the air grew more and more azure.

"Dad-blasted sonofabitch—"

The animal retorted with a clatter of air in its nostrils.

"See what he does? Blows up his belly with air as I tighten the ropes. Then he blows it out and the cinch goes slack and the boxes slide the hell off sideways. It's his trick to defy me."

Isabel was feeling braver this morning. "You must be well acquainted. He has learned how to annoy you."

The packers circled the packhorses, lifting wooden boxes and canvas rolls. They all looked unshaven and red-eyed, except for the very tall one called Francis, who had a gentle smile for her and firm orders for the others. They stood one on either side of each pony and tossed the rope ends back and forth, pulling tight and letting loose by turns. It was like some kind of weaving. Herbie was everywhere, swearing, slapping horses' rumps, laughing his high peal of laughter.

"You know what they're tying? That's the famous diamond hitch. Learned it from the Mexicans," Herbie said. "They charged eight dollars. What a deal. We could never have opened up the Rockies without this knot. How much did the white folks pay for Manhattan? Same order of transaction."

He checked off the grub in his logbook, and then began cursing at the extra bags Maxwell produced. Two pair of snowshoes, four duffle bags and a Kodak No. 8 Cirkut panoramic camera in several rectangular leather cases, one of which contained many cartons of film.

"We thought glass plates would be too heavy," said the professor helpfully.

"That's a bloody relief."

Ready to go, the cowboys pulled their hats down on their foreheads. Maxwell wore a polka-dot bandana around his neck, red and white, and a Mountie's hat, like Wishart.

"You said I couldn't get one of those. How come he's got one?" Humphrey complained. His was a hunting homburg, rounded, with a feather, no protection for his very white skin.

"Won it off me in a poker game," said Wishart grimly.

Isabel's father had prescribed a set of rational clothes for her. These included her brother's scratchy wool pants, drawn in at the waist like a brown paper bag clutched in a fist, hanging loose over her hips and tucked up into tall laced boots; a flannel shirt, feminine with ruffles, at least; a trim jacket; and a bandana knotted at her neck. The bandana was a gift from Maxwell, who seemed to know what was what. But her hat was out of place.

"You're wearing that confection?" said Wishart.

"Is it so bad?"

"You were thinking more of a garden party than a trail ride when you bought it." It was pale peach with a very wide, flouncy brim with a few organdy petals sewn on.

"It will shade her from the sun; she does not want a leathery face," said Humphrey staunchly.

"Mr. Wishart said he will order me another one, more suitable," said Isabel. Then she giggled, almost confident, accepting today the offer she'd been wary of yesterday. "Which horse is mine?"

"Can you ride any better than you did last year?"

"No."

"Take that one."

"What's his name?"

"It's a she. Mousie."

"I don't want a Mousie!"

"Not heroic enough for you? Take him, then. He's Caruso."

Isabel put her left foot high in the stirrup. She hopped once, twice, and then, standing up light and loose, swung her right leg over the back of the pony, landing in the saddle with a thump. "Hello, Caruso. Do you sing?"

"No, he does not," said Herbie Wishart with a crooked smile. "But you are welcome to."

"I cannot," she protested, but he was already walking away. Then he turned his head and winked, and she saw that he was teasing her.

They didn't sing, not in her family; plain folk had no music in Meeting, or anywhere else. Isabel had hopes—here in the mountains women played piano in the bar and miners marched in a band; cowboys sang and packers played harmonica. There was even an opera house, which most people called the band house. The place was bursting with music. She wanted it to sink into her bones and the bones of her father and brother and their man too. Music, and with it a little joy. Let there be a reward for coming again to the Rockies this summer, so close upon the death of her mother.

Waiting for the horses to move, Isabel counted six crates with MUMM written all over the side and was astonished: all that champagne! She said to the cook, in her gently chiding Quaker tone, "How long before that is going to blow its corks and spill on the path?"

How Long laughed. "You start early, making jokes with my name. No, miss, that's only grub—whisky, eggs and a lotta bacon. We like Mumm's boxes. Very strong boxes."

"Oh, I see."

Now it was time. The boxes had been laced onto the packhorses, and with them her father's camera, the tripod and film, the tools, the tents. The packers were hatted and mounted in a doleful line. Mr. Wishart put one hand up over his head and flung it forward, shouting, *Go, boys!* People came out of their shops to wave. The walk down Main Street was showing off, a kind of parade. Yet there was secrecy in it too: all those closely tied bundles and the silent men, faces shaded under felt hats of varying slump. Bystanders might guess the length of the trip from the number of packhorses (ten? thirty!), but they didn't know where they were headed.

The kindly packer named Francis led; Isabel was near the back. She could see ahead past her father, rigid and tilting on his horse. He had aged this year. The first rush of energy to combat his grief had deserted him, leaving him determined but grey. She could see past Maxwell, taller than ever in the prize Mountie hat. Back down the column if she turned her head she could see Mr. Wishart, whom she must call Herbie, a man of winks, hoots of descant laughter and unpredictable temper. He gave slight nods to this or that merchant in the doorways of stores they passed—a man with a green eyeshade at the newspaper office, a baker in an apron. She felt important. This was the town's business; Gateway outfitted the hunters and artists, mountaineers and scientists who came from all over the world to journey up through wet valleys, climb icy slopes in nailed boots and variously discover the secrets of the wild. It was a solemn task, and Mr. Wishart, despite his guff, was the best.

Main Street was wide—as wide as Pennsylvania Avenue—and muddy. There were no sidewalks, and the road surface was used indiscriminately. Buggies moved both ways on either side, tallyhos ploughed along among hay racks, motorcars and riders on horseback; kids playing ball shot back and forth through it all. The street had been cut straight from the base of the big mountain they called Cascade to the bridge. Beyond the river it would meet the Sanatorium. A left turn would take you toward the fancy Hot Springs Hotel. A right turn would lead you around the bottom of Mount Menace and outward.

When they started across the bridge, the horses' hooves made hollow sounds; between the wooden planks were gaps through which one could see the foaming water of the Bow. It was alarming. But Isabel placed her trust in Caruso. He knew what to do, which was fortunate because she was afraid to instruct him.

She jolted from side to side. The movement created friction in a certain area, friction and heat. It was obvious from the backs of the riders ahead of her that most of them were steady and rode tall. Only her father and she and probably Humphrey, who was behind her, lurched in this unattractive way. Use your inner thighs, Mr. Wishart had instructed her last summer; you had to take some of the weight in your legs to steady yourself. She tried squeezing Caruso's bellows-like torso, but she didn't seem to have muscles in the right places. She hoped she could develop them.

This summer would allow much exploration, of her person as well as of the mountains. Isabel was at the brink of her adult life. She would be twenty-one years old in two months. She missed her mother but did not regret her death. She could not allow herself to. It was sudden and made no sense, a subtraction and a reaping, and it had the potential to deform Isabel's life. Despite their professed dedication to Equality and Emancipation, capital *E*s, the Quakers showed a definite leaning toward having a woman keep the house. She would not let the fact her mother was gone turn her into a stand-in housekeeper and hostess. No. Rather, she would make it an opportunity.

Mrs. Hilda Hodgson had dressed in the plain style of her youth, and only her husband's prominence in Washington society as the general administrator of the Fairburnian Institution had convinced her to adopt shiny fabrics, bustles and bows. Her speech was dotted with phrases from the Bible. She gave few commands but was impossible to disobey. She rarely admitted to being a mother, but instead held that she was the "friend" most concerned about her children. They were not instructed, there was no preaching; there was simply an endless *expectation* that everything they did and everything they saw would improve them, or, as her mother had been fond of saying, would *allow their inner light to shine forth*. Even heaven would have no pleasure, as her mother imagined it, was "for your own good."

Self-effacing, Mrs. Hodgson nonetheless dominated her husband, an achievement that made her difficult to love. She was the top of the family hierarchy, sitting above Maxwell and the professor. Three children lined up one behind the other to be greeted in the morning and touched on the head at night. As the eldest Isabel had responsibilities to instruct the two younger. But she was usually found wanting. She tended to rhapsodies and trills of excitement. But education, like life itself, must be a quiet, undistracted waiting for truth. Silence was more beautiful than words.

Mrs. Hilda Hodgson's death had been quiet, that was certain. There had been no music and no flowers: her wish. There was no ceremony: ceremonies were empty forms. Still, it had been an earthquake. An earthquake after which everyone grabbed hold of whatever pillar still stood and tried to keep it and themselves erect. Isabel's father had broken down and cried. This happened repeatedly over a week and ended without discussion. The next week he had adopted a quizzical look and wandered around looking for her, as if she were a lost umbrella. "The gods are against me," he said, his only blasphemy. He did not rage but carried on in that stuffy home as if walls were not buckling, roofs not collapsing.

Isabel had tried to put herself in her father's position. Robbed, as he would see himself, of the wife he was owed, confronted with the unwelcome realization that she, not he, had headed the family. It was his idea to come out to the Canadian Rockies again. Other Quaker families had taken to coming here when the railroad was opened. It suited them. The living was spare and there was science to be attended to; they worked hard at it. Art was frivolous, and they would not devote themselves to such a thing. But in the mountains, beauty involved industry. There were glaciers to measure and rock strata, tossed and bent and exposed, to analyze. And there were trilobites in the rocks, impressions of long-dead creatures with all their secrets.

Last year, when Mrs. Hodgson had been with them, they took the train straight to Laggan and stayed in the Railway Hotel beside the train tracks. The professor had relaxed, and his wife had slept well in the mountain air. The company at the hotel was suitable, even stimulating. Along with others, they rode on the trails among ancient crags and deep valleys whose vistas spoke of the epic battles of geological history. One day they had happened on some unusual imprints. They might have gone right past them if Maxwell hadn't noticed a scrawl that looked like a crab on a chunk of slate beside the trail. The next day they went back with horses and pickaxes. Hodgson had declared the fossils extraordinary, never before seen, having the potential to shake the foundations of scientific inquiry. It was not difficult to wrap and bring a few dozen slabs of slate home. In their Washington parlour, Isabel had spent a little time tracing the strange figures in the stone, and her drawings had been admired.

But her mother found the slate to be in the way, and very soon the professor put the rocks in the museum's basement storage, in their wrappings. At one point he had Maxwell go down to look at them. Maxwell unstacked the slate, and the two of them stood side by side gazing at the still-amazing images on the surface under the grey light. The fossilized creatures were fully preserved and, even in the twilight of the basement, like no creatures ever seen before. The portraits were complete, casts of three dimensions. All parts of their body were drawn in the stone. Not empty like other fossils their age, they were full: one could almost feel the pulse of life.

Right then and there the doctor resolved to study them further and write a paper. But it did not happen. He was a busy man with committees to run. And the resolve faded. Within a few months the stack of slate began to seem unapproachable, even excessive. He was getting old. Did he truly wish to have the bastions of his understanding of the beginnings of life rumbled? Perhaps it had just been the bright sun, or his age, or the unexpected happiness of being in the wild with his unusually acquiescent wife.

And then at Christmas, she died.

Everything changed. Each day going forward; each memory going back.

In January, Hodgson took Isabel down to the museum basement storage to see the fossils again. He ran his fingers over the imprinted figures. They were astonishing, complex creatures. Nowhere in the scientific literature had he seen mention of anything like this: not just the skeleton and shells preserved, but all the soft innards, the complete body of the creature, if creature you could call it. Each one so different from the others, as if there were a huge variety, life forms of untold types. And these specimens had been casually collected, from the trailside. There were more. He must revisit the site. He would bring his family to help him excavate; it would be a way of refocusing after the death. That is what he told Isabel, and later told his son and his butler, and so plans had been made and acted upon, and here they were.

One thing he had been particular about: he wanted to keep his find quiet. He did not want the scientific community to know about it, not until he'd come to his considered conclusions. He had a hunch, he had a glimpse: these creatures could change everything he knew. They were a gold mine, and they were his. It seemed his right, since he had found the fossils. And even more, he did not want the non-scientific community to know. Imagine the wreckage that ordinary unskilled people could make of this! It was in the interests of secrecy that the expedition set out from Gateway, avoiding Laggan and the Railway Hotel and the other scientists and Quakers.

Isabel liked the plan and believed that her father might discover something new, jolting himself and everyone else out of a doldrums that had entered their blood. It was her idea to contract the trail guide they'd met last year in Laggan. They'd gone on a short ride with him one day. They were all romantic figures, these mountain men: runaways from Europe, cultured, many of them; lost boys, educated and yet living hand to mouth, by brawn and instinct. "You give me his name and I'll have Maxwell write him," said her father. His name was Wishart.

A month later, snow fell on Washington—cause for great alarm and the closing of schools and government offices. She asked for her coat with the fur ruff and went out into it, tasting the damp whiteness, scuffing her feet. She came home to a letter from Mr. Wishart. He told her about hearing strange music out on his trapline, violins, out of the east. She hid the letter.

It was a winter of interesting post. Letters also arrived for Dr. and Mrs. Professor Hodgson. Her father read them aloud at the dinner table. The writer, Miss Dixon, was a fellow Quaker, a watercolourist from Philadelphia who had also stayed at the Railway Hotel. Miss Dixon inquired after Mrs. Hodgson's health. She wondered about the doctor's fossils. She asked for his commentaries on sketches she enclosed of alpine flowers—more beautiful than they had ever been in the meadows—sumptuous, rich, puffed shapes in figgy colours, defying the paper-thin desiccated samples Isabel had pressed into the pages of a book. Should they ever be in Philadelphia, Miss Dixon would love to show Doctor and Missus more of her paintings. In the new year, when news reached her of Mrs. Hodgson's death, another letter arrived addressed to the doctor and his family expressing sorrow and sympathy.

Isabel went off wildflowers: too much competition. She did add paint to her tracings of the fossils. The one with pincers she made orange, like a lobster. Then she fattened his tail and turned it into the "parson's nose" on a roast turkey. She put them in turquoise water. How cold the lakes were, and yet once they had been part of a warm sea. She walked down the Mall under skies tossed with cloud and waited for spring to arrive.

When it did, she and her brother were in Rome, dead mother or not. It was time for Humphrey's tour and it was not to be put off. They examined the male bodies painted by great masters and sat in cafés with their chaperone and cups of tea. Humphrey was so quiet he might as well not have been there. Climbing the Spanish Steps in Rome, she thought of *here* and *there*—here the centre, footsteps of citizens over millennia, the tired rites of Christianity, the muddy roots of government; there the ancient, eloquent, untrammelled, untravelled clarity of edges. Washington, her home, some upstart civilization between the two. She felt the sultry hot sun and dreamed of the gentle current in the—what had her father said?—500-million-year-old shallow sea.

In Westminster Abbey the tombs with their brass etchings seemed to her exactly like fossils. *Here lieth trilobites*: she imagined oval mollusks with mysterious teeth along their bottom edge, and beetles with long beautiful hairs curling out from their centre. Humphrey brooded, as he had done all along.

Maxwell met them in New York when their ship docked. He delivered them back to their father, who quizzed Humphrey for an hour and said, "Well, that did not have the desired effect."

"Whatever does thee mean?" Isabel was more inclined to defend her brother than her mother had been.

"Your brother's greatest object of interest is himself. And you are not so very different." He spoke not in a critical way but as if confirmed in his thoughts and even amused, as if it hardly mattered what his son or daughter was.

And you have not changed either, she thought.

*

When she saw Herbie Wishart again, she was jolted. He was a rough character. The hat he was never without, the plaid shirt and open vest, the water-stained and half-laced boots, the pipe clutched between his teeth and sticking out the side of his mouth. His writing was beautiful, that of an educated man; it had drawn her. But his person took her aback.

Certainly he was magnetic, a man whose sheer energy pulled all these men and horses into orbit around him. If the Hodgson family were among his followers it was a case of opposites attracting. Wishart spouted the joys of spring, while they looked wan under instructions to make the world better. Her family officially sanctioned emancipation, education and enfranchisement, and abolition. But was she free? Why not? She could not ask. Her younger sister, Gwen, might: she got away with that kind of question.

Poor Gwen had wanted so much to come. But Dr. Hodgson had decreed that the family would set off from Gateway, avoiding Laggan and the Railway Hotel, riding into their own camp, where they would harvest rocks for the entire summer. He wished to avoid a direct connection with the Railway Hotel and its guests. He would take only his adult children: he did not plan, as he put it, to be a nursemaid. To be a *father* might be another way to phrase that, Isabel thought. So Gwen was left behind at a Friend's farm in the company of other children and would join them at the end of August.

Kicking her heels into Caruso's sides, Isabel sent a silent blessing to her little sister, who would be making sandwiches for the farm lads while the rest of them were riding in paradise. Freedom beckoned. Gateway the town appeared to be far from improving—more the opposite, frankly, a stepping stone to heedlessness, indulgence and misbehaviour. This summer something was going to shine forth and it might not be her inner goodness, Isabel thought merrily. She had no real idea what it was.

Chapter 3
HERBIE

Gateway, May 21, 1911

HERBIE OFTEN THOUGHT BACK to the way it began. He was tempted to say it all began with Isabel. Everything began with Isabel. But it had not. It began not with Isabel. That was the way it ended. It began with the arrival of the gentleman's gentleman, Maxwell. From the start that was strange, in a town where not much was ordinary.

They got the hint something was going on when the black man got off the train at Gateway on a cold May morning. He was an elegant, powerfully built fellow with a light step and an air of importance. For a little town in a valley leading to the main pass through the Rockies, where the sun went down early behind the flanking mountains, it was an event. There were no black people. There had been Chinese railway labourers. And Japanese, although no one could tell the difference. They worked with dynamite. Naturals with it and fast runners, but the truth was that even if they hadn't been, it would have been their job because nobody wanted it. Those were mostly all gone except for a small encampment of Chinese working the tipple. Once in a while a rich American brought a black servant. But you didn't ever see a well-dressed fellow like that walking around on his own.

The conductor stalled with his hand in the air, and the men pulling the baggage dray stared.

Jiminy.

Got off at the wrong stop?

One of them movie people, I'magine.

The kids playing beside the track ran to follow the black man as he swung along the platform. His hat had a narrow fold in the top into which he slid his long forefinger when he adjusted its angle. He wore a long woollen topcoat the way men did in big cities on the East Coast, and polished leather shoes not made for snow and ice. The folks in the station kept an eye on him as he stepped down, waiting for the minute those leather soles hit the snow and he went tits up. But he stayed on his feet, though he held his left hand out flat from his hip like a man walking a tightrope. Then, more dignified and more resolute than any movie person, he consulted a pocket notebook and approached the office of the stationmaster.

What c'n I do for ye?

Gateway the town had seen a prime minister's wife riding on the cowcatcher of the train. It had seen the Prince of Wales disrobing on the platform, and tripping over his feet as he tried to get into Lyall Foxx's grizzly chaps. Lyall wore the chaps to make an impression, great golden furry things with two rows of loops to go around thigh and ankle, and claws at the bottom. The prince had fancied them. So Lyall stepped out one leg at a time. The prince tried to get them on himself. Crowds of people watching His Royal Highness putting his foot in the loop and nearly falling, and reaching under and around to fasten them in his crotch.

Not only that but Gateway had seen Anglican ministers preaching to the Indians from the caboose, and the odd morose Englishman setting out to drown himself in some frigid lake. They usually proved exceptionably durable, however, and got dragged back to life by one of the locals. It had seen the Swiss mountain guides arrive in their suit jackets and waistcoats and ties and knee pants and feather-brimmed alpine hats.

Still, the arrival of Maxwell was a moment.

Could you direct me to the nearest boarding house for gentlemen?

Hotel don't open for another month. The stationmaster gave the black man a long, slow stare and did not elaborate. Let him wait. The black man did so patiently, slowly letting the felt hat settle back onto his head.

There's Mrs. Workman two streets over. Other than that there's Dr. Smallwood and the Sanatorium. He didn't suggest the Hot Springs Hotel because they likely wouldn't let Maxwell in, or the Three Sisters because who knew what would happen to him when the miners got drunk. The Sanatorium, if you're feeling poorly. It was for invalids and alcoholics. He assessed the man: didn't think he was a dipsomaniac. It'll be Mrs. Workman you're after. Number 6 River Street. That way.

I thank you most kindly, sir.

Maxwell turned smartly in half a circle and strode the length of the station in the blaze of sunlight that had just made it over Miners' Wall. He got to where the wooden sidewalk ended and took a big step onto the packed snow. Whoops. He skidded about three feet and the arm that wasn't carrying the smart duffle flew up. It was the moment they'd all been waiting for, but no, the gentleman—you had to call him that—managed to get his balance, sledding on his shoes, turning back to acknowledge that all eyes were on him and lifting the finger to tip his hat again. Then he headed toward Mrs. Workman's house with a reined-in step.

Number 6 River Street was a log cabin near—guess what? Its owner was not anticipating a guest, and especially not one of Maxwell's complexion. The widow covered up her shock with some officious searching for a book and a key and then marched him up to the front room on the second floor. At the door to the room she told him she and her late husband had homesteaded at the foot of Cascade Mountain. She would save the part about how he died for later. There were five children. The gentleman emerged five minutes later looking even cleaner and smarter than previously, if that were possible, and asked if she could direct him to the establishment of Mr. Herbie Wishart.

I shoulda known it was him you'd be wanting, she said, or something like that. Four doors down, last of the log cabins on the riverbank. Corral full of ponies beside it. You'll hear the noise. What size are your feet?

The boots were not up to Maxwell's standard, but he was glad of them, at least he said so. He set off not looking up at the peaks with their load of snow flashing in the sunlight but looking down, concentrating on staying upright over varied surfaces from deep sticky snow to mud to streams of water over evil black ice.

His landlady watched his back. He's got to be an advance man, said Mrs. Workman to the neighbour going by looking for the cows.

Maxwell did hear the noise—men cursing, also the wail of a phonograph. He recognized the music. He approached the door and listened until a break in the racket allowed his knock to be heard.

Mr. Wishart!

It had been a shock, and Herbie admitted over the years he hadn't handled it perfectly. He was drunk: what are you going to do? It wasn't even spring, and the man caught him by surprise. He yelled through the shut door.

Was a man by that name lived here but he's gone clear out of his head with drink. Come back next week—better yet, come back next month!

But then one of the players decided to exit. The cowboy opened the door and staggered out, leaving it ajar. Don't go in unless you're ready to lose all, he said to the stranger.

And this spiffy-looking negro fellow stepped over the threshold.

Mr. Wishart?

You're looking at him.

Wishart was laughing, having won. He pushed back his tree stump. Two other men with several days' growth of beard remained around the table with cards scattered on it. He was suddenly conscious that the place reeked of whisky and piss.

We've had an exchange of letters. I represent Doctor Professor Hodgson of the Fairburnian.

Wishart squinted into the sunlight coming through the open door. It occurred to him that he'd seen Maxwell the summer before. With the American family up at the Railway Hotel at Laggan. He'd guided them a day and had noticed the handsome young lady and her strict mother. Kind of a stiff crowd, he recalled. But for the girl, he wouldn't have cared if he saw them again.

Maybe he wanted to put the fellow in his place.

Looks like we need a fourth. Will you join us?

Maxwell stood there, hat in hand. He gestured to the Victrola. Now I recognize it, he said. Chaliapin singing Godunov.

Wishart took that for a yes and pointed at the overturned chair. Someone threw another log on the fire. Maxwell removed his coat but saw nowhere to hang it. He laid it carefully across the sofa. Then he asked politely if they'd take American funds.

He had good luck with the cards, turning up high hand after high hand. This went on for a few hours, and his card-playing friends were showing signs of disgust.

Who did you say you were?

Maxwell. Gentleman to Hodgson of the Fairburnian.

Jesus H. Christ, how had this bugger snuck up on him while he was having a game? Hodgson was Herbie's big customer. They'd signed a letter and he'd taken his money. Not interested in hunting. Liked to look at rocks, he said, take pictures, do a little painting. This year he was coming with his family for a whole summer's camp.

But it was far too early.

You're not Hodgson, he said stupidly.

Not at all, said Maxwell. I am the gentleman's gentleman.

Come again? It was an expression he'd heard but not for a long time.

I am in charge of his household and of his journeys, said the man. With your cooperation I would like to begin making plans for our expedition.

Herbie sent the man back to his boarding house and said he'd come along shortly. He boiled water to shave and drank coffee and washed and shook his head from side to side to clear it. He felt vaguely one-upped. Wait until he got him out on the trail; this Maxwell would see who was in charge.

But nothing fazed Maxwell. They were walking down the street the next day and a woman wearing a blanket over her dress accosted him. Thief! Those boots belonged to Henry Workman. He was wearing them when he was crushed by that buffalo.

Mrs. Workman hadn't mentioned the manner of her husband's demise when she loaned him the boots, Maxwell murmured. The widow's children followed him across to the Vienna Café, past the station, where most days he stopped in to send a telegram, and down to the trading post, where he bought his own boots. Once he got them he set out on trails twenty miles long and returned looking fresh as a daisy.

If he's the gentleman's gentleman, I can't wait to see the gentleman himself, is all Wishart had to say as he counted out more dollars lost to Maxwell in poker.

It had been a wait of about a month.

At first glimpse that morning, the Doctor Professor, as everyone addressed him, seemed older. He was pale and stooped. A man at the height of his career, a scientist who met with presidents and opera singers, said to be dedicated and strategic. But stuffy. Herbie didn't take to him any more than he had to his man. The feeling must have been mutual. Hodgson looked offended by the guide's mud-splattered cowboy boots and the grease on the vest he never took off. Maybe it was unspecific: maybe he always looked offended. Or the cloud of pipe tobacco bothered his nose. Wishart offered his hand.

"Sorry about the smoke, but it keeps the flies off. You may want to take it up yourself."

"Oh no, oh no, I shan't—delicate lungs, you see."

Behind him was the tall silent son, wearing boots to the knee and that hunting homburg he'd glimpsed the night before, with a large black brush on the side that made him look like Kaiser Wilhelm II. His name was Humphrey.

And behind *him* was Isabel. In full daylight, she appeared to him in a pop, the way a flame jumped up in his pipe bowl when he sucked on the stem. He remembered her as he had first seen her, the coltish eagerness as she peered over the shoulder of the men in front of her, the deep-set blue eyes, and that crazy tongue in her head, *thee*ing and *thou*ing as if she were in church. Just that one day he'd spent with the family, the summer before. Months later, he'd written the letter, confiding a secret he kept from most people: that he had heard violins at Sawback Ridge. He wasn't really sure why he did. Call it loneliness. He spent weeks out on the trapline in winter. While he was snowshoeing, he wrote letters in his head, the words coming out fluidly with the rhythm of his loping. Letters to heads of companies inviting them to tour with him, letters to Parks men telling them they knew squat about the place and what they should do with it. Letters to the girl he'd left at the docks in England. And a letter to this one, who was a greenhorn and a poor rider. He got quite prosy describing the wonders of his world, which she would never know.

Once he stopped moving, the letters usually went out of his head entirely. He never mailed them; he never even wrote them down. But this time he must have needed to tell one living soul about the symphony of great violins soaring across the star-decked sky. Or maybe he sensed that Isabel was one who would listen to him and believe. He was canny like that, with people and animals. Even after he got back to his little trapper's cabin made of logs cut with his axe, fusty and rank inside, piled up with horns and skins and traps of various sizes, and started a fire and sat back to replace the netting on his snowshoe with a lace of goat skin, the letter was still in his head. It was still in his head when he got back to Gateway two weeks later. He sat down with paper and pen, wrote it and put it in the mail.

Why? Maybe just to show that the mountain man she'd met smelling of horse and tobacco had sensibilities. In later years, when he returned to that act in his mind, he could see the devilish hand of fate moving his pen. But even that would have been fine if he'd just kept the piece of paper in the personal file in the bottom of his trunk. But no. He got the envelope and the stamp and took the walk to the post office, bewitched and beguiled as he was, though he never would have admitted to it. He should have left it alone, but he didn't. In that small act of posting the letter he encircled Isabel, and whipped up the whole cruel symphony of events that was to come.

Chapter 4
THE RIDE IN

The Passes, June 22, 1911

As THE PACK TRAIN CAME OFF the bridge, Isabel looked back at the river. It would wind eastward through the foothills, race over prairies and eventually join the Mississippi. So said Herbie Wishart, and she'd seen the proof of it on his maps. Turning to the west she could see up the side of Mount Menace. The trail would have them wrapping around its base. They passed a last trading post, its veranda crowded with a rampant stuffed bear and a rack of beaded buckskin jackets, fringed. The general merchant gave a last wave and went inside, shutting the door behind him.

Then they were riding in sunshine on a narrow track out to the southwest toward Whiteman's Gap. She was slightly breathless. It was the jostle of the horse, which she tried to lessen with her own body. Riding was work. You couldn't just sit there. Or maybe it was fear. Now the horses had begun to pull upward on a slight incline, and the cooler air blew at her open throat. No, she would not admit to fear. As their pace picked up, her hat brim fluttered; she risked letting go of the reins and looping them over the saddle horn while she tied the ribbons under her chin.

Mid-June was barely spring out here. The track grew wetter. In the muddy bits the horses' hooves sucked and made holes. They went around the worst bumps, but it was not possible to soften the ride: the track was full of potholes, and the loads swayed from side to side. The flies were terrible. Only Maxwell did not swat. He let the flies settle on his temples and around his neck. He let them bite. When they flew off they left a thick circle of blood like the wax seal on a letter.

"You're covered with flies. Brush them away!"

"With respect, I've eaten my fill. Now let them eat theirs."

Charles Hodgson tried to resist swatting his own flies but was unable to, which made his children smirk.

The rock faces they passed glittered with snow melt. It was a sharp, clear, open-sky day made for leaving dust and town and home and rules behind. Isabel expelled everything stale and constricted and drew the sweet air right down into her lungs.

It was a long ride through the Gap. Once they reached the other side they started rounding the base of the endlessly long and lopsided pyramid of Mount Menace. At lunch they dismounted gingerly and hobbled around camp for half an hour before they all remounted and rode on. This time Isabel was near the front of the pony train. At three in the afternoon they came to a rubble field, where it seemed half the mountainside had collapsed. They moved through it slowly, the ponies picking their way with clever feet. Mr. Wishart walked beside her, leading his horse. Finally they came out the other side of the rock slide and went briefly into trees. A few hundred yards of soft trail took them to a steep pitch called the Staircase. At the top of this was a notch they would pass through, and on the other side they would be at the beginning of a long ridge, he said. But first, the climb.

"You're a slave-driver, Herbie Wishart," Isabel complained, as the guide caught Caruso's reins and pulled him into line with the others, tying them tail to reins so they made one long string.

"That's my job. Put your jacket on or you'll be sorry."

"But it's so beautifully warm!"

He pointed to the cold threads of snow that had appeared in the breeze.

The Staircase was narrow and as steep as a ladder, ending at a piece of sky. Isabel watched the riders ahead of her. As each horse took the last step to the top, the wind struck it, shooting its mane horizontal. Each rider appeared electrified, hair and hat strings and fringe flying. She got the message and, as Caruso trudged upward, pulled a scarf out of her saddlebag and attempted to tie it over her hat. Too late. Within steps of the top the wind hit. It was shockingly cold, taking the breath from her throat and freezing it before she could shut her mouth. The garden party hat levitated for one exquisite second, and then was ripped off and flung back through the pony train. She shouted and reached with her hand, as if she might grasp it or signal to one of the men to catch it, but then thought better of that and turned the gesture into a wave goodbye.

Like some deluded, feminized bird of prey, the gauzy peach hat whipped over the trees and then low over the rock slide they'd just crossed. Then it rose and flew off.

Waiting on the ridge ahead, Herbie Wishart did not manage to suppress his smile. "The girl doesn't think I'm going back to get the damn thing, does she?" he said to Francis Erwin, safe that in the gale no other ears could hear him.

"We've got a way to go before dinner." But he looked as if he might consider it.

"No, no, don't go back," shouted Isabel. "We must go on." She clung to the saddle horn, her face white and streaked with water—not tears, she insisted, hearing him. She had finally managed to tie the scarf over her head and the jacket was closed, but she looked frozen.

They rode along the ridge unable to speak further, all uncovered bits of skin being pitted and burned from the hail. Off to the right was a string of lakes, barely visible through the chain mail of stinging drops. Isabel opened her mouth and shut it hastily when bits of ice flew in. Caruso was flagging. Wishart gave him a slap, and his step picked up.

They persevered, fully exposed on the ridge, and then in an instant the hail was gone. But the wind still blew, striking at them as if with a blanket, *whomp*, *whomp*, in rhythmic strokes. It served the purpose, however; within twenty minutes the sky had become a bright benevolent blue, a true smirk, as if it had never delivered those bullets. The wind stopped, and at the back of the train some cowboy was singing. Isabel, bedraggled and joyous, smiled her bravest smile.

They climbed until late in the afternoon, when they came to another field of rubble, another rock slide. They traversed it slowly. The sun was at its height and, like a sound itself, ricocheting around the walls. They faced a moonscape of dry rock. Far below was a chain of small, chalky blue lakes, each apparently about the size of a teacup, known as the Magic Lakes. They worked their way above it, nimble cayuses on a narrow rim of rock. The sun went behind clouds and the air grew cold: they passed mounds of snow.

When they reached a spot of brief respite, Wishart rode back to see how the Hodgsons were faring. "Told you this was the long way around."

But the professor was radiant. "We're being stripped of our essentials," he said.

Maxwell rode at the back in his shirtsleeves, untroubled. He looked as if the worst of the weather had taken a curve around him, and hummed hymns under his breath. Wishart himself never wore much of a jacket; he was warm-blooded, always too hot. But he hadn't met a dude that way before.

"How long 'til we get there?" said Humphrey.

The cook shook his fist. "Now you too," said How Long. "And your sister! Everybody make same joke of my name." He pointed. The Fist had appeared ahead. "We stop when we get there."

They entered the first pass. Fat marmots covered in their winter fur, a village of them, sat camouflaged in the doorways of their tunnels. Their whistles echoed from the rock walls. The Magic Lakes at the far end had grown from a series of soup bowls to the size of three washbasins. They were making progress. But at the height of the pass the snow was three feet deep: the horses couldn't walk through it.

Herbie stood contemplating. Damnation! He resisted the urge to tell Hodgson and Maxwell that he had known it was too early to set out, and why go the long way when they all could just have taken the train to Laggan and gone in from there? Why had he let these eggheads tell him how to do his business?

"Shovels?" said one of the cowboys.

"Yup. And an axe."

The cowboys grumbled as they unpacked. Maxwell watched for a minute and then got possession of one of the shovels and set to work. Snow flew away from him in all directions. Wishart got the axe and chopped the thick layer of bark off the oldest fir tree he could see. He ended up with two elongated rectangles, slightly concave. He instructed Maxwell and Humphrey to untie the crates from the ponies' backs. Using the same ropes, he lashed the crates to the dugout. When the time came he'd have the horses pull them, like a sledge.

"Easier to walk through the packed layer of remaining snow and pull a load than to bear it on your back," he explained to Isabel.

She was touched by his concern for the horses and said so.

"My bread and butter," he muttered.

Isabel found a sunny rock and sat on it; Dr. Hodgson poked around at the strata and squinted into his binoculars. How Long made coffee and distributed cookies—they were dry, and the trip hadn't even begun. In a couple of hours the snow was cleared and packed enough to allow them passage. Hodgson and Maxwell went first on their snowshoes.

Wishart led the ponies, whose feet sank only a foot or two. After that they pulled the crates through on the dugouts. Isabel and Humphrey came last, easily walking in the trail that had been made.

"That was Beguiling Pass," said Herbie, looking back as the cowboys began to retie the diamond hitches. "Let's keep moving."

The first Magic Lake, when they reached it, was rock-bound and solid turquoise, with its own small iceberg floating in the middle. They walked to the edge and got down to let the horses drink. They all found rocks that fit their length and stretched out, absorbing the warmth. They wanted tea, but Wishart said they had to push on. And so they did, until they reached the last lake in the chain.

"There'll be fish in there," Maxwell said.

"No, no fish. That's just a landlocked pond of melted snow."

"Oh, I think there's fish," said Maxwell easily. "Shall I catch some? We'll be too high after this." He found himself a spruce limb, asked How Long for a string and some bacon, and borrowed a bullet from Herbie's revolver. He set off with the pole and a couple of rough hooks. When he returned there were three handsome trout slung from his bow. How Long gave a shout of perturbation.

"There's no fish in that lake," How Long said, shaking his head and looking sideways at Maxwell. "*Doan* trust that man," he muttered as he got out his knife to clean the trout.

They ate. It was seven o'clock at night. There were hours of sunlight left, so they pushed on. The trail wound nearer to the base of the jutting sheaves of rock. This close they did not look so monolithic. There were ways up; there had been traffic here—mountaineers, hunters, Indians maybe. They passed between two tall, thin rocks. These were part of the approach to the Fist, and were known as the Pallbearers.

"Who named them?" said Humphrey. He showed the strain of the long day, his cheeks squared and pinched like a washer on a screw.

"Likely the survey fellows when they had to bury their friends." It was not a good a joke, judging by Humphrey's face, which tightened by half a rotation.

Beyond the Pallbearers the trail came out on a flat balcony below a twenty-foot, near-vertical wall. From there it narrowed and cut around behind the wall through a dense cluster of stunted trees. Wishart whistled. He went to take a close look at the wall. It was threaded over with juniper roots and stumps; niches and crannies made it look less sheer from close up. He didn't recall this. Or he did recall it, but not that it was quite so difficult. Again, he wished he'd not let these dudes choose the hard way. Everyone waited for him to speak.

"Well, I figure we can get the people up this way using ropes, if you're prepared to climb."

They were all prepared.

"We can take the horses up there?" said Maxwell, pointing to a narrow section at the side where the larger trees began.

"Dubious."

"We've got ropes; we'll pull them," said Maxwell.

Wishart had been guiding nearly a decade. He considered himself experienced. But he'd never lifted horses with ropes. He didn't know why he said yes: Maxwell was persuasive, that was it. Or maybe he was showing off for the girl.

They got Isabel and her father up; that was the easy part. But it took all the cowboys—a human chain gang including Humphrey, who was curiously animated by the task—to push and pull the belly-wrapped ponies, legs scrabbling, up the side wall. One of them fell and landed on his back at the foot; very luckily he wasn't hurt. It was ten o'clock by the time they hoisted the last pony over the edge and the last couple of packers clawed their way up the wall. Wishart pulled off his hat and slapped the mosquitoes away from his temples.

The long June day was nearing its end and the dark was finally coming down. They were partway up the Fist, at the flat, horizontal piece that from far away looked like the folded thumb. The trail from here led around to the back of the hand, where the slope was less steep; another half a day would get them down and over to Mystic Lake. They pitched their tents and made camp for the night. They were crowded and cold, but How Long's fire was bright. The professor emptied his carpet bag, put on all the clothes he had brought and retired immediately.

Isabel sat close to the flame, shivering from cold and from the thrill of it, her hands clasped around the tin cup of tea and whisky. She looked back east, wondering if their fire could be seen from Gateway. Humphrey was silent with relief at being off his horse. Wishart sat with them, his face burnished by the firelight. This was the moment when, on every trip, he told stories.

"Tell me how you came here, Mr. Wishart."

"Oh, Herbie's gonna tell you. Don't you worry about that. No escaping from it," muttered How Long.

"How I came here? By a sheer stroke of the best fortune that ever waylaid a man," he said.

Chapter 5
HERBIE REMEMBERS

At the Fist, June 22, 1911

He couldn't believe his luck. Looked at all those trees and big old rocks and pinnacles and saw scope for a man of his abilities. He'd been living with his uncle back in the old country, and he got into mischief. The family was of substance, occupied the first few rows in the church. He was the black sheep. Used to go truant from school, get off into the woods on the Marquis's estate and trap partridge. Snare rabbits. They told him to keep out, but he guessed the fish and wildlife needed sharpening up.

Uncle and his wife tried what they could, but Herbie was running wild. Uncle threatened to send him to Australia. No sir, that's where you send the criminals! They ain't caught me yet. If you got to send me anywhere, I'll take Canada. They bought him a ticket. He was eighteen, had a girl who was sweet on him who came to the boat to see him off. I'll come back in six months, said Herbie. Well, he'd not been back in nearly a dozen years.

He got on the train in Montreal, got off in Winnipeg. Stayed in boarding houses and spent his money on drink. Hadn't a care, do you see? When he got short, he went down Main Street to pawn his watch and chain. At the station there was a cattle train. The conductor said, Kid, do you want to go west? He got into the caboose. At Calgary he got out and had a walk around. He could see mountains farther on, so he got into the caboose again. At Siding 29 someone shook him awake. It was a new conductor. Where you going?

Not much farther, is what I'm guessing, said Herbie, now that you're onto me.

He gave Isabel a wink. Charm, that's what they call it over in England. Gift of the gab. Had done him proud these long years. She blushed.

Kid, that's about it! the conductor said and tossed him out the door.

Herbie stumbled out at midnight onto the station platform and looked around, and by the light of a gargantuan silver moon saw the Siamese-triplet mountain they called the Three Sisters. Nuns, that is, not regular girls. Jesus, those nuns. He should have known it for a sign.

A sign of what?

Sign of the women who were going to trouble my days from then on until forever, he said, winking again, more broadly this time.

The mountains were darker than the blue dark, their three peaks with white veils draped overtop gleaming under the moon. He walked a little way looking for a place to sleep and came upon a hotel with a hipped roof and a veranda. He had no money, so he went around the back and opened the door of a storage shed. There, he was startled to see a corpse lying on a buffalo robe. The dead man had a thick head of hair twinkling with hoarfrost and a few layers of plaid clothes and feet that stank so much his boots had taken themselves off and were standing by the door on their own, tongues hanging out, whining.

No, it was a couple of dogs whining. Herbie couldn't see in the dark, so he lit a match. The face was brown from sun and blue from the cold. He leaned closer with his match to see. The corpse sat straight up with his eyes closed, pulling up the rifle that lay by his side, and with perfect aim pointed it right at Herbie's third eye.

No offence, said Herbie.

The corpse opened his eyes. They were the same as his face, blue and brown, one of each.

Shut the damn door, it's damn cold outside, the dead man yelled. Then he folded himself back down with the rifle glued to his side, hoisted the blanket over his shoulder and rolled over.

Herbie backed out of there expecting a shot to his chin. On the back steps of the hotel was a Chinese cook rocking back on his heels and slapping his belly in amusement.

That was me, said How Long.

Didn't know you were listening!

How can I help it? Anyhow, I need to keep you honest.

Don't call me on it when I start to lie, said Herbie, getting up to stretch his legs and refill his pipe.

I said, said How Long, You drop in visit Sam Gallant? You brave man. He sleeping.

And *I* said, said Herbie, Whoever he is, he's not much of a man for sharing.

He's Sam Gallant. The mountain man. Outfitter. Takes tourists out in the wild. Finds the passes through the mountains. They'd all be dead, the soldiers, the surveyors, if not for him.

But Herbie was tired. Where can I doss down for the night?

Try ice-house?

You got some terrific sense of humour.

Take room in hotel?

You can see I'm lacking funds, Mr.—

How Long, name of.

Very pleased to make your acquaintance, Mr. How Long. I sense there's a story there, but first and foremost I am in need of a bed. Herbie could speak that way, educated, and it never failed to surprise him how it worked for him, out here.

How Long let him into the storage porch off the kitchen, which was still freezing cold, but it did have a roof. And in the morning he brought coffee.

Herbie took his mug out into the sun. The mountain man was out there, awake, with his hat on, brim adjusted so that it dipped over his eyes, and holding out a tin mug. How Long brought him coffee too. The man pulled out a flask and added a drop of whisky. Herbie did a good imitation of the voice, bass-toned and groggy.

Who the hell are you? And what are you doing here?

Herbie Wishart—thought I'd take the train west. He spoke in falsetto, for laughs.

Well, you're late to the party. All manner of folk coming in since this railroad. Regret I ever pulled Major Rogers out of Bath Creek.

Wishart didn't know what he was talking about, so he kept quiet.

I got you pegged, kid, fer one more remittance man. 'Cepting you're not quite a man yet, are ya? Place is crawling with you Englishers. Gallant walked away, and then spun around to face Herbie. Not me. I was born in Upper Canada. Bonehead, Ontario. Came out to the West at seventeen. Liked horses, so I got myself one and rode out into the prairie. Found a ranchhouse at dark. Cleaned stables for a year and decided to join the North-West Mounted Police.

Maybe that's what I'll do. Eager, kid's voice.

Can ya ride?

No.

You best learn. In my day there was a big ring near the barracks, all dry and hard. They said if you can ride around it and take that jump and you're still in the saddle when you get back here, you're hired. So I did that. And I was good with horses, so I ended up looking after some.

I'm better at hunting, said Herbie.

"Here I thought *you* were the original mountain man," said Isabel, "but you are telling me there was one before you, one you modelled yourself on?"

"Yep, there's a few before me. But Sam Gallant, he was the best. He was my idol. He's still out there too. I was lucky to have caught him on one of his rare reflective mornings. He told me about those days when the prairie was open; there was no one but the Indians, the 'ordinary people,' he called them, that had lived here always."

Isabel waited for more. Humphrey was dozing, his head bobbing over his tin cup. Herbie Wishart's smoke mingled with the smoke of the campfire.

"Before the railroad, there were buffalo all over the plains. Enormous herds of them darkening the foothills. And they came right up into the mountains along the river valley. Some places, along the tributaries, you can still see the marks of their hooves. And Sam Gallant—he'd seen 'em. That was before the whole species got wiped out. People said the Indians did it, but Sam said he didn't see why that would happen: they'd been hunting 'em with their horses for a few hundred years with no discernible effect on the population. Sure! No sign of them dying out 'til the white man came. You know they put a bounty on the animals south of the border. Piles of bones as tall as a man. They used those bones for china, did you know that? Sure, that's why the buffalo died out. Sam was the first one who told me that. 'Too many big shots sitting in the passenger cars on the Canadian Pacific Railway poking their guns out the windows, if you ask me,' he said."

Herbie looked broodily into the fire.

"Sam Gallant said, 'Kid, you're looking for a life in this place, you needed to be here back then. It's about over now.' He was smiling, so I couldn't be sure he meant what he said. He said those days the sun shone down on the grass like a mirror. Down in the valley they used to get mirages. I've seen them too. One day we all came out of the Three Sisters Hotel and we could see the whole of Cascade Mountain hanging upside down in the sky. Thirty miles away it was, but repeated overhead just like in a fine glass. Trees, valleys, rivers, all of it. Not a word of a lie."

Isabel breathed deeply. "Oh. You don't say."

"I do say. Lately we don't get those mirages because the air is filled up with smoke and dust, and the flat ground, where there is any, is planted. But I'm telling you the truth."

"You haven't said what happened with Sam Gallant."

"I told him I'd been snaring rabbits since before I could walk, and he said that if I was still alive come summer I could join his outfit."

"And did you?"

"No. I was young and stupid. I figured I could manage on my own."

The story was over. Herbie pulled out his harmonica. He pulled the pipe out of his mouth and put the harmonica in front of his smiling lips.

Isabel lingered. "What did you do then?"

"Got myself a job working for the CPR, loading boxcars. I tell you, if you have never loaded a boxcar, you can't appreciate how big they are. I worked at every little stop going up the eastern side of the Rockies and down the west."

He began to blow, then stopped.

"It was loading boxcars I heard the greatest tenor ever. Built like a tree stump. He was working the next boxcar over, bending double and hoisting barrels up to the car, over and over. He must've started it to give himself momentum. '*O sole mio.*' He threw his head back and stood up. His voice boomed and melted all over the little valley. Every man there stopped what he was doing and lifted his head."

"He starting to lie now," said How Long.

"And those notes raced down the long string of cars. They leapt from one to the next. They lit up the shadow-bound little town where the sun didn't reach the ground until noon and went behind the mountain at three. In the dark station waiting room folks looked up. The notes began to rise on the air currents toward the mountain ledges. A herd of sheep heading toward the pass took fright. A black bear slapped her tumbling cubs and got them across the stream. And then the song stopped. The foreman appeared, said, 'Back to work, Caruso.'"

"That's my horse," said Isabel.

Herbie tipped his head toward her and started in on the harmonica again. "I know," he said. "You can read his name on his bridle."

"Is that all?"

He finished his song and gave a grin.

"I said to him, 'What are you doing? With that voice you could have a great singing career.' 'Never got a chance!' he said. 'I love to sing, but I got to earn a living, feed the wife and kids,' he said. I wanted to hunt up in these big forests; I knew I was an artist at hunting the way he was an artist at singing. It got me thinking about Sam Gallant and his offer to give a greenhorn a start. I wasn't going to end up like that boxcar Caruso."

He knocked the ashes out of his pipe and stepped away to get more wood to bank the fire.

Chapter 6
SWAN STORY

Near Mystic Lake, June 23, 1911

In the morning they worked their way around the crown of rocks that—from afar—were the clenched forefingers of the Fist. On the back, the trail descended. Hodgson was eager to get to his chosen spot: he kicked his horse in the sides, setting it off in spurts. They passed a big black boulder that seemed to have rolled from some other landscape. They walked for half a day and then began to climb a treed slope to a pass between two mountains. The way became narrower and steeper, and the snow-covered slopes seemed to close in on them. They reached the top and stopped.

"You remember the last pass was Beguiling? This one is Bewitching," said Wishart.

"What's the difference?"

"This one is more so."

Their way forward was blocked by snow, but this time the digging went faster. The snow was lighter, colder. Maxwell found a tree for the sledge, and by late afternoon they were through. They reloaded the horses, cowboys throwing the ropes over the ponies' backs with speed. They had walked for only half an hour when the slopes fell back on either side and the way opened up ahead. Wide and clear, the trail led to a great open bowl. At the other side of it lay a round, still lake. Beyond that, the mountains rose again all around.

They stopped at the sight. This was the Snow Bowl; it was a small universe, a circle at the edge of a circle, enclosed in a circle. It could have been drawn with a compass. It was filled with sun—the white traces of snow that remained were being greened with new growth. The shore of the perfect round lake was flaked red stone, and in the still cup of turquoise water sat an iceberg in its last glory.

"That's Mystic Lake. The Stoneys call it Medicine and speak of it with awe," said Wishart.

But this was of little interest to Charles Hodgson, who was off his horse and scanning the rock formations high above with his hand over his brow.

"We're almost there!"

Isabel looked up. This was where the fossils came from? She could see nothing. Maxwell pointed to where the rock strata rose and fell in a crumpled arch a fair way above the treeline. A very fine line among the rocks leading past it was a trail. It came from over the mountains that enclosed the Snow Bowl.

"Sam Gallant made that for the guests at Laggan. It's only a day's walk thataway."

Hodgson walked in circles of nerves. "We got here." He seemed to assess Wishart more positively. Had he doubted?

"Not yet. It's farther than you think."

And it was: they walked for several hours to cross the Snow Bowl. It had the feel of an amphitheatre—the Roman Forum, said Isabel. But it just kept on; it was enormous.

On the other side, Mystic Lake was sombre, set deep in splinters of rock, the remains of a landslide. When Isabel walked to its edge and looked deep into the water she saw trees below the surface, white skeleton trees standing upside down, as if they had dropped into it from every side. They hung like the sticks in a game of Chinese pickup, their straight trunks crossing and recrossing, their branches reduced to silver spears floating on clouds of miraculous green that bloomed deep in the water. They might have been angles of petrified jousting poles disappearing downward to whatever unplumbed depth. Then the sun faded in cloud and dark welled from beneath: the lake grew threatening.

There was just enough flat red rock at its edges to walk around it. Humphrey wanted to. It would have taken less than an hour. But Hodgson could not wait to get up to the little trail, no more than the faintest thread through the loose shale, that led upward.

"Take us up to the treeline and then leave us, Mr. Wishart. Maxwell and I will make camp."

"The patch of snow up there is bigger than it looks," Wishart said. "Probably two feet deep. You may have some work to do."

"That's why we brought the shovels."

The guide squinted at the packhorses and calculated the speed with which they could move once the camera, the boxes of film, the bacon, the canvas, the sledgehammer, the pickaxe and pry bars, the snowshoes, the canvas rolls and duffles were lifted from their backs.

"We'll take the easy way out in the morning," he said. The Hodgson party seemed keen to get rid of him. He wasn't sure how they were going to get on, but How Long was there, and the rest, he figured, was Maxwell's problem. To tell the truth, the man was irritating him more than a little with his know-it-all remarks. This was a fleeting thought, not one he admitted to at the time, but one that, in the years to come, was to return to him, making him question why he'd left them on their own, if there was malice in it. Was he that kind of man?

"Yes, stay tonight, Mr. Wishart," said Isabel. "You can tell us the rest of your story."

"Oh, that would take a long time."

*

When he approached the Three Sisters Hotel he saw packers tying champagne boxes onto the sides of little cayuse ponies. Herbie figured it meant Sam Gallant was in the neighbourhood. Sure enough, there was the hat in the bar, dimpled crown, battered wide brim tipped down over one eye.

Remember the greenhorn?

Naw. Meet a dozen of 'em every day. He didn't look up.

You offered to teach me horses if I'd hunt for you.

Bleary eyes, one blue, one brown, looked up and then turned back to his glass, and he grumbled. Setting off for a month with a damn millionaire and his damn kids, and I just lost a goddamn cook's helper.

Not my strong suit. I never knew much about cooking.

Well, that's how you learn, kid. Can you ride at all?

Not too well.

Then you're going to have one helluva time.

Herbie had his dog by then, Fella, and Fella came too. He figured the dog had more smarts than he did and would get him through. Lucky the light lasted in the sky so long, because it was eight at night when they first made camp. How Long got the fire going and gave Herbie chores for making dinner, but Herbie didn't shine at them. Ma and Pa Millionaire were in the tent making funny noises. Finally Gallant gave his hat a twist and told Herbie to take charge of the kids.

The ponies were wandering loose, out of their traces, so he took the kids off after them. They stopped complaining then, which made him happy until one pony ran off. He went cursing after the thing over downed trees and piles of rocks, and he was thinking all the time what Sam Gallant would do to him if the pony got his leg stuck. He followed it to the shore of a little body of water called Nickel Lake. It looked inviting because of its blue-green colour, but it was flipping cold; just a couple of weeks ago it would have been frozen.

Anyway, at last he captured the pony and brought him back to the lakeside, where the boys and their sister were sitting throwing stones. He found a canvas boat tucked under some tree roots. He guessed it belonged to Gallant and was the means of transportation for the party to get to the other side tomorrow. He unfolded it, brushing out the spruce needles and making sure it was watertight before he launched it.

He told the kids to climb to the far end and sit down, being careful not to tip it. When they were settled facing him, he gave the thing a big push. Two boys and the girl jerked forward and then backwards and flipped off the end. This struck Herbie as pretty funny. They were too shocked to scream. He let them think a bit before he clambered to their end of the boat and pulled them up, one by one. He got them back to camp all wet and chattering, but Millionaire Pa was well into the champagne, which was not champagne but whisky packed in the boxes the packers preferred. Herbie swore he'd saved them, not flipped them in the lake in the first place. It was all a matter of emphasis.

How Long had his own problems: Gallant had packed two hundred pounds of bacon and one tin of jam.

"Remember that?" He pulled his pipe out of his mouth and shared a laugh with How Long.

"A month on the trail," said the cook. "Gallant no brain. He drank that much he not know what he doing!"

Seeing a way he could improve his standing, Herbie set off with his gun. He went back to the lake. A huge flock of birds that looked like swans had landed on it. It was getting late then, and the sun was gone. The birds sat out on the water, drifting in a little haze. Herbie had a strange feeling, like he'd stepped into a fairy tale. If he'd had his druthers he'd have gone after something a little harder to find, but time was a-wasting, so he shot one. The rest of them flew off making a great fracas. He had to get the boat out again because the dog wouldn't bring the bird in. When he found the white feathered body floating among the weeds it proved to be a huge thing with a neck like a bull's dong and wings that had to be six feet across. But he did land it and drag it back to camp, by which time dinner was over. It was lights-out and everyone was in their tents. Only Gallant was sitting by the fire waiting for him.

What's that you got? Goat?

No, it's a swan. Thought it would help with the food supply.

Swan? Sweet Jesus Christ. You shot a swan?

The hat went back a couple of inches. Two half-demented razor eyes, one blue and one brown, clapped his. Despite himself Herbie was nervous.

You shot a swan? Gallant got to his feet. You shot a swan. He took a few steps toward him. He saw the big bird dragging.

Yeah, I did. Pulling it out of the lake was about the same as pulling out the twelve-year-old kid.

Gallant bent over the bird. You didn't. You piece of dung. That's a *Trumpeter* swan. Almost human. Kind of a magic bird—don't you know your fairy tales over there in England? Gallant swiped off his hat and began to pace. He slapped his thigh with his hat. His voice broke. The flock rose up and flew off? You know I've been seeing 'em here ever since I first came.

Oh, swans like in the ballet? asked Herbie. That uncle of mine back in the old country was a great fan and took me to see *Swan Lake* in London. I knew when I saw the birds out on the lake in the mist it reminded me of something. He looked down at the snakelike neck of the bird, twisted now and stiffening, the upcurved black bill so prettily cupping the perfect white of the face, the drop of red on the face now matched by drops of blood on its chest.

Heard we were short of food, he continued weakly. Fella was whining and edgy. Time to get out of there. Herbie was planning an escape involving that rather straightforward pony he'd been riding, when Gallant flew at his throat and knocked him in the dust.

Hear me, kid? It's a *Trumpeter*. I never saw those birds here again after the railroad. He rounded his terrible head on Herbie. Do you know what I'm saying, boy? He reached for his rifle and raised it.

How Long, drying dishes, didn't look up. Herbie had to call off Fella. He was a good dog but considered this to be aggression and would have been happy to tear Gallant's throat open.

You're saying you never saw the swans here since the railroad.

I'm saying they disappeared! They took other routes! They didn't come here. I didn't see them! And tonight, tonight, they came back.

Herbie was starting to get the point.

They came back, and you, you piece of cow dung, you unhatched weasel of a greenhorn, shit-for-brains tenderfoot Christly misbegotten sonofabitch who knows nothing, you know nothing about these mountains, went out by goddamn Jesus Christ, took your gun and *shot* one!

Herbie's rendition of Gallant's dialogue must have been good, because How Long was shaking with laughter.

I'm saying when I came upon this lake, they were here. They greeted me. I never saw them anywhere in these mountains afore that. And then they were gone. They're shy. They found another route. But they came back. Just this one time. For me. They were here. Until you shot one! I heard them fly off. Oh yes, I did. They're gone and they won't come back; they'll go somewhere else and I'll never see them. He sobbed. You idiot. You're fired. I won't have you on this trip. You pack up and be gone.

Eventually Gallant wound himself down and fell in a heap. How Long retrieved the outfitter's soft and dinted and dusty felt hat and rolled him under canvas. The millionaire faces that had poked out like turtle heads from their tents pulled back in. Fella turned around in a dozen circles and flopped: crisis resolved. How Long and Herbie started plucking the feathers off the swan. They were huge and white, and Herbie thought they'd make good pens, so he saved a few.

In the morning Gallant was sober. He took all the guests out on the trail and let How Long know that if Herbie Wishart deserted this trip, as sure as Christ he, Sam Gallant, would personally track him down and shoot him where he stood. Guaranteed.

"The swan meat, when they finally got to roasting it, was tough," said Herbie. He put down his pipe and pulled out his harmonica. "It was so tough we cooked it a while longer. And we cooked it longer than that. No matter how long we cooked it, the flesh of that swan was like leather. You could not get a knife in it and you could not get a fork in it and you could not get your tooth into it. The tougher it was, the longer we cooked it. Turned into a lump of shiny black coal, it did."

"Lying now," said How Long, but he didn't need to.

Isabel was smiling into the fire. This was what she liked about his stories: at the end they went crazy.

"The lump of coal got up and walked," he said. "Walked as far as Laggan and lay down, and where it lay down the miners found a new seam of coal. It turned out it was the best seam in the Rockies, and they mined it for a dozen years 'til they closed it down 'cause it was haunted. And you could hear nothing but swan songs in the heart of the mountain. And there was a lake down there, and on it were swimming all the black swans of the world. So says Herbie Wishart. That's it for the night!"

He stood up and gave a wave before backing off into the darkness with his harmonica at his lips.

Isabel went into her tent and fell asleep listening to the wail of his playing. She played his story over in her mind, too, admiring the waltz and sudden stops of his style: "time was a-wasting, so I shot one," "the white-feathered body floating among the weeds." Words, too, were plain in her world. It was new to make music with them.

For his part, Wishart blew and sucked on the mouth organ until he was tired out and then lay down on his sleeping roll and tossed a bit. He was edgy. None of this trip was going according to plan. He didn't have control. If you hire an outfitter, you don't send your butler ahead to do the planning. Herbie was irritated, too, by the needless tough climb, the simpering son and the patronizing professor. He reviewed his plan to leave them How Long and a couple of packers; he and Francis and the others would go back. Let them set up camp themselves, he thought again, if they're so smart. He'd be back during the summer with provisions and to see how they were doing.

At dawn he got up and tied the remaining packs on his horse. The only one of the sleeping party who acknowledged Wishart and the cowboys was Maxwell, whose elegant arm waved from the door of his tent. The group climbed the flinty slope and took that narrow hiking trail the other way up out of the Snow Bowl and toward Laggan. The last thing Wishart said to Francis before putting his head down along the horse's neck in the eerie sound box of that mountain bowl was, "I did warn them, didn't I?"

Chapter 7
THE QUARRY

Above Mystic Lake, June 24, 1911

How Long made breakfast, expertly wrangling the frying pans, bacon, camp coffee and flour for pancakes. Humphrey sat wrapped in a blanket by the fire. He was getting a cold.

"Do you think we can find the place again?" said Hodgson to Maxwell. He sat facing the mountainside where they'd been, his eyes fixed on it.

It was only a few feet off the track where they'd stumbled on the fossils. The three of them, he, Maxwell and Mrs. Hodgson, had been out riding. Nobody came this way. The route ran through scree mostly above the treeline, crossing a smooth forty-five-degree angle of mountainside through the spectacular mile-wide gaps between Mounts King and Regent. To Hodgson it was obvious that great bands of quartzite, which had been sandstone millions of years ago, had been forced up, exposed to view and then eroded away between the great peaks.

The agents of erosion—snow, ice, rain—were still at work. He could see a line that he guessed had been a sea beach, below which everything, all of this—the Snow Bowl, Mystic Lake, their campsite and half the mountain—had been covered with water. Mystic was the last remnant. People knew this: he wasn't the first. Across the other side there was a trilobite field that had been discovered by some Canadian geologist. But it was pretty picked over. This side was ignored. It was Maxwell who noticed the slabs of rock that had fallen from higher up.

"Look at that," he said. "Do you see?" He pointed to some loose shale a few yards from his horse's foot.

"Oh yes," said Hodgson. "A fossil."

"Must've been brought down from there in a rock slide." Maxwell pointed higher and waited for the remark to penetrate Charles's often abstracted mind. "Think we might take a look?"

They had, and a year had passed with all its incidents and here they were back again.

They were all hungry and wolfed down How Long's breakfast. After coffee Maxwell and Hodgson climbed up with their shovels. The spot was hard to recognize, because a layer of thin white snow had fallen and lay on top of the winter's snow, which was frozen hard. Maxwell identified a spot. Hodgson looked over his shoulder one way and then the other, concerned about being detected. He was doing nothing wrong: he was a scientist. They were in the open, there was no one around, and the snow flurries hid them nicely, they thought. A giant ram lifted his head but did not seem perturbed.

They determined a place to dig. "I'd help but this sixty-year-old back is sending me messages already from the ride in."

Maxwell crouched on the hard rock, put his ear on it. He pushed away the top layer of snow. He dug down with the miner's gloves that Herbie Wishart had sold him. They had a forefinger and a thumb, and kept his three other fingers in a kind of hoof. He dug to his elbow, then deeper. Eighteen inches, in some places two feet of snow. Might as well get to work. Charles was examining the layers in the rock wall. The mountain sheep continued to paw and eat the sparse grasses sprouting between the rocks. The dominant ram aimed a sidelong glance at Maxwell in tacit acknowledgement of his activity.

Maxwell shovelled for a couple of hours. He wasn't tired, but Charles was exhausted from standing by. By the time they got back to camp the snow was thinning out, still falling but without wind and in wet clumps. The Tree brothers had built platforms of thin branches to keep the canvas tents off the ground. The fire was crackling, and the gentleman's gentleman got out the first bottle of whisky.

"It's not even afternoon yet."

"For your back," said Maxwell.

Hodgson sat very still then, sipping. The rest had coffee. It was quiet, quiet in the falling snow.

"Summertime," mused Isabel.

"Yes, and we'll feel it in just a few hours," said Maxwell. "I can see it coming over there." He gestured toward the west.

But he was wrong this time. All that came was more snow. It was too wet to work, and each of them went inside to read or write or dream alone.

The next day proved Maxwell right, and after a cold start the sun brought heat at midday. Digging snow under hot sun confounded the mind; they had all seasons at once. Sun burned the backs of their necks; ice chafed their forearms. Hodgson unpacked his camera and set it on the tripod. He took pictures of the ring of peaks that surrounded them, beginning the rotation that would take him full circle. Isabel sat drawing and said very little. Humphrey's cold blossomed, and he was preoccupied with sneezing and his handkerchief. He would use it for several hours and then walk down to Mystic Lake to rinse it in the frigid water, come back and stretch it on a rock to dry.

Days went by with Maxwell still shovelling snow from the indent where they had found the fossils the year before. At last he got down to bare rock. It was wet and filthy in the little cleft. But it seemed he had located the place: the loose slabs of shale were full of surprises. Isabel and Humphrey began scrubbing imprints with a potato brush and a small dish of water, revealing perfect specimens, inches-long animals intact and all parts accounted for, caught mid-gesture, crawling or dining, undigested meal still visible in their stomachs.

Isabel spoke to the entombed animals tenderly. "Yes, I remember you," she murmured. "From last year, yes, I've sketched your sister. You were supposed to be swimming in a shallow pool of sea water! And here you are at seventy-five hundred feet?"

Or another one, so fresh, so delicately drawn into the mud that had solidified around it. "It's you, isn't it? Five hundred million years, you say? Not so long, not so long. And your name? We've no idea. We have to give you a new one."

Her father's shadow fell over her.

"We will name them for where we've found them."

They'd spent two weeks already in camp when they saw a party approaching. It was just two people, on foot, no horses. They came over the ridge to the south, where Wishart had departed. Maxwell, Hodgson, Isabel and Humphrey were in the quarry. Hodgson was peering into the viewfinder of the No. 8 Cirkut, his head under a cloth. Humphrey was breaking slate. Isabel too. Maxwell got out his fancy German binoculars and had a look.

"Man and a woman. Walking slowly. Out for a stroll."

"Where have they come from?"

"Railway Hotel? Tourists?"

"Do they see us? We're quite a bit above them."

"We've nothing to hide," said Humphrey. He took a seat on the edge of a large round boulder.

"If they don't see the quarry, they'll see the camp and the horses."

"Maxwell, go down to the camp to see if How Long can get some tea."

"Humphrey, why don't you?"

Humphrey tossed his pickaxe, not happy to be doing errands for the butler.

Below, How Long already had the kettle on.

"It looks like we're getting visitors."

"How did they know we're here?"

How Long gestured around the great amphitheatre. He creased his face in a look that said, *Are you dreaming?* "Everybody know."

It was anticlimactic to say hello after the long, visible approach. The woman was in a walking skirt and a pert hat, the man in churchy clothes. When the two were within hailing distance, Humphrey raised his arm. They both raised their hands in return salute. The tea was ready. Maxwell, Isabel and his father were still up at the quarry, clearly visible from the camp.

They all shook hands as if it were normal to be making introductions in a tent on a mountain slope. The visitors were brother and sister, more Quakers, from Philadelphia. Phoebe and George Dixon.

"We met your family here last summer; we've corresponded," said the woman.

George took photographs. Phoebe drew wildflowers. She was older than one would imagine, watching her climb. She was rail thin, and her face ruddy but un-aged, one of those spry, dry women whose body signalled that no interference had been made. She enjoyed her tea but, with her brother, kept looking up the mountainside. When Maxwell didn't seem to be laying down the shovels, and Hodgson remained fixed in his posture behind the camera, George asked if he might go up to them.

"Fine," Humphrey said. The man set out, but no sooner had his father and the butler spotted his approach than they set down their tools. They did not want their work observed.

Humphrey and the woman were alone. Phoebe spotted the sketchbook.

"Do you draw, then?"

"My sister does. I try, but I'm not any good." He sniffed and dug in his pocket for the handkerchief.

"I doubt that," said the older woman firmly. She extended her hand for the sketchbook, and Humphrey surrendered it. After a few minutes' examination Phoebe looked up.

"You're not too bad. Fine observation. In the field it's difficult, of course. Here they come now."

There was an awkward greeting between the doctor and Phoebe. She seemed suddenly to remember what she knew, and expressed her sincere condolences on the loss of his wife, their mother. After that there was silence. The quarry workers were dirty and exhausted. Phoebe and George soon stood to say goodbye, promising to visit again.

Summer took hold, and for weeks the family was encamped in the dimple in the mountainside below the quarry. There was water for the horses, and a few trees for protection, the ridge above them and the Snow Bowl below gradually emptying of snow and filling with flowers. After rain they dried their canvas tarps over tree branches. At first, light remained in the sky until eleven o'clock at night. They sat around the campfire as carpets of sparks unrolled overhead. But steadily the days grew shorter. Isabel missed Herbie's stories.

Humphrey got up early, before How Long, and rekindled the fire. He helped with breakfast and then sat staring downhill. He no longer worked in the quarry: his father had upbraided him once too often. Once, at breakfast, the watercolourist from Laggan made an appearance above. They marvelled: she must have left Laggan at three o'clock in the morning. Even when Miss Dixon was not much more than a dot on the slope her mission spoke to the very air she moved through. She could have been rolling on wheels.

When Humphrey spied her he went into his tent and changed his clothes. (He had only three sets, and he had not washed them. It really was not a change but an exchange, one set for another.) He stoked the breakfast fire, got warm water, shaved and brushed his hair. He laced his boots, by which time he could see that the woman had progressed halfway along the scree.

Isabel, who had taken a dislike to Phoebe, disappeared up to the quarry. The new tea was made and Humphrey was sitting pensively on a log when Phoebe arrived. She had come to sketch the flowers in the Snow Bowl. Would Humphrey join her? He did, and they wandered down into it, Phoebe bending and looking, straightening, picking the small blooms, examining them.

Humphrey followed, carrying her little folding canvas chair. He even painted, a little, using a brush and the tints she carried in her paintbox. But he did not paint flowers. He invented maps, they being the prettiest things he had seen in these parts. She painted the flowers on the spot sometimes, but more often stared at them to memorize the depth of colour, and then put them between the leaves of her sketchbook. Again, she raised her head often to see what was going on in the quarry. At last someone signalled, and she exclaimed, "Oh, look! They're waving us up."

At the quarry, he, Isabel and Maxwell stood back while his father took Miss Dixon along the piles of rock, showing her the fossils and lecturing as he loved to do in a way that wearied his butler and children, although Maxwell's unimpeachable behaviour never revealed this. Hodgson seemed to have decided, on this her second visit, that he trusted her.

"Does thee see? Here is one animal, less than an inch long, with many radiating legs. You might say they are almost like the petals of a daisy."

"I do see, yes. I do."

Its body was an oblong, narrowed at one end, impressed into the rock with a thickness almost as great as its length.

"And look at this fellow. Does thee see? He appears to be, at first glimpse, a dirigible sailing. This helmet shape on one end, and the tiny flippers on the other look almost like a propeller—see? Put thy hand on it."

"Yes, yes." Phoebe Dixon reached out tentatively. "May I?" she said, as if he already owned them. As if they were sitting in his parlour and not on a rock face baked when in sun and gripped by ice when not. "Touch it?"

He nodded, flattered. She put her hand on it. Her fingers ran over the indentations in the rock.

"They died and remained so perfectly intact? How would that be?"

He explained that this was a trove of annelids, Middle Cambrian fossils. Most fossils were simply hard shells and bones. In this case one could see a complete picture of the animal. He didn't actually know how they had come to be perfectly preserved, with all the soft tissue intact, but it made the find particularly fascinating. "A sudden collapse of the earth above into the pool where they were swimming is, I suppose, one possibility. A mudslide bringing instant death and entombment."

He stopped over a new animal, never seen before, which he had taken the trouble to name after a nearby peak. "We call this fellow Regent," he said, tapping the rock with his cane.

"How fortuitous it was," said Phoebe, "that you, the doctor professor and quite possibly the scientist in all of North America most capable of identifying them, were walking here with your late wife and came upon them!"

"My gentleman was along too," said the professor.

Maxwell cleared his throat. "The shale had dropped from above," he said. "Maybe snow brought it down."

They had located the layer of limestone and shale that bore the fossils; it was above the trail, and in it they were finding more. Mollusks, mostly. They were unlike any form of life Hodgson had ever seen before. Nonetheless, he thought he could identify, perhaps, the male and the female by the shapes—proboscis for the male, womb for the female. He felt sure their existence would reveal new facts about the way life advanced from a few cells to the vertebrates. But it was not straightforward: there were so many wildly different, seemingly unrelated creatures.

Phoebe was a short woman. She had to hold her hand up to shade her brow from the sun as she gazed up into his face. "It is staggering to imagine them living here, these marine animals. So high up! A tropical sea!"

"Yes, an ocean lagoon. That's where this type of life develops. And then the mountains were forced through."

She looked around at the peaks of black rock.

"God must have had a hand. In burying the life. And in revealing it, perhaps."

"I believe that too, Miss Dixon. God's hand is here. Thee sees it clear as day. But what exactly God was doing as he moved and created, we don't know."

Hearing his father using *thee* and *thine*, pitching his voice low and tipping his head toward the diminutive lady, Humphrey had an uncomfortable sensation. So what is happening here? he thought to himself in disbelief. She has intentions! She can't possibly. She's fifty years old. His sister was not paying attention; she had turned away and was banging at the slate. Humphrey countered to himself, How old is fifty? She's unmarried; she manages the house for her brother and father. A man would give her a new lease on life.

Maybe she just wants to live, he thought, more forgivingly. There was a lesson in that.

Chapter 8
HUMPHREY

Below the Quarry, July 1911

SUMMER WAS HALFWAY GONE when Herbie Wishart reappeared with Francis Erwin and a ten-pony pack train. How Long and Humphrey were alone in camp. The others were up digging in the quarry.

"Just passing by! We're heading to the Brazeau to find us some sheep for Gus to paint."

"I hope you've brought some spuds," said How Long. They were running low on supplies. There were no more fish: not even Maxwell could find them up here. Isabel had seen them arrive, and came down from the quarry. It had been a month now, and she was starting to wonder when that new life of hers would begin. She covered her mouth with her hands and laughed when she saw what Erwin was bearing on his saddle horn. Her hat.

"Where did you ever—?" she said, as Erwin extended his hand, in it the tangle of straw and net.

"I ran across it, miss, is all I can say."

"It blew down to the base of Mount Menace. Took it for an eagle."

"We thought we were going to lose him when he scaled the tree with the thing nested on top. I don't know how he ever spotted it. Must have had an eye out the whole way. Now I can see why," said Gus, taking off his own hat and smiling at Isabel. She was an attractive woman, especially in those pants she had taken to wearing.

Gus Henkel was an artist. Isabel knew that. Herbie had mentioned him; he'd come from Germany wanting to shoot animals to paint and had hired the outfitter. The two of them were going off hunting in the haunts of the Dall sheep and grizzlies. His manner was courtly, his assessment cool.

Presented with three men, all of whom were flirting with her, Isabel blushed hard. To hide it she reached for the tattered hat and pressed it down low over her brow, making them laugh. She fingered her hat. It was in a poor state. Its crown was pushed through, and the brim, once elegantly wide, was crushed and appeared to have been nibbled on.

"Starting to look more like a proper mountain hat," said Herbie, as the other men faded into the background. He gave Erwin a push in the middle of his back to send him off.

"I've been needing it. The sun is very strong."

"You'll be getting the one we ordered before long."

"I hope so."

The professor and Maxwell came down. They'd been breaking shale. But they were beginning to dream of dynamite.

"You've got to have expertise for that," Erwin said. "You could set off slides."

"I'm sure we can manage," said the professor.

"With all due respect, we don't have expertise," said Maxwell. "It's not our field."

"That's a relief," said Wishart. "I didn't know there was an area wherein you had no expertise." He spat and touched his hat. "I'll see if I can bring you up a miner when I pass the next time."

"Did you bring anything beside the hat and the spuds?" said How Long crossly. "We need bacon, and the dried fruit's all gone."

Erwin produced a couple of bottles of whisky. "We suspected supplies might be running low."

Humphrey took to getting up to watch the sunrise. Dawn came abruptly in astonishing shots of light from the east, lighting peaks at random and blasting the cloud to orange. He'd reset the fire and put the water on to boil. It was a race to beat How Long to this task. Then, as the cook got busy with breakfast, Humphrey would sit on his boulder and watch the day begin.

A tent flap lifted. A long and elegant dark-skinned hand, then a leg in red underwear appeared. Maxwell emerged, this tall ebony man looking like a god in saggy red combinations, and stretched to his full height in the cool new light. He maintained a fiction of utter solitude, splashing himself and singing hymns under his breath and getting fully dressed before acknowledging the young man.

Humphrey drank coffee and read the months-old newspapers they had packed in. Why, he had not understood until they got there. But now he knew: they were to be used to wrap the fragments of shale they were going to pack out. He enjoyed the randomness of the news. The United States had sent troops to the Mexican border; the French had sent theirs to Fez. There were many stories about aviation: dirigibles crashing, biplanes taking the aviator down, someone else trying to get airborne after many failures.

The professor now made his exit from the tent. His long underwear was twisted around his hips and his toque covered his ears. Maxwell made an effort not to smile.

"Seven," he said. He and Humphrey had developed a way of communicating with each other without saying the words of the message. They made a list of commands, one to ten. Seven meant *Avert your eyes.*

After the others had breakfasted and set off for the quarry, Humphrey lay on his back on the slope and wondered about flying machines. Would they ever fly over these mountains? These very peaks? He had taken no interest in these stories back home in Washington. Now he read and reread them avidly. He, too, could pore over history, he cracked to his sister, even if his interest went only a few months back, as opposed to—how many was it? Five hundred million years. *The Cambrian Explosion*. Who cared?

He and his father were not speaking. In the evenings, Humphrey and Isabel sat together, staring into the fire. She was becoming a determined quarry worker, and their father often praised her at his expense. She had gone a khaki colour that looked healthy but would not be approved of in Washington drawing rooms.

"Thee needs that hat," Humphrey said, becoming his mother for an instant.

"It wouldn't help. The sun bounces up from the ground; I can't keep it off my face."

Humphrey admired Isabel; he didn't mind that their father preferred her. Of course Isabel insisted it wasn't so. He unburdened himself about how he hated his father, how cold he was after their mother's death.

"Remember what he did that day?" Humphrey stared moodily at the blank canvas of his father's tent.

She nodded. The professor had taken the news standing up. He had walked all over the house, long after the doctor had gone, the mother-in-law had been called in and the servants had sobbed. He walked with purpose from room to room, but each time he entered one, he seemed to forget what he had come for.

"He stood at windows and at doors looking out," she said.

"He looked everywhere else—then finally, after hours and hours, he looked at me," said Humphrey, "his misfit of a son, as if he were seeing me for the first time, which perhaps he was."

"Humphrey, thee is not a misfit."

"Yes I am."

"He said God was against him."

"That part was good," said Humphrey. "But then he took himself in hand. He stifled his grief, and then Maxwell stepped into the hole she left."

Here, too, in the camp under the stars, Maxwell took over. The giant space in all directions allowed him to expand. Getting up with the dawn was only the beginning. He pushed and cajoled Dr. Hodgson from breakfast until dinner. "Doctor Professor," he would say, "you are not only a good geologist; you are a great geologist. You can climb up these few feet to examine this strata and tell us what to do with it."

"You forget, Maxwell. I am a man in my sixties. I can't clamber up these goat tracks the way you and the youngsters do."

But still, he did get up the slope to a few hundred feet, and he walked along carefully watching the strata, as Maxwell watched him, ready to catch him if he stumbled.

Quietly Humphrey and Isabel agreed that their father was aging. He was turning into a fussy old man. He seemed tired, too tired for physical work. But in his weakness, he grew manipulative. He had them all working for him, and he was closing his grip. He became animated only when he was pointing out the rocks and the fossils "trapped within them."

"Do they look 'trapped' to thee, Isabel? They don't to me. They look as if they left their stamp proudly and for a reason. Or as if they had left their positions for a minute and would come back soon to jump into those hollows."

His father never thought Humphrey had much of a head for science. On the other hand, said Humphrey, he had a hunch that the professor himself hadn't exactly grasped whatever story had surrendered these entombed creatures to their sight. He doubted God's hand, however. To him they were much older and much more convincing than God. To him the only question was, How do these creatures relate to us?

Are we what they have become? Or because they were stopped here, stopped and buried, are they some part of what we might have become, but failed to?

Other times, Humphrey and Isabel spoke about their trip to Europe. The trip must go ahead no matter what, their father had said. As if Europe hadn't been there a rather long time—as if it might go away, Humphrey laughed. "Father sent us because he could not bear to see us mourning when he didn't allow himself to indulge."

"Thou is meant to be grateful," said Isabel.

He admitted to liking the Tuscan castles and the tumbling, sunny green hills outside Florence. But in the churches, the chill mouldy air made him feel quite sick. He knew that the cathedral was shelter, and sanctuary, and had been for centuries. But they just made him think of death.

"Thou sounds a little truculent."

"Then I am," he said. "And don't come at me with the *thee*s and *thou*s. I'm not really a Quaker, you know."

"What are you then?"

"I'm an atheist."

Isabel fell silent as Humphrey continued. He didn't enjoy, he *endured* the tour. He heard the necessary, and he saw the necessary and remained in reasonable cheer, the novelty of each day preventing him from collapsing to his true sad level. He really wanted to be at home. But at home there was nothing for him, and very soon after he had returned to Washington they dragged him here.

"And one more thing, Isabel: dost thee—I mean, do you—think it is possible that Miss Dixon is courting the professor?"

She was stung at his switch to the formal "you."

"I think it more than possible," she said. "I think it probable."

"How very"—he searched for a word—"enterprising." For some reason he felt like crying. He was sorry to hurt his sister.

"It is possible," he said, "to feel really confined here, which is strange considering the"—he made a series of throwing gestures, as if he were sowing seed—"vastness." Yes, he ought to have been thankful. He was finally over his cold. He hadn't worked very hard; he had learned something about wildflowers and how to paint them. But he could hardly say it was what he wanted to learn. He'd much rather explore the mountains, the trails and the passes.

"Thee must do that, then," Isabel said.

He would. He had begun to feel he needed action, to flex his muscles, to ride a pony fast and far.

Chapter 9
THE SHALLOW SEA

The Quarry, August 25, 1911

SUMMER WAS NEARING ITS END. Herbie Wishart had come up from Laggan with a Gateway miner who was experienced with explosives. The family had seen them approach, the back-and-forth sway of the heavy-set miner, the man leading his horse.

Joe Mariner was the miner's name. He was an Italian, judging by his accent. He said very little, and stood back, thickset and short and bandy-legged, the way miners were meant to be. Wishart said he was a genius: in the tunnels he went ahead of the others and set the dynamite so that the rocks parted and fell in the precise way desired, revealing the coal seam. "He'll be able to fix you up fine; just show him what you want done."

"Have some coffee. Then we'll walk you up to the quarry," said Hodgson. "If you can loosen some of that rock, we'll be very happy."

Mariner took the tin cup and looked up at their work site. "Easy," he said. "On the surface, in plain day, and no overhang to fall on you."

"Don't be so sure," said Herbie Wishart. "I've seen a gunshot in winter bring down an entire mountainside of snow."

The day was radiant, with that still halo the Rockies could create out of snow, hot sun, rock and chalk-blue water. The light seemed to come from all directions. There was no wind. Time stood in abeyance. The camp at the quarry had become an intersection: there met the long road from Gateway, the short road from Laggan and the even shorter steep path up to the quarry itself. The past, the present and the future met there too. People who had been little more than strangers were drawn together, their lives tangled by what would happen that day, so that although they went on, separately, in different directions, they only pulled the knot tighter.

For fun, Isabel had repaired her hat, sewing the brim back on, weaving dried flowers into it. She put it on her head, and they went uphill to the quarry, where Maxwell pointed out the places where he and the professor had determined that the seam would be fossil-rich and they wanted the bank opened up so they could uncover more of the strange and plentiful creatures they had surprised in their prison of shale. Dr. Hodgson was gesturing widely but letting Maxwell do the talking. Isabel stood by with her gloves on.

"Just come on it, did you?" said Mariner as he pulled his tools out of the saddlebags of a patient cayuse with one white eye. "Just walking by, were you?"

"We were. Frankly the professor was more interested in the trilobite bed across the gap." Maxwell pointed to the mountain facing. "But then he saw—we saw—a large, very complete figure on the surface of one of these slabs of shale. It had fallen down from above. Just off the trail—"

This was Wishart's first trip uphill to the quarry. He kicked at the trail. "Made for the tourists, when the train started bringing them through. Sam Gallant cut it. He wouldn't have taken note of any fossils, that's for sure." He glanced admiringly at Isabel. "You're a bit rakish in that hat."

She shook her head.

"It's the mountains," he said, looking back at her father. "People come to life. Old fossils and youngsters too. Happens on the trail. Likes and dislikes. Developments of affection. And disaffection. Oh yes, sure."

Hodgson did not acknowledge this observation, but seemed to see Isabel for the first time. "You're wearing that hat!"

"Mr. Wishart ordered a new one, but it hasn't arrived," she said. Would her father ever be pleased to see her there beside him at his work? His face was silhouetted and featureless in the sun with his propped-up hat brim. When he pushed the hat back, the top of his forehead showed, a white flag. When he turned to the side, the hat and he himself looked battered.

"Going to get interesting this morning when the banging begins," Wishart offered.

Mariner started asking technical questions. Maxwell pointed to the strata that had to come out, where they thought it led.

"You'd better position yourself above, not down below, then," said Herbie to Isabel. "Stands to reason this stuff isn't going to fly, it's going to fall."

Isabel let him guide her by the elbow to the right. He handed her off to Maxwell, who drew her farther away while Mariner unpacked his sack of dynamite sticks. She felt odd. There was that glow of sun on everything, blurring the silhouettes. She could no longer hear what the men were saying. She could see Maxwell striding straight up on the goat trail and then pointing down from his king-of-the-castle position thirty feet above their diggings. She saw her father look at him and nod, agreeing. Just exactly who *was* Maxwell, beyond and before being a gentleman's gentleman? They said he had a military background, but was that common, black men high up in the command? She didn't think so. She gave a thought to her little sister, Gwen, left behind in Washington for safekeeping. She smiled across at her brother, a very slim young man with a bizarre hat. Mind you, everyone had a bizarre hat.

Her father was letting Maxwell do the talking again. Joe Mariner looked from one to the other mildly. He seemed to know what he was doing. He set the explosives in the rock and gestured to them to get out of the way. He was the best they had, the guide had said of the man with a rough style and short stature. Her thoughts drifted to Miss Dixon. Phoebe Dixon had her eye on Isabel's father. He's all yours, she thought. You and your "honoured to meet someone of your reputation," your "fascinating and so brilliant!" You can look after him. You can be his hostess and housekeeper. It will set me free.

"This is gonna scare the blinking bejeezus out of the game clear down to Mystic Lake and farther," Herbie shouted. "Cover your ears and keep 'em covered: there's a big echo. And sit down, why don't you?"

Isabel sat and looked down the mountain. It was such a disturbed world, such a torn-up, moody, swept-clean, frank and physical world. And caught in its own halo. Yes, that's what it was. She saw little drawings, little engravings, and leaned closer. There were more of these creatures right beneath her feet. Swimming, her father had said, in their private sea. Which was very hard to imagine, way up here against the perfect blue sky.

It had been flat and tropical green. Minding their own business, these little crayfish and jellyfish had been. Peaceful as can be. A backwater, that many million years ago. She had already forgotten the numbers. Now the country was in peaks and folds of white, as if some enormous hand had taken sheets of paper and crumpled them and tossed them down. But no, the mountains had been pushed up, not set down, her father said. The creatures willy-nilly had found the folds between, where the water stayed. They'd crawled on the bottom and darted through the crevices. But here, the swimmers had frozen in their tracks.

What was the catastrophe that seized them mid-stroke as they lazed in their lagoon? Did the ice age come all in an instant? Or was it slow, a long, deliberate squeezing of the life out of all these happy tropical fellows. Each one was so finely, finely made. No damage to limb, if there was to life. She could see a couple now. With waving tentacles and funny long claws and helmet heads. Forty legs. Eyes on stalks and tails with arrow points. Frozen still. She bent right over, closer. That was the question, a question of time. How fast had it happened when the mountains were pushed up? It could not have been an instant. It might have been a million years. Or a break, an earthquake, a great and enormous upheaval, a sudden suffocation for the tiny creatures.

Herbie came for her again, moving her a few feet off, where she stood.

"What are you looking at? Found some more? They're telling us that this was an ocean, long time ago?" he said. "I don't grasp the sense of that one, do you?"

"That's what I was thinking! If it was an ocean, how did these animals get all the way up the mountain? How did the land get all tossed up like this?"

"Well, they're saying it was lying flat at the time," said Herbie. "I got that much." He pulled out his pipe and turned his back on the dynamite layer.

Isabel looked at his hands as he took out the matches. They were lovely hands with long fingers. Quite unsuitable, she thought, for the work he did.

Joe Mariner walked up to where Maxwell stood, on the level above the quarry. Maxwell was pointing and calling while her father down below was giving directions of an opposite kind. Mariner ignored them both. He had made his own calculations. He got out the dynamite stick and placed it carefully in a crevice, where the explosion would be most effective, just so. He lit the stick. Herbie had edged a little to the right so he could light his match and then his pipe, but instead of stepping out of the wind, he stepped into it, and just at that moment Joe's lit stick of dynamite caught. There was a flash and a bang. The bang echoed all across the valley; the mountain seemed to shake and shimmer with anger; it hadn't been so rudely shocked since it was a sea.

Wishart jumped about ten feet above himself and passed Isabel in the air. His pipe on fire, it flew off like a bird. His shoulder or his hip or his leg swiped her and knocked her down the hill. He landed farther down and bounced up immediately, shrugging off the punishment to his body and turning around to see what damage he'd done.

Isabel lay on the mountainside, her cheek downhill against its sharp coldness. She was aware of a certain rock sticking into her hipbone and another in the centre of her shoulder. But she could not collect herself to adjust her position, to turn away from the pain. She was swimming in it; bright pain and a shallow sea. The sun came through the water and sent shafts of light, prisms of colour, down to the sandy bottom. Along it crawled creatures, crablike and festive. She floated over on her stomach and peered at them. They were not actually crabs, she saw, now that she looked at them more closely. They were more like segmented beetles, oblong, with a waist, and a rounded helmet making the front end larger than the back.

She moved her arms and legs as if swimming. Here was another creature, a great appendage coming from its forehead—if that was a forehead—waving, and extending something like an arm, a single arm with open fingers to pluck. She watched as it caught one of the fast-moving crabs, held it and drew it back into itself. The hand disappeared under the helmet; the crab disappeared, in half, then its second half disappeared. One Arm was eating it.

Isabel squirmed, trying to swim backwards, away from it. But spinning up behind her came a great nautilus, a swirl of pink and silver, like a glorious knight on horseback. It rode with its top toward the sun. As it passed her, she looked directly into the centre of the spiral that was its torso. (She supposed it was a torso. Did one look at these life forms as if they were human? Did one import ideas of mouth and anus, of sexual parts, from one's knowledge of human anatomy? She sensed she was making a mistake but did not have the will to change it.) Lining that centre was a round jaw with a row of sharp teeth. The nautilus bounced lightly as if riding on a carousel, making little forward progress, its narrow bottom end trailing a little.

She propelled herself away from it, to her left. On the sea floor she caught sight of a set of glassware with cone-shaped bowls and wide rims. It reminded her of something. A cocktail called a martini. Was it in Italy she had seen these martinis being drunk? Or New York? Men standing along a bar. She had admired the glasses, their slim long stem propped between second and third fingers, their cold (she could see condensation) conical sides resting in the cup of the hand. Below her, the martini creatures stood on their long stems, waving to her in a little turbulence that suddenly welled in the sea.

She could feel the sun on her back. She could hear voices a long way away. She had been knocked into the tropics. She kept swimming. She passed a creature with an elephant's trunk, feeding itself, curling—what?—into a lower lip. Maybe some of that creature shaped like a loaf of bread. Those must be lobsters; certainly they were lobsters. And ahead she could see a true marvel, an animal that loomed above the bottom-dwellers. It stood on pointed chopsticks, a dozen of them or more, that moved stiffly so that it appeared to march like a small regiment of soldiers on patrol.

There was no haste, and there was no noise in this pastel world. She came alongside an egg-shaped creature all covered with scales. Its narrow feathered fingers stretched upward, reaching for the light. There were creatures like clouds, sailing forth in a loose group, waving their tasselled tails. She swam in their wake, chasing them the way she herself was chased in dreams, feet lifting and falling but propelling her not at all. The clouds moved away from her, and now she came upon a cage, a box made of lace where tiny silver fish slid through its walls.

It was marvellous here. She did not want to leave. But she was being caught, dragged, perhaps by a current. She was suddenly heavy, out of the water, and in pain.

Her father was there. So was Maxwell. The intense young man bringing his face up very near to hers, to feel her breath, was, she supposed,

Herbie Wishart. The dynamite fellow had lifted her and set her down with her back against a rocky outcrop. She put her hand up to her cheek: it was pocked with gravel.

"She's fine," said Humphrey. "Do you see, she's trying to fix her hair."

"Water! Someone bring us water," said Herbie.

Her head lolled, and his hand went behind her neck. She could feel her father's irritation. Why was he angry? she wondered, her eyes shut. Was it because she was slowing down the work, or because the outfitter was touching her? Or because she was nearly dead? She was feeling languid and enjoying it.

Maxwell's soothing voice broke into her swoon. "Take her down to camp and How Long will fix her up."

They put her on a pony, which was painful in a distant way.

"The explosion has revealed the fossil-bearing band," Maxwell said. "A little to the north." And they moved off, her father's voice echoing in the remorseless rock.

Herbie had to sit behind her to stop her from slipping off.

"Are you all right, Mr. Wishart?" she asked. "I believe thee went on fire."

"I am just charred a little and madder than a hornet, ma'am. It was my own fault. Happy to see you unharmed."

"Thou took the greater fall."

"I'm chuffed to hear you *thee* and *thou* me—does it mean we're friends?" he said.

"I can walk," she said. "I'd much prefer it."

"Your father said you should ride." He held her on the saddle with a firm hand around her waist.

The pony clopped along on the sheep track. "Where did the animals go? Did they scatter?"

"Oh, not far. They've heard the odd loud bang before. Thunder and the like, rock slides, avalanches," said Herbie. "The furniture moves around here from time to time, you'd be surprised. They're pretty good at knowing what's a danger and what isn't. Though they do make the odd mistake." He started telling her about the ones who just stood there and let you shoot them.

"Doesn't sound very sporting."

"Don't tell the chaps from New York," he said. "They think they're brilliant."

"She knocked me out," Wishart said later that day and for the next week, the same old stale joke, until it became obvious that it was a very bad joke and a worse time to make it. "Isabel knocked me out when we first met."

But it was he who had knocked her out. And what a headache she got! Even so, she spent the rest of the day insisting to everyone that she was all right. She did not need to be taken down to Laggan. She did not need to see a doctor. A slug of whisky was what she needed, Wishart had said. Maxwell had looked repeatedly, searchingly, into her eyes. There was a scratch on her cheek, a bruise on her shoulder, and another one on her hip that no one was allowed to see. Her belly was hot, as if it still lay on that tropical ocean floor. They told her she must not, whatever she did, go to sleep. Then her father and the butler and the two men from Gateway went back to their quarry.

Humphrey kept an eye on his sister. She was chilled: he made a bed for her by the fire and covered her in blankets. She was thirsty: he brought cups of tea. She felt languid, a carryover from the world she had been visiting. She tried to tell Humphrey about One Arm and the crab. He listened. She dozed a little and tried to return to the warm sea, but it was stubbornly elusive. "Are you hurting anywhere?" Humphrey kept asking, waking her.

"It's fine. Thee can go back to work," she said.

"I don't work, you know that," he said miserably.

She gave him a hurt look at the word *you*.

He yielded to her wish to go back to the old family way they had spoken in childhood. "And I won't leave thee. I will talk to thee and keep thee awake."

They spoke of Rome and Florence, places they had seen only a few months before. He remembered how golden Italy was. She said that the gold there came from rocks, while here, though beauty was everywhere, there was no gold. There was black and white and grey and some red-brown. Gold was old, he said. It is about ruin and decay. That's why Italy is gold. There was yellow here, a lemony yellow. But it was not the old gold; rather, it was fresh, like an egg just cracked. He had seen it in the deep little hearts of the wildflowers: in fact July was all yellow, in the flowers. Isabel had never heard Humphrey talk about colours before: he had learned it from Phoebe Dixon. He then described the pearly marbled sculpted forms of Rome—muscled bodies, thighs, chests, hands with softly curling fingers. Humphrey confessed he had not been himself on this expedition. He had been moody. But he felt better now.

Isabel kept squeezing Humphrey's hand and then nodded a little and woke up to discover it was a rougher, sinewy paw, Herbie Wishart's hand. They, too, had a lovely chat, although later Isabel could not have said what it was about.

By dinnertime they allowed her to get up. She walked in circles, a little distance back from the fire. She was only slightly dizzy. Her father was writing in his diary. She wondered idly if he would make mention of the accident. She wandered behind where he sat at his improvised camp desk, a folding metal table, like a general might have in his campaign tent. Looking over his shoulder, she saw the words *block of fossiliferous siliceous shale*. Nothing about Herbie being tossed by an explosion, or Isabel being knocked over by the outfitter and fainting. Nothing about Isabel at all. She approached the fire, sat down and frowned into the flames. She suddenly remembered what she had been thinking about before the explosion: Phoebe Dixon and her father. The older woman romanticized him, a great scientist, a grieving widower. She did not know his ruthless side. Her father was giving little thought to Phoebe at present, but Isabel imagined he soon would get the idea that the lady could be useful.

Her skin felt warm, even slightly burned, by sun and fire and wind, by the excitement of the day. This was good. She didn't care to preserve that white, white skin. The women here let the effects of weather show on their faces. Phoebe Dixon was all browned and lined, and Dr. Hodgson was not disapproving of that lady.

"Miss Hodgson is restless," Maxwell said.

"I'm trying to find the best place to stand," she said. "The wind is bringing the smoke around."

He nodded solemnly. "Just don't drop off to sleep." They had all agreed that she was not to sleep heavily for the next twenty-four hours. Which was too bad because she would love to return to her tropical backwater and its elegant, fantastic inhabitants.

She stood up again and stepped away from the fire so she could see the moon. Behind her, Maxwell and her father were making plans with the guides.

"There's no need for you to stay around, Herbie," said her father. She knew he wanted to pack up as many of the newly exposed fossils as they could. "We'll leave in two days and meet you halfway." There was some talk about the trail they'd take: obviously, with a heavy load this time, they'd go out the short way. This was Friday. The twenty-fifth. They would rendezvous with him at the place called Nickel Lake near Laggan on Monday the twenty-eighth. Just over the ridge, around the back of the next mountain. Humphrey said he knew where it was. Maxwell and her father knew too. Once they'd met, Herbie would take them into Laggan, help load the fossils on the train and take the horses back to Gateway.

So the summer was ending. Isabel felt very sad. Herbie and Joe

Mariner were off leaning against some trees and smoking. So his pipe had been rescued. Mariner was saying how he doubted they'd disturbed any snow up above, but he'd never blasted up high before. You never knew. The red glow of Herbie Wishart's pipe bowl swayed in the air. Careful not to step on a twig, she advanced toward the enticing red dot.

"If you think you can sneak up on me, you got another think coming," said Herbie without moving a muscle. Then he pulled the pipe out of his mouth and laughed his high laugh. "I can sense a bear half a mile away in the bush. I've got the instincts of a primitive man."

"Are you meaning to entice me?" she said coyly, and then wondered where she got the nerve.

He had bagged a sheep that afternoon. She'd heard his shot; it echoed. Both she and Humphrey had stood up and shielded their eyes to see. He climbed nimbly up the slope to where the ram had fallen. He checked to see if it was dead. Then, when the body was barely still, he cut open the belly. Isabel blenched. It was a betrayal of their pact with the animals. The animals that had decided they were not dangerous.

"Why did you kill the sheep?" They were innocent, just figures on a hillside. They were silent and went about their business, minding no one.

"So we can eat," he said shortly.

"Who do you mean when you say 'we'?" she said.

"Folks in Gateway who I give it to. Or dudes like you."

"Is that allowed in the national park?" she wanted to know.

"It is not," he said. "That's why we don't do it in the national park."

Joe Mariner winked at her.

"Is this not the park?"

"No, ma'am. Not here. It starts just beyond the quarry. Right here they were just over the line. Do you see the line?" he said. "It's drawn right there in the ground."

She felt they were laughing at her. "If there are no stories tonight, I will retire," she said, retreating.

Herbie got serious.

"We could ride you down to Laggan first thing in the morning and see the doctor."

She shook her head no at him from the door of her tent, then turned and lifted the flap of canvas, staring into the darkness. She hesitated then and looked back at Herbie. She caught the expression on his face, one she had never seen before, of tenderness and concern. She wanted to reassure him. She blew him a kiss. It was a bold gesture, but she did not regret it for an instant.

No one stopped her going in.

Chapter 10
HELEN WAGG

Ottawa, August 31, 1911

On the very last day of August, Mr. B came into the office with a dark, stiffened face. She'd seen it often before. He got headaches and he was unwell for weeks; she knew of no other way to describe it. She had already decided to hold off their daily meeting before he called her into his office.

"There has been an event," he said.

"I take it not a good one."

"No. I had a call from the minister."

He gestured to a seat. Usually she didn't sit in his office but stood, and they sparred that way, somehow more at ease with each other. Sitting meant this was to be serious.

"Do you recall our American scientific friend who was visiting with his family for the summer? The archaeologist or geologist, whichever. And his family. From Washington. Bigwig Fairburnian fellow. We heard through the grapevine."

"Yes, yes, Hodgson. Dr. Hodgson. Of the Fairburnian. Excellent reputation. Top of his field. Also very well connected. The president and so on."

"The very man."

He reached out to his leather-trimmed blotter and began moving the slips of paper that she had tucked around the edges, little things for him to remember. His eyes remained down when he spoke.

"Well. He's lost."

She had a vision then of an old man—he was sixty, she was less than half that age, and forgive her, later in life she chided herself for this, but she imagined a man so old he might have wandered away from camp in his dressing gown.

"Oh no. Oh dear, oh dear." She thought of bears. She thought of him falling down a cliff.

"Actually, not just him. The whole party. Son and daughter, a Chinese cook, a couple of cowboys and a string of packhorses. And his butler, for the love of God."

"Oh, that's just too dreadful. How could they be lost?" she cried. "Didn't they go out with a guide?"

"They did, as a matter of fact. The guide is one I believe you're familiar with. One Herbie Wishart. They went out with him, but apparently they were coming back on their own. And they didn't show up at the rendezvous."

Helen grimaced. She knew Wishart, all right. At least as well as you could know a man who wrote you letters but whom you'd never seen in the flesh. "How did you hear that?"

"Got a telegraph from Laggan. Minister says he's going to have to issue a statement," he said unhappily.

"Why?" she said. But she knew why. It was a matter of public interest. And both she and Mr. B knew all too well how unpleasant this could be for the Parks branch.

*

Helen Wagg loved her job. She loved being a single career girl and living on the second floor of a brick walk-up with a leaky ceiling in Ottawa, close enough to walk to work. She loved Parks, she loved her boss, and she loved her role as his right hand. She still could fall into happy daydreams thinking of how it had come to her.

Not so long ago, she had been assistant to the assistant to the personal secretary to the minister of the interior. Her job was deciphering the minister's execrable handwriting and reading newspapers. If it continued she would need eyeglasses by the time she was twenty. When the personal secretary left with a blonde, everyone had moved up a peg, but not Helen. This type of thing went on: it was a sign of the new century, which was in some way dragged down, Helen thought, by the last. In the twentieth century men up and left their jobs with blondes, yet when they did, and a vacancy was created, women in the civil service did not pop up into their places like corks. No. Bowen, the assistant to the personal secretary, became the new personal secretary, and a new *man* was brought in from the side to be Bowen's assistant. She was to be kept down in a very nineteenth-century way. She had carried on with her work, alone.

Then they sent Bowen off to Mexico. He was to investigate the idea of Canada sending its trouble-making, freedom-touting, nude-marching Doukhobors there. This was apparently a serious possibility. Anyway, Bowen went off, and she was alone with her deciphering and her newspaper clipping, and then suddenly on a spring day he had appeared beside her desk. He extended a wrist—white cuff and gold cufflinks with the initials *JB* engraved—and brushed away some newspapers to take a one-cheeked perch on the edge of her desk.

"Are you fed up yet?" That was how he greeted her. As if he knew her frustration, and knew she was meant for more. "So what's been happening while I've been gone?"

"You're back!" she stumbled. "How was Mexico?"

"It's a fine place for sunshine and moonshine, but we won't be sending our citizens there," he said. "There's no work for them. They would be reduced to peons. Slaves on the big estates, that's all they could be."

Helen giggled. She always felt like giggling when Bowen was around. And he was not afraid to stretch the truth to make a point. He was a man for escapades, he was. And he was sitting on her desk with his Mexican tan and saying, *Are you fed up yet?*

"A little fed up," she said. "Perhaps, yes." But she didn't know if she should admit to it, or what she was admitting to being fed up *with*. She smiled, and when she did she could tell by the stiffness in her cheeks that she'd been holding a poker face for the weeks he'd been gone. She really did admire Mr. Bowen. He was so healthy-looking. His brown hair bristled and his neck was full and strong above the tight collar of his shirt, and his brown eyes took her in and spoke back to her, full of messages and mischief—oh, she had no idea really what they were full of, but they were eyes she could not keep her own eyes away from. Because he was dead serious, of course. It was just that he was so different from the dedicated civil servants who couldn't say poop if their mouths were full of shit. He had been a newspaper man in his previous life.

The truth was that yes, she was a lot fed up. With clipping newspapers. With not bobbing into place. But she was a little nonplussed that he had known, and she continued to smile meekly up from her desk, the surface of which was adrift in newspapers. She hid her hands. She was always slightly ashamed that they became so dirty with printers' ink. Then she thought, Damn it, he's asking. I'm going to ask back.

"With what, Mr. Bowen? Am I fed up?"

"Fed up with politics."

"Oh yes, well, if you put it that way." Politics was their bugbear. They were here to do the work, as far as she and the other civil servants understood. Politics entered it unhappily through the elected representatives of the people. These representatives were regarded as difficult, stubborn, ignorant, sometimes unpredictable—and hence, there to be manipulated. If the department failed in its efforts to manipulate, that was politics.

"Because I have a proposal for you," he said.

"Oh?"

"You know since we've had our vacancy, unnnh, I have been offered two choices, one being Parks, the other being Waterfalls. I have it in mind to choose Parks. National Parks. A new branch, unnnh. Would you like to come over to it and work for me?"

"Why I—" she said. And then she thought she should display a little caution. "What, may I ask, is a national park?"

He laughed broadly. "That's why I like you, Helen," he said. "You put your finger right on it." And he picked up her hand from the desk and brushed the end of her index finger with several of his, which were rough and dry and tobacco-stained. "I don't know what it is either," he said, "but it sounds easy."

Since then the country's mood, and certain events, had come together at the right moment. The Dominion Forest Reserves and Parks Act had been passed, setting aside seventy-five hundred square miles for independent management, removed from all other acts but the Criminal Code.

It all had to do with the conservation movement that was sweeping North America, a continent once seen as vast and unbreachable. But in this new twentieth century a different idea had taken hold. Everywhere, politicians and the people themselves saw limits to the bounties of nature. Birds, game, wilderness and Indians were "gone," or at least "harnessed," or more frankly "disappearing." Hence the setting aside of a preserve.

The size of this kingdom was beyond imagining. It had begun with Sir John A. and a little bill setting aside a few square miles as "national park" around a hot springs near the railway line. These springs had been discovered by a couple of track builders, but the government had stepped in to claim the place. At that point it had nothing to do with the disappearing wild but with the feeling that if money was to be made from this springs, then the government ought to make it. There were at that time only two primitive bathhouses, but the crowds were coming. Miracles were being reported; pilgrims threw away their crutches and put up tombstones to their rheumatism. People too poor to pay for lodgings camped out in tents.

Before too long the reserve was increased to 260 square miles, with more land added farther west. But that was small potatoes compared to this new act creating the Rocky Mountains Park out of what they used to call the Canadian Pacific Railway Rocky Mountains and Hot Springs Reserve. It was a land area three hundred times the size of the previous sanctuary. This necessitated a new department, and because of the business with the blonde, it was handed to Mr. Bowen, who was proposing that Helen bob up like a cork into her rightful place.

"Yes," she said. She would like to come over and work with him.

Within two months the staff of six had moved to this new building. None of the staff knew anything about the territory of this new national park. Forests had been in charge for the last twenty-five years, and had done absolutely *rien*. There was nothing out there, of course—a mission and a little Indian settlement at Morleyville, some coal mines, a small town at the Three Sisters and another at Laggan, and so on.

Her first task in the new branch had been to inspect the timber leases. Because, as Mr. Bowen had said, those timber companies were on sufferance in the forest reserves. They did not own the land they cut trees on. The government owned it, and the companies had leases. Mr. Bowen wanted those timber companies out. He was very clever. He had no doubt that the lumber companies were breaking the terms of their leases left and right. They were only to take out dry timber. But of course everyone knew they were taking out fresh green timber.

"It only stands to reason," he said to Helen. "They will do whatever they want because no one is looking." She was to go through those leases and see if there were any ways in which they'd broken their promises, and then give back to Mr. Bowen a list of the ways. And she did that, finding a great many inconsistencies in the reports that had to be filed citing their sales and areas of cutting. There were nineteen violations, to be exact, and the government went ahead and cancelled those leases. Just like that. It was quite a feeling. She, Helen, exercising that power, being the unseen hand that caused that edict to be sent out.

Satisfied with her work on the timber leases, Mr. B told her, "Your next task is to find a better name than Parks. We've got to, unnnh, capture the imagination of the people, and especially of the members of Parliament, because they will give us our budget. The idea of a park is nothing to them. They'll, unnnh, think it's just the sort of thing you see around town with benches and flowers."

She giggled, but it was true. She sat in the dripping heat of July in Ottawa, in her second-floor office in the Birks Building. Park, she thought. Park. Park, park. Not a royal park. Hyde Park or Richmond Park. Or St. James's Park. Nor was it Central Park. Not Park Avenue or Park Lane. Not Stanley Park. Or one of those European game parks with animals that the nobles could shoot. Close, but definitely not what was intended.

She hadn't realized how literary the whole park idea was. Not Mansfield Park. Or Eden, for god's sake, though you'd think it was, to hear them talk. *That* was a park. This was the Rocky Mountains Park. A *national* park, but still tagged with the *P*-word.

It was a lousy word. They both agreed it was a lousy word. She and her boss, the brilliant and open-minded, strategic, good-humoured and always energetic James Bowen, agreed. Helen Wagg rocked back in her chair. She put the end of her pencil in her mouth. She chewed and no further thoughts came. She was afraid she was going to fail in this second task, this all-important task of naming that had been given to her.

Helen was a reader. She loved novels. She had lived through them during childhood: English novels of the nineteenth century on hot summer days in the shade. Russian novels in translation on winter nights at the library. Even Canadian novels, although they tended to be moralistic. *Black Rock*, for instance, by Ralph Connor, was about miners in the mountains and a beautiful Scottish widow who stayed behind to save them. These days the shelf of books in her garret (she liked to think of it as a garret, although the roof of the house was flat and the ceilings quite horizontal) was stacked with poetry, because usually after work she was too tired for a full page of sentences. She had a great respect for the persuasive power of words. There had to be a stronger one than *park*.

Preserve?

Expanse?

Playground?

Sanctuary?

"Mr. Bowen?" She tapped gently on his open office door. "I don't disagree with you that it is a paltry word, *park*. But if you were to ask me what I think, I would say that one word or another in isolation cannot make or break our case." She always used the subjunctive in presenting an idea of her own. She actually couldn't remember where she had learned that trick. Perhaps she had read it in a book about women joining men in the working world. But perhaps it had come naturally. She presented all her ideas this way, and they were very often successful.

"What is it you're suggesting?" he said, his keen eyes remaining on her face.

She lost her nerve then. "Nothing really, just thinking out loud." And she backed out of his office knowing she had to find a word.

Helen was also a pacer; she paced. Luckily, the office allowed for it. There was a door, and beyond the door a marble corridor, a strip of tile overlooking the staircase with its brass bannister and a window giving onto the building across the street. Here in the corridor she could walk up and down, and she did. No help. There was another place Helen liked to pace and that was over at the House of Commons. She returned to her desk, sat down, stood up, straightened her stockings and her dress, and walked out the door again. She was often asked to go over to the Commons, so no one thought to intercept her.

What was a park, after all? The dictionary (she had consulted one first thing) said it was a place where military vehicles were kept. Well, not anymore. If asked to say in her own words what a park was, she would say this: A park is an area of land set aside for the public to enjoy. A protected place.

Protectorate?

No, that actually was a political entity, and she wanted to avoid that.

Pleasure ground?

That was in the initial legislation, but it sounded a bit dated, did it not? How about *pleasure dome*? A bit Coleridge? Involving mind-altering drugs? She had not studied English literature for nothing. She felt a longing to see the poem. There was a good deal there to consider: had Coleridge perhaps been thinking of parks management when he wrote his lines "In Xanadu did Kubla Khan / A stately pleasure-dome decree"? No, it was another of those opium hazes he put himself in. Still, "romantic chasms," "caverns measureless to man," "a sunny pleasure-dome with caves of ice."

She walked through the East Block and into the Parliamentary Library; the spines of books surrounding her, she walked its curved aisle. Nothing spoke to her.

Playground. But that took her to women and beatific-looking, curly-haired children. Swings and teeter-totters and wailing toddlers. She was allergic to those. No, we didn't want snotty noses; this was a wildlife park. This grand new area cordoned off, a kingdom to run: a haven, a place of beauty saved from the ravages of timbering, mining and industry, whatever terrible activities were got up to out west by people trying to make a living.

No. This would be a place where beauty was reserved or preserved in an ideal state for people to enjoy. There would be grand scenery. And wild animals. The animals were to be kept wild. No. Not "kept" wild. That in itself was a contradiction. The animals were to *remain* wild. Although they would be available for viewing. And posing for pictures. People liked to have their pictures taken with animals. She stayed at the library all afternoon, and when she emerged, she realized that it was Friday.

Weekends were slow in Ottawa. On weekends, Helen felt the lack of a spouse. She wrote to her sister and her mother; she cleaned her apartment and went to the market for food, and listened to the radio at night. Her Sundays were not quite empty, however, because her uncle lived in town. He was an odd man, Uncle Fitz, a sophisticate, her mother always said with distaste, escaped from the farming community of Lowell in southern Ontario to university and then to something obscure in the public service. Which was fortunate because when Helen came along and no one knew what to do with her, he could be sent an appeal.

It was he who had got Helen the job. Picked her up at the train station in the capital city and carried her bags to the little apartment, looked up at the stain in the ceiling and warned her about the leak. Every Sunday he had her over for lunch in his Rockcliffe house. It made an anchor for her empty weekends. Saturday night she stayed in, and the next morning she brushed her hair and ironed a fresh blouse. This Sunday she marched up Uncle Fitz's front steps and patted the dog—How do you do, Jimbo?—causing a cloud of hair and dust to rise up from his back.

She sat with her sherry. Her "aunt" had given it to her and left the room. They were an unusual couple. They had no children. The house was full of newspapers, and books were splayed open on the piano stool. No children, but they had each other. Helen appreciated their oddness; it lent them an air and ensured that they had sympathy for her, a working girl. However, they were becoming more odd, and that worried her: would they go from an endearing eccentricity to the kind of thing that would embarrass her? It was getting close—they were wearing stained clothing, mouthing antisocial beliefs and letting their house fall into disrepair.

There were African violets on the windowsills. There was dust on the varnished tabletops. The couches were covered with dog hair. She would be sneezing before long. Her uncle stepped in the door. Its dark wood trim seemed to set him in a portrait frame, grizzled, bright of eye and wide, although his tight belt and the pants it gathered around his waist made it look as if he'd lost pounds. He walked for miles in the Gatineau.

"How's the job, Helen?"

"I am enjoying it very much, thank you, Uncle Fitz."

"Are you making me proud? You know I want you to make me proud."

"I hope so, Uncle."

"Excellent. Enjoy your sherry. I'm just finishing up some reading and will be with you shortly. Where's Stella? Stella?"

"She's getting the dinner." Slowly. It was already nearly two in the afternoon.

Helen pressed the crystal sherry glass against her top lip. She could feel her eyes starting to water. She tapped the cushion on the sofa beside her, and a cloud of dust rose from it. Stella entered the room looking harassed.

"Helen, I heard you thumping. What can I get for you?"

"Oh nothing, it's just—I'm allergic to dust; perhaps you could take the pillow away?"

Stella gave her a hurt look.

Lunch would be substantial when it came, Helen knew; her weekly Sunday lunch was worth turning up for. Uncle Fitz was too, even though she did not believe, as others in her family did—not yet, not on your life, not ever—that her bookishness, her seriousness about work, her intelligence (people always said!) and the way she loved to debate the issues of the day would consign her to a fate like his.

The bell tinkled, and they assembled at the table, the boiled lamb congealing in its fatty skin as Stella trundled back and forth like the housekeeper she had been, with plates of cauliflower with asparagus sauce, new carrots and boiled Spanish onions with parsley sauce. Helen and her uncle bowed their heads for a fast grace.

"Rub-a-dub-dub, thanks for the grub," he said, and Stella, standing by with hands folded, laughed merrily.

She was plumper than he but not fat, just happy looking, and her face showed tan as if she too had been walking. What did they do? Collect rocks, watch birds? No one did that but them.

"That's a bit disrespectful, Uncle Fitz."

"We don't believe in God, do we, Helen? Stella?" said Uncle Fitz. "Nature is God, don't you think?" He picked up the gravy boat and began to pour out the caper sauce. "Now tell me everything."

"I carried out my first task well." She told him about the timber leases. "But I am failing in my second, I'm afraid."

"You aren't. I simply can't believe it."

"I will. Unless you can help me."

"What is it, girl? Don't be shy! Don't hold back." An open mouth with a rind of lamb in it.

"What do you call that?" She pointed out the window to the boulevard with trees and a circular flowerbed. Actually the flowerbed wasn't circular: it was in the shape of an insignia of some kind, one you wouldn't recognize.

"It's a park, my dear. A very small one. It may be a parkette."

"Or a parakeet," said Stella.

"A square, you know—but it isn't square, is it?" he said.

"A playground? But no. There's a sign right on it. You only have to go to the entrance to see. 'Active games prohibited,'" said Stella.

"Let's face it. It's a park. And *park* is too small a word." Helen placed her fork on the side of her plate. She had promised herself to eat lightly. Uncle Fitz dug in. "It does not suit these giant preserves we are making, and that we shall continue to make, to save the land, save nature, from progress. We need to call them something. *Park* is just too . . . mundane."

Uncle Fitz put down his fork too. "Well now, then that's your task, is it—to make a new word?"

"To make the whole idea more evocative. To give it a ring. To lift it into the imaginations of the people of this country. And the members." She couldn't help it but her voice began to sing out in a kind of imitation of her boss.

"Is that what Bowen wants you to do?"

"Yes. You see, we need to capture imaginations."

"Who was Mungo Park?" said Stella.

"Went down the Niger in a canoe, didn't he? Stuck on a rock. Shot at by natives. Drowned himself, if I'm not mistaken. Not sure he's the origin of the term. Stella, do sit down. And eat with us. I've begun to feel this is very awkward, you standing on guard as we feed. As it were." Uncle Fitz had a telegraphic style.

Helen blushed.

Stella looked about to cry and took herself off, sliding the pocket doors open to leave and sliding them closed behind her.

"Uncle Fitz, you've scared her off. That was very mean. Not like you, I have to say."

"Mean? I am trying to be kind!" Fitz roared. Helen shrank. "There are things you simply don't understand, my dear."

"You think?" She had an impulse to tell her uncle all. But she could not. Not take the risk that some conservative, antique part of his personality would be tipped over and old morality would spill out. She might have told him that she understood everything about his love for his housekeeper and his difficulty in moving her into the category of wife. People did have affairs, she knew about that. She had watched it unfold in the office. So had Mr. B, but of course he would never do anything like that. That made her feelings all the more potent.

She was bursting to tell it: she was enamoured of her boss. Oh, not in that way. You couldn't imagine that sort of thing with Mr. B. He was religious, but he didn't go to church. He believed, but in his own way. He believed in the power of being in nature. (Though he hadn't been *in nature* very much himself, she had to admit.) He believed it could persuade people of God's goodness. It could show us his plan for the universe. Helen took his words to heart, like the poems she'd learned in school: the air and the smell of the pines put new life, new fire in his blood. There would be no blondes in his life; he was a God-fearing man, and he was married.

But her uncle was not. She remembered the conversations between her parents, cryptic but easily deciphered—about how the housekeeper was no longer a housekeeper, and was it right to go on seeing Fitz, and her father saying, of course he could do what he wished, he had the money, and her mother sniffing, "As if money had anything to do with it!"

She could not tell all to her uncle.

"Helen, I think it is too much for your superior to expect you to reinvigorate a tired word. That is surely beyond and past the call of duty. You must tell him that."

So she had gone back to Mr. B saying there was no better word. *Park* may have been a paltry word but it was the word we had. It was the word that had been given. And it was already in place. That counted for a great deal. She was not sure it could be bettered. All the points her uncle Fitz had rehearsed with her. "I think that it is in the *sway* of words we'll find our power, not just in one or another *term*. A park is a park. But we are not limited to one word. We can *describe* the park."

"True." He had given his head a little sideways jerk, one of his ways of saying she was grand, and put out his hand—not to touch hers, but to lay it flat and open on his paper-covered desk—and said, "Why don't you write me something?"

Helen was overjoyed. On naming she had failed. But Mr. B was a forgiving man. He had given her elaboration; he had given her seduction by words. It was easy to write; it was only taking down the phrases that spilled from him when he got going. His passion welled. He had a vision: mountains, endless and eternal and belonging to all, and never, ever to be used for any other purpose but to enlighten and benefit the people. She toyed with Wordsworth's "something far more deeply interfused" through wild nature and the great solitudes. William Blake's "A Robin Redbreast in a Cage / Puts all Heaven in a Rage." Ernest Seton Thompson's "Turn but a stone, and start a wing." And of course again Wordsworth—"mid the din / Of towns and cities" the "sensations sweet, / Felt in the blood, and felt along the heart"—returned to one.

She got most of that down.

And Mr. B was pleased with what she wrote.

"Miss Wagg, I accept that you turned your second task on its head, dexterously. We have ceased to search for a name. We have a name, and now, thanks to you, we have persuasion. There is a third task we must accomplish"—it was like a fairy tale, she knew that, and that made it even more fun—"and that is to create an *argument* to sell the concept. To the members. To make it come alive to them. To give them reason to wholly jump aboard. You see, because they are jaded, those men. The point being"—he often used that expression—"that we will need to drum up support to vote us a large appropriation of money from the legislature. We will need funds. You are persuasive with your words. But they are not in themselves sufficient. We need a rationale. Do you understand? A compelling reason, one that will get those members up on their feet." And Mr. B said to her, "Go and dig! And bring back anything you can that we can use."

So she had dug. She wasn't sure what he meant by "anything we can use," but she read reports about Indian reservations (not good) and timber reserves (no) and treatment for eczema in hot springs baths (perhaps of interest, but not entirely savoury). She liked it when Mr. B asked her to dig. He was treating her, she thought, like a journalist, and a journalist was one thing she would have loved to become when she graduated from the University of Toronto.

She took two stenographer's pads out of the supplies cabinet. Not that there had ever been one bit of stenographic work in her job description. She was proud of that. It was sometimes hard to make people fully aware of this. But being graduates in the first decade and a half of female students at the University of Toronto had been arduous enough, when memory was still alive of the few women allowed entrance being kept in an antechamber off the lecture hall and required to goose-neck around the door to hear the professor. These humiliations were made much of by male students, eighty percent of them laughing about the fact that there were no women's washrooms and ten percent using the hostility of their fellows as an opportunity to present themselves as being among the very few who accepted them and wished to help. The other ten percent were embarrassed by the whole thing and therefore ignored the female students altogether.

On the positive side, the few women—a matter of tens amid thousands—had befriended each other, and now Helen had an excellent collection of friends scattered here and there scrounging for work or admittance to professional schools. She had been proud to be able to tell them—she hoped it wasn't boasting—of her job in the civil service, gained through influence of an old family friend (she didn't name her uncle), and especially that it involved no secretarial work.

On her lunch hour she went again to the Parliamentary Library. To go there was reflex, meaningless, like needing to put on your glasses before you could have a serious conversation. She found the old legislation from 1900, before she had started with the government, saying, "the Park embraced . . . several Noble Mountain Ranges . . . 65 miles of Good Roads and Bridle Paths have been made." Blah blah blah. Nothing close to a seduction or a rationale.

Escaping the walleyed gaze of the librarian and the expanse of brown leather book spines, she went out the front door, crossed two streets and climbed the stone steps of the Ottawa Public Library. A young mother came out the door with children, the little ones holding hands. Helen smiled distantly; never had she imagined herself to be in this woman's shoes. Helen was a different breed of woman altogether. Yet this place was more propitious, of the people, as the park must be. She loved public libraries and felt at home there, having spent as much time as possible inside hers in Lowell during childhood, hiding from active games. She did not like to run, to jump hurdles, to skate, to swim, to play tug-of-war, to break out in perspiration, to compete on a team, to ride a horse. All of these activities brought her horrors. The more she avoided sports, the worse it was when sports were forced upon her, until eventually a nurse took pity on her and named a malady that kept Miss Helen Wagg permanently off the field hockey pitch.

Still, she was not feeble, and the stamina that her teachers and parents had wanted to instill in her by having her chase around in muddy fields with a stick had instead been built carrying stacks of novels home and chewing pencils fiercely and refusing to give up until she found what she wanted. "Dig" may have been a metaphor today, but the energy required was not metaphorical.

"Anything we can use" was very broad. He meant anything that could capture the imagination of the quarrelsome and stingy, corrupt and troublemaking members of Parliament—anything that could make them come together as one to raise their hands and vote dollars into the budget of the new Dominion Parks branch. Beauty was good for the soul, but who could convince these men that they should allocate money to preserve it? They believed that the country was endless, stretching off to the west where the sun set and where they'd never been, that there was plenty "out there" to give away as a reward to any industry that wanted it. You sent out regiments if people got out of line, or if traitors were bred. And you made money, which would all come trickling happily back east.

She had found her way to some musty volumes of the American Scenic and Historic Preservation Society, and began reading through the minutes of their annual sessions. She came upon a spot where one fellow—she imagined him as old, pompous, bewhiskered—stood up (wheezing before he spoke) and said, "I remind you that these beautiful places are worth money."

The sun came around the back and lit a lovely path from her window across the grass. She took out her pencil and opened her stenographer's pad, although she was certainly no stenographer, and she got the sense that she was rising yet higher above that position even as she wrote "worth money" and the reference.

Sunday lunch again.

"I approve of your Mr. Bowen," said Uncle Fitz. "Unfair assignment, asking you to invent a new word. But making a case by which to wrestle money from Parliament? A worthy exercise. Words can be so empty, my dear. Ideas will invest that word *park* with grandeur. Potential, that's it."

She tried him with the notion that had come into her head in the library, a cloudy but shaping thought. She quoted from the records of the Scenic and Historic Preservation Society of America: *These beautiful places are worth money!* "If we could sell it to Parliament as a profit-making scheme . . ." she said.

At this Uncle Fitz got very excited and slapped the table and invited Stella back in from the kitchen (because she had declined to eat with them). He beamed at her and said, "Helen has had a first-rate idea! That's the ticket, Helen!"

The thought of which emboldened her when she went into the office on Monday morning. She confided her idea to Mr. B, who loved it. He was always so good. It was his thought that they could make the calculations. And they worked it up, comparing the money that could be got from tourism to the entire wheat crop of the West. Out of it came the calculation for which they both should have been famous, which was this: whereas wheat fields were worth only $4.91 per acre to Canada, scenery was worth $13.88.

And much more could be computed, now that they had a few hard numbers. For instance, the secretary of the interior in Washington estimated that, formerly, over $100 million a year had gone to Europe as people holidayed. But the Americans had succeeded in redirecting much of that home to their own parks. In that vast and wealthier country the annual number of visitors to parks was 278,000. But already, in the smaller, less-populated country to the north, Canada, 120,000 people visited their own national parks each year.

Mr. B got out his slide rule. "We've done forty-three percent of what they did. Very, very good!" He whistled and performed another operation on his slide rule. "Using the same ratio, we can say that our Canadian parks will be worth somewhere in the neighbourhood of forty-three million dollars."

Helen's eyes popped.

"Get it down and get it in the annual report. The editors will love it. I can see the headlines tomorrow."

Numbers were good, but Helen needed to couch them in the kind of language that tugged at the heart. *Our national parks are vast treasuries to which we can return over and over to fill and refill our cups to overflowing with vigour of every kind—of the body, of the mind and, yes, of the spirit. It is as if we get blood infusions from the pines and the ozone.*

"Let's not talk about blood infusions," said Mr. B. "It makes people queasy."

"I thought nature was red in tooth and claw."

"I know, but let's not have it red just here. I'd prefer to go more mystical."

He was right about the headlines. It went in the *Halifax Chronicle* and the *Edmonton Bulletin* and in papers between those centres. Not only did the newspaper editors across Canada give them headlines, but they all wrote editorials to say what a wonderful investment the parks were. The eyes of the members of Parliament began to spin in small gold circles, and the branch received its first appropriation.

In the mysterious workings of Nature, wrote Helen, *the time for Parks has come.*

Chapter 11
THE TROUBLESOME EVENT

Ottawa and Gateway, September 1911

And now, when summer was nearly gone, a call from the minister. Important Americans had gone missing. Members of a fossil-hunting expedition had failed to show up at the rendezvous point with their guide. Yes, she knew Wishart. And she badly wanted to blame him.

Contrary to her first idea—that the kingdom of the Rocky Mountains Park was pristine and empty and traversed only by innocent wild creatures—people did live there. All right, the Indians were now out of it, but there were hundreds of regular people, some more unsightly than others, all living off the people's territory, breathing its hallowed air, shooting its wild creatures, grazing their horses and calling for the streets of their little towns to be paved. More of them, mostly foreigners, were working underground in the coal mines so the trains could run. That she could understand. But on top of that, quite literally, it had become clear that people were needed to serve the tourists, as guides and innkeepers, provisioners, what have you.

Little by little, a population had grown up, and it was without humility.

The people were a determined bunch with a talent for self-preservation, not to mention self-promotion. They were town boosters, it was a type; she knew what she was dealing with. They had themselves a newspaper, even. A person called Lyall Foxx owned it. Where he had got that extra *x* she did not like to think. Only a couple of months ago there was an editorial in the *Gateway Trumpet* that stung:

> *Mr. James Bowen is Commissioner of all the great national parks of this country, which makes him a King with divine rule over us here in the Rocky Mountains Park. But unlike God who sent his son, he has never set foot in Gateway. We find that a little odd. Maybe he's waiting for an invite. Well, here it is. Come and get a look at what's happening. Meet the folks! You might even step up and offer some assistance to your subjects. True, Ottawa is one hell of a long ride. James Bowen sounds off about the beauties here and how they are good for the soul of man. I guess he's seen the pictures. They look real purdy. Maybe that's why he stays out there in the East. If you get up close you'll see the sewage in the stream and the bears in the garbage . . .*

Helen had a special dislike for Foxx as well. But he was outdone by this Wishart man. From time to time he wrote to Mr. B, wanting more room for hunting, or cheaper game licences, or just to tell him what he should do with this paradise in which he, an Englishman, had set down his roots. When Mr. B asked Helen to respond, and she did, Wishart started writing to her too. He had a nerve, considering that he was engaged in prohibited activities in every season. He was quite open about it: everyone knew. He trapped in winter and complained about the park's boundaries cutting him out from his territory—"his" territory! If he wasn't trapping, he was cutting timber where he wasn't allowed to and floating it down the river to the Kananaskis. He was grazing his horses where he wasn't supposed to; he was building his trapping cabins where he shouldn't; he was thoroughly annoying, and he wrote a very good letter.

His missives charmed Mr. B; her boss loved to read aloud, admiringly, Wishart's descriptions of dudes on the trail.

"The man's got a gift," Mr. B would say. "Listen to this—'He climbed up on the horse like a swami assaulting the hind leg of a camel.'" And he would laugh with delight, taking off his glasses and placing his fingertips in the inside corners of his eyes—to stop tears. Since Mr. B's laughter was highly cherished by Helen, she took to disliking Wishart, who made it happen far more easily than she did.

If you took his letters seriously you'd think the whole of Gateway lived on whisky. He described the curling games that had become popular in town. "We used the ice down in front of the Sanatorium because it was handy to the medical supplies, if you understand my drift. Thing was, some of the fellows who were signed in for treatment got the idea. I was buying my whisky when I heard the most awful crashing coming from the ward, so we dashed up to look and found in the corridor several dipsomaniacs in their well-vented nighties having a bonspiel of their own using those tin 'rocks' that were generally kept under their beds." Mr. B leaned back in his chair and shook with laughter, and despite the fingertip trick, tears would spill over his lower lids.

But he was not laughing now. Helen Wagg frowned.

"Why would this important party of scientists go out with that buffoon?"

"I suppose because he's the best," said Mr. B mildly. "Finds the game, you know. Knows the trails like nobody else. Made half of them. Good man in an emergency, I hear. Not to mention that he tells a good story. Do you remember the one he told about the time when the grizzly came out of the stump?" Despite his anxiety over the bad news Bowen smiled reminiscently at an incident he looked ready to relate.

Helen tapped on the edge of the desk to bring him back.

"But these are scientists, not hunters. What were they after?"

"Well, that's just it. Fossils, it seems. Wishart sent the telegraph but won't talk to the press: he's being uncharacteristically shy. Says the party camped for the summer on their own, looking at rock formations with a big Kodak No. 8 Cirkut. Said they knew how to get out, but they never made it to the meeting place. There was a storm, so he waited a few days. Then he went back in to their camp, but they were gone. Vanished somewhere in between, is what he says." Bowen put his middle fingers to his temples and rubbed absently. "I expect they'll show up soon."

Helen wondered how far it was and how a party of five, plus cowboys, plus horses, could disappear. "What kind of a storm?"

"Real blizzard. First of the season. Early." He had begun to have his faint look. "Helen, can you do a little damage control?"

And so she spent the day calling newspaper editors, to accomplish the opposite of what she normally attempted, which was to fan the flames of curiosity and drama. She was fanning all right but with a thick wet cloth, which she then dropped on top of the story, putting it to bed, she hoped. Bringing down the tension, using phrases like "probability there was a misunderstanding" and "a bit of difficult weather," and inserting the word *yet*, as in "have not turned up at the rendezvous *yet*."

But they did not turn up that day, or the next. The week went on. And despite her best efforts, she could not tame the reaction. Herbie Wishart went quiet: she got in touch with Lyall Foxx, who said Wishart was out looking. Her wet blanket was getting singed, in fact burnt right through. Newspapers across the country began to get excited. She had thought the editors were her friends; they regularly took her releases for copy. But no, these men were faithless! No sooner did they get wind of this accident— Accident! Who said it was an accident? The party was simply late. Or it had decided to take another route. It was a big place. They would turn up. There was no evidence of misadventure, and certainly not of foul play. But by Friday the story had moved from the inside pages to the front page, above the fold.

"Celebrated scientist vanishes in Canadian Rockies."

"What befell doomed party?"

"Blizzard, bears or avalanche?" That was the beginning of an editorial out of Montreal.

"Are Canadian parks safe?"

Of course they're not, she fumed to herself. If they were safe, what fun would that be? To make them safe there'd have to be regular patrols on the trails, and that was an absurd notion. Some crackpot in the West got himself on the line to a New York reporter and suggested that the expedition had been sabotaged because "the fossils belonged in our country, not yours." Somebody else thought they might be spies, with that big camera—but what would they be spying on way out there?

That Friday was the day before the Labour Day weekend. It had been a week since the Hodgson party failed to show up at the meeting point. On Saturday *The Washington Post* got in on the act. Concern was expressed for the eminent archaeologist and his family. The reporter wondered if their northern neighbours were holding the visitors hostage, as if the Americans had ventured out of the known world and into a barbarous empire where no person or animal could be trusted. Then the cowboy newsmen in Montana and Colorado began to run with the story of the mishap—all right, she was ready to call it a "mishap."

Monday was quiet—the holiday, no papers. Tuesday Helen came to work and called in every favour she could remember, telegrammed every conservationist friend she had on file, and had Mr. B do the same. But they were losing ground. Washington was unhappy. The public was concerned, and the rumble about the safety of the parks was becoming louder. Wishart was nowhere to be found, and the Hodgson party had been missing for eight days.

The story had traction south of the border. The press was definitely not friendly to the newly formed Parks branch, the only national parks administration in the world. All that conference attending and mutual planning with their friends in Yellowstone. All the poetry and the nights around the campfire. All ready to blow sky-high. The Mounted Police were called in to search; the problem was, the only person who really knew the trails was the guide who'd got the party lost. And he was being surly and taciturn. To go out on a search the Mounties would have to leave their horses behind, because despite their reputation for fancy dancing, Mountie horses were too tall and clumsy for the rocky trails.

The first big break came when one of the lost saddle ponies turned up in the corral at the hotel at Laggan. But nobody was sure how long it had been in there, and the animal couldn't talk.

As it happened, the blizzard turned out to be not a freak one-shot whiteout, but the first shudders of winter. A week later wind and snow were raging up in the beyond, to hear tell. Snow was filling the valleys and blowing between the peaks. Snowfall even buried the rail line. It would end, the locals insisted. It would end and then would come the famous "Indian" summer. But by then it might be too late.

Helen tried to protect Mr. B from the worst of it because his headache was fierce. She thought each day the expedition would turn up. But the Hodgsons stubbornly remained lost. Rumbles from the United States grew more threatening. At this point Theodore Roosevelt promised to send up some of his riders. "Call off the dogs STOP What's the use of troops STOP," Herbie Wishart telegraphed. "None of them knows the backcountry and I do STOP."

"Do not obstruct the search STOP," she telegraphed back. "Comply or you look as if you've got something to hide."

As soon as the sky cleared Herbie and Francis Erwin went back to the site. In the snow the whole terrain seemed transformed. It was so utterly changed it seemed as if there'd been a rock slide above the campsite.

"Oh, holy shit," Herbie said to Erwin. "Look at this. The whole slope came down."

"It did," said Erwin, "but who's to say when?" The layer of snow made it hard to tell. He didn't see any uprooted trees.

Herbie pointed out that you wouldn't, because they were above the treeline. Erwin was a thinker; he should have figured that out. "I'd say it's recent."

"Recent, I don't know. In geological time a couple of seconds is a few hundred years, right?"

They smiled sardonically at each other: they'd taken to speaking in Hodgsonisms.

Herbie scrambled on the slope, kicking at rocks. He was ready to strangle the Hodgsons; he was sick with nerves, and he was angry at himself. The summer had gone well; he'd hooked up with a few good customers. Since the beginning he'd left the Hodgson party to look after itself. The plan for leaving was clear: meet Monday at Nickel Lake. But no, a balls-up. What had he done wrong? He was looking for the hitch. The mistake. Could this be it? Using dynamite had brought down a rock slide? But Joe Mariner was the best. Joe knew what he was doing. The miners put their lives in his hands when they went down in the mantrip.

A couple of days later they brought him up the blaster. Mariner scratched his head. He had a good look. He said he was no expert on dating a rockfall. He stood pointing with his short arms. But even if he *could* say it had happened a week ago, say, at the end of August, he couldn't see how his blast over there was connected to a slide over here. He would have admitted a mistake if he thought he'd made one: he was a straight-shooter. But the slide was too far away. There was no fault line connecting the two slopes, the rock strata were all going the wrong way, and nothing he could see related the quarry to the slide.

"Are you sure?"

He shuffled his wide feet. Who could be sure? Okay, he supposed it was possible that the vibrations from the dynamite could have caused it. You just never knew. This was a surface slide. Overhang let go.

Might have had nothing to do with anything except that suddenly an age-old balance was tipped. Or the wet from the snowfall, the wind, loosened that little wee bit that tipped the balance. An act of God, no one's fault.

"I told you everything's a risk, Herbie."

Had he told him that?

"Look, the Gateway mines have one of the best safety records anywhere. But I'm always afraid when I blast. Fearful, you know? Mountains got their ways. Their secrets, you know? Strong places, weak places." Mariner squinted across to the peaks. "Old, old mountains. Complicated set-up—rock on rock, water, cracks, boulders. In the mine, I tell you I can sometimes feel these old guys fighting back. Well, they would want to, wouldn't they?"

Herbie closed his eyes against the vision that arose. The old crags and ridges splitting open, raining boulders and stones. If a slide started coming at the Hodgson party, no one would know which way to run. They were so heavily burdened with the damn fossils. Maxwell marshalling the young ones, the professor shouting to get the fossils clear, the horses panicked and rearing, great rocks beginning to bounce over their heads. The professor down like he was shot, Humphrey galloping clear on his horse, and Isabel. What about her?

What came next—a clump of people and horses effectively stoned to death—was horrible to conceive. Herbie couldn't even think about it, much less talk about it. He shared with no one that he was awestruck by the *irony*, that the Hodgson bodies should be pressed down under tons of rock in the same way the fossils they'd prized so highly had been pressed down by some ancient onslaught of mud. Perhaps it was divine retribution. A cosmic rebuff to their explorations.

He did not wish to make further searches. It gave him the willies. He concluded that no one had escaped. And he grieved for them all. He just wanted it to be over. He figured people would come back at some point and move the rocks. The bodies must be underneath. But for now, attempts at recovery were not recommended. So said the police. So said the Parks officials. Could set the whole thing off again.

But what did the Mounties know? What did Ottawa know?

People asked him all the time if they had looked. Well, of course they had looked. Because the first snow eventually blew off and Indian summer did arrive. There were search parties—scientists, Americans. Folks from the Fairburnian. Even this new bunch of hopped-up cops called the Federal Bureau of Investigation. Suspicions of espionage. Other agents trying to undermine the United States of America in its sacred scientific quest. But even the FBI could see it was unlikely. Nobody spoke to the Stoney Indians, possibly an oversight, but on the other hand nobody spoke any Stoney, plus the Stoneys weren't overly talkative.

There were those, Phoebe Dixon among them, who absolutely did not believe the Hodgson group was buried under rock or snow. To them, the whole rock slide story was a red herring to distract from some event where humans were at fault. And the truth was that the longer the rock slide idea was around, the less convinced of it Herbie was himself. There was no proof. Not a speck of evidence. As an explanation, it seemed too convenient. It took all the responsibility off the expedition members themselves. And let's face it, Maxwell was overconfident. They were greenhorns—except for How Long and the Tree brothers, who were not making the decisions.

He found himself back up at the site. He had a good look at the rocks. With the snow gone, the edges were exposed. He walked over them. They were worn. And there was lichen. Yes, it was a rock slide, but from many years ago.

This could not be the burial ground.

But if it was not, where was the Hodgson party?

Could Maxwell have misunderstood about Nickel Lake? Had something scared the horses so they bolted? Had something led them to take the long way out? Walk through the Snow Bowl and along the ridge? Take that turn at the rock wall? If they had turned the wrong way—hard to imagine but possible in a blizzard, maybe even deliberate—they'd have been headed not down to Gateway but upward and north. They would have been in for a long struggle with those ponies and the weather. You didn't have much time up there when winter came on.

Chapter 12
GWEN

Gateway, September 10, 1911

THE PLEAT BETWEEN GWEN'S EYES deepened as she searched the station platform. She could not see her father, who was tall and stood out in a crowd. She could not see his square, flat face with the waxed moustache and pulled-in chin. She could not see Maxwell either. Then she spied the four-horse tallyho with SANATORIUM HOSPITAL written on the awning. A man in a cowboy hat was driving the horses.

Gwen shouted and stuck out her hand to flag him.

"Don't point, Gwen," said her chaperone.

"We're being met by a Mr. Wishart," she said to the driver.

"I beg your pardon, ma'am, but I doubt it," said the cowboy. "Unlikely to get here. I've come for yis. Sanatorium, is it?"

"We're staying with Dr. Smallwood."

"Like I said." The cowboy had a crop of whiskers and bad breath and a couple of teeth missing. He pushed his hat back off his forehead to get a better look at them. "Doctor's kin, are ya?"

"Not that doctor."

The driver had a way of solemnly attending to his horses and the clomp of their shod feet, while at the same time aiming practised lines back over his shoulder to the passengers up high on the seat behind him. He delivered the advertisement the way he always did. "You got baths there in Turkish, Russian, tub or douche style. The water comes from the hot sulphur springs. There are trained nurses."

Gwen thought perhaps someone was sick. "Why do people go to the Sanatorium?"

"Because they're fat. They need to work off the effects of rich living. Okay, a few for rheumatoid arthritis. Others are just off their heads—the pressures of modern living. Others are"—he turned and gave them a wink—"dipsomaniacs! You know?"

Gwen didn't know.

"Tell you, last winter one of them dipsos who was longing for the bright lights of town escaped through a window wearing only his glamour gown. They went after him, afraid he'd die of the cold. He didn't, but one of the nurses did."

Gwen was shocked. "She did?" Then she said, "*We* are not ill!"

"No, ma'am, you aren't." Making conversation, he said, "So the Hodgson party didn't show up. Bad for business that!"

The chaperone took the girl's arm above the elbow. "I'm sorry, I don't take your meaning, sir."

"Didn't show up at the rendezvous. It's all in the news."

Gwen seemed not to have heard. "Will my father be at the Sanatorium, waiting? And my sister?"

"No. Not at this time," said the chaperone.

They travelled down a wide, muddy street to a square box of a house, unpainted, with a large veranda on which people sat in invalid chairs, covered to the chin in blankets. It was not warm. There was the sound of running water from the swift, bubbling river only yards away. Trickles of water ran down the rocks beside the house from the mountain above.

The maid insisted they come to the dinner table.

"The doctor'll be late. He's always a half hour late," she said. "I'm going to serve the soup."

They looked at the pictures on the wall. That must be him, performing surgeries in what looked like a boxcar, standing in profile beside a high bed flanked by women in white veils and white, full garments.

"Do you see? Four nurses with him! All in white," the chaperone said to Gwen.

In half an hour the doctor came through the doors; the chaperone stood up. He was the senior man in town and not acquainted with the Hodgson family, but he had agreed to host them here, considering the situation. He thought it odd that the girl had been allowed to come. Dr. Smallwood surveyed the two. The maid whirled in with his soup. He had a job to do, but he would eat first.

"What do you know about the place you've come to?" said the doctor, hoisting his soup to his mouth in the way of a man who typically ate alone.

"You sawed off a man's leg in a boxcar."

He was only too pleased to tell the story. Twenty-five years earlier, when they were building the last section of track, men were dying of Rocky Mountain spotted fever, and from the blasting, but Dr. Smallwood was able to keep this figure very low. They lost only four men.

"Four deaths is four families left without a father, four mothers without sons," chided the chaperone.

Several of them were Chinese, the doctor said in a mitigating way.

"When is my family coming?" said Gwen.

"We will discuss it after dinner."

It was while tending railway workers that the doctor had heard about the hot springs. Some of the fellows saw steam coming out of the side of the mountain. When they reached the spot they found a deep, odiferous pool half-covered with fallen timber and jumping with tropical fish and almost hot enough to boil.

"There are tropical fish here?"

"Oh, many varieties. You can find them down by the fens." Not to be sidetracked he went on. "When the area became a Hot Springs Preserve, I got permission to build a sanatorium."

"How does the water get hot?"

"It is simply snow that seeps into the mountain, drains down, meets the core of the earth and percolates back up, piping hot and smelling like rotten eggs. At first it was just a hole there with a ladder you had to climb down. The prime minister's wife herself climbed down it."

There was a respectful silence.

"What is this meat?"

"Elk," said the maid.

"Did you shoot it?" said Gwen.

"No, not I," said Dr. Smallwood. "But someone did. Probably Herbie Wishart. That's the man we're waiting for."

The light began to go not long after dinner; summer was ended. Half-heartedly they tried to dispatch the child to bed, but excited by the thought of seeing her family, Gwen would not go. There was a card table the doctor looked at out of the corner of his eye; he normally played poker at this time of day. Then came a knock on the door, and a man was led into the parlour, his hat twitching in his hands. But this was not Wishart either.

"This is Mr. Erwin," instructed the doctor. "He's one of our best packers. Excuse me a minute." He pulled Erwin aside. "Any sign of them? What am I to tell her? Why have you left this to me? Where the hell is Wishart?"

"He's searching. I don't need to tell you, he's taken it to heart, Doctor."

"Come and meet Miss Gwen Hodgson," said the doctor.

Francis Erwin bowed to Gwen grandly and took her hand to his lips. He answered the doctor's question while still smiling at the girl: "Wishart will be along in just a day or two."

"What is he doing?" said Gwen.

"Searching," Erwin told her, straight on. "I was too."

"For what?"

"For your father's party."

"Why?"

"They left their camp but did not arrive at the meeting spot. We think they may be lost."

Gwen pulled in her chin abruptly. She looked like her father then. "They can't be lost," said Gwen. "They're likely just dilly-dallying."

"I'm sure you're right," said Erwin. "You know all about dilly-dallying, don't you? Do you know how to ride?"

"A little."

"That's a start," he said. "Perhaps someone will teach you."

Gwen looked hopeful. It had been a dull summer. The trip west, begun ten days ago, offered excitement.

"Better you than the profane Herbie Wishart," said Dr. Smallwood.

People were angry with this Herbie man. Gwen picked that up. "Can't he ride?" she said.

"He's a good rider, but he's colourful," admitted Erwin. "And besides."

"Besides what?"

"He swears a lot."

"I should like to hear that," said Gwen.

"Miss Hodgson," said Dr. Smallwood with an air of gravity. "We must warn you. This is a serious situation. We are all concerned about the welfare of your father and the group."

Gwen raised her eyebrows in the doctor's direction. She had taken a dislike to him, and a liking to Francis Erwin. That's the way she was, always picking favourites. Her mother had scolded her for it. The more she liked one, the less she liked the others.

"I can see that you are worried," she said evenly. "But *I* am not going to worry. They'll come in good time." She suspected they had gone on somewhere interesting and left her behind.

"We don't know where they are. That is, they haven't been seen for a time. The Hodgson party. Your father, your brother and sister, Maxwell and—who was with them? The cook. The cowboys."

Gwen did not seem to grasp it.

"They didn't show up at the rendezvous."

"Perhaps they moved on to another camp but the guides didn't find the trail." Gwen was calm and smiling.

The doctor kept talking. The chaperone looked guilty: she had heard the news and kept it from her charge. Erwin turned his hat in his two hands, around in a circle once, then twice. The maid folded her hands in a neat triangle on her apron. Well, Gwen had her faith. Her family would return. There was some mistake, that was all. She stood, silent and a little white.

The next day Francis Erwin took Gwen riding. She stood beside her horse wanting to mount but not knowing how. Francis made long rides, days and days long, he told her. Being a packer was seasonal. He and the other guides stretched out the season as long as they could, taking to the trails in May, when they were mostly deep in snow, and staying out on the traplines until November. He spoke of this softly while fixing the stirrups for Gwen. She eyed the horse, which seemed small to her, smaller than any horse in Virginia.

"This is Brownie. Go around to her nose and make friends," he said, and so she did, though the horse chewed and spat, trying to dislodge the bit. Francis made a cup of his hands. Gwen put her wrong foot in.

"You'll be turned around facing backwards if you do that."

She gave him the other foot. He boosted her up, and she swung her leg over and landed with a sigh—air puffing up in her skirt—looking pleased.

"Next time wear some of your brother's trousers."

Late November and early spring—those were the times when he was able to get off by himself. He would go to one of the usual camps, a day's ride away, and leave his horse there, take only some water and biscuits, and head up narrow rockfalls or along ridges away from any known trail.

He went behind and untied his own horse, Cymbal, and mounted without seeming to do so. He just walked onto its back.

They ambled side by side along the river path in Gateway, Cymbal's and Brownie's hooves beating *onetwothreefour*. She asked him the names of the mountains. He showed her the Fist, and Mount Menace, and the Three Sisters—nuns they were, he said, not sisters like she and Isabel were sisters. Then he winced, as if he shouldn't have mentioned Isabel. Gwen noticed that. She pointed to each of the peaks, wanting to know their names. No names, he said, just Big Sister and Middle Sister and Little Sister. Then she wanted to know about the big white spaces between the mountains—and was that Whiteman's Gap? Yes, it was. And where did it lead? And where did the passes lead? And where is the farthest place, over there, she said, where there are no trails and no passes and where nobody goes?

"That's the Inaccessible," he said.

"Why is it inaccessible?"

"Because you can't get there. It's the glacier tops. Nobody can."

"Is that true?"

"Well, almost," said Francis.

"You have been there," challenged Gwen.

"The Inaccessible," said Francis, "is a kingdom where the animals rule themselves." He once saw, high in the saddle between the peaks, a big grizzly herding mountain sheep. Yes, he did. And that's no surprise. Grizzly is king.

"You saw that just once in all the time since you have been here?"

Once was all he was talking about.

"What is it like?"

"Very moving and beautiful."

"Is that why you came here?"

"It isn't," said Erwin. "Why I came. I didn't know about the animals' kingdom until later. I came for another reason altogether."

"Why did you?" Gwen began again. She knew he was from somewhere else because of the way he spoke—cultured, her mother would have said. He must have left it all behind.

"I came for a different reason than most people come," he said.

She seemed to accept that. They clopped along farther, past the little sandbar islands in the river and toward the rapids.

"Why don't you take Cymbal up to the Inaccessible, where animals rule themselves?"

"Because he might get ideas. You know, he's not far from wild himself. He's an Indian pony from Cochrane, and they get them from the wild herd."

"Are there wild horses?"

"Yep. They run near the Ghost River. And over in the foothills that you passed by in your train. Herds of 'em."

Gwen went quiet, thinking of wild horses.

Then she started up again. "Why do most people come?"

"You'd be surprised."

"I might."

"They come for the same reason your father came: looking for something."

There was a silence. She seemed to sense he didn't know how to fill it.

"But that's not why you came here."

"No, ma'am." It was hard to remember that she was twelve. She was very composed.

"Why, then?"

"I came because I had a broken heart."

"You did?" said Gwen admiringly. It seemed like a very good reason to take up life far from where you began it. "I wonder," she said, "will that be my story too?"

Chapter 13
HERBIE'S SEARCH

The Quarry, September 13, 1911

HERBIE DIDN'T SHOW UP THAT NIGHT, or the next, to meet Gwen or Dr. Smallwood. He stayed over at the Hodgson camp. He found tent poles cast aside and the peg holes kicked over neatly in How Long's way. Not much else. They had packed up before they left. They weren't in a hurry.

Higher up, in the quarry, he looked again at the garbage they'd left: a couple of lids, one two-fingered glove, a sardine tin with the tiny key and a coil of sharp tin, a folded and sodden Washington newspaper from the previous May. He examined the splintered bits of rock. The shale that had been blown apart by the dynamite looked familiar—some of it had hit him. It had landed ten to twenty feet above and below the explosion. He kicked around, feeling the immensity of the open bowl stretching beyond and below. He imagined the symmetry, the combinations of force and release that kept these towering piles of rock in place. Had the party somehow endangered the balance with their charge of dynamite? Was the mountain "fighting back," as Mariner had imagined? He entertained the thought that it was a spiritual thing: they had angered the mountain. His Stoney friends would say so.

He scanned the neighbouring slopes. The rocks took up their positions and seemed to have been there for millennia. He walked the square area of the digging. In how many years would these disturbed layers look just like the other fractured, bent and twisted layers? How many years would pass before the dynamite blast disguised itself as just one more event of geological time—one that had done its damage and become part of a larger story?

He felt sick. He felt sorry. His anger flitted around like a great raven and tried to settle on Maxwell, who thought he knew everything. The raven cawed and the great wings flapped as if that noble head were too small a perch for it. All right. Maxwell was an easy target, but knowing it all wasn't a capital offence. He was a smart man. He would have done his best to get them out. The words went through Herbie's mind, words that he liked to repeat when he was leading new dudes out: "Nature has a lot to teach you. Learn from it or be a fool. And a fool has a short life around these parts." He was saying that to himself, but had he said that to them?

He noted that the friendly rams were gone and wondered if it meant anything more than that winter was coming on. They'd be moving toward the Pity Plains, where the snow barely fell and when it did fall it didn't stay. Finally he lifted his eyes to gaze across at the great slopes Dr. Hodgson had been photographing. There was one high, thin line that might be a goat track. What if they had tried to get out that way, to avoid losing altitude in the bowl? But he had seen horse tracks going the other way. Could there have been two exits, two halves of the party setting off in two different ways—and two calamities? Or one half turning against the other?

The track went halfway across and then stopped. He got on his horse and headed up to it. The slope was bare at the top, clogged with snow at the bottom. He rode a long way across to where it dead-ended in a snow mass as hard as concrete and probably ten feet deep.

It was the wrong time of year for avalanches. Still, it was more feasible than a rock slide, and harder to verify. Horses, fossils, guides—all could have been taken by surprise in an instant onrush of snow. He got off and scrambled over the surface, looking for something sticking up, a horse's hoof, a tent pole, a can of film. Nothing. He ventured onto the slope looking for traces. Nothing. He took off his hat and sat there for a long while. An avalanche could have carried them with it, down the steep side to the treeline below, where it still had the power to knock down spruce and scatter itself into the bowl, and even the lake. Deep, violet (today) Mystic Lake, filled with upside-down, whitened timber.

That fall day on the mountainside he became convinced he'd found the secret. He went back and brought out the Mounties again. But they weren't going to absolve Herbie yet. Mystic was now frozen. Again there was no evidence, no trace that whatever disaster had occurred had swept the Hodgsons, packers and horses all away. And again, on sober reflection, Herbie wasn't sure either.

This was the hell of it: nothing remained, and no theory accounted for the vanishing. Herbie tried to make sense of it, to settle his agitation. There were plenty of ways to die: they could have wandered onto a glacier and fallen in or got into trouble with animals; someone could have got hurt and the rest perished waiting in the blizzard for rescue.

That night he rode back to Laggan. He sat smoking his pipe outside the Railway Hotel in the dark. He liked to say he had never felt fear. But this was fear. He was terrified—for their lives, sure, and also for the life he had created for himself in this place. This could ruin him. He was about to go to sleep under a tree when the telegraph came from Erwin: the Tree brothers had shown up, together with the two saddle horses.

In the morning Herbie rode back down to Gateway to see them. They met in the dark of the bar of the Three Sisters Hotel. The Trees had never been talkative. They were fidgety and took Herbie's rebuke with sullen faces.

"Nothing we do, boss. They listen nothing." James and Jonas, those were their names. Not their Indian names but the names they used when working as packers. Good men, both of them. They said Maxwell had told them to go ahead on the day of the rendezvous. They had packed out most of the cookstuff and the tents. The party would follow in a few hours. They set off toward Laggan and rode right into a bad snowstorm. It snowed all that day and the next. They never saw the others again. Maybe, they said, the professor and his party had tried to go the long way—very difficult, especially when loaded with rocks, but they were that stubborn.

"What took you so long to show up?"

"We waited at Laggan—didn't see them, then we took our time. Followed the railway cut, stopped to fish at the lakes. Spent a couple of days tracking a bull moose."

Herbie wasn't sure he believed that. How could they not have heard?

"What were they doing when you last saw them?"

"Loading those ponies with more rocks, that's what they were doing."

It made no sense. Why, if they were packing out so many rocks, didn't they keep Jonas and James?

The snows continued, a foretaste of winter. Later, come October, there would be a patch of warmth, maybe even a few weeks, before the deep freeze set in. In October the larches would be yellow, like torches in the high meadows. He'd go out searching.

But for now Herbie waited in Gateway. He sat in the bar in the Three Sisters Hotel. In the Map Room he pulled out Sam Gallant's curled, singed, drawn-from-memory images and compared them with the pale blue government-issued railway maps. He knew the terrain, he just didn't recognize it here. Here it was just veiny blue lines on white paper, names of rivers—Mistaya, Athabasca, Brazeau, Clearwater. Little teardrop lakes. Nothing to indicate where the shoreline was the sort of muskeg that could swallow a horse; nothing to show the burnt forests that stood like armies holding up spears, making every step a do-or-die event.

There were a couple of other maps—plain white, with black lines and cross-hatching to show the hills. Here was one by an early geologist sent by the railroad. It had more character and presented a litany of pitfalls: *Falling Rock, Soft Dunes, Stinking Water.* It struck him how simple and elementary were the names they'd given these places. *The Ram's Horn. Black Mountains*. It was a kind of blueprint for wilderness; it could be anywhere. How simple and childish they were in approaching the great mystery, he thought in a rare moment of humility. Only the Indian names made sense: *Wiwaxy, Yoho, Takakkaka*. And the maps were changing, becoming more and more businesslike. New this year was a coloured map, all marked in squares and rectangles of pink, pale green, pale yellow and green. Made it look very simple.

He felt helpless, and he did not like feeling helpless. Whisky was one recourse, but even he had to admit it was not the perfect solution. He had nothing to do. Well, there was one thing. He forced himself over to the doctor's house to meet Gwen. The little sister. He was three days late.

He found her in the doctor's dining room after dinner. He was astonished to discover he was tongue-tied in her presence. She was like a young princess who had been crowned queen far before her time, taking on her mantle, prepared for its burdens, her small torso held erect, her face showing no weakness, only a variety of patient inquiry, as if they were all a little dim and she wanted to hear them out for their own sakes. He supposed it was her faith. God had selected her for this. If that was the way she wanted it, fine. At least she didn't blame him. An aunt showed up, all decked out in black, and then, thank the good Lord, the child went back to Washington.

Herbie stayed around the Three Sisters, avoiding daylight, avoiding the Dominion Parks lady, Miss Wagg, who sent out increasingly cross telegrams from Ottawa. He was suddenly famous, a controversial figure, impugned by some sources, exonerated by others. His buddies dropped in at the bar—the whole town knew where he was—to suggest crackpot ideas of what had happened to the party and to offer hope. Even Foxx held out Herbie's innocence.

"These fellows were too smart for their own good. I figure they've gone off somewhere to hide their treasure trove of fossils. They'll show up," he said. First kind words the man had ever aimed at him, but they were a little too easy. People rarely showed up two weeks later in the Rockies. "Weather'll change and we'll get out and locate them."

Herbie itemized in his mind the numerous fatal accidents that he had nearly had: The beautiful spring day when he sat on a cornice like an angel's wing and brought the whole thing down on top of himself, but managed to crawl out. The time his campfire set alight the spruce tree hanging over it, and the fire spread to half a dozen trees, and if it weren't for a helpful wind he'd have started a forest fire. The day the grizzlies came into camp and frightened the horses, which ran off. Well, he had been spared. Any of these could get one person, maybe two. But How Long, Maxwell, the professor and two adult children were gone. Not to mention the horses. He shed tears for his horses. Four of them. Including Mousie and Caruso, two of his favourites. He'd bought the string with money from England that came his way when he was twenty-one.

"I dunno, Lyall," he'd said. "The party must've split up. And got lost from each other. One or two of them here and others there: wasted their time looking for each other."

Erwin came in to see him. "We need to think from their point of view. Put ourselves in their moccasins," he said. "Once we have their motivation, the plan will become evident."

Herbie appreciated Erwin. God for some reason had endowed Gateway with a gaggle of Oxford graduates who had found England too small after the Boer War and come west. They were all strapping young men. They raised the tone. But in a crisis, and when he'd been drunk for a week, he was not up to Erwin's level in talking philosophy.

"Bullshit, Erwin. All the plans in the world mean crap all in the mountains. Snow comes or melt starts, rockfall or avalanche, you go blind, die of thirst or go mad—your mind is a leaf in a snowstorm."

"We'll get out there again."

"Yeah. I'm waiting for the weather to break. Let's just hope they can."

"They must have left a trail."

"Yeah, Erwin, sure." He humoured his pal, but he knew how keenly nature disguised its wounds. Without walking over each square foot of mountain, picking at the lichen, wiggling every rock, he could not find it.

"You will. You're better than anyone," said Erwin.

"No. I spent ten years learning this place. What is that? Three seconds of geological time? What do I know?"

Herbie lifted his head and looked to the small square window bright with the flying whiteness of the squall outside the hotel.

"I was knocked out when I came to this place. All wide open. In England it's all about *you can't do this*, *you can't do that*. You know. Here, you got the right to go out into the wilderness and camp under the stars. Shoot game for food. The right to get lost and freeze to death, that's yours too. But all you have to do is learn the place, respect it. I messed up, Erwin."

"You're doubting yourself, Herbie. I've never heard that before."

"And what happens when I mess up? That's when we discover we got government. Ottawa wanted us to be wild so they could put a fence around us and start charging admission. Now Ottawa wants safety. How's that gonna work? Naw, it's bringing the whole circus down."

That was the worst night. He drank the full bottle of Seagram's.

He barely made it back to his cabin beside the river. As he passed the corral he wondered hazily if he saw an extra head or two. He went inside to bed, but after fifteen minutes he got up again—damned if that wasn't Mousie.

And it was. He was outside the fence leaning in, trying to get in. Skin and bones.

Chapter 14
BUFFALOED

Ottawa, October 3, 1911

Now it was a whole month since the disappearance. The office of the Dominion Parks had barely kept its head above water: Helen Wagg was still breathing, though she was sputtering a lot. She was on the telephone ordering supplies when into the office on the second floor of the Birks Building waltzed the member of Parliament for the West himself. Frank Oliver, another newspaperman, famous for having taken the first printing press out to Alberta on an ox cart. They said the wheels made an awful creaking noise. He was their man, having worked for the creation of Rocky Mountains Park, and had put Bowen in the job.

Oliver eased in the open door, bypassing Helen to set himself in front of Mr. Bowen. That bothered her. He had breached the invisible beam that joined her to her boss. *No one* got to him without going through her. And if it did happen, they had an understanding—an unspoken understanding but real enough—that she would rescue him. She walked past the open door and saw that Mr. B was looking beleaguered. So she stepped into his office and stood against the back wall.

"Having a spot of bad publicity, are you, Bowen? I do feel for you. When you get those newspaper fellows against you it sure can mess up a man's plans." Inside joke, ha ha. Oliver was a bit of a squeaky wheel himself, with his frothy white handlebar moustache and his thick black eyebrows pulled down over a neat, well-proportioned boyish face. "I have an idea here for what we can do to help you. An exercise that will get the public onside."

Helen sighed audibly and folded her arms. He was talking about the buffalo. He'd been on this hobby horse for months. How a few of those kings of the prairie had miraculously survived the holocaust. How a French guy living in Flathead, Montana, working as a border agent, had sent word that a rancher had this big herd, the only ones in existence and all. But he was finding their keep a tad expensive and wanted to sell. She went so far as to roll her eyes when she heard Mr. Oliver say, "How about we bring some of those buffalo back? If the tourists don't love 'em, the Indians can shoot 'em for food. I can get you the money."

"I don't see," began Bowen, "how this can—" But it did not lessen the flow.

"I spoke to Foxx, you know the chap—newspaper man from Gateway?"

"Yes, he just—"

"Foxx thought—"

"Wrote a rather nasty—"

Now Mr. Oliver was laughing. "Foxx says, 'Holy hell, what does that man think he's got there? Some kind of Noah's Ark?'"

"Editorial claiming—" said Bowen.

"They make a good deal of fuss out there already," said Helen. "It's best to ignore them." But it was not her place to make suggestions.

"Hear me out, Bowen. I'm trying to help you."

Helen and Mr. B gave in, leaned back, pretended to be receptive.

"So Foxx sent a couple of Indian scouts down to Montana. No, I'm telling you the truth. The first thing, he told them, is to ascertain their pedigree. 'Cause we all know buffalo have been gone, as in *documented* gone, *officially extinct*, for nigh twenty, twenty-five years. So where'd they come from, these buffalo? They could be imposters, you know? There is a creature called a cattalo, a mix, not good enough for the wild."

"Exactly," said Helen. "But they're the real thing?"

"Listen. A Pend d'Oreilles Indian, name of Walking Coyote, went out on one of the last big buffalo hunting trips. He killed a lot of cows. They massacred the kill right on the spot and loaded the meat and parts they wanted on their saddles, and the calves just hung around bleating and looking mournful.

"When he and his men turned their horses toward home, four of the calves trailed after them. They followed Walking Coyote all the way to his own corral; his kids came running out to meet him. And they wanted those buffalo calves for pets. Now the hunter felt bad about the death of their mothers, so he agreed. Ten years later the calves had grown up and bred among themselves, and now there were thirteen. Everyone swore there were no interlopers in that bloodline, straight from the wild animal on the prairie.

"Well, by that time—1894, say—it was painfully clear that the buffalo had been exterminated. Walking Coyote had done a great thing the only way most people ever do a great thing, which is by accident. He had kept some of them alive. But he couldn't sell them for food because they were the last ones. And he didn't see himself breeding buffalo back to life, and anyway he needed the money. He sold ten of his purebred buffalo to some local ranchers looking to make a buck.

"So these ranchers keep the herd for another, what is it, seventeen years, and they keep it quiet. Today it has reached seven hundred and they want to sell. Okay, all right. I know what you're thinking. Here's where Foxx's scouts figured the ranchers diddled the deal, because even in twenty-five years you can't breed to seven hundred unless you're a rabbit. He suspected there was some cattalo in them. I choose to disremember it."

"I'm afraid I still don't see how this helps us with the Hodgson expedition."

"Look, it's easy. I'm in favour and Foxx is in favour, and Parks needs a good-news story."

He swivelled around and looked at Helen. She hadn't known he even realized she was in the room. "Here's where you lot come in. Get out in front of this scheme. Say it's been hatching for a year, which it has. We'll bring back the wild buffalo to Gateway. What a story! Dominion Parks buys up the last remaining herd, the last *buffalo* in North America! Good story? Right? Newspapers love it, *right under the nose* of Uncle Sam—who, I happen to know, badly wants these animals but is unable to move quickly. And I will bet you dollars to doughnuts that the ensuing headlines will knock the lost Hodgson expedition off the front pages."

It was a crazy scheme but they said they would think about it, and Frank Oliver swept out the door. He nearly took out the telegram delivery boy, who often came by.

The train station was only a couple of blocks away, but the boy was sweating as if he'd run miles. No wonder, in the pillbox hat and the grey flannel suit with knickers. He handed Helen the paper wordlessly. She tore it open.

One more horse returned solo to corral STOP
Name of Mousie STOP Humphrey Hodgson rode it STOP
Mousie aint talking STOP
Wishart

The Hodgson expedition was a tragedy, and a public relations disaster, but it had finally begun to drop below the fold on the front pages and then into the back of the news section. This was bound to bring it back again. Helen gave a thought to poor Humphrey, for whose fate this did not bode well, and folded the telegram tightly once, twice, three times.

*

Because the weekends dragged, Helen had cultivated interests in the capital. She had joined the Cycling Club, but found it was not to her taste: there were too many sweet young ladies, and gentlemen who doted on them. There was a club of university women, such as herself, and that was more suitable, but even there a great many were married and mothers, which made her impatient. Helen was twenty-three years old. She was unlikely to marry, now. This could not be denied, in 1911. She was an object of pity, but she didn't mind; in fact she pitied those who pitied her. Her sights were set higher, on a career in the government, and her work was absorbing and hugely important.

What Helen did on Saturdays, since the club activity was not a solution to the long and empty day, was travel around Ottawa taking in the sight of its inhabitants at work and play. She rode the cable car to Rockcliffe Park and watched the wealthy play at golf, for a little. She walked along Metcalfe Street and looked in shop windows at enormous tented fur coats, showing up now in preparation for the winter season. She sat on the grass in the public gardens and gazed over at the water in the canals and at the ducks. When the grass got too prickly for her, she stood and walked more, this time passing in front of the Château Laurier and having a look at the Grand Trunk Railway station that was rising, columns and all, like a great temple across the street.

This Saturday was no different, and she wandered, thinking as she did that perhaps this activity, which had been devised to connect her to ordinary people—as if she were a nun let out of her convent!—had the opposite effect. Watching a boy with a hoop and a stick run circles around a woman—his nanny? not his mother, she thought, because the woman's complexion was rather dark—Helen came face to face with her essentially saturnine nature. She was alone, an observer, separated from this clatter as if by a window. She might knock on the glass, but she would not be heard. She could watch, and she did watch, unseen.

The glass gave her a cloak of invisibility. Was it a prison? She didn't feel imprisoned. She could take note, she could examine and theorize, she could compose sentences and opinions. She had a handbag but stuffed nothing there, not a notebook; the notebook was her mind.

She left the little park and walked over to the lawn in front of the Parliament Buildings, where she sat. Notebooks were not for her. She saved her thoughts and delivered them to Mr. B on Monday morning. This way it was almost as if her weekend had a purpose—to continue their conversation, left dangling on Friday afternoon. She would tell him about the bored boy with his hoop. She would express her views on the railway as temple. The beauty of the circular flowerbeds in front of the Parliament Buildings. She stood and dusted her skirt for grass clippings and set off for her favourite stop in all of her rambles, the Byward Market in Lower Town.

The noise hit her first and then the smells: cattle protesting and chickens squawking. There was a lumber mill behind the shops, and the dust from its blades lifted above the roofs in a swirl of hot air. The Casion Theatre was here—not theatre of the kind she would like, of course, but a burlesque hall. That woman with the very red lips (so early in the day!) emerging from an upstairs apartment must be a dancer appearing in the show. A fiddler sat on a stool with his hat on the street in front of him, sawing away as if his life depended on it. Maybe it did. She dropped him a dime, and he looked wildly at her. He could not stop playing. *It was as if his fiddle were driving his arm, and not the other way around*, she imagined saying to Mr. B.

The sawing down of great forests, the draining of lakes and rivers of fish, the skinning of mink for their fur: this was what she knew, what she saw. The countryside abandoned by its keepers, who turned into this raucous mob: this was the inheritance of the city. If all these people could magically get on that train and be carried west, what a great change that would be. If when they arrived in the west they could see *what once was*: the simple prairie with the great herds of beasts covering it, the thunder of hooves, the racing Indian on his horse speeding alongside, between the train window—her glass pane had become a window on one of the cars now, and she was behind it, in the jolt and metal squeal of wheels on tracks, in the flash of sun, moving west—if all that, would the world not be improved?

Her normal lunch was a ham sandwich purchased at a French-Canadian charcuterie inside the market building, and she fought her way there, through crowds of women with baskets and raftsmen looking to be cured of a hangover. They worked in the bush all winter and came into town for the spring and summer months, where they caroused and fought and patronized the prostitutes. But it was fall, and soon they would pack up and go. The Jewish barrow boys—men really, not boys—stayed in a line down the centre of the glassed market building, a two-storey cathedral to crops. A turn of phrase she might share on Monday?

Sandwich secured, she retreated to the corner of a table and began to eat. A pair of lovers noodled away not two feet from her. Disgusting, really. But the type of thing she couldn't repeat. Not to her boss. There were constraints on her conversations with Mr. B. He was a married man, so of course not innocent. He never spoke of his wife except to give the impression of frailty there. She never doubted that he was unhappy. Of course he deserved better. The man at her table tightened his arm around the waist of his lover, getting his fingers caught in various pleats and fasteners. The woman settled closer against him.

So that was physical love. She did not envy it. She loved Mr. B, but not in that way. On a higher plane. She would not express personal feelings aloud, of course—not on paper, not in the words her life depended on. There was no question of him expressing anything. He was too fine a man to behave as others had done and abandon his family responsibilities for a woman he met at work.

No, the feelings they had for each other found expression in their mutual passion for the Canadian national parks. She could imagine his thoughts on how the fine champagne of mountain air would heal the broken souls she saw around her: the dirty man with the sole of his shoe flapping loose, filtering crumpled paper for a mouthful; the loggers who had begun to fight (who had the money to go to the tavern and get the first beer?). Even the tired farmer's wife with her eggs to sell: she had the out-of-doors, certainly, but farmland was not pure; it was full of dirt and manure and exhaustion and sadness.

Helen did not speak feelings but sublimated them in the written word. Writing was a powerful weapon. There were others who could write too. Her mind leapt to that Wishart fellow, the guide who had abandoned those poor Americans on the mountain. He was a wordsmith. Broad humour, coarseness was his area, not something at which she excelled. Thinking of that buffalo caper about to be launched, it occurred to her to send Mr. Wishart along. He could give a colourful account, which might be useful.

She thought Mr. B would like that idea.

Chapter 15
THE HEIST

Flathead, Montana, May 1912

Report on the Buffalo Heist
by Herbert Wishart, Esq., Outfitter
Gateway, Alberta

The Canadian posse headed south by train, a case of whisky on the seat beside us. We'd get out at every station platform and Foxx would make a show of twirling his pistol. Sure! Demonstrating how cowboys shot into the platform to make the tenderfeet dance. I can say I grew a little weary of the spectacle, but when we arrived at Flathead I had something better to look at. We met up with the ranchers' cowboys, about forty of 'em, mostly part Indian. I watched them ride. Oh boy, was it pretty.

The Indian cowboys gave Foxx a bronco that had no intention of taking a rider, and then they sat back to watch the fun as Foxx got himself bucked off—but he didn't. He held on and held on for just as long as it took, flying out of the saddle, hat off, fringe up, back snapping, head lolling, left arm out like an airplane wing and whipping like a lariat, but he held his seat and finally the horse just wore himself out and stood still. After, the cowboys accepted him into their roundup. He and I were the only white men to ride with them. Why they never gave me the test I'm not sure. My horse was as easy as pie.

We rode out about twenty-five miles and there they were, all shaggy brown and hump-shouldered, prehistoric-looking with that big head and the ragged ruff hanging down. Big feral smell such as I've never before encountered: multiply a bear by a few thousand. They moved like a slow stain on the grass, could make you seasick to watch their backs, thick and dark. When they got it in their heads to run, it was like flowing water. Then all at once they'd stop. Dead, on a dime. Force of nature. But if you got up close and looked into one of their squidged-together little eyes, you saw an old fart from a London gentleman's club, a guy in a wingchair nodding, everything the way it used to be, obstinate, arrogant, never-had-to-worry kind of fellow. But gentlemen they were not, I was to discover.

Foxx and I followed instructions from the Indian cowboys, but it seemed to me nobody knew the right way to round up buffalo. First of all, forty-two of the chaps on horseback made a big horseshoe surrounding the herd. The buffalo just stood and stared. This is how the creatures got themselves shot by the bounty hunters. But we weren't out to kill 'em, just needed to move 'em along, take 'em back home. No dice.

So the lead cowboys figured they'd cut out maybe a hundred at a time. That involved a few fellows riding straight into the crowd, shouting, pushing, clapping them on the back. I tried it. The beasts pressed so close together, you couldn't part 'em. Eventually with a lot of shouting and swinging of ropes we did get around a group of them. Then we made the horseshoe again with the open end of the horseshoe pointing in the direction of the railroad station.

The creatures made as if they agreed with the basic plan, or at least didn't care to acknowledge if they didn't. And slowly, you know, stately, they walked. We couldn't be rushing them. We couldn't be letting 'em get the idea we *had* an idea. We had to be subtle and keep the pressure on, but nothing sudden. It took a long time. You gotta enjoy that, being in the saddle, silent except for the noises the herd made, little rumbles between the bulls, bleats from the kids, juicy farts from the tail end and such, under the hot sun, beautiful country. Let your mind roam. Not a bad thing, to be a cowboy.

And this went along fine for a time, the buffalo just minding their p's and q's, munching on the grass, and the young feeding, now and then one of them breaking into that rocking-horse trot they had and then slowing down. But what happens is that before too long you get to the edge of their land. Were there fences? Naw. Were there lines drawn on the ground? No. These creatures just got rules. And when they got to the edge of what they deemed to be their land they all stopped. Still. As if there were a baton lifted somewhere up in the sky. They all stopped. All of them, rows and rows back, they went still.

It was uncanny, the way this stillness settled on the herd. Like they shared a nervous system. I've seen goats following their leader. I've seen men do it too, the best-trained of armies back at old Buckingham Palace and marching down the Cromwell Road. But soldiers could not compete with this team. *Pre-cision*. They all just stopped. Still. So we stopped too. Until they changed their one mind, there was no way you were even going to *think* about moving them.

We rode up and down a bit, shook out a bit. Nothing. Did the buffalo take their commands from clouds? *This is far enough*. We couldn't fathom it. I figured there was no leader at all, just something in the blood that felt the soil their hooves had churned before, and when the end of that came, said, *We didn't walk here*. Not a step farther. To a fellow like me, lived all my life with wild animals, figuring the way they think is a matter of interest. I know with sheep there are leaders and the same goes for elk and caribou. Bears and cats are loners. But those buffalo moved as a single thought; that was something I'd never seen.

They stood and then, what do you know, began to inch their

hooves slowly around in a half-circle, on a dime, I tell you, inch by inch until they faced back the way they'd come. One hundred and eighty degrees. You could have got out your compass. We weren't too happy.

We brought our horseshoe shape around to stand in front of the guys who'd been in the back and were now in the front, facing home. We shouted and danced around a bit, waving and firing in the air. They did not like that. From their dead stop one guy charged us, driving head down. We bolted. And then those buffalo took off, nothing stopping 'em; even if they came to a slough, they just ploughed on, the mass of 'em spreading and then narrowing their herd to accommodate a riverbed or a bluff. Oh, it was something to see. And by the end of the day we were back where we began.

We stayed in the saddle all night. I don't know how, but we weeded out and wove around and got some of 'em heading back to the railway station. Those railway cars you constructed especially, reinforced on the side, paid for by the people of Canada? Note I said that: sides reinforced. You can kiss them goodbye. We had a chute with some ropes to get the animals lined up. Well, the first bull just blasted down the chute, up inside the railway car and kept going right out the side wall. The ropes busted and the car blew up as if it had been dynamited, boards flying everywhere, horses and cowboys scattering, and that was the end of that. A riled buffalo very easily gets out of hand.

We drove the next bull down the chute into another car and he bucked up somehow and busted his little legs, which did not look as if they were up to the job of carrying him. Had to shoot him.

Took a day but we finally got most of those creatures loaded. And that was only the first bunch. After the boxcars left, we thought again. It wasn't healthy, rounding them up and driving them to the train station. Driving that opinionated herd across the border? Would have taken years. Why? Because it wasn't in the direction they wanted to go. In the end we tried a convoy of wagons, sliding them in easy. One at a time. Little by little.

The Buffalo Heist, as it has come to be known, took forever. But we did load all seven hundred and got them across the border and up into Canada. King of the Prairie, being shipped back.

What did we say, we lost only one man and four buffalo? I didn't know the man. He got caught in a stampede and squeezed off his saddle, trampled to death. A messy one. Out of the seven hundred, seventy-seven came to Gateway, to the paddock we built at the foot of Cascade. Anyone who goes by could see them placid creatures enjoying their grass. So it is mission accomplished. Not that I wanted to do you folks back east any favours, but I heard there was celebration in Ottawa.

Respectfully submitted, as above.

The Buffalo Heist succeeded in overshadowing the Hodgson expedition for a time. The big animals settled down in their paddock. It backfired in one way, however. Teddy Roosevelt was furious because he wanted those buffalo for his own country. Well, he had his chance, didn't he? said Helen. They all felt quite smug in Gateway. Parks was happy that a lot of people went out to look. But it was a bit disappointing. It wasn't as if they were wild and running in the millions; it was just a few hundred bewildered grass-eaters whose hooves dug up the ground. Interest in buffalo dies down quickly. Interest in tragedy, however, is like dipsomania: leave it alone and you might think it's gone, but one little drink and it comes roaring back stronger than ever.

The winter was quiet, and the year turned to 1912. In July Commissioner Bowen went out from Ottawa to Gateway, bullied into it by Foxx and his editorials. He announced the opening of a road from Calgary into the park, something the motorcar clubs had been wanting. In response to lobbies from the logging folk and the hunting folk and the water power folk, the park gates were moved west; Gateway was no longer inside but outside. He okayed another road that would go over the mountains to the south. He hired more wardens from among the fellows who were giving up guiding and packing as the horse trade declined. Erwin took a job. He came into the bar and showed Herbie the cunning little water pump he'd been supplied: you could carry it on your shoulder. Commissioner Bowen had the idea to build phone shacks about thirty miles apart, up and down the valleys, so they could call in, say, if there was a fire or other emergency.

Those telephones were inhabited by devils. Herbie knew, because as soon as they went in he rode up to have a look. The little cabins were handy enough if he needed a place to sleep, though he was used to dossing down under the big spruces. But the phones were another thing. They changed the backcountry, where he'd been so happily beyond reach 'til now. One night he ducked into a warden's hut up through Whiteman's Gap and lit the fire and helped himself to a drink. He lay down to sleep, but the phone rang. He picked it up: no one there. This happened over and over until he didn't pick it up anymore and sat shouting at the thing and stomping on the floor under where it was attached to the door frame. He had it in mind to beat it to pieces but figured he was in good shape with Parks for the moment so he'd better not. But it was spooky. He couldn't discount the possibility that someone was lost out there and calling for help. The phone went all night, and he couldn't get a wink. When he got back he asked Erwin, who said it had happened to him too. Nobody calling, you understand, just sharp little rings. Erwin said that it was electrical and caused by northern lights.

Herbie, too, was restless as hell. No business came in. He went up to the Spray and set out a trapline; in the cabin at night he talked to himself out loud and was surprised to discover that the words that came out were his uncle's. "No more of this wheezy guilt, lad. You got plenty other emotions to choose from, like pissed-offedness." Well, he was angry, no question. He'd spent a decade building a reputation, and it was shot thanks to the Hodgson group, with help from the stupid Parks bureaucrats meddling in mountain affairs they knew nothing about.

He could lose his whole business over this. Even if he stayed afloat, he'd have a stain on his reputation. He had been party to a horrendous misadventure. And now it was written in the blue air between him and the mountains—they were dance partners: Herbie Wishart and the Hodgson expedition.

And there was another feeling, a craziness that had him racketing around the bare walls: plain loneliness and hunger for a woman. He hadn't wanted a wife the past ten years. Outfitters like him had no time for one. But a need had been awoken. It was crying out. It had its roots in the mishap. It was here even in this faraway, brand-new, almost paradisiacal world. He had a longing for a female.

When he was in town, he spent evenings in the Three Sisters bar. He came out of it one night, and there was the big moon hanging over the mountain of the same name, those dominant nuns. He asked himself if those bleak harpies were going to be the only women in his life from here on in. He sat on the veranda for a time in the silence, looking at the horses, seeing how the blue moonlight tied their shadows to their feet. His pony, Major, rattled his nostrils in a friendly way and whinnied softly. Isn't it time to go home? "In a bit," said Herbie. "I'm thinking."

He listed the women in his life, one by one. He had a mother, true, a lady for the parties she was, maybe not too interested in his wee self but up for a lovely time. She had needed a bit of guidance, he could see now, and she hadn't got it from his father, who died young of drink. Then there was his aunt, who wished to reform him: full marks for trying. He remembered that girl who was very keen on him when he embarked for Canada. She was probably still at the port, awaiting his return.

Women: he'd grown up with the fragile, spoilable type who bloomed early and settled into matrons. Here he'd encountered women of a different stripe. They seemed larger and took up more space. Mountaineers, horsewomen. Even the local wives with their children were redoubtable. They made him nervous, carrying rifles, wearing big boots.

Herbie whispered, "I've been careful. Gotta be. These women can take you down, Major. You're attracted, you're entranced, and you do unwise things. You can't let that happen. You have to stay in control, old boy." He took Major by the bridle and patted him hard on the side. "On the other hand . . ."

A cowboy came out and grinned. He understood the need to talk to your horse.

"Go on, get lost," said Herbie.

Major shook his bridle and huffed.

The problem of women. It was a conundrum: how could you keep them out and keep them in at the same time? That was what marriage was for, he supposed.

He began to walk with the horse, leading him home. "To be truthful," he said, "it isn't just any female I want. It's Isabel."

He'd never said it or even wanted to. The thought of her pierced his alcoholic muffler. He was lonely for her. How could he be? He'd hardly known her. Did he love her? Oh Christ, an ache was in him. Oh, if he could see her, seat her on his horse, get up behind her the way he had. He could hear her sweet voice and that quaint way of talking, *does thee* and *could thee*.

But that was ridiculous. Because she was dead. She had to be. When he looked up, the Three Sisters peaks were leaning over him cruelly, white-topped, shocking in the darkness, laughing: they had given, and they had taken away. She was dead. Gone to those cold, overbearing nuns. What a waste, that beautiful, eager little filly.

Can you fall in love with a dead woman? Could the woman he loved be dead? No, the heat of his desire gave her life. But he was stricken. He would swear until the end of his days that he never felt fear, but what else would you call this? A chill into his very gut. Ghastly thought, ghastly punishment: that Isabel was gone and the bleak nuns were his destiny. That his heart had gone there too.

No. It could not be. He would find Isabel. He would find her, or at least find out what happened to her.

There it was, a purpose, a vision of his life going into the future. He welcomed the vision because to tell the truth he'd been down and wasn't at all sure there would be a future for him.

Major's hooves and his boots made the only sounds on the wide, empty street. He was afraid he was sobering up. Okay, this was poor, he thought. So desperate, he was sizing up the local peaks for their feminine qualities. Time for bed. There was the corral.

Chapter 16
THE BUTTERFLY LADY

Assiniboine, August 1912

Next morning he stopped by the Vienna Café, which adjoined the post office. Pappos was already up baking the bread, and gave him his mail. There was a letter asking for his services. It was from an English lady.

Mrs. De la Beche Nicholl wanted a guide to take her butterfly hunting. He was inclined to think it was some New York big-game hunter pulling his leg, probably put up to it by Foxx, who loved to make him look the fool. But no, the letter was serious; turned out she had got his name through scientists who had been up the summer before looking at worms that lived in the ice. Always something to see in the Rockies. Apparently she was not put off by the Hodgson balls-up.

He needed the work or he'd never have taken the job, by which he meant that if he hadn't been desperate because of the Hodgson debacle, he'd never have agreed to spend eight weeks with a female Britisher whose game was no bigger than a postage stamp. But he said yes, and she paid his price. They set it up for the month of August.

When he first saw her, she was walking west along the railroad track from Laggan, with her butterfly net at the ready. Something hilarious in the vision and he'd started to laugh: that weapon, a wisp of white against the steep grey canyon walls.

"Mr. Wishart?" Her only words. "I expected you first thing."

"Sorry, ma'am, I had to ford a river, and with the ten horses it took all morning."

She was an old biddy to him, but that was because he was barely thirty. She was sixty-five, bloody ancient at the time. She was small and wiry, and if the butterfly net weren't comical enough, the beat-up Panama hat, the black widow dress and the hobnailed boots made him scratch his several days' beard. The ear trumpet she carried in the other hand topped it off.

"Does that thing work?"

"Look at me when you speak," she said.

Which he took to mean it didn't. So it was a kind of accessory? He thought he detected mischief in the bright eyes, but he couldn't be sure. And he was never sure, over the months of their friendship, if she could hear him cursing out the horses. If she did, too bad: that kind of language was the only thing they listened to.

But face to face and aided by the ear trumpet, which was almost as long as her arm and which she kept tied to her belt, she could hear just fine. Nuisance, she'd say, raising it like a salute, so he felt he had to stand to attention. He had to stop himself from saluting back.

Her name was Mary, but she said he should call her Minnie.

"Might as well get going, then," he said. He'd made camp at Wapta and he was a bit concerned; missing How Long, he'd had to hire a new cook.

They walked back to the Railway Hotel and she got her bags, and he tied them up with the other bundles on one of the ponies. She had a tin box she wouldn't let him have, insisting he put it behind her saddle. The ponies were short, but even so she needed to put her hobnailed foot into his cupped hands. She hardly weighed a feather and tried to sit sideways.

"No, ma'am, that will not suffice," he said. "You got to put your leg over."

"You think I can't," she said, and jumped down. She gave him the other foot, swung her right leg in a big arch over the back of the animal and landed astride, kicked the pony and cantered off. He stopped laughing. She was a good horsewoman.

"I guess you've been riding to hounds back in Old-ee England-ee," he said.

They had sussed each other out in the first two minutes and not liked what they'd seen. She said, and she kept saying, that she wasn't English, she was Welsh—but if she imagined that made a difference, it just proved the point.

"You're right, Mr. Wishart. I was mistress of the hunt." And she followed that with a sharp assessment of him: "Lincolnshire, is it? What brought you here?"

With her high-up politician for a husband, her split surname and her fluty voice, she was one of those people he could actively hate. But he minded his manners. To her face you had no choice. She was imposing. She told him that once, in Spain, a whole crowd of people had surrounded her and marched her into town and set her up on a stage because they took her for Queen Victoria. He asked her if she'd been wearing that Panama hat that looked as if the horses had got their teeth in it.

"As a matter of fact, yes," she said.

They went up Healey Creek to the meadows and stopped at the little lake, where he took pleasure in pointing out the immense grizzly tracks in the mud. She didn't flinch. Mrs. Mary De la Beche Nicholl didn't scare easily. Herbie knew because he tried all summer long, with talk of circling wolves that attacked in packs and bull moose that charged you on the trail. Cougar—you won't feel a thing, he said. Quick as a wink, he jumps on the back of your neck, bites through and snaps it. You're on the ground, your horse bolts. No pain, it's all over.

"Hmmph," she said. "And the collection case?"

"You won't have given it a thought."

"I'm giving it a thought now," she said tartly. "If anything happens to me, ship it back to Wales."

"Right-o."

All day it was strapped to the back of her saddle across the horse's rump. She took it with her when she crawled backwards under the canvas at night, and it was the first thing she looked at when she stuck her head out of the tent at dawn. And in between, times were not infrequent when he—who had gone eye to eye with a charging bull elk, who was the man to come to if you wanted to shoot big game in the Rockies—stood by and held the damn thing.

During the first couple of days she showed him how to use the butterfly net. And as often as not, when she saw some little blue petal of a thing go by, she got him to go after it.

"Go by" didn't actually describe what the butterflies did. These things were uncertain in their progress, jerking up and down and sideways, and landing for no reason that you could see and leaping vertically too. Hunting them was like playing badminton.

A big animal you get a sense of what it's after; you can get a fix on where it's going. But with butterflies you had nothing to go on. You stood and waited, holding your net like a bat. You saw one and it was gone. But then in a minute the object of your desire would falter back your way, and you'd leap up and make a rapid swoop with the handle so the net floated over it.

It was a short-lived sense of victory because once the thing was in your net you had to be sure it stayed there. The trick was to turn your wrist with a snap. She showed him: she was expert at it, he had to say. "It's just like casting a fly," she said. So she could do that too? She could.

He'd taken no notice, before, of how butterflies moved. They were restless and unpredictable and could vanish at will, a sky-blue thumb-sized slip of paper exploring minute blue forget-me-nots at the edge of the stream one minute, a falling leaf the next. But now he did. The big ones flapped in your face like bats. When they landed they went suddenly still.

God, if folks could see him. She handed him the net and pointed to the stream, at a place where it was carving a gully down a slope at forty-five degrees to the horizon, and asked him to get a couple of those little white ones. And then she got out her camera and took a picture of him clinging to low branches, sliding down wet rocks, leaning over the brink.

The first butterfly he caught in his net (he wouldn't hazard to name it) he stared at a little too long and it fluttered out. Damn. He watched her again. Twist your wrist and the butterfly falls down into the sock, then take the rim in your hand and fold it over the opening so there is no getting out. Often the creatures didn't try: they went absolutely still, as if they had a sixth sense of being enclosed and had no desire to bash their fragile wings. She taught him to reach in and hold the creature by the body. You couldn't touch the wing because the colour came off on your fingers. It felt like dust but it wasn't; it was little scales, she said, that made the colour.

It faded when the butterfly was dead. He knew that happened, from birds he'd shot.

They chatted about what she saw in them.

"They are little miracles," she said. The caterpillar takes months to develop but adults "fly" only a few weeks, from late June to early August, or early August to mid-September. Flying means being alive for a butterfly. During that time they need to visit the blossoms, which is why they develop colours to fool their predators—mice and rodents—into thinking they are part of the plant. The colours are also meant to attract the opposite sex.

"Hmm," he said, unconvinced, being wise to the games animals played as prey and predator. "But it makes them more obvious when they move."

"They can camouflage themselves. Notice that when they fold up their wings they look completely different from when their wings are open? One side is bright, one drab; one side is striped, the other is all swirls."

He got to watching them. Sometimes they seemed to be breathing very gently.

When he caught a prize for her, she laid it on a piece of paper in the bright sun and examined it with her magnifying glass. Then she consulted her blessed book. She cried out, "This may be a brand-new species; I don't see it here." Such excitement you'd have thought they'd come upon a clutch of bighorn rams snoozing. She kept staring at it through her magnifying glass, which was firing the sharp late beams of sun. He told her if she didn't watch out, she'd set the thing on fire, and he went for a walk to the lake.

When he came back, she was sitting on a folding stool. In front of her was another stool with a little pile of sugar on it. Herbie had a devilish sweet tooth that was never satisfied on the trail. He licked his forefinger and stuck it out the way he'd always done, to put it in the sugar and get a sweet coating he could suck off. And whack, out came the ear trumpet faster than he could see and cracked him on the wrist.

"Don't touch!"

"Goddamn!" he said, rubbing his hurt wrist. "You're worse than How Long. We that short of sugar?"

"It's not sugar. It's potassium cyanide."

"Are you setting to kill me, Mrs. Mary De la Beche Nicholl?"

"I wouldn't waste any on you, Herbie. It's for my butterflies."

He took no offence, and later in the evening they had a conversation about killing. There was a lot of killing in what he did. It meant little to him at the time. Most of it was for food. He wasn't cruel. He always travelled with strychnine to finish off the animals in the traps.

He told her about the time he had the little bottle in his breast pocket and leaned over the frying pan. A drop fell. He thought it must've come off a tree, snow melting. Straightened up, looked—you always checked out what was behind you—nothing, but no branch either, funny, but he let the thought pass and he leaned over the pan again and there was another drop. It sizzled and gave off a bit of an odour. He put his fingers out to pick up the bacon. Then he figured it out.

He got her laughing, and some of that grimness went out of her mouth. He thought he just might with any luck get through the month.

He waited for her to get tired, but she didn't. Next morning big old Assiniboine was clear and dominant, twice the size of anything else and like a pyramid, drawing them. They had a break at Citadel, where he spotted a big ram looking down on them from a chimney rock. But no time to investigate: she had him running around with that net looking for something called an Astarte.

When they got up to its base Assiniboine had disappeared, a habit it had. Thank god, he thought; it meant she wouldn't insist on going up it. They made camp amid clouds of mosquitoes. The new cook got water from the creek and brought out the pile of saucepans from the pack. He was busting out the bacon when she came bouncing in all excited because she'd got one.

"*Chrysophanus snowi*," she said, writing it down carefully in her ledger, "alias *Lycaena cuprea snowi*."

Darned if he knew why the things had an alias, is what he said to her.

She'd had something to say then, about his ignorance. He knew he was ignorant, but he didn't like to hear about it. However, at a later point in their journey she had praised him for stick-to-it-iveness while pushing one of those packhorses up a steep slope. "You've got a bright future, Herbie Wishart."

Nice to hear while you're staring up the wrong end of a horse.

"Tell you the truth, Minnie," he had said, "my future got washed out with those Hodgsons disappearing."

"Oh, nonsense," she said. "You're young. It will be forgotten, and you'll get ahead on your merits."

That was welcome news. He was in a bad patch, for sure. Maybe she'd been sent by his guardian angel to get him out of it. She cut him down to size, but she also taught him some lessons. He figured out the fact that folks he guided also had some kind of expertise and that he could learn from them. People said Minnie's collection was on a par with the Rothschilds'. So did the Rothschilds have a big butterfly collection? He guessed that they had all the butterflies money could buy.

Maybe it wasn't such a waste to spend a summer with her. After they got back, she took a few days' rest at the Hot Springs Hotel, and then they rode in to Lake O'Hara.

Chapter 17
WOMEN

Lake Louise, August 1912

THE LOWER SLOPES WERE BURNT TIMBER, and butterflies were all over. They passed and paused through the scorched black and spiky trees, jerky as thoughts. As the party climbed, getting away from the burn into the growing forest, they didn't see as many, and she worried. He told her there would be flowers up in the meadows, and that made her happy.

They made camp away from the shore in a small meadow. The sun came down there late in the day, and it was protected and warm. The first thing she pointed out was a hummingbird, feeding at a clump of Indian paintbrush. She was charmed by that bird, a precise ruby-coloured speck of life against the hard cliffs and the rough overhangs. She wasn't a gusher, but he could tell by the quiet that came over her that the wilderness was speaking her language. The new cook went off to catch a bit of dinner in the stream, but this time the trout were eluding him. So Minnie got out her fly rod and made three damn eloquent casts and caught as many trout.

Herbie himself fried them up over the fire with some bacon. Later, while the cook was washing up—she offered to help, but he waved her away—Herbie walked Minnie over to the lakeside and waited to hear what she'd say. It was a perfect, aquamarine mountain lake with towering rocks and snow above. There was nothing else, not a hut, not a hotel. It was an enclosed world.

He showed her the dipper bird sitting on a rock in the fast-moving water, grey with its darker head and long beak, how it dove and swam. She seemed to like the signs of violence in the place, pausing over an upturned tree, the underside of its root ball turned up perpendicular, a clump of earth still attached.

"Struck by lightning probably," he said. "It makes a tree jump up like that." Because of the shallow earth over rock: the roots didn't go down far, but spread sideways.

That piping voice went completely silent. An excellent sign.

They got going the next morning up toward Opabin. When they reached the flat rocks, she signalled that she wanted to stop. She swung her leg over and slid down the side of her big mare. Herbie looked sideways at her waist, buckled with brown leather and hung with various tools of her trade. She had six children well into adulthood. Must have been made of durable material.

Still, he kept a close eye.

They took a barely worn trail through spindly trees. It flattened out, and there were huge rocks dotted here and there. Probably from the glacier's retreat, she said. He heard a whistle, and there was a marmot sitting on a moss bank sounding the alarm. Fella, be still, he said, and the dog whined but held its position.

She got her net and went scrambling where the rocky creek spread itself very thinly over red rocks, just deep enough to wet your boots. There were paintbrush and violets, aven and crocuses, and other flowers he had no name for. He watched her closely. She could fall and twist one of those well-funded ankles; she could land on her bottom in the creek and get soaked to the skin and catch her death of cold; there were a dozen ways a day might become fatal or close to it, and none of them would be easy on him.

When she took off up the bank, grabbing onto inoffensive little bushes that were not going to hold her weight, he began calling out precautions that went unheard. On a mossy overhang she stopped and looked back at him and shouted, "I'm sorry, Herbie, I cannot hear you; as you see, I am a little deaf."

"Yes, you're deaf to any damn thing I want to tell you," he answered. "You infernal, irritating old woman."

She beamed.

Trouble was, he was not accustomed to anyone whose functions weren't functioning up to snuff. That sort didn't as a rule show up for guided hunting in the Rockies. But here one was. The huge brass ear trumpet, as long as a Winchester rifle, which she was continually lifting to her ear, tied up one hand and did not help in a climbing situation. He tried it and found it worse than useless. He heard before using it the horse's snorting, the twitter of a small bird, the high kyrie of an eagle somewhere watching, the warning peep of a ground squirrel as it stuck its head out of a mound. With the trumpet in his ear those sounds were blanked out. She, too, was silent, moving up the hillside, intent on her chase. It unnerved him. In the same way, it was going to unnerve a bear.

A little white fluttering thing led her on a chase that day, settling and allowing her to come close, then lifting off and moving in its aimless, up-and-down, sidewise way, up into the dark straight trunks of the black boreal spruce, with the black moss hanging from them, undisturbed probably for centuries. Though she was stealthy with her net, the butterfly was winning. Minnie grew pink under the Panama hat and veil; damp spots appeared under her arms. He did not ask himself what the hell she wanted with so mindless a thing, because he knew: chasing them gave her a thrill. The thrill she got was just as great as the thrill he got shooting a moose that was wallowing in the muck.

"A hunter is what you are," he said to her later while the cook was getting dinner and he was sipping his whisky and she was staring dejectedly into the fire. "A hunter whose game got away."

"Oh come, don't demean me: the aims of science are higher than that, although I must say"—she examined her leg where it had met a sharp rock—"I am showing signs of the struggle."

The aims of science, balls. But he did enjoy her company. She didn't say much around the campfire before they both turned in, either, which was fine with him. He didn't have to entertain.

But when they did talk, it counted. One night, she confided, "You know, Mr. Wishart, at home I often feel that I am separated from my family by my deafness. They do not take the time to include me, and as a result my understanding of my children has suffered. When I am out here, this handicap does not figure. I will make no concession to it at all. So you'd best not."

"Okay."

He took her up to the ledge above Opabin. They had no luck for a couple of days. They began to spar.

"I am not going to be happy until we get that Astarte for the British Museum."

"Why should it be in the British Museum? Why not here where it lives?"

"It's a short life span; it'll be gone in a week anyway," she said.

"But wouldn't it reproduce if you left it here?"

"In the same way I could say to you about your mountain sheep, why should they adorn your wall—?"

"How do you know I've got a wall?"

Getting no answer he slid twenty feet down to the horses. Something flashed by, and she swooped for it, those little battered black leather boots sinking into the loose rock, lifting then sinking again as she went over backwards. He ran back up to where she lay and seized her around the waist, pulling her down to the flat and setting her on her feet. She stepped away from him and straightened her bodice.

She had caught it.

The weather changed. First it was the wind. Herbie recognized that key of howling. Frigid air was coming. Sure enough, within an hour it was freezing cold and the rain came down, with thunder behind it. He and the cook hauled in more firewood and built a blaze right in the doorway of Minnie's tent. She took a glass of spirits—she who did not drink!—and retreated for the night. He could see a candle in there and knew she was writing in her diary.

The entire next day rain poured down on them. They spent it in camp.

The next day was clear, and she was up before he was. He made a big pot of coffee. She'd had time to catch up on her notes, she said.

"Do you know what we've caught here?"

"I don't," he said. The sight of her there, tight little bodice and ragged Panama hat, her earnest eyes looking up at him from under the brim in the first sun, made him smile.

"It's not an Astarte. It's a Bog Fritillary. With excellent markings."

"Whoop-ee!"

They went back, and higher. They walked below curtains of steep grey rock with pockets of snow halfway up. They had to ford a stream. He picked out a part where you could jump from rock to rock and handed her a stick for balance. She used it to lengthen her stride, but once she got to the middle for some reason she threw it down. She seemed not sure which way to go: she looked upstream and down. He told her she could stay there and he'd get the pony, but of course she didn't hear. She just picked up her black skirts and set off wading, stepping into a place where the water came nearly to her waist. The current was strong, but she held on. When she got to the shore she found herself a patch of dry rock and sat down. She removed her boots and set them a yard in front of her and lay flat on her back to dry out.

The thing about dudes, he always said, was that not everyone liked the place once they got here. He might see, in a group of twelve, twelve different reactions. Some were frightened and almost affronted that their race and church meant zero. A few were overly bold, launching themselves up scree slopes or into streams without taking the measure of what they were up against. A lot of the hunters fell into that category—figured a gun gave them godlike properties. Others were wary but could be coaxed out of it. A very few, like Minnie, just stood and breathed it in. The wilderness settled deep inside them and found some echo. To those he was partial.

She had taken herself off on one of her jaunts, poking her face into a flower here and her toe into a moss bank there, her silly net propped up on her shoulder, when he saw the bear. The sow was browsing in much the same way she was. Bear and matriarch were moving toward each other without knowing it. He shouted to warn both, but neither paid any attention. The bear turned and moved toward her, and he couldn't even shoot it because Minnie was in the way. He ran along the creek to get another angle. She was a huge silver-tipped grizzly, and who knew if there were cubs around. She stood there swaying and sniffing and probably spotting with her poor eyes the ratty straw of the Panama hat bobbing silently on the other side of a bush.

Herbie had his aim, but he couldn't keep it and look where he was stepping as well; he slipped on a wet rock and fell forward into the stream. The gun went off as he was falling. At the sound, the bear packed up and moved on. Herbie surfaced and watched from the water.

At least Minnie heard the bang. She looked up and saw the grizz depart, and then she walked over to watch Herbie get out, dripping. "What'd you tell that fellow?"

"He's a she. Oh, I said, 'You don't want that one, she's Welsh.'"

That was it, she had no nerves. Never got scared, and she could make him laugh.

They took the gentle route down from Louise because there might be butterflies along the way. Minnie said she had climbed in Montenegro, in Bosnia, in the Pyrenees and in Spain, first with her husband, but later he did not wish to travel. In his later years he was not well. Their travels then were mostly to spa towns in Europe, where Mr. Nicholl looked for a cure. That was not Minnie's idea of adventure, but she had been devoted. And when he died, she put on her widow's black. Then she went out mountain climbing.

She saw a couple of butterflies and made her strange approach to them, poising like a cat and then whipping the net, flicking her wrist to keep the thing in its trap. Then the killing jar and the collection box. All this while hardly pausing in her conversation.

That last night Herbie played his harmonica. She waited until it went silent and then asked him about marriage: it wasn't on his mind, he swore. But when it came to his mind, she said, and it would, would he bring his wife on the trail? Absolutely not, he said. She won't be one of these independent ladies like you. His mind clouded up again with Isabel, just when he'd managed to forget. Minnie was gentle with him, as if she knew.

"Oh, but I didn't start out this way," she said. She'd begun with her mother telling her to put all thoughts of herself aside once she was married. "'Put your husband first and then your children. And be sure it is in that order, because no husband wants a rival in his child.'"

"I tried," Minnie said. "I can say that I honestly did try, but I didn't really want to succeed! A marriage of two equals was what I wanted, and a soulmate and an intellectual companion."

"Lucky you didn't expect too much," he interjected.

"What hurt me the most was that when I spoke to him about my qualms about God, he would not debate."

Could you beat that? Women! Who could ever guess the stuff they harboured against you. She still sounded surprised all those years later, with the husband dead and gone.

So he said to her, "I feel a certain pang for this John you married and his long-ago unpleasant discovery that his wife was a woman who could do just about anything and probably better than him." When she laughed he continued. "I'm learning a lot about marriage," he said. "Still, I doubt I'm going to put it into practice."

"You'll be sorry if you don't," she said.

Why they talked like that might seem a mystery, but it was part of mountain life. To her, he was out of time and place—a man on horseback in a wild corner of the empire. To him, she was a listening ear, even if deaf. He said things he needed to say to another human being but didn't dare say to anyone he was going to see again. When you can hear the other guy's farts emanate from the open tent flap, you get to feel close—in a temporary way.

"Let us talk a little about the tragedy," she said. That was how people referred to it now.

"Do we have to?"

"I know scientists can be very single-minded. I don't blame you for the loss of the Hodgson folk. You probably had very little control. And besides, we all take the risk when we come out here. That's the exhilarating part. No one to blame if you don't come back!"

"I wish that were true," he said.

"It is."

"When we get back, I am going to write all my friends to say you've given me an excellent tour," she said.

And she did that. Put out the word among her friends and fellows that Herbie Wishart was the guide you wanted in the Rockies. She came back a couple of years, and her important friends followed. They were people he could learn from, artists and scientists. The businessmen came later, politicians and company presidents. Hard to believe that he—Herbie the truant and poacher—should appeal, but he did. And he got himself a method for self-improvement: he broadened his mind while they broadened their horizons.

But this was all to come. That night at the end of their first month-long pack, Isabel rose to his mind. He felt the longing as he said grimly about the Hodgson party, "They won't get the best of me. I'll find them. Find out what happened. If it's the last thing I do."

Part Two

Chapter 18
SETTLING IN

Gateway, July 2011

IT WAS 5:30 A.M. To see the sunrise Nancy walked around the back of the old hotel and looked west. That is correct—sunrise, west. You got used to that kind of thing in the mountains. *Bass ackwards*, as Grandfather Herbie would say.

She had always been the early riser in the family. Now, mere weeks into the family's tenure at the hotel, she was claiming the dawn. At this moment a far peak to the southwest was on fire: no sun in the sky but a big hit of it on rock and snow. That peak was called the Fist, and that's what it looked like: clenched knuckles of rock pushing straight up out of a wide upturned sleeve of trees. Granite, crumbly, deemed unsafe for climbing a century ago, but studded all the same with old pitons, expansion bolts and weathered slings left by rock climbers.

Only the first joint of the index finger was lit, but in minutes the tip of the second finger flared, then the thumb crossing the others, then the third and fourth knuckles. Nancy went back inside, got her coffee and stood looking out the kitchen window.

The sky was a cool pale lavender. It had rained in the night. Silent, small predawn creatures were about, a hummingbird on a dead branch at the top of the birch tree practising liftoffs, a vole in the garden. And the rabbits. Twenty years ago someone let loose a few tame bunnies. Since, they had multiplied to become a scourge to local gardens. A black one near the station, a white one in the park, several on the lawn across the street. One street over, behind the station, a neighbour crawled out of the orange tent he'd slept in the past couple of nights. His wife had told Nancy he missed camping and slept better in a tent than anywhere. She looked away to give him privacy in his blue mechanic-style jumpsuit as he circled his tent, plucking at the folds to let the water run down.

The sun's fiery hold on the Fist had increased. The light now illuminated all the knuckles and the back of the hand. You could see layers, depth: two slabs overlapped and the first laid down its shadow—one vertical ridge became a tendon in the wrist. The neighbouring mountains now appeared: front and centre was the Three Sisters. Her father's complaint was always that they had jinxed him. Three daughters and no sons—too many females for him to control. A joke. Her grandfather had said the same about the jinx, though he'd had only one daughter.

As she watched, the honeyed light worked its way down the facing slopes, finding creases and opening dark passages. She could see Whiteman's Gap, through which the pack trains had once wound upward and mountain bikers now toiled uphill in gravel dust. To the north and west, the front ranges, starter peaks named after British royalty. Beyond that, range upon range of full-out, grand-scale mountains. And beyond them, over the Summits, the place they used to call the Inaccessible. She wondered idly if it still was. Of course not. It wasn't then and it surely wasn't now; it was studied by legions, landed on by helicopters, driven over by giant-wheeled buses.

An inaudible plane left its vapour trail overhead. The thumb and knuckles of the Fist had shaded from pink to granite grey. The sun in its trickery hit Miners' Wall straight on, bringing it forward, a placard held up by a line of stagehands. The scenery was moving into place for the grand performance. And it came: all the mountains suddenly were lit in the first yellow light. Wherever you were, you stayed in place to watch. They held the light for minutes only. Nancy drank her coffee and waited.

Now it was over. The fire of sunrise was out. The yellow slid down toward the treeline and soon buried itself in the absorbent green-black forest. A curtain closed on the uplands even as it opened on the town below. Just above the river on the nearby flanks, you could see, still, the wooden mine portals, abandoned, along with the web of tunnels reaching back into the mountain and under the town. Walk north for fifteen minutes and there was a mine under you. Walk south or east, same thing. The tunnels under the town gave her father his other favourite joke: *Don't undermine me*, Walter would say, *I already have been!* It was a metaphor. But not by much.

The air was cool. The streets were silent except for the thin scraping of the cross-country skiers' training skates as they went by, aiming for their little drag strip beside the parkway.

Iona wheeled into the kitchen on her walker, looking stricken.

"Where's Ann?"

"She's here. She arrived last night, remember?"

Mistake. You didn't say "remember?" to Iona, because she didn't.

Iona looked skeptical, spun her walker on a dime and headed back down the hall. Nancy looked at her departing form, bent forward in an *S*, white knuckles on the handlebar. Her own hands clenched in sympathy: hold on, Mum! She had declined in the past few weeks, but mostly Iona was still herself.

Lynn was at the deep double sink set in the linoleum counter, looking out the window at the park. Her daughter and her grandchildren had come. She was the only sister to have children, and the only one who attempted to keep house. She leaned forward, trying to lift the sticky old window frame. Nancy helped; they had to get a hammer and bang, but they succeeded. Instantly the piping sound of children's voices entered.

"What's all this?" said Walter, coming up from behind. Life in a family of four women had made him the outsider. *Don't mind me, I only work here*, he used to say. "What you call them? Those three-wheeled things?"

"Troikas."

"Yesterday when I took your mum out for a walk, we met some woman running, with a dog on a leash and pushing one of those troikas at the same time, blocking the path, all over both sides of it, couldn't control her dog, baby in a plastic bag. Dangerous!" he said. "She could have knocked your mum down."

He turned and left them. Nancy and Lynn locked eyes. You had to give him credit. He had transformed himself into a caregiver. He was in charge of Iona. All day most days. It was his job now, and like all his jobs this was one he did very well.

Iona had got herself into a stuffed chair in the lounge. Nancy approached with a cup of coffee. Her mother looked up.

"In my dream last night I was singing. Singing away just like a bird! In the bar right here!" said Iona.

Nancy sat beside her and touched her thin wrist. The tawny-spotted hand lifted and fell in greeting. Her mother's wedding rings stood out, huge above the sunken flesh ridged in sinews and veins. Her own hand was plump compared to her mother's, but it too bore deep lines within deeper lines, some running across, some running lengthwise.

There were no wedding rings on Nancy's hand. Once, years ago, Iona had protested Nancy's husband's treatment of her: "He hasn't even given you one decent piece of jewellery!" A big stone meant something in her mother's world. But Nancy had never wanted that mark of ownership by a man. Before and after her divorce she had worn many rings—turquoise and silver, tiger's-eye from India, coral from Hawaii, gemstones she picked up on her travels. But not diamonds.

Walter patted the front page of the *Gateway Trumpet*, folded on a footstool. "The King Is Back," said the headline. Above the fold on the front page was a photograph of a bear, staring out candidly.

"Whoo. Big one. Where was he?"

"We never had trouble with bears. But if we did, we'd of shot him."

"Dad! He's magnificent."

"Gonna get hit if he keeps thinking he owns those railway tracks."

"The CPR should clean them up so they don't attract animals," said Ann, ready to start a fight.

Walter took his glasses by the right temple and pulled them down his nose. "You probably don't agree with me. But they should just get these bears and put them somewhere else. Leave this valley for the people."

"You mean leave it for the trains? And the transport trucks going over the Rockies?"

"What else are you going to do? It's how you get to the other side of the country."

Walter put down the paper, stood and walked to the door, withdrawing from the fray. Male subtracting himself. The dominant male, the affable male, the brooding male: most types had been represented over the years, but all were somehow tangential. As Lynn's daughter, Mellow, came in from the park and sat, pulling her three-year-old girl onto her lap, the room rearranged itself neatly and efficiently like a stage set for the next act: women through four generations. It seemed a moment to mark.

"Coffee?"

"I'll have some."

"Let's make another pot."

Lynn went to put it on.

The tribe, Nancy decided, felt overwhelmingly female. Female and restive. Each member endlessly aware of what went on inside the others' heads and hearts. How did that happen, how had they learned to read one another? Or rather, how had they failed to learn to let one another go unread?

There was something.

Something in the women, an inability to fit, an anger that arced over generations, a refusal to give in, give up. The way they sought to be equal, demanded it, or renounced the struggle and soured. Sabotage: their strength, their competence, their cleverness worked against their simply having successful careers or successful marriages. Or being happy.

Yet that was not true, because they enjoyed themselves. Friction enlivened them. At some point every day they would erupt in laughter. Giggles, they used to call it. As kids they had "got the giggles"—irresistible, unstoppable giggles. Walter hated it. Once Nancy giggled so hard and for so long at the dinner table that she was sent to eat in the garage. Was that normal? Was it really joy, or was it nerves, hostility, defeat? What had it been about?

It came from Iona, Nancy decided. Or perhaps it came *through* Iona, from her mother, her father, this town, even this hotel.

In the veins of the Three Sisters Hotel, and despite a couple of cleanings—once before it went on the market and a second time before the Mariners moved in—ran the dirt of decades. You could see it by pushing the side of your forefinger along the deep wooden windowsill. If you probed one of the creases between logs with that same finger, chunks of crumbly matter came out. That wasn't only dust. It was mortar, dried and collapsing and smelling like beer.

"What is this stuff?"

"It's just age."

"How do we get rid of it?"

"You don't. It'll never go without the whole place falling down."

"You can try vacuuming."

"You'll have to get busy," said Walter from the doorway. He hated to see an idle woman.

"It's a huge job."

"You're looking for something to do. Nancy can organize it. Lynn can come up on weekends and cook. Your mum can supervise."

He'd left out Ann. "What about Ann?"

"She can protest it," said Walter, and they all laughed.

"You think that's a joke? If we try to modernize there will be issues with the park or the town—wait and see," Ann said.

"It's not in the park."

"They'll have issues. Same if we tried to take it down," she added. "What we're going to need is someone to guide it through all the hoops."

Walter summoned his old pal, Fred the Fire Boss. Fred arrived on the veranda in half an hour.

"The kids are asking," said Walter. As if they were kids! "How do we improve the life expectancy of these logs?"

Fred had taken up log cabin restoration in his retirement. "You don't need experts. All you need is elbow grease," he said.

They took a tour up to the third floor. Ann bent down to look out the windows.

"This feels like maids' quarters in Paris." You could see light through the floors. You could see it through the log walls. "How would you ever heat this place in winter?"

"Tear it down and sell the property," muttered someone.

But Fred was talking preservation. A simple first step was to wash the logs. Here's what you did: first sweep the outside with a stiff broom: you could get a handle extender at Home Hardware. Get up into the eaves and check for wasps' nests. Wear gloves. Then wash the logs with water and dish detergent, maybe add a little bleach. If any of the logs were in really bad condition, then you might need to replace them. He knew a place where you could find some old logs, up a little farther into the mountains. Guy had been keeping a stack of them, intending to build, but he hadn't, and he might like a little cash . . . You needed a good length for the front here—that might be a problem. You had to get up on ladders and scrub every inch with the soapy water. Starting at the top would be a good idea, he thought.

The sisters began to smile at each other, imagining what it would be like to be up there on ladders. Fun if the weather held.

Then you could get a pressure hose and rinse them. Not too much pressure or you'd damage the wood. Maximum fifteen hundred pounds. Oh yes, some of those machines went up to six thousand. You'd blow a hole right through the hotel if you kept your nozzle pointed at any one place too long. You wanted to look very carefully to see if you had bugs in the logs, but he didn't figure that happened around here so much because of the cold winters.

Walter pointed out that he could do the hosing-down part himself. Lynn would consider coming up weekends. Ann would do the desk work from Ottawa. Nancy said nothing. She had come out in early June, had supervised the move and was still here. She noted that no one in the family gave any thought to her time, as if it were completely unoccupied, as if she had come to stay, which was by no means certain.

"Finish that and your logs will be fresh and clean. Let them dry and see what you've got. Might be some damage near the foundation where the snow builds up," Fred said, downstairs now and looking around under the veranda.

"Foundations? That's not good," said Walter.

"It looks as if the previous owners shovelled the snow to prevent it melting in."

But farther back in the basement, under the bar, there was water damage that went back decades. All those floods. Still, you could get the foundations repaired. He guessed if you did, the building could last a couple of hundred years. In passing, Fred said he didn't know why Walter hadn't taken the trouble to find that out before he paid for the hotel, but he guessed it was an emotional decision. That was a dig. Everyone knew Walter never made a decision without a good reason.

Walter coughed.

After the cleaning, there would be chinking, and then there'd be oiling or staining the logs. Do that and they'd last forever.

"I don't know about that roof either," said Fred. "You'd have to look at it. Depends when it was put on. Happen to know?"

The telephone rang. It sat on the bar, which had doubled as a front desk and faced the lounge and the fireplace. It was an old phone, but it had a new number, in their name, and it surprised them with its ring. Nancy picked it up, said hello and then started digging with her toe at a chipped linoleum tile.

He had a voice that was not North American, although he had no accent that she could discern. Its timbre was unusual; it had depth. There was no edge; the voice was not urgent. Perhaps that was the strangeness. It rolled out slowly, but with determination.

"Is this the household of Mrs. Iona Mariner?"

"Who's calling, please?"

"I am trying to reach Mrs. Mariner or her family," continued the voice.

If at that moment Nancy had to guess the purpose of the call she would have said that it was a roundabout message from the old country like the ones Grandpa used to get—that one of the mad English relatives had died and left them a share in the carrier pigeon stable that had served the king, for instance. But not this call. There was a certain familiarity in the man's tone, although he was a stranger.

"I'm sorry. I don't know who you are."

"I'm Kaz Otaka."

"Oh yes. You spotted us at the Wolf Den."

"You remember." And he paused. A little expectant. As if he thought, or hoped, that recognition would dawn. It did not dawn.

"What is it you want?" Nancy said. She felt annoyed, and reluctant, although the man seemed to be quite nice. "I'm Nancy Mariner. Mrs. Mariner is my mother."

"Yes," said the man. Pleased, a little. But distanced, a little. As if a barrier had risen between him and the person he intended to reach. "You are her daughter. Well," said Kaz, "may I backtrack for a moment?"

Nancy looked at Iona. Her mother had the coffee cup in both hands and was trying not to spill as she lifted it to her lips. "All right."

"Some time ago, in 2004, an act was passed in this province to open the adoption records. I signed the register to find my birth mother. This information is given to all adoptees unless the mother vetoes releasing the information. Perhaps you already know this. Your mother did not veto."

Nancy wandered as far behind the bar as the old telephone cord would allow her. She looked over it to the lounge; the windows could be deepened by cutting out several logs, she mused. It would be very pretty. They caught, from here, the glint of the creek. A deeper window would catch more. The water stirred and flashed. She turned back to the telephone.

"Is it possible," she said, carefully and politely, "that you have been given a wrong lead?"

"I don't believe so," said the man. "Miss Iona Wishart has for many years been known as Mrs. Iona Mariner."

Nancy did not want this call. She could see what was coming. "She's not *known* as Mrs. Iona Mariner, she *is* Mrs. Iona Mariner." She put her hand out and fingered the small holes in the logs—wormholes? Maybe they were. She felt a wobble in her knees. "I can't speak to you now."

He was very polite. "Shall I call back in an hour?"

That seemed a bit soon. Nancy wandered out onto the veranda. Her mind was blank.

Her mother had arranged herself with a newspaper and her magnifying glass when the telephone rang again. Nancy picked it up and then went to stand before her mother. A certain quiet fell.

"There's someone on the phone for you."

After, Lynn said it was cruelty. "You could have given her a heart attack. Suddenly like that, out of the blue."

"So I should protect her from the phone?"

"She's old."

"I noticed. What's your point?"

Lynn just stared.

"She's old but she's not an invalid. She's quite capable of taking a phone call."

"Of surviving a shock like that? You don't know." Ferocious look.

Nancy couldn't exactly hand her mother the receiver; it was on a long coiled cord and didn't reach. Iona had to get up, settling the newspaper in the wire basket of her walker beside the big round magnifying glass, release the hand brakes, give a push and step carefully up to the wall. She took the receiver in both hands and turned her back to the walker, positioning her tiny hips on its padded seat in that guilty way she had; Walter had told her a hundred times it was unsafe for sitting. Nancy stood close by, looking at the floor.

"Hello?"

Iona sounded so young and eager. There was not a quaver in that voice. A listener who couldn't see her could imagine spark, even energy in it. Perhaps that was what happened with the caller. He knew his own age, but not hers.

"Pardon me?"

Nancy was watching intently from across the room where Iona had been sitting.

"I can't hear you very well. Please speak up."

Poor man had to shout it. What did he say? Something like *My name is Kaz.* Lynn had come in from the kitchen, where as usual her head had been bent over the sink, and was listening.

"I see," said Iona. There was no faltering in her composure. None whatsoever. "No, that cannot be." She paused. A delicate little cough of embarrassment. "No, I am afraid that won't be possible. But thank you very much for calling."

She pushed herself to standing and, one hand holding the receiver, the other gripping the handlebar of her walker, turned in place with that still-evident delicacy—*stepstepstepstepstep, reach*—and held the receiver out to Nancy. "Can you take this, please, dear?" Looking at the ground a foot in front of her wheels, she made her way back to her chair, turned on the spot again with those small, exact steps, and backed toward it. Nancy sprang to get her arm and lowered her weight—what was it? Maybe one hundred pounds? Iona landed with a gasp.

"Boom!" she said.

They all smiled in relief.

"Could you give me back my newspaper, please," said Iona. Then, "I dropped my handkerchief; can you pick it up for me?"

Nancy saw that the call had ruffled her mother's feathers. But it seemed that things would go on as usual. She swept her hand down to floor level. She did not resent picking up her mother's handkerchief; she resented that to do it she had to let out a little groan.

"What was that, Mum?" said Lynn.

Nancy handed the handkerchief to Iona.

"Why do you ask? It was nothing. Thank you," Iona said. She dabbed at her nose.

"Nothing?"

"Well, perhaps not exactly nothing. But—" said her mother, looking straight ahead. Then she shut her lips firmly.

"What was that?" said Walter, coming into the room.

"He wanted to speak to me," Iona said with an air of importance, like a child, "but I don't know him. He had a funny name."

"Somebody from the paper," Nancy said.

"Your mother's been famous ever since they published that picture," said Walter, buying it. "Does he want to take your mother's picture? Sounds like he might be brave enough." Iona was vain and hated most photographs of herself.

"That's funny, Dad."

He left the room, and Nancy sat holding her mother's hand. They all waited for a break in this odd tension born out of nothing, a random phone call—well, not quite random, but certainly unexpected—in the chilly old hotel with its smell of woodsmoke and damp on a peerless summer morning, a little less blue than the one before, with a barely detectable haze, a cast forming overhead.

"I'm going to go shopping, Mum," said Nancy.

"Don't go," said her mother. "Don't go just yet." She held up her hand. "How do you know that man who called me?"

"He's called before. I spoke to him."

"What did he want?"

"To come and see you."

"Did he know my father?"

"I don't think so."

"Then why?"

"Do you really want me to tell you?"

"Yes, I do."

"He says he's— Well, no, I can't explain it."

Iona gave a little cry of annoyance.

"What's all this again?" Their father strode into the room.

"Nothing," said Nancy. "Mum was confused."

"I'm not confused. At least, I don't *think* I'm confused." Iona's lips widened slightly into a smile.

Her daughters smiled too. One of Iona's little jokes. Little ironic self-contradictions: *Don't tell your father, because he thinks I'm a snake in the grass.* They used to be frequent. Everyone always laughed at them.

Mother and daughter held each other's gaze.

Lynn, out of focus in the background, said, "Well, whoever it was, you told him not to call again."

"No, she didn't," said Walter.

"No, she didn't, quite. She just told him it was all a mistake, and it would not be possible."

Chapter 19
HOW LONG

Gateway, June 1919

Herbie Wishart was on the veranda of the Three Sisters Hotel, soaking in the sun and breathing deeply, fanning the flames in his heart of something that might just become happiness. He watched the cars fight their way around the horses, which owned the street—not paved, despite Foxx's protests, and ankle-deep in mud. He had hopes that some packers would show up. He was itching to get on the trail.

The war years were over. The winter was over too. You could feel the crackle in the spring air; you just knew that miles up in the beyond, the top level of snow had begun to melt on the glacier and find its way down through the layers and out from under the ice pack. Not just that season's ice but the ice of an awful decade.

And he saw this familiar figure walking, little guy, wiry, wearing a tweed cap with a brim, not a trail hat at all, but one that a miner would wear. He had it pulled down over his eyes. That in itself was nothing unusual. Identity had always been fluid in these parts: new fellow comes into town—you don't ask where he's been before; another fellow up and disappears one night—you don't ask much about that either, unless he's absconded with the payroll, which did happen.

The little guy came closer and he looked familiar; Herbie was about to shout out, but the fellow's eyes petitioned him to hold it. He thought, No, it can't be, but it bloody well is How Long and he doesn't want me to let on. Herbie didn't move a muscle as the man came up the stairs and sat down in the corner of the veranda. Herbie had a moment of doubt. Was this specimen his old friend or not? He was dark-skinned, could have been Mexican or Indian, but he didn't have their ways. Herbie had worked with How Long a hundred times, and the more he watched this man, his face kind of puffy as if he'd been beaten or had taken a bad fall, or most likely had been frostbitten and the blisters had changed the shape of his face—the eyelids swollen and droopy, the lips collapsed around what appeared to be a toothless mouth—the more spooked he got.

"Can you bring me a coffee?" the stranger said in a low voice.

Herbie took off for the kitchen. No one was in evidence, so he helped himself. Seemed like he practically ran the place, he was there so often, but that was another story. His hands shook while he poured out the coffee. It was not so much the arrival of the missing man. It was that Herbie had sensed it, he'd felt the quiver: something was about to happen.

God knows he'd been wishing for a break. The guiding business had fallen off with the war and not come back. The old gang of wranglers and guides had broken up. Men went overseas for the fighting. Some of the best were killed, like Francis Erwin. Other boys who used to guide around here, like Jim Crockett, were wounded out. Parks gave him the job of warden at Flannel Creek. He used to show up out of nowhere like some shade when you were on the trail, take a look at what you were doing and dissolve back into the trees. The wardens were all a little crazed, mind you.

There had been death close by too: a favourite fact of his was that during the war years more men died in the Gateway mines than in Europe. They blasted and dug like moles all through it. Of course they had help from the prisoners, Ukrainians, who were suddenly enemies although they'd been in Canada for decades. One of them died. Damn decent of the mine to have an investigation. Not much of an investigation, but they did have one. The conclusion was that it had been an accident. Well, of course it was an accident: who is going to choose to be in the chute when a tonne and a half of coal slides down it? You also saw them in chain gangs, expanding the golf course, safer work.

He'd been able to keep going, just barely, with his American company presidents and scientists looking for ice worms. He liked to blame the collapse of the outfitting business on those cars that were all over the roads, scaring the horses. In many spots new trails needed to be built. Recently he'd had words with Parks about how they should fence the highway near Lake Louise. He despised the car tourists. You could drive through in a couple of days and say you'd done it.

He thought How Long took sugar in his coffee: he'd give the fellow some and see what he said. When he went back out to the veranda and handed over the mug, he remembered that morning at Siding 29 after he had surprised Sam Gallant in the ice-house. How Long had come out the back door of the hotel and given *him* a coffee. Herbie felt the symmetry, and as How Long took the mug the same recognition came into his eyes, and the two of them exchanged the merest look of amusement that clinched it: this man truly was How Long, no word of a lie. But Jesus, Mary and Joseph, he'd been lost for nearly a decade.

"Christ almighty, you said you'd meet us on Monday, August 28, 1911, at Nickel Lake. Where the hell have you been?"

"Wishart," he said, "I come back from the dead." He gave a pathetic look. "You protect me, Herbie?"

At that Herbie figured How Long had gone to where the fairies live;

he wasn't all there. His anger drained away. Lucky he had experience with animals and knew to wait until How Long settled, which he did once he downed the coffee.

"Don't worry, old chap. There's no danger now. You're back in Gateway, though I don't know how you made it."

"The others didn't?"

"Not that we seen."

"Not the professor or Isabel, or Maxwell? Humphrey?"

"Listen, buddy, where have you been?"

"With the Indians," he said. "That breakaway group of Stoneys up around the Pity Plains."

And that figured. Beyond the Summits. Beyond the Inaccessible. That just figured.

"Holy jumping Jesus Jehoshaphat, how did you get all the way out there?"

How Long held out his mug for more coffee.

The professor and Maxwell had delayed the departure two days. Then there was snow on the trail to Laggan. They insisted the party go back the way they came, the long way. No reason was given except that they had missed the rendezvous already. At this point the Tree brothers took their ponies and left. Maxwell made sure the ponies remaining were loaded with shale. They got as far as the steep cliff where they'd lifted the horses on the way in, and stayed there a day with Maxwell and the doctor arguing, trying to figure out how to take them down, and a blizzard began. They ended up realizing they couldn't get down, and so they took the trail at the top that led off to the north, the one no one ever took. Maxwell said that they could get to the back of the storm that way. Hah. The back of beyond was more like it.

The wind-borne snow made it nearly impossible to see. The trail led around the edge of a deep chasm and backed right up against the rock.

The snow was slippery and turning to ice, and the heavily laden ponies stumbled and slid. The professor and Maxwell pulled out their snowshoes and went on for a way, but it was too dangerous to continue and so they returned. Together they found a bit of shelter against a bluff. There was flat ground for maybe thirty feet in front of the wall, so they unloaded the ponies. There was no way to build a fire; they were above the treeline.

But not far above. For once Maxwell seemed content to sit. How Long left him and the others huddled and went back the way they'd come, scrounging to find dead branches to start a fire. When he got past the chasm, he zigzagged around and pulled at the base of some little scrub pines. With the branches in his arms, somehow he made it back to where the others had been. They were gonc, ponies and all. The wind was blowing, but he found it impossible to believe their footsteps had disappeared. The snow still flew. He ran in one direction and then another. Ahead, their thirty-foot camping spot narrowed to become a ledge.

"Goddamn," he said to Herbie, "in that kind of weather you can't tell if you're going up or down."

Herbie knew the feeling.

How Long figured then that they had no way of seeing the trail or finding a pass in the snow, so they were just following their noses. In the same way he had no way of following them because their snowshoe tracks had been blown off already, and the horses, well, he couldn't see their prints either. But he thought that, far ahead, when the swirling snow allowed him a bit of vision, he could see a wide expanse of trees.

He had two choices: to go back to where he'd parted from the others, or to go forward to where he thought Maxwell and Hodgson might be. He went forward. In the weeks to come he had plenty of time to regret that decision.

He made it to the trees, figuring the others would be there, but there was no one. Shouting was useless in the wind. He doubted they could be far away, so he tucked himself in at the base of a big fir tree with drooping branches, covered himself with boughs and just about kept himself from freezing. He had whisky in his pocket and chocolate.

"You know me and my pockets, Wishart—"

Oh yes, Herbie knew: How Long had the most fertile pockets. In them on this occasion were bacon rinds and potatoes going to seed and fish heads; to these were added the everyday essentials of flask, fish hook, dried apples for the horses, string and knife. And maybe a piece of ginger candy. It's a miracle the bears didn't sniff him out.

He tucked in for the blow, eating snow and chocolate, and dozing on the whisky. He was managing fine, and he assumed the others would be too, either back at the pass or nearby. But three days later, when the blow ended and the sun lit vast new unbroken slopes of snow, he could see that wasn't likely. The path dipped below the treeline where he was, but in either direction it rose. There was no protection: within a hundred feet the walls of rock slanted up either side. The trees became small and thin and within five hundred yards had disappeared.

He could see no one, hear no life. The sun was relentless. He felt as if bits of glass had flown into his eyes. He could barely take a step; the snow was that deep. He spent a day tying branches to make himself snowshoes. He fit them on his shoes and walked a bit. Had the others got back to the rock wall? It was a faint hope. Had they managed to scale these slopes and reach the plain? They had snowshoes, but the horses didn't. Those poor cayuses—where were they? In the storm, had Maxwell loaded up the rocks on their backs again? If he had, the beasts were probably frozen to death. He wasted some energy getting incensed that Maxwell had taken them straight into the storm. Served him right if those fossils were now buried beneath feet of snow.

When his vision started to go he went back to his tree. For a week he was blinded and could do nothing but cry. The water seemed to help his eyes. He made an eyeshade of fir twigs, but that wasn't good enough, so he tied a bandana over his face and cut holes to see through. He was deplet-ing his supplies but at least his vision began to return. One twilight as he sat very still, his crying done, waiting for death, a beautiful little ptarmigan came to sit between the rocks. It must have been surprised by the early storm too; it still had its summer plumage, hadn't turned white yet.

Next day he made a snare. The project kept him alive for a few days. The ptarmigan stayed near, and he caught it. "Bird saved my life," he said. He had to kill it, though. He felt very bad about that, cried some more. But then he wrung its neck. He was determined to cook it, and that pushed him to get a fire started in the dry needles under his tree. That took another day. One day after another passed, and he discovered he was still alive. He began to plan. Was this a summer storm or the beginning of winter? That was the question. By then, he thought, it must have been September. He ate his bird and gave up on the bloody Hodgsons. They must have got out and left him for dead.

But one day a warm wind came up from the south and the snowpack began to shrink away from the tree trunk. Now came the Indian summer he'd been waiting for. He decided to leave his nest and go back to the fateful cliff, see if there was any sign of the party, and then head toward home. He was sure he started walking that way, but those warm spells were always set with huge winds. The blow pinned him against the rocks. It seemed impossible to go back—too much of an effort heading into the wind. He could hardly stand. To save energy he decided to head onward. Now he could see that was another bad decision. But at the time it felt right. He could make out the trail at the other end of the narrow pass, and thought it must go somewhere.

So on he went and on, and perhaps he had gone a little crazy. After some days he met the Stoney hunters, who fed him and took him beyond the Summits and over the Snow Dome and down the chute of the Pity River to the plains. It was a good place, warm, flat so you could let horses run. Sam Gallant had a trading post, though he wasn't in it at the time. There was an encampment of Stoneys there for hunting season. Not many of their women had come with them from Morley, so How Long cooked.

"I wasn't hiding, Herbie. Nobody came looking."

But if he had been it wouldn't have been hard to escape detection in that company. The more he thought about it, the more he was certain that there was a curse on the Hodgson expedition. He was superstitious and he'd never trusted Maxwell, he of the poker face and perfect manners. Seasons followed seasons: word got to him that they had disappeared. Then he couldn't return: he'd be wanted by the law. He'd be blamed for the loss of the others. He knew it. He renamed himself Snares Ptarmigan after the bird that saved him.

Finally he'd been at the Pity for so long he thought it would all be forgotten. Horses, rocks, Maxwell, professor, young lady, young man—finished. "I'm not lying, boss," he said. "Believe me."

Herbie figured "Snares" had got himself a wife among the Stoney or he would not have stayed so long. And that he was drinking up some of that liquor that Sam Gallant packed in. Asked him, and he admitted it. About what happened, Herbie did believe him. Mostly. But there was something fishy. He wasn't telling everything. So he asked How Long the question he'd been pondering for ten years.

"So tell me, How Long. I've had a lot of time to think on this. And there's only one reason I can come up with for the whole disaster. Did you all leave the camp together?"

It wasn't a question you'd ask an experienced mountain man. Nobody split up on the trail, ever. But he had to ask it, and when the answer came it seemed as if he already knew it.

"No, boss, we didn't. When we got up that day, the boy and the girl were already gone. Waited a couple of days and never saw them again."

Herbie told How Long to turn himself in. He'd vouch for him.

Herbie had no idea the Mounties would give How Long such a hard time. They said it was because he'd been hiding out all this time: he must have been guilty of something. Really it was the Stoney up there at Pity

Plains they should have been quizzing. And Sam Gallant, who had to have known How Long was there. And in fact they did send out a team of Mounties to go there by road, in from the north and east, but nothing came of it.

Eventually the Tree brothers came in and swore as they always had that they'd left the party before it decamped, that there was no one but How Long and the family with the packponies, and that the professor had been acting like a crazy man, shouting that he would go to any length to get those rocks out. So it made sense that Humphrey and Isabel had gone ahead, or gone for help.

And it was hard to believe that the little Chinese cook had murdered four people, stolen their fossils and hidden their bodies. The only sure thing was that he had survived alone in the high peaks, only to be rescued in a poor mental state by native hunters. The Mounties and even the Americans had to let it go, finally. But for the town of Gateway the question of the Hodgson expedition had risen anew.

Chapter 20
GWEN

Gateway, Summer 1920

THE GIRL CAME OUT FROM WASHINGTON in summers. She had been doing it since that first time, when she arrived to meet her brother, sister and father and was disappointed. It seemed odd. She had no real ties to Gateway. Foxx even complained it was bad for business. It was Erwin who convinced the town to see it her way. He was Gateway's philosopher, and Gwen's chief defender. Shouldn't they be kind to her? Was it just possible that they were annoyed by her presence because it kept the whole tragedy alive? And where else did she have to go?

Family, they said.

Think of her logic, he told her detractors one after another: her family disappears, so she decides to attach herself to the place where they were last seen. Out of love. Out of loyalty. If she were ever to meet any of them again, it would be here. He would do the same, Erwin said. The Washington people, from what they heard, were a bit frigid. She needed warmth and life.

And it was easy to like the girl. She was not a figure of despair. She was a buoyant, busy little person who seemed convinced that her father, brother and sister would reappear. She liked to walk the trails; she wasn't afraid of the wilderness, unlike some city people. Erwin helped her become a not bad horsewoman. Dr. Smallwood boarded her every summer, and it began to seem natural; the chaperone was no longer deemed necessary.

Then, in 1914, Erwin went to fight in Europe. The summer after, a gaggle of Gateway mothers turned out at the station to greet Gwen's train. They felt sorry for her, abandoned again. She charmed the town—she taught Latin to the miners' children; she held sewing classes; she took little troops of girls out picking wildflowers along the river. There was an intensity in her daily enthusiasm: behind her back more than one woman worried that she tried too hard, and that the grief would catch up to her one day.

You could tell her nothing; she was fierce, but at the same time delicate. Best to watch out for her. This protection became Gateway's undertaking: be nice to the poor Quaker child whose family was lost in an avalanche. Or was it a rock slide? Or did they wander off in a storm? That mystery had never been cleared up. Certain people befriended her: Phoebe Dixon, the spindly grey-haired artist, was one. Phoebe had let it be known that she was to have married Doctor Professor Hodgson; Gwen would have been her stepdaughter.

Then How Long made his miraculous reappearance. Someone had to tell Gwen. Phoebe Dixon was the main candidate, but she declined to break the news herself. She nominated Herbie, whom she'd never liked, and got Dr. Smallwood to ask him.

"Jesus, Doc," said Herbie. "You can't get a pastor?"

Herbie had been walking around Gateway with a cloud over his head. But now, with How Long's explanation of events, opinion was shifting in his favour. Still, he drank, and when he drank he showed off, telling stories, playing his harmonica. No one knew that he blamed himself.

In fact he longed to speak about the expedition. If Erwin had returned from the war, he would have confided to him that the tables had turned: he the hunter felt as if he were being stalked. Not by an animate creature, not by ghosts: it was not as simple as that. By darkness. There was a space of great unhappiness in his world. It was off to the side, just behind or ahead of him. It was a great gaping hole. If he looked he saw it, and if he didn't look he might fall into it. It was like one of those pits they dug in Africa to catch the big cats, the elephants. They'd dig a hole and cover it with branches so you could run toward it not noticing, but then one step and it was just air underneath that fan palm; you went down with a roar, thrashing. Then what? The men came to the edge with spears?

The pit tempted him. A kind of relief lurked in it and the mockery it made of his success. Sometimes he could dispatch it. But then it would appear again, in his peripheral vision. The dark place, waiting, soft as a bruise. He faced it, sometimes. They are gone. I know I am guilty. He would argue with it. No, not *guilty.* They did it to themselves. But I am *responsible.* He fell into it. I took them out. There were signs. I could have listened. I could have done otherwise. I might have— And he wondered how he could possibly have avoided the disaster. He could have insisted they come out when he left, that night. He could have ridden in immediately when they didn't show up at the rendezvous. Hindsight was a wizard.

He tried to get out of the pit, but he could not. He had spells, then he surfaced. The sun came out, the spears were gone.

A woman would be good for him, people said. He argued. But I'm a guide. Guides don't marry, and if they do they have to marry cowpokes. Friends said he needed the companionship when he got home, and he denied it. But he knew they were right. And there was the pit. It was his pit now and would be with him. It threatened to change his idea of who he was. He was a mischief-maker and a problem kid in the old country. Came here and was like a man reborn; he had talent and ingenuity. It raised him up. Now this came to plunge him down. He thought being good would help. He did good deeds. How Long wanted work, but no one would hire him, so Herbie helped him set up a business selling fresh vegetables from the Chinaman's garden on the tipple. He also got him work making deliveries of fresh milk and butter in a cart pulled by a husky named Drago.

Going to see Gwen Hodgson would be a good deed. Herbie remembered going over, hat in hand, to meet her on the last day of August, eight years ago, a couple of weeks after the disappearance. She had been remarkably poised, tiny, with little buds where her breasts would be. Not at all like her sister, who had been willowy; this girl was compact and staunch, a small, wilful, righteous girl. He had gone over the events with her then, though he did not for the life of him remember how, and he would do it again.

If he had been a man who felt fear, he would have feared that Gwen was an opening to the pit. But he was not such a man. He understood that she suffered. He dared to imagine he might speak to her of his own suffering.

Herbie appeared at the doctor's house and took the girl for a walk along the riverbank. It was a fine summer night, with the moon rising quickly in the east. An eagle swooped down to pluck a fish from the water. He took that as a sign of good luck. And their talk did go well. He explained, as he had before, that he had arranged to rendezvous with the family at Nickel Lake. That they had said they knew the way. That he had waited a day, two days, and when they had not arrived, he had ridden in to find the camp empty. Now he knew what had happened. She raised her pleasant, smooth face to his while he gave How Long's story about the trek, the blizzard, the heavy burden of fossils, and getting separated from the doctor and Maxwell, never to see either of them again. It was certain they had perished.

She listened carefully, patiently, holding her questions until the end. Then she said, "And what of my brother and sister?"

He had a choice. He could lie to her and say they were all together, and all gone. That might put the matter to rest. Might. Or he could tell her the truth. And lessen the attraction of the pit. Good man levels with survivor. He was certain she could cope with the truth. She had that curious serenity. She had her faith.

"How Long says they left the camp on their own, two days before."

There was a flicker, a sign of human frailty.

"What does that mean, Mr. Wishart? My brother and sister left separately?"

"Please call me Herbie," he said.

He smiled into her eyes and felt as if he were truly himself for a moment, no more acting.

"I tell you this because you are grown up now. I don't know what it means," he admitted. "Why they did that. Were they going for help? Was there an argument of some kind? Did they even try to get to the meeting point?"

"They must have!" She was looking at the water as she protested, and her voice rose alarmingly.

For the first time he thought she might lose control.

"I don't think so."

"But why?"

"Because they would have got to it."

There was silence. The water sucked at the bank, and farther out it rushed. In between there were eddies and swirls. It was muscular water, thick as milk and tinted like sky and moving fast. You did not want to get in its way.

"We did find signs of a rock slide. However, if they had been hit there would have been evidence. The other possibility is that they took a wrong turn. And were lost." Now he ventured further into his truth-telling, this new activity. "One thought I've had is that they deliberately avoided notice. Got out somehow and did not want to be found. Was there any reason— Is there anything you can think of?"

"I was twelve," she said shortly.

There was another long silence while the water chucked and whistled at them like a nesting bird.

"What you're telling me is that they could be alive."

Was it? No, no. It was not what he wanted to be telling her. Quite the opposite. He wanted her to accept their death. But she had read his thoughts, which were the opposite. They could be alive. He'd been pondering it ever since How Long told him. The idea of two disappearances, the young adults one day and the older ones two days later, beggared belief. But it was the only explanation; Humphrey and Isabel must have done a runner. He gritted his teeth over that, and that fierce oath he'd made to himself to find Isabel flared again in his chest.

But he had not intended to convey this to Gwen.

"I don't see how they could be alive," he said.

"You don't have to see how," she said gently. "And neither do I. It is not given to us to know the why and wherefore. What is given is to see the possibility. We must have faith."

Gwen was twenty-one years old, Herbie nearly double her age. They spent time together that summer. He did not talk about his pit, but he felt she knew.

There were times when, walking the streets of the little town with him, she looked up into the crags of the mountains, saw the faint mist of snow flying, and felt an urge to walk out there and keep walking, to be lost in the swirl of wind, to sink, to lie, to become whiteness. He could see it in her; she did not need to tell him.

He knew she was tempted to let go of her burdens. A shaft of bright sun made her disappear. So, too, did the depth of the darkness. Beyond the little grid of streets, the house lights, the noise of a car door shutting or a horse whinnying, the sound of the band escaping from the doors of the Opera House, beyond that sprinkle of human affect, there was nothing.

No, my girl, he would say when she gazed in a greedy way up toward Whiteman's Gap and asked why they couldn't go for a few nights' ride. Home for you, he would say, steering her back to the doctor's house.

Once he took her down to Dead Man's Flats to watch his cowboys catch the wild horses that ran on Pigeon Mountain. Another time they went to the movies that were shown in the Opera House, with Mrs. Hawrelak playing the piano. They picked wild strawberries and hiked up to Noisy Valley a couple of Sundays when he was in town. Times he wasn't, he had the odd sensation of missing someone. Yes, he did, he missed her cool, clear company and the calmness of her face. She did not get rattled. He told her that she had the gift of a wonderful temperament. She denied it. "No, no, you have no idea," she laughed. "I keep my worst habits under strict control." But she said this with the wind blowing her hair all over her face and one foot up the hill, like a climber. She said her strength belonged to God. He thought that was nonsense, but for once he stopped himself from saying what he thought.

One day they walked three-quarters of the way around Johnson Lake. At the far end there was a little shallows where a pair of loons was fishing. They sat on a rock, watching.

"The loon is an odd bird and terrible eating: one of my scientists told me they're as old as dinosaurs," he said. "They mate for life."

One of the loons dove and then the other and she watched for them: the water was perfectly clear. The two birds dove and criss-crossed the bottom of the inlet, always within sight of each other. Their necks lengthened and their feet went back, and with one swipe of the wings they were propelled for minutes, feathers glued against their bodies. They were illuminated where the sun hit the light-coloured mud of the bottom, the male with his bright white necklace, the female more monochrome.

"They've become fish," she said in a whisper, as if her voice might scare them off. He liked that.

Who was this girl, after all? She didn't talk a lot, but when she did it was worth listening. When he thought of her he thought of her in negatives: she had no airs; she was unspoiled. She was not flirtatious. He saw nothing of the pompous father in her, and none of Isabel's giddy receptiveness. She was like a photographic plate, a species of light, all white haze, a shape inside it that you could not read. She was raised in a big city, by powerful people, although the most powerful was gone, which must have created a vacuum. Did the remaining family treasure her as the only survivor, or resent her as the reminder of the lost? She never said a word about what waited for her in the fall. In Gateway she would never escape her own story. Perhaps she didn't want to.

He wanted to take her in his arms but resisted. From a stalwart child she had turned into a shapely woman. Although she and her sister were not alike in any other way, they shared that curious magnetism: you wanted to kiss, crush, consume their sweetness, drink them in like milk. He'd had women, of course. That was a practical matter, and he dealt with it in a practical way, with willing barmaids. But this was desire of a different sort. He burned to fold her in his arms and bring her to his chest. He wanted to ask her the question: Who are you, Gwen? He tried it out in his mind. Then he tried it out loud.

She turned her calm face to him as if she was grateful to consider it. She cocked her head, listening to he didn't know what. Then she laughed.

"I am that bird," she said, pointing to a raven on a treetop. It flew off, followed by another. "And the other is Isabel." She put her arms around his waist and laid her head on his chest.

He patted her back. It was not the way he'd hoped their first embrace would be. But he felt a jolt of desire. He told himself to wait: she was innocent.

And the question remained unanswered. Who was she? A brave adventurer who wanted to break away from her birthright, as her sister, too, had wanted? He imagined the home in Washington: eggheads, gentility and thick pleated curtains with floral patterns, then this Quaker thing with its bizarre Meetings. Could she be a zealot? He knew Quakers: good, solid, right-thinking people who worked hard. They had no "side"; they did not put themselves above anyone. They were not, generally, otherworldly, although she sometimes had that air about her.

It wasn't until they were at the train station saying goodbye that he took her in his arms impulsively. She felt good there, small and firm with a bit of sway, like a sapling. The rush of desire bowled through him again. This tending of Gwen had become a bit of a sacred task. He had not factored in lust. Perhaps it was his reward for good works.

The winter was long, as it always was, and made longer by her absence. He wrote her a letter. He took it to the post office and remembered the letter he'd written to Isabel about the music at Sawback Ridge. *Violins. Coming out of the east and sweeping across the sky. Getting louder and swelling over my head. I swear to it. I had never heard that music. I listened for a few minutes, and then it was gone. I thought maybe I was going crazy. Folks do out here.*

He hadn't heard that ethereal melody again. The music he heard now was earthy and urgent. This letter was different. He wrote to Gwen about ordinary things—how the trade was coming back now that the war was over, the bridles and cinches that he'd ordered, his new ponies and their stubbornness. He wanted her; he could feel it in his gut when he handed over the envelope.

In three weeks he got a letter back. It was straight to the point.

Dear Herbie,

You asked me to tell you who I am. The answer is that I do not know. But I offer you this. When I was born, my mother consulted an astrologer. She did this in secret because of course my father would not have approved. Here is what the astrologer wrote.

She had copied the page in a careful, unnatural hand.

Gwenneth Hodgson is a sensitive creature, quick to be hurt and slow to heal.

She will be loyal and true to her commitments but will keep her feelings hidden—perhaps for longer than will be useful. I see a creature full of contradictions and a life the same.

She will have no taste for luxury, preferring the glories of nature. Hard work will fill her life, and for that she will be grateful.

Yet there will be times in her life when she is not able to work, perhaps due to ill health.

She will be strong and of independent mind. Yet she will adhere to old scripts—not scripture! But scripts she herself has written fiercely.

She will be beautiful in the best possible way, caring nothing for it. Her nature is passionate but difficult to rouse.

She will have good fortune in many things. But notably not in one area. In her family will reside her greatest unhappiness.

She will respond well to love and care and will never fail her loved ones, forgiving them and remembering them throughout her life.

Does that help? she wrote.

What the hell? thought Herbie when he read it. Were they engaged or something? He found the astrologer's message silly, an affectation. He feared a trap and went riding in the backcountry. She's just a kid. I should hold back. I'm getting evil looks from the doctor, who hates me anyway. But Erwin didn't come back from the war. She has no one else.

That June marked a beginning. There was a special stand for returned soldiers opposite the Three Sisters Hotel. The CPR was using lantern slides and motion pictures to ramp up its publicity campaign. And it was working: last year just about the only money he earned was the twenty-five dollars he got from selling the skull of a grizzly that he shot on Healey Creek to the British Museum. But now a teacher booked with him to bring up a dozen schoolgirls from the States. Anticipating the surge of business he ordered some teepees from the Stoneys.

He even got a letter, on that Parks letterhead with its fine cursive font, from J.B. Bowen: "I hope to visit Banff sometime before winter comes and look forward to meeting with you to discuss the outfitting business in relation to the national parks. I am eager to cooperate with guides and anyone else who has projects designed to increase the tourist revenue of the Dominion."

It seemed that he was out of purgatory; he was becoming a person of note in the area. He bought up more stirrups, quirts and rope. It was full steam ahead.

But he did not forget Gwen. In the summer when she arrived in Gateway she brought a large steamer trunk and no relatives. He reconsidered: she was an eager, free young woman at the edge of the wilderness where women were rare: an opportunity not to be missed. They began to see each other again. And seriously. They would marry. It seemed the best solution.

"Solution for what?" How Long asked him. "What is problem, boss?"

Put on the spot, Herbie admitted the problem was that he needed a wife, one who would put up with him. The problem was that the one he wanted was her.

He did not go to Washington: she did not want him to, and he was happy to avoid the trip. This was perhaps short-sighted, he admitted later. What does your family think, your aunt? he asked. She said the family was upset because she was marrying out of Meeting.

Well, if that is all, Herbie said.

They were married in the little Anglican church left by the missionaries. The remaining packers, Lyall Foxx, How Long and Dr. Smallwood—most of the town—cheered as they came out of the church door on a brilliant summer day.

*

It was a love affair. Herbie brought Gwen to live in his log cabin by the Bow. He found the way to unlock her passion: it was to be quiet and gentle and patient. If he let her have her head, everything was simple. They visited the ice-house, where the ice he had cut in spring lay in sawdust so it stayed frozen all summer. They went to the mushroom patch above Mineside to fill their baskets. The Finns down there invited them to use their sauna, women on one side and men on the other. Then they came home and fried the fat, pale fungi, not worried about poison: there'd be no poison in this place. She liked the ponies that were corralled next door. She often went out to feed them apples and stroke their noses. She asked him which was the one that came back from Mystic Lake. He pointed her out. Not Caruso. Mousie, nonchalantly chewing grass. Only once did she seem odd, and that was when he caught her at the corral in earnest debate with a pony, smiling and scolding. He'd had to shake her shoulder to get her back.

But that did not happen again. His wife fit right into life in Gateway. Everyone knew her already and watched over her. Which was a good thing because he was out on the trail for a month that first summer, with the president of Royal Tomatoes. There was good money in those long trips: judges, company executives, doctors. He charged each of them $175 a week, all in.

His business grew like wildfire. He had hung on through the lean, and now he was one of the few guides left. With his modest, strong little bride he was sitting high and pretty. He discovered a talent for self-promotion. He could write, he could talk. He worked his connections as soon as he made them. Fellows who'd had a good experience in the Rockies gave him the names of their friends, and as soon as they did he'd sit down at night and send off one of his charming epistles. There were other guides, but they didn't have his style nor were they so lucky with the animals. No, you couldn't call it luck. It was more than luck. It was that sense he had, of where the game was. The sixth sense. He boasted about it to Gwen when he got back from a pack, taking her on his lap. A vigilance that woke him from a dead sleep if a bear came within half a mile, he said. And then he knew their habits, you see; he could predict where a bear would go better than the bear could. He was the better hunter.

Nonsense, you had a gun, Gwen would tell him. That's the only way you got to be superior to these magnificent creatures, she would say, looking at the trophy bear head that hung over the door.

Those were grand times. But there were signs. Ominous signs. With his instincts, how did he miss them? The answer was he didn't miss them, really. He picked them up and then wilfully ignored them. The little gavotte with Gwen and the ponies. The advent of cars.

He had seen changes coming, but he didn't want to. Foxx did. Foxx, who'd been running guides himself, got out of the horse business and into motorcars. Herbie thought he was nuts. He himself was not good with cars, couldn't get their temperament. If he ever got behind the wheel he ended up down the riverbank or nose into a tree. He didn't think the Rockies could do a thing to you if you just drove by them. But Foxx went into cars and buses while he, Herbie, worked the pack train business, seeking out the hunters and big spenders.

He had the idea of visiting sportsmen's clubs down east. Aldwyn, a dude from Manhattan who ran a steel company, agreed to take him around. He took one of his cowboys with him, for colour. But it was taking Gwen to New York that was his first big mistake.

Chapter 21
THE LOST FILM

New York, Fall 1922

The Salmagundi Club was full of men in white dinner jackets and bow ties, and while this apparel had not been unknown in his past, it was strange to him now. Only the prospect of a big commission to take half a dozen of them minus their ornamental wives out to the Brazeau this summer kept him from undoing the cummerbund and loosening the damn collar. That and the appreciation he'd had from Gwen when he emerged from the hotel bathroom so clad.

"Oh my," she said. "Wild man visits Manhattan."

He didn't mind that. Didn't mind her fussing with the pleats on the front of his shirt one bit.

"This is not who I am, lady. Don't you believe it for a minute," he said.

"I know who you are!" She laughed and turned her back to him. She had her hands up around her ears and was fiddling with a clasp. A cloud of blonde hair in his face. "Can you do this up?"

She called him *you*, not *thee*. She was adjusting to the big city, was that it? Or was she feeling distant? He never knew. He did up her necklace, looking down on her bare arms and chiffon-draped shoulders, and then down into the tight-boned bodice squeezing her small breasts.

"What is it?" he said, turning her around.

"Peridots and seed pearls," she said carelessly, adjusting the pendant. It brought out the green in her eyes, which shone but whether from chill or excitement he wasn't sure.

"Where did you get that?" he said.

"It was my mother's."

It hadn't occurred to him that she would have brought her jewellery to the Rockies. But of course she had pearls and the like: he wondered if she had Isabel's jewels too, and where she kept them. His twenty-one-year-old bride in a log cabin in the Rockies had her secrets. Did she also have the secrets of that other girl he'd never really known?

"Putting on your airs and graces," he said.

On the way over in the cab, his hunting buddy Aldwyn spoke into her ear, looking like he was going to take the whole shell-shaped morsel and swallow it. Herbie minded but tried not to. He was deafened by the honking and the rumble, city noise he'd suffered for two weeks now. And during that two weeks his wife had opened like one of the butterflies the dear old Welsh lady had told him about, losing the fuzzy camouflage and becoming a flapper with pale pink skin and a flushed neck—an urbanite, alighting and feeding on the city sights.

Aldwyn was trying to talk the chairman of the opera into booking a month's trip next summer. He got Gwen and Herbie in to hear Caruso, the real one. Even the cowboy got a pass for rehearsals. After that, he disappeared every morning. And Herbie'd have to go rousting around to find him and say, "Where you been?"

"Oh, Mr. Wishart," he said, "I been to hear an angel sing."

He would tell that story when he made his speech to the club tonight. How he heard the other Caruso singing as he loaded that boxcar on the CPR main line. Music seemed to go with the mountains. Those Italians! The railway recruited them to work underground. When the day shift was over, they washed up and played in the band. Not a word of a lie. That was the romance of the Rockies: transformation. That was the romance of the big-game guide. The beauty and the fear.

In the foyer he loosed her arm, and she was led away to the powder room.

"Not your usual way to spend a Friday night, Wishart?" said Aldwyn.

"Nope, nope, usually just sitting round the campfire listening to the wolves."

"Try this Glenfiddich. A cut above your Seagram's."

"I don't mind."

He was a kind of mascot here, but it was good for business; he had to play along. Besides, he liked the men: their bluster, their bulging necks. He was a spider in comparison, particularly to Aldwyn, who was a great big guy impressed from some college football team into the top ranks of Morgan Steel. Aldwyn came straight up the middle of any room. Doors seemed to blow apart in front of him, displacing any person or thing that happened to be in his way as he took on the room and its occupants.

The wives were different. Fragile little Frau Aldwyn emerged from her powdering activities. She wouldn't do him any good if he were stranded somewhere, unlike Gwen, who could handle a log house, a hailstorm, a horse. Not that he would let her out on the trail.

They'd had the conversation on the train coming across Canada, one that they'd touched on in letters. She mentioned that he'd pursued her since she was a child. He admitted to pursuit. At least one letter of pursuit. But not over years.

She smiled. "You wrote letters."

"But that was only the last year."

"Before too," she said.

"What letters?" Because he didn't remember.

"There was one about the violins you heard when you were way out in the backcountry and all alone, the sound that came over the sky," she said.

He had stared. He opened his mouth to say, *But I wrote that letter to Isabel*, and then shut it. So she had read Isabel's letters. Not for the first time he had the sense of an elusive third in their marriage.

Although they were married, and happy—he would say to any who asked—he felt he hadn't really run Gwen down yet. It was the same in any hunt—there was chase, evasion, reappearance in the open, running off, repeat 'til victory. And all the time the ending was foretold to both predator and prey. The marriage business hadn't worked out the same way. Once they walked out of the church, he had expected the hunt to be over. But this one seemed perpetual. She had leaned away from him in the jolting compartment and stared out the window. Sulking.

He was firm about the ruling: she was not allowed out on the trails. Nothing beyond a day's ride.

"But I'm a good rider. You said so when we met." She pouted. "You liked my spunk. That's what you called it."

"I did, darling," he said, drawing on her spine with his fingertip, "but it's one thing for a girl, quite another for a wife."

"You don't think I married a hunting guide to have a soft life?"

"No, I don't. There will be lots of times like this summer, when I'm out on a trip and you'll be managing on your own. Mind you, you've got half the town to help you. You're independent, and I like that in a woman."

"But not so independent that she goes into the backcountry?"

He went quite still. "Oh my god, no. Not a chance, lassie."

She had looked out on the rock shoreline running past, unremarkable at that point because there had been days of it. He thought she was going to argue with him. Which would not have been a good idea. It was a small compartment and sound carried. He had never been known for having quiet arguments.

"We shall see," she said softly.

*

All along the length of the narrow dining room the hard, dead gazes of mounted antlered creatures, on either side and evenly spaced, crossed in the otherwise empty space. It was like an honour guard—deer from Vermont, moose from Maine, antelope from New Mexico, a grizzly and a wolverine in perpetual snarl. Gwen turned back momentarily as if she might escape, muttering that it felt like a tomb. Aldwyn chortled and put his hand on the small of her back. Herbie's scruff rose, and he delayed a bit, taking note of the names on the brass plates beneath the trophy heads; they all belonged to fellows he could look to as prospective clients.

Down at the end was a familiar face, Gus Henkel. Herbie had been taking him out for years. Now Gus was getting famous; he kept a studio here in New York and a house in Gateway for the summers. Ulla, his wife, and Gwen stood together complimenting each other on their jewellery. He didn't mind: Gwen could use a friend. But Gus made Herbie twitchy.

Gus had a tight face with a square white forehead like a blank sheet of paper. His eyes were unreadable. He pushed his hand forward and stiffly touched Herbie's shoulder. His manner was guarded, despite his avowal of friendship. Wariness had crept into their relations. From Herbie's point of view it was that Gus was a reminder. He'd passed through the Hodgson camp that summer with the pack train. He mentioned it from time to time, usually in the context of how he was and that he knew how to get in and out of the wilderness alive, unlike some others. Christ, surely Gus knew enough not to mention it tonight.

He came forward telling the company how he and Herbie went way back. How when he was just a young man from Germany wanting to learn to shoot, he went to a ranch in Montana. But the rancher couldn't hunt anymore; he'd been mauled by a grizzly. Somehow Herbie got wind of it and wrote offering him the chance of a lifetime to hunt in the vast northern Rockies: a month in the haunts of the Dall sheep. "Threw the letter in the garbage," Gus was telling people, "until Ulla said, 'Wait a minute, look at how he writes; he's an educated man.' She was the one made me take up the offer. This is your man. The best big-game hunter in the Canadian Rockies."

Herbie cringed. He knew his background was to his advantage: the wild-eyed mountain guide, under the whisky and behind the pipe smoke, was that familiar character, the well-bred Englishman. Yes, he came from a good family and went to a good school: he would admit to that. Excepting he couldn't sit in school. He kept playing the truant, didn't he? But it was a good school he played truant from and a good accent he sassed the teacher in. He hated relying on old country credentials. Where he got his education was from Sam Gallant, from the old trappers, from the Stoneys. He was a self-made man, a mountain man, and he had no use for old country smugness.

This city did its work on folk. The man he'd stretched out with for a lunchtime snooze, hat down over his eyes, sketching tools on one side of his saddle and gun on the other, was now loudly listing his art degrees. In Berlin, he said, he had learned to draw animals using the kaiser's livestock as models.

"What livestock? Cows?" said Herbie. "Pigs?" To general merriment.

Gus then reminded the boys that Theodore Roosevelt had invited him to lunch, and that he would have joined his Rough Riders to fight in the south but they had wanted a trooper, not an artist, although he counted himself an ace shot. "Even then," he said, "it was disease you really had to fight and not the enemy, and for that bullets hardly mattered." Ulla stood a pace behind her husband, smiling, hands folded as if she held a little posy in front of her navel. "Roosevelt and I have a bond," he said, "that of the great hunter and the great statesman."

Speaking of bullshit, Herbie gave his talk emphasizing the music of the mountains, and it was a hit. He got the opera man's card and wished them all happy trails. "See you in the Rockies!" he said. But as he told Gwen, watching from bed as she unclasped the necklace and dropped it into the velvet, he would be glad to get back to Gateway with his wife and away from these name-droppers.

The green went out of her eyes with the peridots gone. She slid into bed. "Will you?"

"Yes. How about you?"

That canny face, lifted to his, that impossibly smooth and untroubled look. "I don't know."

Was she going to revert? He made sure she had enough fun to tire her out. It was one nightclub after another. The next night they had tickets to the Floridian Room on Broadway, where the Great Charlotte was performing. It was freezing in the bar. Gwen with those bare arms had to keep her fox stole spread over her shoulders. It was a nice pelt, that one. Aldwyn was still leaning over and shouting into her ear; you couldn't whisper because of the rumble of expectation, the clinking of glasses. Then there was hissing as women told other women to be quiet.

The Great Charlotte was what they called a figure skater. She came out on a round, sunken dance floor made of ice, hard and white, with baubles of light criss-crossing its surface. She was a German lady dressed like a creature from a fairy tale, with filmy layers ending above her knees and white laced-up skate boots, and long hair that flew out behind her when she stroked around in the big circle. She was an athlete—strong thighs—and could twirl on her sharp toe-point with one leg up to the sky and her head down on her knee. She could jump, scissor her legs and land moving backwards. Herbie was impressed but not as captivated as Gwen, who could hardly breathe while the performance went on.

"Here we are in New York," he said, too loudly, causing people around to glare, "watching someone skate on pretend ice when we could be home skating on our own real ice with the mountains above."

She shushed him, and Herbie, who was always thinking up ideas for his business, began to daydream about building a special round skating rink high up on one of those mountain lakes, or maybe even right up on a glacier. He could take up a shovel and an ice scraper and a lot of sacking to cover it so it would stay smooth. And he could bring in entertainers: wouldn't that pack a charge for the tourists?

But the kicker of the trip came the night they were sitting around a table, probably ten of them. Gus got in his cups—okay, they were both in their cups—and said he'd come across something out in the back-country that might interest Herbie. Might interest the *search parties*. But he wanted to tell Herbie first. Herbie grabbed the artist by the arm and pulled him out of the room, out onto the sidewalk.

"What the hell are you doing?" he said. "Not in front of Gwen."

"You don't even know what I'm going to say." Gus adjusted his belt; it was always a little high on his hips.

"Anything upsets her. Any part of it." He took out his pipe and lit it. He fixed a fierce eye on the German.

"You know how I follow the goats up over the passes?"

"Do I know, Gus? I taught you."

"Well, I followed a herd up, out beyond the Summits. And I stumbled upon something curious sticking out of the snow, in under some big trees. Half covered by branches. Square corners, didn't look natural. Dug it out, had a look. And would you believe? It was those camera boxes of Hodgson's and the cans of film."

Herbie got out his tobacco pouch and tamped a little down into the bowl of the pipe. His heart seemed to have dropped a couple of inches in his chest.

"Jesus H. Christ, so they got way up there."

"Yeah. No sign of anything else. I looked."

They stood together, looking down at the New York pavement.

"No—remains nearby? Or horse remains?"

"Not that I could see. Course they could have been dragged off." The pipe flared.

"That thing makes an awful smell, Wishart."

Herbie kept his eyes on his pipe bowl and sucked the flame down in.

He could see the professor in his mind, standing like a crane behind his tripod, his hat brim curved overtop of the viewfinder, the prized camera rotated half a circle, its accordion folds opened. What had he been taking pictures of anyway? The rocks, Wishart, the rocks, he'd said. This magnificent panorama tells the story of earth.

"You picked it up?"

"No. I couldn't carry it." Gus looked evenly at Herbie in a way that let him know he'd made a strategic decision not to, that it might be better where it was. Gus, always playing games. "I couldn't carry it. I brought back some of the cans of film. But I know exactly where—"

Herbie played along. He told Gus he'd done well to keep it quiet. For now. It was just the sort of thing that would set off the whole search frenzy again. He should have thanked him, but he didn't want to think he was in Gus's debt. His wariness notched up, and he forced a smile.

"I'll have a look at them," said Herbie. "And we'll get back up there this summer."

He guessed he had to tell Gwen. He didn't know any better at that point. He tried it in bed, when he had his arms around her, holding her against his chest.

"Gwen, honey, your friend Gus was telling me—"

"He's not my friend."

He didn't know why he began that way. Except that he was still feeling like the rube among the sophisticates, and he thought he had detected, between Gwen and the artist, a glimmer of a smile indicating that this was their world, and that Herbie was a kind of amusement. He checked himself.

"Our friend Gus said he came upon a box of stuff beyond the Summits. The camera. Film. Your dad's."

She went very still. For a minute, and longer. Too long.

"Darling. You seem upset. It's just a camera." But it wasn't "just" anything, and he knew it. She stared into the distance, the way he remembered from when she talked to the ponies. "Tell me what you're thinking," he said urgently.

She flung herself out of bed. He got into his flannel robe and stood beside her. She took a long time about it. He gave her a glass of Scotch. That seemed to bring her around.

"You know," she finally said, "I can see him. Standing behind the thing, looking over the top of the box. He's got one hand laid on its side. Possessively, like it was a woman's cheek." She laughed a little, and a tear came out of her right eye.

She turned to Herbie and smiled. He was relieved. It was going to be okay. But then she turned away again. "I remember he set the tripod so that he could look comfortably along the angle of the accordion. It was a special camera for taking three-hundred-and-sixty-degree pictures. The tripod had a circular top so that the camera box and accordion lens could be swivelled; the photographer moved around behind it. He always had to dance to make sure he didn't trip on the legs. He was clumsy."

She seemed calm enough.

Herbie remembered too. "He had trouble setting the feet of the tripod on the slope so the camera would be stable. Then he'd put the grey cloth over his head and disappear under it. He became one with the proboscis of the thing. He and it would look like a circus elephant—all flapping ears and pleated trunk."

"He set it up in the back of our Georgetown house. He looked into the treetops of Dumbarton Oaks. Then he could see over the housetops below us and toward the White House. He could see the Washington Monument." She giggled.

Herbie had never been to Washington, but he smiled along.

"He even got permission to take panoramic pictures of the city from the top of the monument. He had a perfectly clear image of all the buildings, their gables, their rows of little square windows, the clock tower, the smokestacks. There were stripes of lighter then darker brick, fading into a mousy brown where the buildings in the back became indistinct. Beyond that was flat farmland."

It crossed Herbie's mind again—hell, he wasn't the first person to raise it—that the man was a spy. But that was crazy. What could he have been looking for when he set up his camera on the mountainside? He wasn't a spy; he just acted like one. He was a scientist, that was all, with an enquiring mind.

Gwen changed: it was as if someone threw a switch. Now she was angry.

"How could it be just sticking out of the snow? Didn't anyone ever *look*, what was it, nearly ten years ago? What if it had turned up then?"

"Gwen, even if we'd found the trail two weeks later it would have been too late."

He wasn't sure about that; he said it to pacify her. How long had the party wandered? Where were they going? Why up there? He soothed and petted her; it was hard work. It was hours before she crawled back into bed, and he couldn't say anything had been accomplished.

On the train back to Gateway with his silent, fuming wife, he had a lot of time to think. A couple of things came to mind. One, his wife was a handful. He hadn't known that when he got into it. But luckily she was a woman of passion. He loved her. And surely that was the most important thing.

Two, the Hodgson episode wasn't going away. He hadn't expected it would. But he thought it might lose its potency after the marriage. And it had subsided. It subsided, but like most things lost in the mountains it was preserved and what with wind and melt and erosion and the actions of animals, it eventually resurfaced. Spooky. The lost appurtenances of the expedition were coming back: the horses, How Long and now the camera.

It was eerie, in a place so vast and untrodden: nothing much sunk in. There wasn't soil to sink in. There was nowhere to hide. Rectangles were a giveaway. The corners of anything man-made stuck out.

And Gus had the film. Herbie didn't like that.

He doubted there would be anything to see after nearly a decade in the cold and wet. Still, it existed—a clue, a footprint, a statement.

Of course Gus was on his side. If there was a side to be on. What was he afraid of, after all? Gus had offered the film to Herbie to examine. Might as well look at. But Herbie didn't want to be in a conspiracy with him, against Gwen or anyone else.

Back in Gateway, Gus brought the film over to Wishart's house. Herbie had warned Gwen that it would be useless. And it was. The unexposed film was in flat, yellow cardboard boxes with the name Kodak in red on the top. It was wet, no good at all. The exposed film was in cans, wound. These cans, too, had got wet, and the joins were rusted. But Herbie got oil and worked off the lids. The film Gwen pulled out of them was a furry grey, like something from a grave or from the bottom of the sea, like the intestines of some great creature or machine, in loose spirals with white notches on their edges. Gwen rolled and unrolled it.

"Ruined," Herbie said. "Can't be saved, I'm sure." Never mind that Gwen was exposing it; it must be gone anyway. It cracked and broke. You could see, if you held it up to the light, rocky skylines, like the jagged scratch of a seismograph. Gwen fingered the film, saying nothing. There was so much of it.

Phoebe Dixon came. "He was only taking pictures of the mountains," she said, glaring at the men. "Just out of interest in the rocks. It was nothing secret. He wanted the whole scope of it, three hundred and sixty degrees, complete. That's why he brought the panoramic camera. He was planning to take it home and use it to write about the spot, to offer conjecture about how this fossil bed came to exist."

Phoebe sat beside Gwen, and Gwen laid her head in the older woman's lap. She stroked Gwen's hair. "I looked through the viewfinder with him. Your dad would tell me how the swirling patterns in the rocks were the deep roots of the mountains. He said the strange folds told stories of tremendous pressure, of boiling rock that became so hot it flowed like honey, one continent into another—" She broke off, then started again.

"The articles he never wrote. The ideas he never formulated. It's a great loss to science."

Gwen stood up and gathered the spent coils in her arms. They unwound and fell in slippery loops.

"Let's get rid of it," said Herbie.

She wanted to keep it. She insisted that one day it would reveal its images, that mountains and cowboys and bighorn sheep would magically appear on the grey ribbons as bright stains. The negatives would reverse of their own accord and reveal a narrative to rescue her family from oblivion.

Even Phoebe tried to disabuse her of that idea. "It won't," she said. "It's not physically possible."

They all agreed that the camera belonged to Herbie's wife, as the survivor. Gus said if he came across it again he'd bring it back. "Oh no," said Gwen. "Go immediately and find it. I must have it."

"It's not a walk in the park," said Gus, eyeing Herbie. "But I will. I will try to get back there."

But Herbie had misgivings: if the film caused this much emotion, what would the camera itself do? Gwen went to bed, and Herbie slowly wound the exposed film back into tight spools and put it in cans, which he placed on the top bookshelf. In the morning Gwen was strangely elated, buoyed by the thought that further discoveries were close.

Herbie watched his wife carefully for a week. He saw her go surreptitiously to the tins of film on the shelf and finger them. He worried. It was becoming clear that she was not the hardy little pioneer he had taken her for. No matter what he tried to do to make her forget, his actions become fuel for her insane hope.

To him the film said one thing and one thing only: the party had gone up to the Summits. But who knew why. Late at night, over a whisky, when he was honest with himself, he wondered why he expected Gwen to forget what he could not.

*

The baby was born in spring. They called her Iona. That summer Herbie was out with pack trains most of the time. He asked Gus and Ulla to watch over his little family. Herbie had told everyone his wife was not to be excited. But Ulla Henkel was Gwen's friend, and friends didn't follow the rules. That he did not discover until much later.

Ulla was tall with a rangy frame, confident, sharp-tongued, the type you could see in gumboots striding through an English swamp picking up dead ducks. She did not shoot, however; she left that to her husband. The couple had built a house on River Street, only three doors away from Wishart's cabin. The impression of glamour they gave was dimmed with proximity. Gus was as dependent on Ulla at home in Gateway as he was fiercely free of her when he was out on a trip.

His studio was filled with animal heads and full-scale taxidermied specimens. Ulla called them corpses. She brought him coffee at two-hour intervals.

At three in the afternoon she chased him out with a broom. "Get some sun before it disappears!"

You could hear him down the whole row of cabins: "Why have I been saddled with this stupid woman who does not understand art?"

And Ulla shouted right back: "Because you don't have the brains you were born with, and I'm the one who puts you to rights. Now git—"

"Let me finish the hoof before you—"

"No! Git, the time has come."

Gus went to the river to wash the paint from his hands and the guts from his boots. He clipped the paint from his beard and changed into cleats. Then he went off to take exercise, which he did with a butterfly net on the lower slopes of Mount Majority.

At that point Ulla walked up to Gwen's door. Ulla had dogs, and Gwen had Iona to walk in the pram. The gardens of Gateway were very pretty: miners' wives arrived with rose clippings and sweetpea seeds from the old country. They tried hollyhocks and succeeded with delphinium—dahlias were no good here and roses needed babying.

Gus would come back cheered from his butterfly hunt. At five o'clock he and Ulla set off to the Hot Springs Hotel for tea. When Gwen saw the pair walking toward the bridge she would put on her own kettle. The sun was gone by then, behind the mountain. The evening hours were lonely. Gwen would nurse her baby. She read aloud to her. Or she might cry softly, wishing her sister and mother, anyone, were there. Iona was quiet.

Ulla might go past later and look in the windows. Gwen would be playing house—that was how Ulla described it. She would have opened her trunk and put on her white satin dress cut on the bias, or her long black velvet with the deep vee neckline. The clothes were a little out of date; perhaps they were Isabel's. She would be looking at a book as she practised dance steps.

Of course it was odd, and word went around. Gwen was a romantic, they said. She was strange. She spoke to herself; she sometimes glittered and sometimes wept. People said she had not recovered from the tragedy, that they understood.

What they did not realize was that there was purpose. Gwen was teaching herself to dance. When he came back, she put Herbie through his paces. Slow, slow, quick quick. They rolled up the rug and rested their cheeks side by side. He held her in his arms and hoped that he had her all. He was an excellent dancer.

Chapter 22
HELEN REACHES THE WEST

Gateway, July 18, 1924

THROUGH THE RAIN SHE HEARD IT COMING, a clamour of brass instruments. Then she saw it. Twenty marchers in blue uniforms. An open wagon behind them with a rectangular box inside, women sitting with it. Behind the wagon a crush of people moving up Main Street.

"If you didn't know any better you'd ask what were they celebrating," said Pappos. He stood in front of his Vienna Café.

"You gotta admire the spirit. It's a long march from up there in the rain."

Herbie Wishart led, and she followed, pushing through clusters of locals on the sidewalk to where the parade took a turn onto a track heading toward the wooden enclosure that was the cemetery. How odd that it was at the heart of the little town, cheek by jowl with what was now known as "the business district." It couldn't have been the best place for burials, because it was low and, as Helen knew, subject to flooding.

The crowd, in fours and fives, wedged itself between the stone gateposts. People held umbrellas over their heads, but they were wet anyway, and undeterred. What was the tune they played? A polka maybe. And the instruments—a tuba sticking up there, a few trombones and trumpets, a snare drum to keep them in step. Cymbals, a glockenspiel. It was a racket, that's what it was—a drenched racket.

"What on earth?" she said to Wishart.

"Miner died in the chute."

The mourners took the cemetery path, four abreast, pushy trombones out front, the rest in no formation at all, just a clump, closely followed by a snake of men, women and children, at least a hundred and still coming past the gateposts. They were dressed in their dark best and, now that the rain was stopping, slapping the sides of their coats and shaking out their hair. The sky was clearing and the brass instruments glistened. The band wound down one side of the little graveyard toward the back, the *gawdawful noise*, as Herbie Wishart called it, becoming more concentrated as the gaps closed.

There was a grave dug at the back, and that's where the crowd was heading. Now it was some kind of aria from an opera they were murdering. A man strode up holding his ears, silver-haired with an aquiline nose, elegant.

"Foxx," said Herbie.

Helen was surprised. He didn't look the way he wrote.

"Don't bother showing off. We all know your ears are tin," shouted the guide.

A man in a painter's apron splattered with blood came up from the riverbank. Miners and their families poured in the gates, now arm in arm like protestors, which perhaps they were; they looked more angry than sad. The coffin was a plain one.

"Hope it's tight," said Herbie, "all this rain."

Foxx said, "Well, you know who makes 'em? Moro, the cabinetmaker. Italian, that's how he gets the business."

"Trust you to be thinking about trade."

"Not the railway?" said Helen. The CPR owned the mine.

"Nope, they don't provide a thing." Herbie looked at her. "Now there's a matter you lot could address."

She wasn't responsible. But Parks had given the CPR permission to run that coal mine; the railroad owned the end of the town that housed the miners. It was intended to be a model mining town, with quality two-storey homes, church and meeting hall, electricity and running water. A charming addition to the tourist attractions. And the music: that was intentional. Someone high up had been in the Italian army and said he could bring over men from the military band.

Herbie took his hat off and nudged Foxx. "Show a little respect for your neighbours," he said.

Foxx banged his hat with the back of his hand. "It happens to be the middle of July, and there are tourists in town."

Helen could see his point. It was a bit unsightly.

"They need a cemetery up there at the mines. Stop bringing their dead down here."

"Of course they should. Ground is all dug up and ready for it." Herbie grinned. "There's your next editorial, Foxx."

Foxx took it straight. "Not a bad idea."

"Yes, it is a bad idea," muttered Herbie. "There's so much water in the ground over there, you can't bury anyone. It's half the reason for the accidents—coal is tough to get at."

The cemetery was filling, the wagon drawn up to the open, weeping hole in the earth. The band's sound had improved now that the musicians no longer had to march and blow at the same time. The boys in shorts and woollen caps, the girls in white dresses with black coats and stockings, and their parents in sober suits with long jackets and buttons down the front, straw hats with small brims and flowers on the side, all formed up into a tight wedge at the back of the graveyard. Out of their midst stepped the priest from the Catholic church. There were crescendos of "Ave Maria" and then the "Hallelujah Chorus." A few minutes of silence while words were said.

To Helen it was theatre; the widow held firm between two of her friends and clutched the hand of the smallest child while the two older boys looked off to see where their friends had gone. One woman's chalky white face pressed into the shoulder of another, who held her; voices rising not in wails but in shouts of anger again. His family propped up and held in place by neighbours who lived the same life and stood to have a similar death, going down into the earth every morning, swinging the pickaxe, lugging the coal, up at the end of the day to the public showers, where—despite the hot springs at the other end of town—there was never enough hot water. Homemade wine. In winter, hockey games against other coal towns to work off the rage. And a day like this, saying goodbye to the one whose work earned their food, their house. What would happen now? They couldn't stay in the company house or shop at the butcher without being on the payroll, could they?

"This part you can almost endure," said Foxx. "It's what comes after."

"As if you've never a drink taken."

It wasn't long to wait. The few words were said and the coffin lowered by ropes, men slipping on the wet earth. Those beside the grave watching intently until the box settled and weeping as burly miners picked up their shovels. The clay soil sticking to the shovels. The wooden box recording the strikes of the clods of wet earth—splats, really—and beginning to disappear. Helen couldn't help making mental notes. But this was not the sort of thing she could write about. Maybe Foxx shrank less from decorum than from shame.

The crying at least stopped: that was over. Now came the carousing. Bottles of homemade hootch came out of the shoulder bags. The close pack of people began to loosen up. The latecomers were out the cemetery gate first.

"Gotta get back fast," said Herbie, moving behind her and pushing her through.

"Where are you taking me?"

"Where everyone's going. The Three Sisters Hotel."

The band struck up in a rendition of the *William Tell* overture. Holding arms, leaning heads together, shouting words in Polish or Italian to their children, the men and women surged back along Main Street. The crowd swelled over the tracks and took seats on the station benches. The evening sun sent its long, flat rays out from beside the Fist although it was after eight at night. By the time Helen and Herbie got there, the mourners had reached the veranda of the hotel. Half a dozen men were sent in to order whisky while women unwrapped cloth bags containing bread and sausages.

Foxx had taken cover, but Herbie was by the batwings shaking hands. Helen didn't know where else to stand but at Herbie's elbow. He eyed her and laughed.

"We could go into the bar, and you'd be right in the heart of it."

Helen must have looked frightened.

"You aren't the first fragile lady we've had out here. People send them my way, only the good Lord knows why. I'm like as not to kill them."

She flushed. "I am not fragile," she said. This was 1924. She had a responsible job and was extremely capable.

And she did not wish to be protected. Her bushy hair was coiled into something like a snail's shell and clamped to the back of her head. Over the past decade, due to the pressures of work, she liked to think, a bright white streak had developed, growing out of her hairline on the left side. Against the jet black it made a strong impression. If as a child she was frail, that was over, and Helen was proving herself worthy of Parks. For instance, although she'd never been on a horse before, she had ridden that day for the first time and stayed on. Of course when she got off she fell down. Herbie laughed at first, thinking her legs had just collapsed, but he sobered when it turned out she was in a dead faint. She revived quickly with whisky. That was a couple of hours ago now, and she had gone to the Hot Springs Hotel and washed up and here she was, in the middle of a riot.

Herbie should not confuse her with his wife, she thought. He had married since they first crossed paths, by letter and telegram, in 1911. A much younger bride, she'd been given to understand, who now had a two-year-old child. While Herbie was away, she stayed alone in the log cabin by the river. "She doesn't get out much," Herbie had said. She had the feeling that the wife was tenderly held, somewhat of a pet in town. But the key information had not been imparted. It was only when she got here that Helen learned Herbie's wife was Gwen, the youngest of the Hodgson family, the only survivor.

How surpassingly strange that he had chosen to marry her.

At the entrance to the bar she found herself pressing hands and tearing up in sympathy with the mourners. Herbie was introducing her as "the Parks woman from Ottawa who works for the commissioner." He said her express mission was to grasp what it meant to have a coal mine, an elegant hotel, cowboys, sport hunters and real people in a town in a national park. Of course, the real people were the most trouble. They all loved Mr. B. But Helen was his voice; she was the one who'd written all his speeches, so they should've loved *her*. But they didn't know that.

At last all those who were going in were in. Herbie put his hand on her shoulder. Space had opened to give her a seat at the bar. She took it. Gingerly.

"I won't be sitting comfortably for some time," she said, aware that she sounded prim. Before she could drag in a line of poetry about sore posteriors, he got her a whisky.

"So tell me how you like your creation," he said.

She had descended from the train at Siding 29 and been staggered by the place, but for different reasons than the others in her car. They were tourists. She was the expert: she'd written the guidebook. From a distance, admittedly, but with authority, she hoped. The problem was, so firmly had her image of the Canadian Rockies come to dwell in her mind that the reality was a bit of a shock.

First, the mountains: spectacular, of course. And at their feet, the pretty town. Well, perhaps not so pretty: it had no plan; there was no sense to it, and no architecture, except for the Hot Springs Hotel on the height of land to the south and the model coal mine on the benchlands. She supposed you had to count the rather dingy Anglican church built by a missionary. What had she said about him and the Indians? "Their legends remain, but they are now Christians converted by the kindly Dr. Rundle." The Stoneys were "friendly people, honest and simple" with their "glistening brown bodies" and their "ancestral hunting-grounds, though now they live in reservations outside the park."

The Indians she saw on arrival were not glistening but dusty from the ride in from Morley and standing by the door of the trading post looking to sell beadwork. These must be aberrations. She was looking forward to seeing the ones in full feathered war bonnets who did the Owl Dance on the front lawn of the Hot Springs Hotel during Indian Days. She'd seen the pictures. Parks couldn't take credit for it: Indian Days was one of Foxx's notions. He had started it years ago, when a late spring runoff washed out the railway lines, trapping hundreds of tourists in the town. He asked the tribes to entertain, and the result was a three-day festival with hundreds of Indians arriving on horseback and parading in full regalia.

Alas, those Indians were not in evidence today.

In the noisy crowd she felt herself sway. It was the altitude, or the whisky. She had just stepped off the train, after all. Was it two days ago? It had all begun to run together in her head. This was her muse: the place to recover from the ills and strains of city life, the perfect air and the dazzling water to cleanse the soul, the sacred heart of nature. She supposed it was always a shock to come face to face with one's imagined heaven.

Wishart raised his glass in her direction, and she raised hers in return. Mourning, carousing miners shoved her from both sides, and when she tried to lean back she encountered a tuba.

After Mr. B's first time here he had come home rhapsodizing, as only he could, about the scenic thrill and a population that was half cowboy, half climber, where Indians and ladies wore buckskins, and trophy hunters rode beside artists with folding stools and palette knives. She'd been desperate to visit. He had sat on the edge of Helen's desk, clasped both her hands in his and told her about it for an hour. Of course he'd seen little of the town, spending most of his time in the wilds. He had communed with a group of fresh-air enthusiasts, climbers and woodsy types. The Alpine Club, they called themselves. They set up their camp in a different beauty spot each year, and that year it had been at the headwaters of the Vermillion River, ten miles from Castle Junction. Mr. B made the hike, which nearly killed him but made him feel like a god. His feet were blistered and there were terrible mosquitoes, but he had been transformed, he said.

"Helen, you are not going to believe it. They had big tent canopies for eating and lectures and cooking, men on one island and women on the next. They had people splashing and half drowning, running back and forth, nearly frozen to death—you know, the water was only two hours removed from ice." Mr. B's picture included women reclining with sun shades, taking their ease as the sun went down, and cooks toiling over steamy cauldrons.

"After dinner we all sat around the campfire, feeling the warmth of the red flames cross our cheeks, watching the dark slowly envelop the landscape. It was the grandest of luxuries! My spirit was at rest, my mind was calm, my body was exhausted but glad. Oh yes, Helen, that is what we can have after a day of hard climbing in the bright, clean air.

"I listened to chatter about the false steps others had nearly taken, the blisters on their heels and the sunburn on their necks. I said nothing. I was the commissioner no more. I was simply one of them, having shared the risks and the thrills that got us here to this wonderfully remote, beautiful, spiritual centre that is ours, *all* of ours, in this nation.

And that way, being anonymous, I could see the power we hold, we in this department. We can *use* this wilderness. It can make us as a nation!

"I know the secretaries mock us for our love of poetry. So only to you will I say this. I thought of Walt Whitman: 'Now I see the secret of the making of the best persons / It is to grow in the open air and to eat and sleep with the earth.' That's what I thought of."

The whole summer had enchanted him, from his meeting the Duke and Duchess of Connaught and their daughter Princess Patricia, to the local member of Parliament and physician giving him Turkish baths and free medicinal whisky. He had come back believing that all the national parks should be kept in their wild, original state. Not only should the plants and trees and wild animals remain untouched, unmolested, unchanged, but there should be nothing artificial. He was determined to keep it natural, which meant taking the bounty off the predatory animals like wolves and coyotes.

Mr. B said all animals belonged there. That was why the Indians had to be out, or, when in, only displayed for tourism purposes. "There is no point creating a sanctuary in one place if the animals are only going to be slaughtered by Indians in another." Those were his words.

So despite the new road, and the next road that was going to lead off into the southern interior of British Columbia, there would be none of the trappings of town life—like sewers, for instance. No amenities to encourage more unsightly homes and gardens. The locals were a necessary evil—somebody had to cater to the visitors—but let's not make it easy. Tourists should drive slowly through the majesty, so as to have moments in the great solitude, moments to reconnect with the self, to measure the rays of the sun.

On and on he went, and although Helen adored, even idolized, the man, she found herself getting irritated.

"One needs to come to know oneself and one's god," Mr. B said.

But he was not a religious man, was he?

"Solitude can do much for us. Solitude is essential, don't you agree,

Helen, dear? You've touched on this in our writing, I know. I just want to encourage you to say more, to speak more of your heart—"

"I haven't actually been there, Mr. B."

"I know, but you understand, intuitively, it seems, maybe from the books you've read."

"Certainly not from the trips I've taken."

"We must see to that. We must see to your having a summer in the mountain parks before too long, Miss Wagg."

It took thirteen years.

For all that time she stayed in tame Ottawa, in her little apartment in the red-brick walk-up where the ceiling leaked, in a neighbourhood of young families, war widows and aging civil servants. She continued her Sunday lunches with Uncle Fitz until he died. She arranged hikes in the Gatineau with her friends, a select but growing contingent of women working in government. Tuesday nights she had bridge club, same women. Her bridge had improved, and now she was very good. She wrote pamphlets and letters and reports about all this going on in the West, sight unseen. Until now.

Mr. B *had* mentioned that Gateway was a little rough: the streets were unpaved, the garbage loose. The sidewalks were cinder and the drainage non-existent. Certain inconveniences for the locals were inevitable. There were the letters, of course, from Wishart and the editorials from Foxx, but the petitions of those on the ground, so to speak, had to be balanced by Mr. B's ideals.

He had expanded the warden service and got a fire engine. He even made sure each of the wardens had a wireless set. She'd written about it: "They have merely to twirl a few knobs and they can draw on the programs of a continent." Still, it was a lonely life that "appeals to men of education, one an Oxford grad."

Not in evidence either, today.

Of these improvements, she was now forming her own opinion. Wishart reported that the regulations meant the game was coming back—though poachers still existed, he said with a twisted grin. As for the Oxford grad, Helen hadn't actually met one. She made a mental note to ask.

She managed to get another drink and tipped it in the direction of Wishart. "Is it what you expected?" Wishart shouted.

Not actually. Not at all. Not yet. She smiled and waved. It was too noisy to speak. I suppose, she thought to herself, that a certain dissonance may have been created by the very *strength* of my writing skills. *Our* writing skills, as Mr. B always said. Of course she knew the town would be serving tourists and still producing coal. But she hadn't actually cottoned to the mess of human living that entailed.

"How's that guidebook doing?" he shouted.

She wormed her way toward him and found a pocket of relative quiet by leaning over the bar. "The CPR took two thousand copies to give to its top-drawer customers and it's still selling well," she said. On the strength of that, her annual salary had risen to fifteen hundred dollars. Impressed, what? Still, she suspected he was laughing at her: greenhorn, tenderfoot, they had names for people like her. She had been deluded to think she would be heralded, out here, as the one who made the place known to Canada and the world.

"All ready for our trip, Miss Wagg?"

Upcoming was a thirty-day pack train excursion. To be honest, she was leery because of the horse thing. She had been given a choice of two types of tours. The first was Wishart's horse tour. The second was the walking tour, a new thing run by a famous surveyor in the area whose group was going to walk into Assiniboine, the Matterhorn of Canada. That seemed eccentric and taxing, so she had chosen horses.

"I am wildly excited, Mr. Wishart." Steely gaze.

He gave a likeable grin. "You're in for an adventure. And for that, we've gotta get you a hat. You noticed, everyone's got a hat? You didn't put that in your book, did you?" He took her around behind the bar, where she could breathe a little more easily, and she found herself in an anteroom with a table full of maps and a wall of souvenirs and hats for sale. He pointed back into the jostling crowd.

"The hats have many purposes. But from where you sit, just two. One, weather protection. And two, identification. You can tell who someone is from a long way away by the shape of his headgear. Or hers. You can recognize just about anyone coming toward you by his silhouette. You can tell what work a man does by the hat he wears."

"Okay," she said, looking at the man silhouetted in the doorway, "explain to me what his hat tells you."

"That fellow's a packer. See, he's wearing the same Mountie-type hat as me, with a stiff brim. That's so when you ride into the wind it doesn't blow back off your face."

"Packers are cowboys?"

"No. They're a different breed entirely. They've got to know horses, sure, but they're mountain men. Come from elsewhere mostly."

"What are they doing here?"

"Drinking."

"I can see that."

"Escaping. Put it that way. But they've got to work to stay alive. They pick up a lot of new skills, learn how to use an axe, build a house, trap in winter maybe. Now here's someone with a profile that is unique. You see that man, his hat puffed up high with flat dints on the side? Rancher."

"How do you know?"

"I know the guy. But you can tell. Proud. Property owner. Not a wild man; still, he could stand you a fight. Oh sure, some of the bigwigs who come out for some railway event have even higher hats puffed up like stovepipes."

Helen wished she had her notebook.

"Oh yeah, there's all kind of hats. You used to see men around town like Chief Chiniki. Now he tied his felt hat under his chin and wore the brim straight up, like a crescent moon above his face."

"I thought they wore feathers," she said.

He laughed. "You don't see those every day. Now guides—other guides I know—wear a soft felt hat, floppy with an inch-wide brim. They all follow the Sam Gallant original. That hat has moods, oh sure, changeable just like him."

"So is it all about making yourself into someone else? If the hat's not enough, you grow whiskers?"

"Not necessarily into someone *else* but into a bigger and better version of yourself. Growing whiskers will help, but you can't do that, Miss Wagg, and that is my point," he said. "We're going to find you a hat."

She hated to be fussed over, and he had her in a tiny corner closet of a room that was the shop. She felt quite certain this was a manoeuvre he'd pulled before. "I bet you do this to all the girls," she said faintly. He didn't seem to hear.

"Maybe one of these special hats some of the ladies wear. Here. Try this. It's a bit of a floppy hat. The Gateway hat. See that brim?" It was three inches deep. He turned it up and then down. "Now this here's a cross between the campaign hat worn by Theodore Roosevelt's Rough Riders and the Stetson worn by the Mounted Police. You see—the crown can be dented in many styles, and some of them make it look quite dressy. The women who wear them add a leather thong to keep it on when riding or in wind; the broad brim is good in rain."

The charm was quite practised. He was doing his job, even if he had to sell one of Foxx's hats. He hated Foxx, she knew that from the correspondence. It made sense: two men who wanted to run the show, but one of them was an entrepreneur and the other more comfortable with a gun in his hands.

"How did it get to Gateway?"

"People say it was through a party from the Fairburnian Institution."

"You don't mean Hodgson?" To her mind rose a picture of the man, circulated after his disappearance; he was standing in his khakis on the mountain slope leaning on a pickaxe. His hat was high up on his forehead, the brim flipped up like some angel's halo in a medieval painting.

Herbie affected nonchalance and pulled out his pipe. "Naw, he wasn't the original. He copied it from somewhere."

Something hostile in his voice took her aback. The man was still sensitive.

She put the hat on and looked in the small mirror on the shelf. It improved her, but as she looked closely into her own eyes she could see the apprehension. In Herbie's face, too, the mirror found a wayward look. He was not as carefree as he liked to seem. They both looked away.

He turned down her brim. "You're a tad concerned about coming with the pack train," he said. "You know you don't have to come, but I doubt they'll put you up at the Springs for a full month. I can get you a place in town."

"Oh no, you don't," she said. "I wouldn't miss this for the world."

"Then take your hat and go get some sleep."

Chapter 23
LONG LANCE

Gateway, July 20, 1924

She stood on the back balcony of the Hot Springs Hotel looking over the Bow Valley. It was after nine and the light shot out flat in its last hour, turning the river below to silver braids where it wound through the town, but leaving its way forward in shadow. The railway tracks, too, glistened. She ran her fingers through the white stripe in her hair, a habit when words failed.

"Do you like the view?"

She turned. Behind her had materialized a tall, dark-skinned man with jutting eyebrows, wide shoulders, a high waist and pencil legs. He was dressed in a morning coat with white tie and perfectly pressed trousers, the cuffs of which sat in exactly the right place on radiant leather shoes.

"It leaves me quite speechless," she said.

She had missed his name. Had he said it? He stood very erect, his right hand in his trouser pocket and his left hand, with a cigarette in it, held close to his chest. He spouted a line or two about the myriad waltzing waters and the pine-velvet slopes. Her eyes wandered back to that gulf that fell away from the grey stone to the rushing water at the bottom. She felt slightly nauseated. But she could not be speechless for long.

"I feel that I'm in a castle, and below us is a kingdom," she said.

"You *are* in a castle. Yes, I think so. And who is the king?" He stepped to the rail himself and looked over.

She had meant it idly. But he had an intense look.

"Must there be one?" she asked.

"Oh yes. There is always a king. Maybe not in the beginning, here, but since the conquest."

"Conquest?"

"Oh, did you not know? The kingdom was conquered by those rails you see."

She smiled vaguely and turned back to the view. But he did not go away.

"Perhaps I could offer you a drink."

She wasn't sure she was ready for another drink, having had a couple with Wishart, but curiosity trumped her fatigue. Besides, the mosquitoes were out.

"Perhaps I could accept."

She took her hand off the rail and went back inside. The man followed. In the lounge he led her to a stuffed armchair and waved for a menu with a familiarity that gave her a second clue to the fact that he was a regular around the place.

"The railway built this castle, true," she said. "But I don't think the park is its kingdom. This all belongs to the Canadian people."

He drew on his cigarette. "You do know they fed the workers on buffalo flesh, leaving the Indians to starve," he said.

How unpleasant, she thought. What did he want? To take away her enjoyment of the view? "Oh, dear. I knew I was looking at a geographic cataclysm. But not perhaps a human one."

"Then you'll want to hear more," he said. "But you start. Tell me your impressions of the town."

She settled back into the chair, which seemed to swallow her, and let down her guard. "I thought I knew what to expect in Gateway, but I seem to have had it all wrong. Instead of upland meadows full of tiny flowers and peaks scrubbed clean in a peerless blue sky and jodhpur-clad young misses in horse trains, I found grieving miners getting sozzled in the dark reaches of a hotel bar."

"Ah, yes," he said. "The contradictions."

"I did know about the Scottish castle. But it's different when you see it in real life. Leaning over the abyss."

"It's why rich Americans come for the season with trunks and domestic staff."

She looked at him closely. Could he be Mexican? Egyptian? A visiting movie star, perhaps. He was smooth. He made a point of meeting her eyes. Then it came to her: she was speaking to some kind of shill. And she knew which one.

"'Fess up," she said. "You're in the employ."

"And so are you." He put out his hand. "I am Chief Buffalo Child Long Lance. It's Miss Wagg, of course—you were pointed out to me. I admire your work."

"It's not mine, of course, but thank you." She never took credit for the booklet that had come out under the department's name, but she was sufficiently charmed by this agent to acknowledge it with an eyebrow.

"I wanted to hear your reactions on seeing the place you have immortalized—"

"No, no." She waved.

"Yes, immortalized—with your words."

"I realize this has made me a figure of comedy," she said stiffly.

"Not at all, just one who is more prepared than the rest."

She'd heard about Chief Buffalo Child Long Lance: everyone had.

He had been a reporter in Winnipeg. She even recalled now that he was the CPR's publicity agent in Gateway for the summers.

His contract with the railroad gave him a pass to travel on their lines all year long, he was saying.

"Lucky you." It was coming home to Helen that she spent too much time in the office. "How do you earn that?"

"Many ways." One of his jobs was to supply the Indian legends that appeared on the menus. He turned the cocktail menu over to show her.

The Sun Dance

In the days of warfare it was necessary for a warrior to go through this dance in order to attain the rank of a brave. The dancer inserted two strong rawhide thongs through sheaths of flesh on either side of his chest, tied the other ends of the thongs to the Sun Dance Pole, and then danced and jerked upon them until the flesh gave way and he was freed.

"Ouch," said Helen.

"You prefer the dinner menu?"

He stood up and went to the bar. She noticed the fluidity of his walk. An athlete: hadn't she read that he boxed? He came back with the dinner menu. It was illustrated with a photograph of two braves on a grassy knoll with bow and arrow and tomahawk, one pointing ahead.

The Sunrise

The Indian scout had to be a man of invincible courage and endurance, such as Many Shots. The scouts had to get up long before sunrise each morning, steal out under the cover of darkness to the highest point of vantage and lie there in hiding until dawn—the time of day when all Indian attacks were launched.

The legend was served along with Lake Winnipeg pickerel, scalloped potatoes and soup of fresh tomatoes.

They took nothing for granted: a lone, grazing buffalo in the distance or a browsing antelope might turn out to be two Cree scouts concealed under the skin of a bison or a deer. If a yelping coyote or a hooting night-owl was answered too frequently from a neighbouring butte, they knew that these sounds were signals passing between Sioux scouts, who were remarkably adept at imitating the cries and calls of the furred and feathered kingdom.

"That reads very well," she said. "How do you do your research?"

"It's not research. I learned at my father's feet." He pointed to the byline below the legend.

Chief Buffalo Child Long Lance, the author, is a full-blooded Indian, a chief of the Blood tribe of Alberta. He is a graduate of Carlisle, where he gained a reputation in university sports. The chief was appointed to West Point in 1915 but relinquished the appointment in 1916 to go overseas with the Canadian forces. Entering the field as a private, he served with distinction, was twice wounded and returned with the rank of captain.

She sized up Long Lance while sipping her whisky, the third of the night, their consumption precluding dinner. It was hard to credit him as a wild Indian, or "redskin," as her mother would say. Still, he was wonderfully atmospheric. She could make use of him: his suavity gave a delightful twist to the commonly held notions of his race. *Her* race, she had long ago decided, was that of journalist, author, those who wrote things down. Mr. B was a member; he'd come from newspapers, and he was a master of the art of publicity. She did not tire of quoting his advice on how to tweak the interest of jaded editors: every editor was jaded, and every jaded editor was desperate for copy at deadline. Long Lance just might be a member too.

She relaxed.

"You mentioned the rich Americans. They come to the Rockies, I am reliably told"—or unreliably, she wasn't sure—"by Herbie Wishart, with fifty thousand dollars to spend."

"It's true. They dress for dinner every night, the men in their jackets, the ladies in their ball gowns. Come to the ballroom. You'll see."

She sighed. The raw cold rain, the mud, the sobbing, the anger was too vivid to be replaced. She told him about it. "I have been asking myself a question: Do the two Gateways meet, ever, anywhere?"

"Yes, they do. Our guests dance to music made by some of those same miners you saw at the wake. We have a couple of men in our band who spend their days underground. They come up for air at four o'clock, wash the soot off their faces and put on white tie."

The evening began to blur. She knew that Long Lance spoke of the poetry of William Blake, a certain poem called "A Poison Tree." "In the morning, glad, I see / My foe outstretched beneath the tree." He said this fit well with Blackfoot philosophy. He claimed to love opera, citing Nellie Elba as a singer he followed on the radio. Among his other enthusiasms was the New Zealand rugby team. The All Blacks had visited in May, and he got to know them. There were several Maori members.

He said that there was no distance between the races among these antipodean athletes. They had run up and down the mountainside and tobogganed by moonlight up in the passes where the snow was still deep. They had taught him the *haka*, he said, and there in the tea lounge, without warning, he leapt up into a wide stance, feet apart, knees deeply bent, hands on his knees so that his elbows were at right angles. He jumped up and down and roared. He stuck his tongue out and waggled it, rolled his eyes and grunted. Then he sprang out of the pose and went forward to take the hand of a woman entering the room on her husband's arm.

Helen laughed in astonishment and then reddened and covered her face with her hands. Oh yes, she understood his game. He liked to play against people's expectations. They were bamboozled, amazed to be with a primitive talking about stalking bear, and then dazzled by his courtly manners. They turned to putty in his hands. But not Miss Helen Wagg. Not bamboozled. Just—boozled. Watch yourself, she thought.

And so when the chief asked her to go into the ballroom with him, Helen said she was not dressed for dancing, that she could not, not tonight: she must go upstairs and have toast in her room and get some sleep.

He kissed the back of her hand.

"Tonight I am as you see me, and off to the ballroom to dance with the ladies whose husbands are unwilling. Tomorrow I'll be in my war bonnet and full regalia on the platform at Siding 29. The CPR bigwigs are arriving."

Chapter 24
THE PACK TRAIN

Gateway, July 21, 1924

The next morning she got up early. At breakfast she studied the menu. Long Lance's "Indian Medicine Practices" adorned the bill of fare.

> *The medicine man would hold a sort of séance in which he would get in touch with a particular group of spirits and secure a forecast of the fate of the war party.*

The story included the names of Chief Heavy Shield, Stud Horse, Weasel Horn, and Raw Eater. Choices ran complete with pricing:

Stewed Rhubarb with Cream 25 cents
Broiled Finnan Haddie, Drawn Butter 65 cents
Country Sausages with Wheat Cakes 60 cents

She ordered the sausages and didn't eat the pancakes. In the hotel lobby she picked up a copy of the *Gateway Trumpet*. Yes, there it was, the story she'd been expecting: Foxx must've stayed up late writing his editorial.

> *We call upon that great corporate citizen, the Canadian Pacific Railway, to fill its duty to the mine workers. They're the ones pulling profits out of these mountains. And yet when a miner is injured underground, does Papa Choo Choo come forth with doctors? When he dies, does Papa buy the coffin? No, he does not. So we learned yesterday as yet another cortège honked, roared and thumped its way down Main Street. We have all the sympathy in the world for these families. But can't they take their ear-splitting wake somewhere else? Isn't it time for the great CPR fathers to stop railroading their workers? Build a cemetery up at Mineside, please!*

She folded the paper into her purse. How convenient it was for men of ambition to control newspapers. They could ride their hobby horses in public; amazingly the populace accorded them legitimacy and continued to read newspapers as if they were actually statements about news. Mr. B said even the news was "the entertainment business." That had shocked her a decade ago. But not now.

She set out walking. Perhaps she had been naive. And still was. Not naive but a particular type of Ottawa-bred idealist. She passed the hot springs: a mere thirty years earlier this had been a hole in the mountainside choked with rotting logs. Of course that was in a previous century. Now it was the 1920s, a mad bad decade opening and closing its knees, sequins winking, hands shaking. Movie stars dangled their toes in the water from the deck of the Hot Springs Hotel pool. Cars chugged up the narrow road past the park gates and into the long Main Street of town. Drivers leaned out their windows to feed the bears.

She walked back along Main Street through the centre of town and out the other way, toward Mineside. It was her habit to walk: she walked to and from work in Ottawa, and on the weekends down to the falls and in the woods up the Ottawa River. Walking, she could observe freely without being rushed, and she had many of her best ideas. On that Gateway morning she observed the splashes of sun on the peaks, the cool trenches of shadow down here, and the almost animal roar of the water under the bridge. She felt the valley itself and the way they were all held in it, people both rough and polished, foreign and native, newcomers and ancients (she thought of Long Lance), as in a cupped hand, going about their business at the feet of these monster edifices of stone.

Of course it was inadequate to describe a place by saying it held opposites and was composed of contradictions. Banal, and Long Lance had pointed that out. What was it about Gateway that hadn't been said? It had to do, she decided, with how visceral each person's hold was on it. You could feel this tenacity and fervour. Some had touched the peaks and eaten mountain goat soup, others trudged through snow three feet deep and lived to tell the tale, while still others were burrowing in tunnels beneath their feet to chip away coal. But everyone, all of them, had gripped it and the place had gripped them in return. Parks, her branch, had not created but had allowed for this, had permitted this town and all the traffic in it, human, automobile, equine, subterranean and buffalo (what was the adjective for "of the buffalo"? bovidae?). It all came about through raw desire and against the odds of human settlement.

She was proud. Yes, there were some niggling issues. There had been a question about the coal mines. Whether to keep them in or put them out. By moving the boundaries one could do either. And the Indians: "privations of my people," that was Long Lance's phrase. Yes, well. Perhaps unavoidable. On the whole the decisions were, in her opinion, and in the official opinion, correct.

She came to the station. Beside the railroad tracks, the greeting party was mustering to greet the CPR bosses. She ducked away and entered the low fens where the river, divided and divided again, became rivulets between trees and dove under mossy banks, stopping dead at a fern bank and turning back on itself. She kept walking; there was a path around the edge of the woods. Finally the path rose toward the benchlands. Mineside. It was announced by a boarding house, a jaunty and inappropriate line of iron spears and coils along the roof-line, a wide-roofed veranda and hitching posts out front. She came within sight of a school and a church. There were the gabled two-storey homes the CPR boasted of, and the wide streets, which, though muddy, did have telephone poles along them. Certain published words and whole sentences returned to her, as they so often did: she was not quite sure when she had written them but they were hers: "nestling under the shadow of Cascade with its beautiful homes and its teeming industrial life . . ." The women she saw had flocks of children and wore white lace collars and stiff leather boots. They smiled but kept their eyes down.

She walked beyond the houses to where a number of square wooden buildings with slanted roofs and oddly spaced windows stood: one tall structure with a ramp built on wooden stilts looked like a fairground roller coaster. Smoke billowed near train tracks and piles of logs; this must be the mine, but how did you get down in? There must be some kind of hole. She came to a tall black pyramid, taller than the narrow pines that themselves were taller than a house. When she crossed behind it and was hidden from the miners' homes she saw a set of shacks, charcoal in colour, surrounded by fresh green growth. Those were home to the Chinese workers.

This teepee of coal bits, its man-made geometry so different from the hills surrounding, was a slag heap. She got that. She also got the Chinese. She knew there were still some on the rolls of the mine. She hadn't been aware of just how many, that was all. Hired for the building of the tracks, some had remained in the employ of the railroad. They did not work underground, as trust among miners was paramount. As a matter of strict fact they were working not *in* the mine but *on* the mine, scrambling on the pyramid, salvaging. That they were not accommodated in the same model housing as the miners was news to her. She supposed they preferred to live out here? Separately from the others? She came upon the most beautiful vegetable garden. She stood looking at heads of lettuce. Those frothy stems looked to be carrots. A tangle of peas, held up by a little fence.

"Good morning," said a man. "I help you?"

"I was admiring your garden. Very nice. Hard work!"

"I work for deer." He pointed to the tracks between the rows. "They pull out by the roots! Everything gone." He was shaking with anger. "I'm Slippy," he said. "Nothing to sell today. I wish. Ladies pay money; deer, they steal."

"Oh, I'm sorry," she said.

"Give you ginger candy. All I got!"

She walked back with her head down, thinking.

The day of departure Helen was offered her choice of ponies and opted for Elsie. She had her jodhpurs on and got in her saddle all right. She noted a couple of smug smiles among the packers, but she didn't care. Waiting to start, she saw among the milling packers the erect back of Long Lance. He was a confident man; his body oozed it. For the trail ride he had abandoned his dinner jacket and white tie, and also his Indian regalia, now appearing in a shirt with cravat, tweed jacket and pants. Having been instructed by Wishart on hats she examined his carefully—felt, with a lifted crown and fairly wide brim turned a little down in front and on the sides and throwing the upper part of his face into shadow. The Tree brothers—Indian cowboys—wore tweed caps. The packer was Bill Potts, a skinny little guy with a huge hat worn on a rakish slant. It gave him a piquant quality.

"I'm looking for that Oxford grad?" she said to Wishart.

"Sorry, Wagg. The war took care of him."

The rather famous wildlife artist named Gus Henkel, whom she'd first seen in a bloody apron at the cemetery, looked much neater today, his buckskin shirt tucked in as if he needed to show off his trim waist. He wore a firm, stiff hat with its brim downturned like an enormous beak.

She had been looking forward to meeting the Swiss guides brought in by the railway, in their neat and natty waistcoats with the coil of rope over their shoulders.

"No Swiss guides today. They're for ascents. You're not climbing a peak, are you?"

"No!" But she was disappointed.

Their guide was Wishart himself.

Then they were off, twenty ponies in a string with Wishart and his dog, Fella, at the head, making their way down Main Street. She concentrated on staying on Elsie, looking up for glimpses here and there of the frightening grey ranges in the distance. Long Lance trotted up beside her. He talked a good deal for an Indian. She'd always read that they were people of few words. He seemed to have taken on the job of educating her.

Cayuse—she tested the word under her breath. Means a small pony, probably wild, probably obtained from the Indians.

"The Stoneys call them 'sky dogs.' They stole their first horses from the Kootenays. At first they thought they were sacred, they were so powerful and fast. Then they realized they would work. That's how they began to associate the horse with the dog."

It seemed a long time before they stopped for a tea break, but it was only eleven. Lunch came after another two-hour leg: she was in mortal pain after dismounting and eating, availing herself of a nearby bush, and struggling to get back on her horse. She could not imagine how she would get through the afternoon. But she did, and that night fell dead asleep in her tent without dinner.

She rose with determination the next morning. As their second day waned into the long twilight they came near Lake Louise. Long Lance seemed to intuit the pain in her hips and back, and kept talking to distract her. "Above this is an even more beautiful lake called the Goat's Looking Glass—that's where the mountain goats go to comb their beards. We Indians hunted these mountain goats on the steep slopes, jumping them and killing them with knives, and then rolling the bodies down to the streams below so we could butcher them."

He did prefer the bloodthirsty to the beautiful, she noticed.

She must have been asleep in the saddle, a phenomenon she had read about but hardly believed possible, when at last they arrived. Someone took the reins from her. She stood up in one stirrup and tried to get her leg over the horse's neck but it wouldn't go. A voice told her to turn and lay her chest on Elsie's saddle, and grab the saddle horn, but there was still that other leg to be moved or she would stay bifurcated on this beast for life. Someone helped her swing it. She grasped the horn to her breast. Let go, someone said. It's only a foot to the ground. She let go, but she hung, feet dangling above terra firma. Her brassiere was caught on the saddle horn.

For how many summers had she sweltered in Ottawa and dreamed of sitting around this campfire on the ground? Thirteen, to be exact, and here she was, though it was not mossy ground she sat on but a spread tarp in honour of the lady. In truth she was very uncomfortable. She leaned on one arm until her wrist began to hurt. She shifted to the other hip and leaned on the other arm. That, too, was hurting, but she had no choice as her hips were screaming; she doubted the sockets would ever again allow her to sit upright, in, for instance, an office chair. A black-and-white dog came to sit beside her, ears alert. Fella. She looked at him askance. The look was caught. If anyone was going to nail you for giving his dog a filthy look it was this Herbie character.

"I'm just worried about him," she said. "Might he get in a fight with a wolf?"

"Fella will smell a bear a mile away," said Wishart, "and let you know."

Helen gave him a grudging pat, and the mutt shifted his weight companionably into her side.

Wishart squatted on the other side of the dog. He seemed to await a development in their relationship.

"I haven't quite forgiven you," she said. "You never came clean about the Hodgson expedition."

"That is completely false," he said. "I know nothing."

"Yes, you do know something. You were holding back. The whole town closed ranks against us on that one."

"There are people alive who are affected," he said. "Maybe we closed ranks, but we had to. And let's talk about what you folks at Parks did. Bringing in the FBI? They could no more find a lost expedition than dance a foxtrot."

"I don't see who would be affected. They're all dead."

"You're forgetting my wife," he said.

"Oh," she said. "I am very sorry. I *had* forgotten your wife. Now the Hodgsons are family."

"They are, Miss Wagg. That's right. Family." He pulled out his pipe and tobacco. "Anyway it's over. It was a tragedy, but even tragedies have to end. Smoke a peace pipe?"

"I couldn't. I'll drink to it, though."

Helen used her fingers as a comb to push back the wave with its white streak. Springy and thick, it repeatedly found its way out of any hairband, scarf or pin she wore, to pose like an upside-down asp over her brow.

"The Buffalo Heist made you look clever. You're smart men with publicity out here."

"Only as good as you are."

"Bloody geniuses," she said, taking the whisky.

He removed the pipe from his mouth and gave her a wink. Then he put his lips to it and sucked. The flame popped.

It seemed that Long Lance's role on the trip was one of spirit guide. Every night he filled the silent dark with Indian tales. The medicine man, most whites assumed, was a kind of witch doctor, casting spells and causing deaths with his evil spirit power. But no, he was a surgeon, a seeker, a wise man.

"From the time he was a small boy the Indian who would be medicine man would go out on his own into the forest and stay alone, without eating, building the power of his will."

All faces tipped downward to the fire and reflected the orange glow. What was true bravery? he asked. No one took up the question, so Long Lance began to speak of a warrior who had a medicine dream and warned his people away from a massacre. "If you want to go back, you may as well go home and put on your wife's skirt," said the commander. The warrior said he had no wife but he would gladly put on a woman's skirt. Part of the party turned back with him, while the leader who did not trust the medicine went onward with his few stalwarts, only to be ambushed as predicted and struck down. The dreamer-warrior had the courage of his convictions, said Long Lance, and was not afraid to look a fool.

Helen wondered if he had to wear the skirt after all. And, she thought, without the energy to follow it through, what a man of many talents he was, this Indian chief cum publicity agent cum trail rider cum storyteller. He may have been a "natural," as the saying went—good at everything. But he was not a man of nature. There was something studied in his movement, his manner in the woods. She looked at the people who sat around the campfire and wondered whether they saw through him. In part to shield him from their scrutiny, she tried to contribute to the campfire storytelling. The best she could do was quote Arthur Conan Doyle, one of the park's famous visitors. His little poem had come across her desk. She thought Parks should publish it:

I shall smell the virgin upland with its balsam-laden air,
And shall dream that I am riding down the winding woody vale
With the packer and the packhorse on the Athabasca Trail.

Again she slept like one dead in her small tent and could barely drag herself out in the morning.

Chapter 25
SEDUCTION

On the Trail, July 24, 1924

Long Lance hoisted her onto Elsie and patted her thigh. Perhaps he thought he was patting the horse's flank?

She had never been the sort of woman at whom men made passes. Her reaction was to pretend it was not happening. Then he did it again, holding her buttocks in a firm hug to help her dismount. "We don't want to see you get stuck on the horn again!" She caught a snicker between two packers and thought, Of course they know all about it; he comes out on trips and there is always a single woman from the East. He is one of those men for whom a woman is a magnet and a mirror; he is compelled to look good and to prevail. I won't let him touch me again. She would have given him a slap, but she thought she might need his help later.

And she did: after three days on the trail she was depending on it. She and Long Lance shared the long day's ride, making camp, dinner on a tin plate and then the campfire. She sat in a grassy place leaning against a log, unable to move. He brought her tea and brandy. He found her a tarp to keep out the wet. She sat and memorized the scene: men and a few women staring blankly toward the flame, quieted, as if they were basking in sun. The flame winked off the curve of their pipes. It seized the faces, bringing features up startlingly, but it was a shallow capture; the third dimension, from edge of the eye and cheekbones, went into darkness. Clasped hands were lit too. One man had a tin bowl and a white paper in front of him and was rolling a cigarette.

It had been a day of riding through marsh. The only rest they got was when Gus, the artist, went out and shot something and made them wait while he first drew it and then butchered it. Night could not come quickly enough. Now the packers had built a simple arch of cut logs over the fire. On the vertical post on one side was tucked a hobnailed boot hanging upside down over the flame, drying. The metal grid on the sole of the boot caught the light too. On the other pole hung somebody's white enamel cup and ragged towel, washing tools. Wishart's probably. He was the boss here.

Exhausted and limp with the climb, the fording of streams, the *work* of it all, and knowing there'd be the same tomorrow, they sat like children listening to Long Lance's stories. Tonight it was about how an Indian took his family crest from an animal that had come to him when he was sleeping. For the rest of his life he carried its claw or tooth (he didn't mention how the Indian got the token) and drew it onto his teepee. If an Indian didn't have a totem animal, then he had to live in a plain white teepee. She succumbed to sleep almost, but stayed awake to watch.

Chief Buffalo Child: the name didn't suit. The title did, though. *Chief.* Apparently it was hereditary. He had a glitter about him, a physical arrogance, a nerviness, a certain malign grace. He was more wolf than buffalo, she decided, smooth and alone and treading a winding path. Fearless but not, she thought, in the way of a traditional man of the forests. He walked too close to the fire. She noticed that.

Long Lance spoke of "his people," a dying race of natural philosophers.

This won approval almost all around the fire—savages mystified, even revered, in their absence. If the living members of the tribes begged to differ, they weren't talking. The more entranced the CPR bigwigs were, the more distant the Tree brothers became. And Wishart: that had to be an ironic grin folded around the pipe at the side of his mouth. Gus smiled behind his glasses, occasionally jumping in with tales of his derring-do with the gun and the unarmed creatures. It occurred to Helen to question why Park regulations allowed a man from Germany to hunt while the tribes who had travelled these mountains for a thousand years could not.

She knew men like these railway chiefs, moustaches turning their upper lip into a kind of chevron on portly, satisfied faces—they were all over Ottawa. They were getting their money's worth from the man whose face gleamed in the dark as he spoke of maidens and revenge for dead mothers. Long Lance cast a spell of words: he reminded her of herself. And along with this feeling of familiarity came a spark of revulsion, then, as well, attraction. But that would be inappropriate, and she quenched it.

They were not alone with the stars and the silence. There were proprieties. Inflexible ones. She was a professional! But a sneaking voice in her head said, What place have city values here? She could almost hear Long Lance saying this in his storytelling voice. If a man wanted a woman, he went to her tent. Natural. Fulfillment of destiny. Not to mention convenient.

"Time to turn in!" He reached for her arm to help her stand.

Dying race, my ass, she thought. This representative was very much alive. Of course nothing would come of it. The big shots would be with them until the end of the week. In their presence she was on the job, a Parks employee.

And she did turn in.

Then she heard a scratching on the canvas. Was it Fella, the dog? She hissed. A human hiss came back. A corner lifted and a dark head entered. It was followed by broad shoulders, a long body. Long Lance. He came toward her like an alligator on his hands, leaving his legs to drag.

Helen was amused. Not frightened. Curious. Not particularly aroused.

"Chief, what brings you here?"

She could make out his face, sorrowful, and the bulk of him, now resting alongside her sleeping bag. She could not see the edges of him. His look was a bit pathetic, and she thought she might laugh.

"You are a beautiful woman."

"I am not."

"Beautiful and . . ." He groped for words. He was also groping for a part of her, under the puffy sleeping bag. He didn't find anything. "Powerful. You carry a powerful magic."

"Thank you, Chief." It was a little crowded in the narrow tent. She did not move sideways to make room for him, nor did she offer the opening he was seeking in the flannel. She moved aside within herself, stepping back and watching the seduction—the attempt at seduction—from another place. Long Lance pressed himself against her, all hands and breath. It was not comfortable. There was a tension in his bones, a tension to him. She cleared her throat.

He was an attractive man. She had felt the dazzle of him when they were outside in the air. Here, his expertise showed, and it was not to his advantage. You don't want a man to be that practised.

He found something—her neck, actually—that he could get his hands around and pulled her head toward him. He wished to kiss her, and he did. She was slightly delayed in reacting. She had to decide: I will go along or I will not. She had been attracted to him, she was sure of it, and yet now she was no longer. He had found the eyelets and the thongs, and was loosening them. He was climbing into the sleeping bag.

"You shouldn't wear your clothes when you get into bed," he said.

"I'm cold."

"They'll be moist from the day, and they will make you colder."

"Nonetheless, I don't think I'll take them off."

He didn't insist. Maybe he was too proud. She did not resist: she did not respond. They lay like that for a time, and then he said, "I hope I warmed you up."

"Thank you, Chief. You've done the job."

And he was gone.

The following night at the campfire was not as pleasant as the last. There was apparently strife in these idyllic parts. Herbie drank too much whisky and became argumentative. He said that the railroad was hiring inexperienced boys to escort tourists at cheap rates, doing the real guides out of business. "You'll be sorry when we're all gone," he said. "Your boys are taking the wrong passes, crossing the streams at the worst point. Oh yeah, there will be accidents."

"That's the least of our worries, right now, son," said the CPR man. "And I think you've got a nerve to talk about accidents, if what I hear is right."

Herbie shut his mouth, and sat mulling and furious by the fire. Helen let Long Lance's soothing tales swirl past one ear and strained to hear the two camps carping about each other. The cowboys were on Herbie's side and gave long, sour looks to the company men. Gus Henkel was silent, keeping an eye on Herbie. The company men were waiting to hear about a vote.

Everyone had gone to bed that night when the scratch came on her tent and Long Lance crawled in again. Again she did not resist or encourage his advances, but stood back, in her mind, watching and thinking, A chief of the Blackfoot tribe is trying to seduce me. Somehow it sounded better than it felt. It was a difficult situation in which to have dignity, but he did well. Too bad she couldn't write about it.

It was a quiet group that mounted its ponies the next day and rode to Lake Louise. There, the CPR men picked up telegrams: the vote had gone in favour of a strike in the coal mines at Gateway. They folded the papers and looked at each other, and when they got back on their horses they spoke roughly to the animals. Later that day they set up camp near the lake. The whisky came out before the sun began to sink. They dined on elk that Herbie had shot.

The miners were greedy, the executives said. Were they not grateful to be in a model town with electricity? They wanted to keep the wartime daily bonus. They wouldn't take a pay cut. The company had continued to pay it long past the time when the government was passing it through to them. If this bonus were to be paid it would have to come from *company profits*. Which did not seem right, not at all.

Herbie said that pay was not the only gripe: the union complained that the mine was unsafe, that mining up the mountainside was too difficult.

"We can cut off their credit at the store; we can cut off the electric power."

Helen could see two sides. No one wanted a pay cut, or could afford one. The wages should match the level of the town; otherwise, it was hypocritical, wasn't it? But there was that death—it was dangerous, and the railway didn't help the stricken family. The railway should show more care for its workers. She knew what Mr. B would say: A strike would look bad for the park. It will look bad if tourists could see miners' children scrounging for coal on the slag heaps. But her comment would not be welcome here, and so she didn't make it.

"Their strike fund is not ample—only eight dollars a month," said one man. The other shrugged.

She retreated to her tent, where she twisted under her blankets through the night. Her hip joints ached. Her tailbone throbbed. Her thighs were rubbed raw. Her own rhetoric repeated on her, like garlic. *The majestic silence of Nature has riches to bestow on all who listen* . . . Actually, it was quite noisy. There was a wind howling up above, and some horse or perhaps dog was snorting behind her—worse, it was probably one of the bigwigs snoring. *A natural beauty spot, like a master's painting, becomes more valuable the more it is seen. A tourist in the Rocky Mountains diminishes nothing of the great wealth he finds.* Actually, that was debatable as well. Said tourist could diminish the value for the rest of them considerably by getting drunk and obnoxious and bringing his fights with him. *On the contrary his enjoyment increases its value because he must speak of it, and write of it, and therefore encourage others to come and see themselves.*

That night her visitor did not arrive. And this, too, she sensed, was part of his seduction game.

In the morning certain cowboys led the railway bigwigs back to the station at Lake Louise. Helen bent her face into the coffee mug, inhaling with the hope that the sharp steam would revive her.

"What's got your goat? Have you been wrestling all night with the angel?" said Herbie Wishart.

She groaned and lifted her eyes. Long Lance was smiling down on her and the word *wrestling* seemed too frank. They were a smaller, tighter group now. They'd travel faster, said Wishart.

He took them back across the railroad cut and north toward Beguiling Pass. There were rocky gentle meadows on either side of the trail, and ahead the shores of a little lake: the trail worked its way upward slowly. It was, as they all said, God's country—though what he had to do with it, Helen did not know. Mr. B, too, had got religion when he came out here. Helen was the opposite; she lost any she'd had. The country was too rough, taming it too bloody awful, the terrain too obviously not made for man. Unless this god was the prince of hope, expectation, arrival. She supposed that was what he should be. Not that she thought of him often.

What did she think of, jolting silently on Elsie? There was not only the journey itself but the suspense of seduction. Seduction by nature, seduction by natives.

There were no threats—the bears were busy elsewhere, the cougars likewise, the lynx were shy, and the moose were in the marshes. The path was wide enough that she need not be concerned that Elsie would stumble. And her hips—well, her hips once again submitted to the rocking and grinding that would, by nightfall, have her reaching for the whisky bottle. To keep her mind off the pain Helen thought about intimacy, or, if you preferred, intercourse. And its absence in her life.

She was not a virgin. *Let me assure you*, she wanted to say, if that was what they all thought. Sex, the physical life, marital intimacy—this was not unknown to her. All right, she was not married. She did not have the pleasure of turning in bed to see a body beside her, or reaching out for human warmth in the night. She couldn't say she *missed* the pleasure. There had been a few nights of folly in her past, but they didn't matter. *Well, if you must know*, that very uncharacteristic encounter with the French journalist in the Château Laurier when she first came to Ottawa, which had ended in a humiliating tussle in his room. And the other time after a friend's wedding, when she had—in an opposite spirit, one of duty, really—gone to bed with a groomsman. What did matter was that she had been in love with Mr. B for fifteen years. In her way. Perhaps more with her heart than her mind, perhaps more with her heart than she had permitted herself to know. He might even have been in love with her. He was a devoted family man, but his home life was unhappy; she knew that. He lived with his mother and his wife, one of which, she was not clear, was an invalid whose condition required that they all cohabit. Or perhaps the invalid was him.

Sometimes his mood was clouded. She worried for him when his face turned to porridge; he began falling asleep at his desk and finally took a few weeks' furlough. They would speak on the telephone, and she could cover these times. Then he would suddenly be better and back at it, and they would laugh and plot in the office again.

That was really why she had written the pamphlet. He had started the work but was unable, he said, to get through the first few sentences.

She sympathized. "Writing can be very trying for the mind. Not a thing one can do deliberately. One has to surprise the elf of invention."

"There you go, you see, Helen," he said. "*Elf*, I like that. Well put. You have the gift. Take a run at it, and I can jump on board once you've got the first few pages down."

So she had done the first few pages. Maybe too well. Once he saw them he grinned, that square Scottish face breaking into dimples, his chin poking out. "I won't attempt another word. It's all yours."

She saw that she had switched from thinking about sex to thinking about writing. How had that happened?

Had she ever fantasized about making love with Mr. B? She might have. She did have fervent night thoughts in that apartment in Ottawa. But in her imagination his body—so attractive above the collar—had a way of turning into something else, like the body of one of the secretaries. Mr. B was an open-minded man; she appreciated his support and appreciated that he did not mix it up with improprieties. He had discovered she could write and she had discovered she could write, and between them had begun this dance, where she put words on the page and they read them together, touching each phrase delicately, appreciatively, making small adjustments, but few of these, because her first draft was always good. She studded each one with lines from Blake, Wordsworth, Ernest Thompson Seton. Whitman. Tennyson. On those bits they sat back and closed their eyes and breathed deeply. It was heavenly.

And illicit, in its way.

She had told her uncle, in so many words, that her affections were engaged. Uncle Fitz only smiled as if he had expected that, as if it were part of her job description. But that was just a way of putting off the inquisitive old man. She wasn't sure her affections *were* engaged. Her mind was, and her ambition. Her love of poetry. This Indian chief liked poetry too. But poetry was not what was interfering with her composure on the damn cayuse. A restlessness had got into her body. She was excited. A little frustrated. Moving through glorious country nailed to the saddle, held bolt still and upright. She felt staked, a dog leashed to a pole. They rode on, fording a stream, licks of icy water at her ankles. Her white-striped hair bristled at its roots. She was thirty-six. Some might say her youth was behind her. She said she was in her prime.

They reached the top; it had not been a steep climb, although Elsie would have had more to say about that than Helen. A circle of snow lay on the granite mound. She tried to walk on it; the crust broke, and her foot went through. She teetered, rescued herself and made for the prize she had in mind, a sunny chair-sized rock. On each step her foot broke through the corn snow. She had to pull it up from under, hold it high as she stretched forward, and then brace herself as she set it down and, inevitably, crashed through another eighteen inches. She was exhausted when she reached the rock. Long Lance was already there. She could hardly bring herself to call him Long Lance, a ridiculous and suggestive name. He reached for her—strong arm, gracious smile. It didn't matter if they flirted, did it? Who was to complain, who was to know? He'd brought the bowl of stew and a cup of tea.

"Did you know we're heading the way they went in?" he said.

"Who went in?"

"The Hodgson expedition."

"Why would we do that?"

She wished never again to hear about those lost fossil hunters. She hoped she and Herbie had put it to bed, so to speak. Even a tragedy has to end, he'd said. Yes. The incident had brought unwanted attention from high places. Washington had acted as if its most famous scientist had been kidnapped and was being held for ransom, as if Canada had absconded with this man, when, truth be told, Hodgson had been absconding with Canadian fossils.

"They are our property, aren't they, Mr. B?" she had said. "Being in the rock of our mountains?" Or was there some fancy international agreement that indicated anything you found several miles up or several miles down in the earth was yours to keep? It was that way with fish, wasn't it?

"Of course they're ours. And valuable. Even if we've been letting our horses shit on them for several decades," he mused.

"You don't suppose these people's disappearance has anything to do with the fossils?"

"Maybe with the fact that the packponies were laden to the gills."

"Did anyone else want the fossils?"

"How would they even know about them?"

"We're told they were groundbreaking."

"You know I appreciate your bad puns, Miss Wagg. It is not necessary to live up to your name at all times."

"Sorry, Mr. B. It happens when I'm excited."

She had a tendency to recall, word for word, their repartee. But this was not funny. It had been a very sad, very bad incident in the short, grand history of the Rocky Mountains Park. The newspapers went at it again and again, whenever new information came up—a horse reappeared, or the cook. What else was going to emerge, some frozen corpse? Helen herself dreamt now and again of poor Isabel with her concussion, unable to proceed and bringing the whole group to ruin. These dreams, frightening, could wake her out of deep sleeps with a jolt.

"I suppose you know that How Long was with them—" Long Lance inclined his head toward the cook.

"That's the one? But his name is Snares."

"Changed it. You remember—separated from the main bunch. Rescued by Indians out on a hunt," he said. "Those two also, the Tree brothers." He jerked his head back to indicate the two packers. "They were at the camp, took off before the group."

"Christ," said Helen. "Old Home Week."

"Everyone who was in the party and survived is here. Even Gus Henkel. He wasn't in the group, but he went by their camp that summer."

Were they heading for some sort of re-enactment? She did not like the feeling that came over her then.

The rock had become very hard and cold during the half hour they'd been sitting on it. Long Lance extended his hand as if inviting her to dance. She didn't know who started it, but suddenly they were having a snowball fight. Running and shouting with laughter and finally rolling. The rest of the group watched from dry land. Then it ended and back she struggled through the knee-high corn snow, soaking wet.

She swung her leg over Elsie's back. The apprehension returned: where were they heading, and why?

Long Lance patted both the horse's flanks and her own. She was not reassured.

Chapter 26
THE ELF OF INVENTION

On the Trail, August 3, 1924

> *I regret to see more and more a tendency to rush through the national parks. It should take three weeks to go by pack train from Gateway over the Summits to the north end of the Rocky Mountains Park. And what an experience.*

Past Beguiling, over Bewitching Pass and onto a high meadow that unrolled toward farther peaks. It was strange to get up above one's world and find another layer, another world laid out. There were hillocks and bubbles, and the ground had a spongy texture. An eagle gliding over caught nothing because the ground squirrels were allied against it, sticking their heads out of their burrows and peeping to warn each other. Precarious on a bare rocky rise, a herd of mountain sheep paused to look back at them, and Herbie got out his gun. Gus scrambled after him, hiding behind boulders. The pack train stopped while Herbie and Gus got the kill. The artist took his time, arranging the ram's head on his lap for a photograph first, and then taking out the folding easel. When the sketch was finished Herbie got his knife and eviscerated the creature. Snares took the carcass to pieces and boiled it.

"Now you'll be able to say you've eaten goat soup," said Long Lance.

A day's march and farther up to another pass, through it, down again and beyond, toward the northwest. At night the packhorses were released from their loads and their halters. In the morning they came reluctantly to Herbie's curses. One day when they were being roped into their load there was a loud cracking followed by rumbles: white thunder. An avalanche across the gap. The ponies bolted. One of them tried to leap over a clutch of stunted trees, caught his foot and fell; the pack loosened and the goods spilled. The pony cantered off, ropes trailing. Wishart unleashed a vocabulary that only began with *Goddamned sons of bitches, get your sorry asses back here or I'll have your testicles for a hat rack. Whore's tits, hell's bells, Jesus wept, bollocks and balls.*

The ponies recognized it was a crisis and trotted back for reloading.

On they went through another narrow pass, this one with a village of marmots as sentinels. The furry creatures sat in their rocky doorways and whistled. They must be poor eating or Wishart would shoot them, Helen thought. She let her body post from side to side. She was exhausted, out of her mind really, and had no cloak for her emotions. She was often on the verge of tears on account of the scenery. Never said, at least she had never heard it said, was that while riding these extreme and empty lands you confronted your own inner landscape.

Long Lance had taken up his campaign again. Each night he came to her tent and crawled into her sleeping bag. She didn't mind the company; maybe she encouraged it. She couldn't say he forced himself on her. It was not that direct. He wormed his way into the tent, inch by careful inch. Then he pressed himself against her. His body was hard, his muscles tense. He was a beautiful man. But something in the exchange made her skin crawl.

He did not give up, and one night, she gave in. He was insistent, but she knew he did not desire her. He wanted her; there was a difference. It was what he did—he had women. He had had women. He could have women. She did not care to conjugate further, but she did not desire him. Nonetheless, it came to pass that they were having sex. There was a lot of tugging and grunting. Arching and spasms. Feeling of warm gush. Afterward it was as if ants were running over her skin.

The next day was a tough one in the saddle. She was filled with revulsion, for the night before, for herself. Many things she never thought about came to mind. She had always supposed she could get through her years as a Good Person. But now, riding in the Rockies, she wondered. Purity was all around, but she was compromised, alien to it, corrupted and from another world. She was not righteous. When her sister was ill, had she left her job and gone home to help? No, she had been too busy, too essential, in Ottawa. When her father died, had she been there? No, she couldn't leave work. Couldn't leave Mr. B. Was that not hubris, to think she was so necessary to a married man? And now she had made love with a man she didn't love, who didn't love her.

Going further afield, she was a liar. She stretched the truth so often in writing publicity that she routinely forgot what the truth was. She invented. The list went on. She was foolish and vain. She was weak and feeble. She was smug and self-satisfied. The sun flared on the peaks and running water chuckled around her. The bowl between two great chiselled peaks opened up and the horses picked a narrow way through fields of tiny flowers of blue, yellow, white and purple. Tears began to run down her cheeks. She wiped them away with her bandana, as if they were sweat.

She was a false woman. It had never been more clear. No one loved her, not husband or child, or even boss. She had a sister whom she would not nurse, a mother who was critical, an uncle who was forever unloosing cynical advice. Her beloved uncle Fitz was himself a devious man, one who could thrive only among the false and calculating mandarins of government, not as he wished to be seen, romantically involved with his housekeeper. Yes, she loved him, but was this only the love of one unpleasant creature for another?

She was like her writing. Fabricated. Trying to make an impression. Trying to put over a point of view. Composed—too composed on the outside; chaotic within.

They rode on through the bowl of flowers. The trail was narrow, and the flowers of brilliant blue were now joined by taller specimens in peachy orange. Elsie took a little canter; Helen clutched the reins and leaned back, afraid of losing her seat. Wrong! Long Lance took her bridle instantly and slowed Elsie. She looked into his deep brown eyes, sympathetic and unguarded. In that moment she understood he was a fraud himself. When you are a made-up thing it is easy to notice where people have sewn themselves together and the fabric doesn't cover.

She smiled. Straight into his eyes. Warmly.

He touched her saddle and then trotted up the line.

Did they all know? It seemed to Helen that the whole train, horses and people, kept their heads down.

They stopped at the far side of the Snow Bowl. Long Lance rode up beside her. The path was narrow. Their horses' sides rubbed.

"Up there," he said. "Do you see the cut on the mountainside? That was the Hodgsons' quarry."

A barely visible trail led up toward the campsite and the quarry, a razor slice into the mountain. Below it, near a few trees, must be the campground. Wishart and the cowboys put their heads together as if discussing whether to go up. Helen was curious. Surely after all this time, nothing could be left that would offer any clue. She rode up to talk to him and interrupted some fierce words between Wishart and Gus Henkel. The artist cantered off.

"Something's come up. How do you feel about a change of plan?" said Herbie Wishart.

"You've got something up your sleeve!" she said. "What is going on? Is this ride turning into a search party?"

"We're talking about going over the Summits. Across the Snow Dome. Lucky you to be with us. It's a good long way, but we'll get to Pity Plains from the back by the old fur traders' trail."

"Lucky me? If you say so."

"You'd like to see Pity Plains. Magical spot."

She knew of it: it was a bit of a topic back in the government at the moment. A breakaway band of Stoney Indians from Morley was living there. They claimed the place was their ancestral hunting grounds. "Her lot," as Herbie would say, wanted them out and thought the Pity should become part of the Rocky Mountains Park. Or a game preserve: that's what he was angling for.

"Flat ground for grazing and growing. Hardly any snow in winter. That's why you get the game: they can dig up the grass with their hooves. The warm wind from the sea gets in there. Yes, all the way from the West Coast," he said, seeing her incredulity. "Wind blows like the devil. It's so strong I've even seen it freeze a gaggle of geese at the edge of the water. The ice coats 'em, and they stand stock-still until the weather warms up. It's like an enchantment."

He raised his eyebrows and pulled out his pipe, looking down into its bowl as if wonders resided there too. "There are strange colours in the light too. Oh, in winter you see ice whipped up on the lakes into peaks."

What was he after? She didn't trust Wishart.

"Haven't visited for a decade. I used to go see Sam Gallant—he has a trading post there. You'd get to meet a legend."

"Why now?"

"Truth is, Helen, I've been hoping to do it from the start, but I didn't like to announce. There's a lot of superstition around the place. You haven't met my wife, Gwen. She would have worried."

"You're not a good liar, Wishart."

"No? Perhaps not." He flashed his defiant grin. "What a lovely thing to say." He sent out a puff of smoke. "But you present a problem. You see, I'm torn. I do have a plan up my sleeve. Can I trust you to keep your mouth shut back in Ottawa?"

"Yes, you can." Ottawa was feeling farther and farther away.

"You swear it?"

"On Elsie's head," she said. He loved his horses.

"Shall I take you into my confidence, then?"

"Yes, please."

"Here it is: Gwen has been after me to get over to the plains. That's where How Long stayed for those years after the Hodgson disappearance."

"Do you think you'll find out anything about the rest of the expedition?"

"Not likely. It's more what we might see along the way."

Helen imagined frozen corpses. The skeletons of horses, signs of attack by bears. Who knew what clues. She was thrilled. An adventure! She was also terrified. She imagined her own frozen corpse.

"I see." Still, she felt he wasn't levelling with her.

He watched her face. "I think we'll do it. You're a tough dude, aren't you?" He winked. "We've got good weather; let's hope it holds. And a full moon coming up."

"Okay," she said.

He clopped away.

"We'll get to meet the original mountain man," she said to Long Lance.

"Maybe he wants to surprise Gallant. They fell out back in the early days."

They took a narrow, well-worn trail away from the Snow Bowl, in the opposite direction to the camp and the quarry. They walked the rest of the day on a high plain; again, new territory. For Long Lance too, he said. Gus Henkel made little detours off into the trees, kicked the snow in the dips around the larger trunks, and came back shaking his head.

So it *was* a search party. Their path sloped downward, and gradually the flanking rocks drew in on them. Their passage narrowed, and then they hit a wall. They were in a box canyon.

"This isn't it," said Gus.

Gus and Herbie argued. There was swearing and a hat thrown. They retraced their steps to the flat place. More cliffs, more trees: Snares/How Long peered up and around himself, this way and that. He raised his hands: no idea. Gus found a narrow trail leading upward, and they followed. Gus rode along beside them, weaving on and off the trail. Helen fretted. Did anyone actually know where they were going? If relics were around, they didn't find any.

They made camp for the night. It was cold, and Gus and Herbie were hardly speaking.

The next day they persisted in a direction that made no sense to Helen—but no direction made any sense—crossed a pass and came on the west side of a mountain to face another mountain. These were the Summits. And so it went, down and up, a roller coaster, each descent a little steeper, each climb a little higher, their progress punctuated every now and then by a shout from Gus that this might be the place, and a rest while he turned and gazed and turned again and decided it wasn't. This went on for three more days until they came to the highest, most difficult pass of all, and broke through to face an enormous downslope, a wide gap filled with rivers and forest, and a new range of mountains.

On the windward side, the terrain was hard going. They descended quickly and soon were moving through what looked like virgin forest, although Wishart insisted it was a trail. There was always more rain here, and the undergrowth was thick. There were tangles of stubby trees and bent willows and a plant called Devil's Club that grew eight feet high and had thorns on its thin, closely packed stems. She got one stuck in her face. The end broke off, and the bit that stayed with her exuded some kind of poison. She got an oozing red boil on her cheek. It horrified her, and she decided never to look in her pocket mirror again. But before long she had a dozen of these wounds.

The party followed Herbie, walking the horses. The packers and Gus Henkel swung axes; she couldn't manage it. She stayed close behind Long Lance. Tears kept falling on her face. She rinsed her bandana in streams and dried it in the sun, but it soon grew soaked again with blood and tears.

At the end of the day they broke through and scrambled toward an airy upland, gleaming in the sun, splashed here and there with little chalky blue lakes. One boasted a house-sized iceberg. Higher up and beyond was the glacier, Herbie said. They climbed toward it. A feeling of freedom energized the group. It was as if they'd torn the veil of common life and were moving toward the gods. The slope was steep and covered with flowers, and the trail Herbie led them on took hairpin turns, across the angle: it would be impossible to go straight up it. It was exhausting and astonishing to be part of the line of ponies and people zigzagging across the beautiful fuchsia-and-green hill.

Then clouds rushed in, and it began to rain, heavily. They climbed up through the rain, doggedly, silently, looking down as they moved upward. No one slept. They got up before dawn and put in several hours before it got hot. No one rode. The ponies' heads were down.

At last they encountered a well-marked trail coming from the west.

"Now we're getting places," said Herbie. "This is the road."

Road? Helen didn't know there were roads on glaciers.

"Yep. The fur traders from the North West Company travelled it—once a year for fifty years. Brigade left the mouth of the Columbia and travelled to the Athabasca Pass. Met there a brigade from the Hudson's Bay Company and exchanged furs for trade goods and mail."

The road took them between two close-pressed mountain flanks, where the ice ran like a river. The trail was high about the waterway. In places the trees were thick, which made for hard going. But then there was an opening, a meeting of three paths. Three roads, one going south along the high divide, one going west and one east. There were boulders strewn around, green with lichen. The east–west lines were wide and worn.

How amusing, Helen thought, to find a crossroads on this huge unmarked patch of the globe. You never knew what would come from meetings of roads. They were mythical, ominous: one thought of Oedipus on the road to Thebes. The sun reflected off stone and snow. Gus and Herbie wanted to go hunting, so they made camp and took a day off. They came back empty-handed and were grumpy around the fire that night.

"It looks like the trails were made by big mammals. Mastodons, maybe," said Long Lance. "The Stoney people always said there was a huge creature up above. They ran away from it."

"Mastodons might have been here, but they didn't make this track. It was made by traders dragging boats. In some places you can see where they laid down planks for the hulls to run on. They must have been bloody heavy, full to the gills with beaver and bear pelts."

"That's who you should look at when you talk about the game being gone," said Long Lance.

For the next week they travelled at an easy pace, taking time to hunt, and when Herbie got a kill, waiting while Gus sketched it. The days were glorious, sunny, long and windless.

The day before they came to the Snow Dome, Herbie said to Helen, "Don't be like the last lady I took up on the glacier."

"Why, what happened to her?"

"I told her to wait until I could take her down. I went ahead to help two men. She decided she wanted to run. She said, 'Hey, here I come!' Those were her last words. She ran downhill and picked up steam. You hear of this thing called gravity? It got in on the game, and she ran right by me. I tried to catch her hand, missed it by six inches, and off she went. Right over the edge, fell five hundred feet, end of story."

"It's not true," she said aside to Long Lance as they took up their dinner plates.

"Maybe it is, maybe it's not," he said.

"Why is he telling me?"

"So you'll do what you're told."

The next day Helen began to feel that they were in the presence of a being. A being whose size was beyond their measuring, dwarfing the party and even the slopes. Its cold, damp breath filled the air. Its voice rose, the roar of water, the sound an ocean made when you stood on the shore in a windstorm. Water was bursting and running everywhere above them. Some was grey-green and carried silt; other flow was crystalline. A tangle of streams appeared on the slopes. The party stopped briefly to rest. The rocks were grey and smooth, washed with outflow from the snow cap above. A constant roar grew louder. It came from under the ice, a rushing, silty river. Helen looked up.

The glacier. They could see it now. It loomed above them, thirty feet tall, grey and white, fitting around the jagged rocks on top of the mountains and blending into the sky. It was ancient. It creaked and groaned. The air became cold: everyone put on jackets, except Herbie, who stood in his vest and shirt-sleeves, looking upward. It was ten shades of white—blue-white, brown-white, green-white—and many-faced, a god of sorts, weeping in distress and roaring, containing all things.

They all fell silent. The wind blew.

"This is just one paw of the Snow Dome," said Herbie. "It's enormous, a cluster of six glaciers. They all have names. This one is called Philharmonic. Over there is Forbidden." From the dome, he said, water flows in three directions—north to the Arctic Ocean, east to the Atlantic and west to the Pacific. They would cross Philharmonic and walk out on the snout of Mastodon, the one leading to the North Saskatchewan River and to the Pity Plains.

"I'm giving you a sneak preview. Thought you might want to add it to the Rocky Mountains Park," said Herbie. "Apparently it needs protection, although from what, we don't know."

"How could anyone even get here? I may not survive to cross it," said Helen.

"We have our ways. We've done it. Even the grizzlies walk across the glacier. Don't you worry."

The grizzlies did not reassure her.

"Can't you get through there?" She pointed to a steep valley between two peaks.

"No." They all laughed. "That's the Cleavage. You can't get through there."

"Not with horses. You need to be mountaineers," said Gus.

But Herbie looked thoughtful. "That's what they thought they were," he said.

Chapter 27

THE INACCESSIBLE

Philharmonic Glacier, August 10, 1924

THEY FOUND AN APPROACH where the slope was gradual. It was a long, gravelly ramp the guide called the Tongue. It took them half a day to get to the top. Philharmonic was blinding white under the blue sky. It made the sounds of an orchestra warming up, pings and moans, high and low. Its ice gleamed in places; other spots were dull and spongy.

Heaven must be like this, brilliant and treacherous, Helen thought. But of course she did not believe.

Herbie pulled out a supply of cleats for their boots. The sun was hot, and water formed on the surface, making it slick. The ponies' hooves disappeared with every step. He decided that they should wait until sundown, when the snow would harden, to move any farther. They ate a cold dinner while standing. Dark took forever to come, but at last it did, and the moon rose. It was nearly full and like a beacon. The cowboys scouted for crevasses, and Herbie barked repeatedly to keep them all in line, and Helen, terrified, obeyed.

They tied the horses together and walked until dawn and still had not come to the edge. They would not walk under the sun but wait again for it to go down. Helen curled up on a tarp on the ice. The ponies stood and switched their tails. There were flies: how could there be flies on all this ice? She waved her hands wildly around her face. Finally she went to sleep. When the sun was low on the horizon they got up and began to walk again. Helen alternately asked herself what in God's name she was doing there, and congratulated herself on doing her job, exploring the park with a guide. Herbie was right: she could write about it. She could write about it, if she could just find that notebook in her knapsack.

The moon was full tonight, high and cold: they walked on the whitest sections of ice in a pewter light. It must have been two in the morning when they reached the other side. The ponies' legs had been slashed by the ice, and everyone was exhausted. There were no trees, so they rested at the foot of three spires of rock Herbie called the Guardians. They were through the worst.

The next day they worked their way down Philharmonic by making a circuit of its side, following an almost invisible trail. You only knew it was there because Herbie took it; there was the faintest appearance of a narrow line, a few rocks worn or settled, a deepened dip, and something pressed into the slope, a shred of desiccated horse shit. Others had been this way but a long time ago, and they had moved softly.

And all this time Long Lance rode behind her. They had given up the pretense of being lovers, which was a relief. The ride was new to him, but he could satisfy a little of her curiosity about this breakaway band.

"Why do they stay way out here at the Pity Plains?" she said.

"So they can feed themselves. It's their traditional hunting grounds. The reserve at Morley isn't big enough to provide food for the people. So now this bunch decided to stay. There's game in all seasons but especially in winter; the animals congregate there because there's no snow cover, and they can get at the grass. In summer it's a dry place, and flat so they can grow things."

Then came the morning where, around the slant fortress of a mountain skirt, they saw the final climb to the plains. They agreed to make it a long day, rode all day without stopping and as the sun set camped on the first place you could spread a blanket.

Gallant's trading post stood beside a fenced pasture where horses grazed. It was a low log cabin with rows of antlers nailed on the front and sod on the roof. The logs that served as roof beams stuck out ten feet in front, maybe because he was too lazy to cut them, or maybe so he could pound in nails and use them as racks to hang his merchandise. The door was less than five feet high. Any adult would have to stoop to enter.

Wishart, the cook, the cowboys, Gus and Helen appeared like the ragtag ends of some army in a forgotten war. Long Lance stayed back.

Herbie shouted, "Gallant! You son of a gun! Come on out."

But it was an Indian who came through the doorway, bending. When he straightened it was to over six feet. Helen's eye caught the porkpie hat with the braids. "White man's religion has been bad for the Indian," Long Lance had told her. "Don't trust the ones with hair cut at the neck. The best Indians have long hair."

The tidy braids of John Hunter—it wasn't really his name, but that's what they called him—hung down his chest. He wore a necklace of teeth and a belt of bullets. His intelligent eyes settled on the cook. "Snares, you brought them back with you?" he said. "We saved you. Is this how you repay us?"

"These are friends," said Snares. He spoke more in Stoney.

Hunter did not look impressed. He had a judicious manner and spoke like an educated man. There was a mission school at Morley; he had been there.

"Who is she?"

"She's a lady writing books." Wishart didn't mention the Parks connection. "Where's Gallant?"

"Supply trip. He left one week ago."

Herbie swung his hat and looked suspicious. Why didn't they see him on the trail? "Fine, I'll talk with you. Where can we put our camp?"

John Hunter gestured away from the pasture. They went to set up, all but Herbie, who stood talking. Long Lance was walking among the people's dwellings, speaking to the women. Helen took off her hat, wiped the sweat from her hairline and breathed easily for the first time in days.

This was not what she had imagined. The Pity Plains was a narrow tongue of land, flat and planted with crops. Children ran in the grass, their hair carried out behind them by the wind. The river was broad and blue, and the mountainsides that framed the plain were steep. She had thought it would be a patch of wilderness with animals. But no. It was domestic, a settlement, a refuge, a Shangri-La. She wondered why Parks felt the need to get the Indians out. The number of furs sold by Gallant with his solo treks in and out could hardly be a threat to the animals. Whose story was it that game was becoming scarce? Herbie denied it, said he could always find a dozen rams. Mind you, he, too, had his reasons: he wanted the hunting grounds for his dudes. He blamed the fur traders. Parks blamed the Indians. She stood ruffling her hair humbly. Again she thought Ottawa was a long way away.

Before Herbie got to his real questions he asked about Sam Gallant. "How's the wild man?" Gallant had made a deal years ago: he would bring in ammunition, alcohol and a few domestic goods. They would give him all their furs to take out. And he would pasture his horses.

Hunter scowled. "He has too many horses. The band needs the land where he grazes them. We befriended Sam; we built him a trading post. Now he wants us to move."

"How many people are living here?"

"Maybe two hundred."

"More than before?"

"Same families. But they grow." Hunter smiled. And then he said, "What brings you?"

Herbie wasn't saying, exactly. "You seen any white folk around here? Last few years?"

"Who's asking? Your government?"

"Not me! Not on your life. I've been fighting the government since the day she took over." Herbie jerked his head at Helen. Both men laughed at the idea.

"Man and woman, couple of summers ago. She sets up to paint, like him." Hunter pointed at Gus, who was sketching the scene.

"Phoebe Dixon and her brother." Herbie shook his head. "Boy, they get around. She had planned to marry the professor. You know who I mean. The scientist who was lost around Magic."

"We know, we know about the lost scientist, Hodgson. Listen, Wishart, I told those Mounties. I told Miss Dixon. We saw nothing. Find nothing."

"I understand." He paused delicately and appeared to be thinking. "Phoebe Dixon and her brother, that's a hell of a long ride for just the two of them, from Laggan. I wonder what route they took?"

The Indian said nothing.

"Course Gallant, he'd be the one taking that long ride many times, going to and from Laggan. He'd know the shortest route. He'd have seen the lost Americans, if anyone did."

Hunter shrugged. Herbie smiled at him directly.

"You had Snares with you for a long time."

"Our people saved his life. He is grateful. Should be."

"I'm grateful too," said Herbie. "Snares is a good friend of mine." He took out his pipe and started tamping it down. "It's just too bad he couldn't shed any light on the question."

"What question?"

Wide smile from Herbie. "Now that you ask, I gotta say that as a matter of fact we've got two questions. There's what the hell happened to the Hodgsons, and then there's whether you are going to stay here and hunt. I mentioned Miss Wagg here is from Ottawa?"

"What is she doing here?"

"Just having a look-see. She's sympathetic. Has connections." Herbie smiled slyly at Helen. "She thinks the government should just let you be. And certainly doesn't think they should turn this into part of the park. Then nobody can hunt."

He has no idea what I think, thought Helen.

Hunter watched carefully as Herbie lit his pipe. He didn't seem to believe Ottawa would send the likes of Helen to assess, and he was right.

"So we're on the same side here, Hunter. I'm an old friend of your people. I learned the trails from them. When I was just a greenhorn I camped near the Indians, and they showed me. I don't want to compete with your people for game."

Hunter grunted.

"You think I could pay a visit to the men who found Snares? Thank them properly? I'd like to."

Later that evening three Indians approached the campfire: Hunter and two sidekicks. Helen had dug out her notebook and was making like the lady writer in the blue twilight. How Long signalled hello to the two men and then stared into the flames. Herbie had been playing his harmonica. He stood up and went to them. Long Lance and Helen followed, giving Herbie sidekicks to match the Stoneys'.

"Here are the hunters who found Snares."

"I want to thank you," said Herbie. "He's like my brother."

"Him crazy."

"Sure!" said Herbie. "He was. Snow-blind and bushed too. He wouldn't be alive if you didn't help him. We are paying our respects."

The trio didn't move.

"I'd like to know what happened to the scientists and the rest of the party."

The Stoneys did not react.

"You saw no sign." Herbie said it like a fact. But it was also a question. "They were—" Now Herbie's face tightened, and he seemed to be getting emotional.

Helen looked down to spare him. She'd never seen him like that.

"My wife's people. Father, brother. Sister."

The Indians were quiet for several long minutes. When John Hunter spoke it was on another topic. "Our people came here to hunt during the season, for many years. And now, we stay. The government wants to keep us at Morley. It is impossible to grow crops at Morley. There is not enough land. And the soil is poor. There we will starve. That place cannot support us all. This is a better home. Tell us why the government doesn't like that."

"Ah, those Parks men think you're cutting into their crop of game animals." Herbie grimaced around his pipe. "I say there's enough game to go around. Parks needs hunters and trappers. I always tell them. You know about the animals. You watch out for the fires. If people are lost, you find them."

"They make 'game law violations' against me." John Hunter rocked as if with laughter. But he didn't crack a smile. "Me. Our land. Our hunting place."

"Oh yeah," said Herbie. "I get those charges too. But most times they'll drop them, when they want something. Miss Wagg, are you getting this?"

"I am," said Helen. "I understand. You have a nice settlement here. There's no reason Parks should move you off." She folded her notebook shut.

Hunter allowed an upward twitch of his lips. "'No reason.' I tell you, to us, that is the most common explanation of a government decision. 'No reason.' Many things are 'no reason.'"

"I have no power." She raised her hands. "But I understand your point."

Hunter gave her a long look and seemed to decide that was all he was going to get. He turned to Herbie. "You're asking about the lost people."

"Yeah."

"One of our mares found something in the creek. Dug it up with her hoof. One of the bridles the people make at Morley."

He turned to one of his men, who fished it out of his pocket.

Herbie took a look. His bridle. The little bit of tooling on the brow band. He'd had half a dozen of them made years ago. He reached for it and tried to read it. The leather was half rotted. The letters were tough to read. Did that say *Caruso*? He couldn't tell. His throat dried up. He swallowed. Wiped his brow with his bandana. Held on to the bridle.

"What creek? Where?"

"Up high. Few years ago."

"And you told nobody."

"No one asked. Not about horses."

"Can you get back to this place? Did you look for other signs?"

John Hunter said nothing. The two men looked at each other and spoke in an undertone.

"I didn't get that," said Herbie.

"I wasn't with them. Gallant was. I only tell you what they say. They say there were people up high. Trying to get to the other side. Lost. Must have been. But that was a long time ago. There's nothing to see now. Are you going to give that bridle back?"

"No. It's mine. I'm keeping it." He slung the leather straps over his shoulder.

They shrugged.

"Can you say where the stream is? Draw me a map?"

Helen opened her notebook and tore out a page. She tried to hand it to Hunter, but he didn't take it. He spoke to the other men, who answered in Stoney.

Hunter shrugged. "I tell you I was not with them."

"Just the general direction," said Herbie.

Helen handed over the notebook itself and her pen, and Hunter balanced the book in his hand and sketched the river, the trails, a pass, another trail going around the base of a mountain, a small lake, a stream coming out of it.

When Hunter was done, Herbie took the notebook. "Where along the stream?"

Hunter wasn't saying. He gave Helen back her pen. "That's a start. To find the place, you'd have to ask Gallant."

Chapter 28
THE WAY BACK

Pass in the Clouds, August 12, 1924

The next day Sam Gallant came in from his supply trip. Herbie watched his horses descend the path and begin to cross the gravelly edge of the river.

"He moved quickly. Eight days there and back: he's found himself a shortcut. Has to have," said Herbie to the cowboys, walking toward his store.

Gallant was a bear of a man with a grizzled beard, wearing a sheepskin. His hunched body looked powerful, but old. There was a mad look to him, Helen thought. She followed him but kept a safe distance.

Gallant's reaction to the party was not friendly. "What the Jesus, Joseph and Mary you doin' here?"

"Can't believe you're still alive, Sam. Seems like you've become a legend."

"Oh, you don't say? You're thinking I'm dead? What's in that for you?"

"Just taking some folks for a tour." Herbie approached him slowly, steadily, with one hand out, as if Gallant were a rabid dog.

"You better take yer Christly misbegotten ignoramus tourists off my property," said Sam.

"They're not tourists. Per se. This lady's a writer, and that guy's an artist."

"Even worse. What is she, some kind of spy? No, greenhorn, I can spot a government agent when I see one."

Government agent! Helen suppressed a squeak.

"You think you can put one over on an old man?"

"Are we feuding?" said Herbie. "Goddamnit, Gallant, I guess we're feuding. Damned if I can remember why."

Sam tipped up his hat brim. He squinted into the sky. Then he swept the hat off and dusted it against his leg. He was laughing, but it wasn't a happy sound.

"Let me refresh your memory, ya weasel. Ya lose people up in the back of beyond and ya bring the Mounties out, sic 'em on us, few innocent Indian families living where they can actually feed themselves—"

"Sam, you're conflating two unrelated topics."

"Don't give me your vocabulary, kid."

"I never wanted the Mounties on this any more than you did. And it's got nothing to do with moving the Indians back to Morley. Nothing!"

"You want something, Herbie Wishart. Spit it out and be gone."

Herbie did not do as he was told. He began circling. He looked at the horses, at the corral, at the trading post.

"We go back a ways, Sam."

Sam pulled at his hat and shook his jowls.

"You've done well for yourself."

This goaded him to speech.

"I tell you I got no luck with my land. Surveyed off at Morley, an' I'm going get surveyed off here if that like have their way." Sam jerked his head at Helen and Long Lance, having sussed out right away that they were some variety of official. "Don't hasten the day, fer god's sake."

"I won't, Sam. I'm after something altogether different. I confess, I'm still a little curious about the scientist."

Helen's eyes were fixed on Sam's. The chief wonder of the legendary face lay in the unmatched pair: one blue as the river, the other black. She took in his hoary face and long hair, the mad gleam of his smile, his stained hide vest and pants that could have walked a mile on their own. She stepped back a pace.

"I'm on your side, Sam. And the Indians'. And I'm in good with the commissioner, I tell you. Helen here can tell you that. I'll put in a word if you tell me what I want to know. What happened to those folks?"

"You married into the family, I heard, did ya, Wishart? Damn strange."

Herbie pulled out his pipe. "My wife thinks so too."

He got a laugh with that line.

"Well, greenhorn, how'd it happen?"

Herbie looked down and put a match in the bowl. He got that mulish expression on his face. Damned if he was going to tell this man about his desire for his wife, is what it said, if Helen read it correctly. She had begun to suspect he loved the girl deeply.

"She was a kid, Sam. She kept on visiting. I felt a responsibility."

"Damn right you did."

"She grew up, and one thing led to another."

"You thinking you can wash away blood with blood?"

"Don't talk shit to me. She wants to know, and I do too."

"I doubt you can clear your name." Sam grinned. "It's too late for that."

Herbie flared at that one. "My name's clear as a bell, Sam. This is strictly for the record."

"John Hunter told you right. There's nobody up there. No axe murderers, no buried bodies, no spy rings, no thieving Injuns, whatever they've got going out there in the newspapers. Nothing out of the ordinary. Bunch of people get lost, stagger around in the snow, argue about which way to go, lie down and die, end up eaten by animals, not much to say. One of the mares dug up a horse carcass at the edge of a stream. Bridle made in Morley. Could be yours, could be mine. Pile of rocks beside it too, a cairn maybe, or probably your famous fossils."

"They're not mine. Not the fossils. But the horse, yes. It was my horse, Sam. Name on the bridle." Herbie took it off his shoulder and shook it, then pulled it back again, to deny Sam too close a look.

"That so. Well, then, that's right. How d'ya think your horse got to wherever he got to?" There was a cautionary look in his eye Herbie chose to ignore.

Herbie took out his pipe. He got a match from his pocket and tried to light it in the wind, made a little pantomime of it. "That's the question. Isn't it? Wandering. But they wandered a very long way." He went through his tamping, sucking, blowing routine. "Hunter drew us a map too."

Sam squinted across the plains.

"You taught me most of what I know, Sam."

"May the good Lord have pity on you, then," said Sam, lightening up a bit.

"We just want answers, that's all. Wife wants to put the whole story behind her."

"Then leave it be. I'm on yer side, Herbie, just like yer on mine. I wanna believe yer not looking for trouble. So listen. No good will come of digging around. I swear it."

"That's my business. All I need to know is where on this map you were." He produced Helen's notebook. "Show me the dead horse and the cairn."

"That's not all you want, greenhorn. You want to know how I got there. That's the big question. And if I told you that, I'd be giving away my trade secret."

"It's your shortcut, isn't it, Sam? No one could make shortcuts like you."

The men stood looking at each other. They were like father and son, thought Helen, deeply connected, deeply antagonistic.

"I'm asking you. Man to man. You've got a secret way. It's how you get out and back in eight days. You completely avoid the glacier, don't you? Gus here stumbled on a relic about halfway to the glacier. Was that your turnoff? Did they get themselves onto your trail, Sam?"

On pain of death and dismemberment and the promise that they'd never use it again, Sam showed them his route out.

It was still a long and arduous 120 miles back to the Bow. Sam's route took them into the deep valley they'd passed on the way in—the Cleavage, which they had believed was impossible to get through. They went partway in and then, using Hunter's map, climbed a hidden, narrow stack of rocks that formed a staircase Sam called the Spiral. He said his horses could do it and so could theirs. And they could. At the very top they found an airy pathway: Pass in the Clouds.

"Well, I'll be damned," said Herbie. "I've heard tell of this, but I never thought I'd see it."

It was an Indian trading route, long ago. No one used it anymore. It would lead them to the stream Hunter had put on his map, alongside which Sam had put his *X*.

Crossing the pass, they were a silent party. It was technical, tough on the horses and the humans. They were tired at night, and Helen rediscovered her need to write.

There had been more events with Long Lance. He had come to her tent, and they had chatted companionably about the day, and then quietly and with determination he seduced her. The ants did not crawl on her skin this time. They repeated this for several nights until the feeling came to Helen that it must end.

"I wanted to be your friend," she said. "Chief." It sounded preposterous to her, and she felt like giggling.

"But you are my friend," he said, burrowing between her breasts with his noble head.

"I am. It's true. I should say I wanted *only* to be your friend."

"All my women become my friends, when I am ready," he said.

It was the "all my women" part of the remark that rankled, and he didn't even notice. "When I am ready" was just overkill. She should probably have felt humiliated. Others in the pack train, like Gus Henkel, had to know what the only woman in the group did at night. She wasn't especially angry, just annoyed, as one would be with a wilful child. It had been an adventure, but she would call it off before he did, before a more attractive woman crossed his path.

She was freed by this and at night wrote in her notebook, now adorned with the map created by John Hunter and annotated by Sam Gallant. She was becoming a split personality, she thought, and wrote in two ways: one set of words was for "them"—this was how she thought of her employer, and by extension, the public—and the other was for herself. For them she wrote rhapsodies about the park for her next publication, which would describe the lands beyond the Summits and Panoramic Glacier. For herself she wrote about the Stoney, the little settlement, the tall hunter with braids who spoke like a schoolteacher, who knew the mountains and the rivers so well that he could draw them on a piece of paper.

Herbie brooded, in the company of Seagram's. Even now, days after his encounter with Gallant, he was without his usual grin.

"He's thinking about his name and if it's 'too late' to clear it," said Long Lance, watching him. "That comment stung."

In only two days they reached the spot where the Pass in the Clouds trail met the stream. They turned to follow it, and it brought them back to the trail they'd taken going in: they'd avoided the glacier altogether. A few hundred yards away, Herbie thought, was the place marked *X* on the map. There was fresh snow; no horse bones were visible. Herbie and Gus circled, searching for anything that stood out. Helen searched too. Eventually, up against an outcrop, they found a pile of rocks.

The slabs could have been in a natural pile, almost: there was much in these mountains that was neat and geometrical, tidily piled, with corners even. But these—not quite. They had been too carefully laid. One sensed the human touch. Nearby, Herbie found the shreds of a weather-ruined rope. That clinched it.

He held the rope in his hand and stared at the cairn, his eyes watering.

"I'll be damned. What the Sam Hill—? What were the blazing idiots doing way up here? How on earth did they get in here, and where did they think they were going? Jesus H. Christ."

Helen tried lifting the pieces of shale. They were very heavy. With Long Lance's help she moved two or three. Set them side by side and sat down, rubbing off the surface damp and dirt with her handkerchief. She saw the creatures. They were much larger than she had imagined, inches across. Here was a crab, there a dirigible thing with many feet. There were some fringed umbrellas on a stalk, here one with claws. She felt their allure.

"Like prehistoric knights in their little tombs, the brass rubbing on top," she said.

Herbie winced. Isabel had done that. She had spoken of the fossils as if they were the living dead, as if they were a creature she could have known, like a pet, a dog or a cat. It wounded him. Was this her grave, then? He felt the loss not only of her flesh and bones but of the wonder she had shown. He got out the Seagram's and swore at the ponies.

The rest of the party circled the spot for hours, but found nothing else. That night they sat by the fire, united for a time in silence.

"Let's discuss this like rational beings," said Herbie, although he clearly wasn't one.

What news did they have? A second-hand report of a dead pack-horse. The bridle made by Indians at Morley. Well, anyone could have lost that, Sam Gallant or the Indians themselves. Herbie didn't mention that there was lettering in the leather; it was barely legible. A map hand-drawn by a hunter. A pile of rocks bearing fossils, maybe a cairn, marking the joining of two routes. Did they know for sure these were from the quarry? If the rocks really had made it this far, it was some kind of miracle. And why were they left here? Was this the end of the road for the expedition? The destroyed rope was another piece of evidence: a horse or horses had been unburdened, and at least one had been so exhausted and hungry that he died. It did happen. Herbie had lost horses before.

Of the people there was no sign. Gus said that.

Herbie gnawed his pipe. He ran his thumb and forefinger over the letters in the cheekpiece. He had not been able to read them. It probably wasn't Isabel's horse, he thought. How could Caruso have been with Hodgson and Maxwell when How Long had said she'd gone off with Humphrey?

How Long said he didn't know. "Not my job, boss." He didn't pay attention to horses. The Tree brothers did.

And Herbie wondered why he hadn't asked them, back at the time. What had become of Isabel's horse?

He posed other scenarios. Could it have been that the others had followed what they thought was Isabel's trail and found her with her horse, here? Dead almost certainly. They had left her horse, and the fossils that were weighing them down, taken her or her remains, and continued on. But to where? The demon hope began to tingle in his veins again. He was as bad as Gwen. Each of them obsessed, never finding answers, only more questions.

On top of the questions raised by the fossils was the larger question of who should be told.

"You mean what are we going to say?" said Gus.

It seemed they had already agreed to be canny. Herbie was trapped. If he wanted to "clear his name," as Sam Gallant said, they should go home with an announcement: the expedition was trying to get to the Pity Plains on an ancient, half-existing trail, and was lost. Proof positive: dead horse, identified bridle, abandoned fossils. Unfortunately, no bodies. End of story.

Would it "clear his name"? Only to insiders who would understand that it meant the party had wilfully taken an opposite route. It might provide some relief to Gwen, but from what he now understood of her, it might also drive her mad hopes. She would demand a search for the bones.

Then there would be the Mounties, the FBI, the newspapers. It would be a zoo. What good would it do? It wouldn't bring them back. If bones were here, maybe they should rest undisturbed. And if they weren't, they should give up the search. The loss was a cave within him, a well of sadness, but he was used to it: it had inhabited him a long time.

"We don't need to have found this. We could easily have missed it, even with John Hunter's map."

"We could have," said Gus. "We nearly did."

"We didn't find the camera, after all, and you *knew* where it was."

"And just by the by," said Gus, "I don't agree your name needs to be cleared, Herbie. You're still getting the business. You've got the big cheeses writing you and booking you up. You're the best guide in the Rockies. If you can't find these lost people, no one can."

"We found the fossils."

"A few of them. There must be other piles of them."

Herbie remembered how Isabel had swooned over the creatures in the shale. They seemed to carry her to another world. And perhaps they had. She said, that last night, that she didn't want her father to take them, to analyze and classify them. He was too strict, too straight. He couldn't appreciate the lives they showed. *They need not science, but spirit*, she said. Of course she was confused, she'd hit her head; she hadn't known what she was talking about.

"Maybe we missed the spot. Can we agree on that?"

They could. They would say nothing. There was, actually, nothing to report, just a second-hand story about a dead horse and a bridle that had belonged to Herbie. And the fossils, supposed to change man's understanding of how life began. But maybe they were merely a widower's folly, a folly that carried over from one decade to the next. It was easy, sitting in this place so alone, so unvisited, indifferent and withholding, to believe that. None of it would be brought home. None of it mattered now. In deciding this they honoured Isabel, Herbie thought.

They pledged to keep silent. No one would ever say one word about the rocks or the bridle they'd seen on the Pity Plains.

Helen tore the page out of her notebook and put it in the fire. Then she retired to her tent and began to write.

> *This discovery, if announced, would lead to events none of us wants—for Herbie, it would tear up his wife all over again. Long Lance only cares about the Stoneys: any news would call attention to their hunting in the park. And Gus—well, he only cares about his painting. I want the whole Hodgson story to stay buried for the sake of the park. Nothing can save them now.*

The next day a short way down their original trail toward home, they found the camera. Gus saw it and gave a little cry, cantering up. It was in a flat spot, shaded, a good hiding place.

Three boxes, leather, square, like suitcases, were under a tree, in a hollow, sitting in a rim of snow but exposed now, in the height of summer. The largest held the camera. It was like a sample case carried by a salesman. It had metal clips on top and a short leather handle. It was heavy with sharp, square corners.

They stood around the cache, looking down. "Jesus Christ, I remember roping that to the pony," said Herbie.

They felt disinclined to open it.

"It doesn't really change anything," said Herbie.

"No, it doesn't." They had made their decision.

It had ceased to be a clue. It was a memento. It seemed to the party that it proved they were correct; it was an encouragement to continue with the plan they had made. But they couldn't leave it where it was. Someone else might find it.

"We may as well bring it in."

Yes, they would bring it in.

They brought it in.

Helen got off Elsie's back at the Hot Springs Hotel in the company of Long Lance, feeling triumphant—she'd completed a month-long pack trip; she was a woman of the wilderness—and thoroughly compromised. In a number of ways—sexually, for sure, and perhaps morally.

Gus went home to his wife. Herbie rode on to the Three Sisters for a couple of drinks, during which he thought it over. In an hour he was ready to go home.

But first—"Think I'll just stow these boxes in the basement," he said, and took the three boxes down the back stairs of the hotel and stacked them in a dark corner.

Chapter 29
HOME

Gateway, August 17, 1924

Gwen was at the door to greet Herbie with Iona in her arms. Herbie followed the same routine as always when he came back from a trip. He wanted a drink, a hot meal, Iona on his knee for five minutes, a bath, and a bit of kindness from his wife when they got to bed. In that order.

He never talked much about a pack trip. He always said a trip was private to the group who'd been on it, and he never shared well. But that night it seemed to Gwen that he was more taciturn than usual. Yes, they'd got to the Pity; yes, they'd had a run-in with Sam Gallant, but at least the old goat had told them how to get out through a shorter pass, the Pass in the Clouds. Gwen was unsatisfied. She knew they'd been searching. Gus had said he knew where the camera was and that he could find it again. Gus had been on the pack. There had to be news.

"Did you find it?" she said.

"No," he said, over and over.

Gwen was angry: her husband was protecting her, again.

The next day when Herbie took his horse to be reshod, Gwen went out for her routine afternoon walk with Ulla. They each took one of Iona's hands and swung her between them. The dogs were sniffing and peeing on bushes. Gwen went in to buy some fresh bread at the Vienna Café. Pappos was at the counter. Gwen made a wistful remark about her older sister, how if Isabel was there she'd be an aunt to the little girl. She patted Iona's head and said how glad she was they still could hope.

Ulla was shocked. In her view, in the view of everyone in town, this hope was unhealthy. That was when she opened her mouth. How many hundreds of times in years to come did Herbie wish Pappos had shut Ulla up? Pappos always said he would have, but it happened so quickly.

"I suppose, Gwen, that you will be able to put this behind you now that bridle of that horse has been found."

Gwen's wallet fell to the floor and coins rolled out.

"What bridle? Where?"

Gus had just mumbled this to Ulla the night before. She was not really clear about the details. Or that it was a secret.

"The bones of the horse—Herbie's lost packhorse—on the trail to Pity Plains? And the bits of leather with the buckles?"

There was a scene: Gwen screaming, panic in the café, Pappos calling in Constable Fury. Herbie was nowhere to be found, of course. Someone handed Iona off to Ulla, who stood with a strange stricken look; she'd put her foot in it. And Gwen, poor little Gwen, was striking everyone who came near with her fists.

When Herbie got home, he found Ulla in her kitchen saying poor Gwen was laid out half dead in the Sanatorium. He was on his horse in two seconds.

"They found her sister's bones!" said the nurse when he ran into the ward.

"Where did you hear that? We did not!"

Gwen was lying on a cot. He could see her face and she could see his.

For one minute he thought she believed him innocent. Then he understood. She saw guilt on his face.

"You lie! You were always a bad liar, Herbie Wishart," she said firmly.

He stood over her bed. Under his eyes she closed her own and lay, shut down and grim. She did not look at him. She did not give him the satisfaction of shouting. She did not throw a shoe the way she had before, charmingly, looking him in the eye and then at the last minute changing her aim and dropping it on his foot. She did not shout, *Why didn't you tell me?* as she had once before, although he knew that she was just as angry, enraged, in fact, because it was her story, her property, and he had presumed to keep it from her.

"It's not your sister," he said. "It's just a rumour among some Indians about a dead horse. Don't you think if the bones were human I would tell you? But a horse? It would just upset you. And see? It has!"

She did not list his failings one by one. She held back. He knew that if she allowed it to, her rage would fill the hospital and fog the valley in great dark rolls, and he would be rolled in it as in the smoke of hell: he would fall at her feet in sorrow. She did none of those things. She closed her lips firmly and lay on her back like a brass rubbing on a tomb. Like the Lady of Shallot going downstream. He could have withstood blame. But instead there was this, this *act*.

He took a chair and sat by her bed. She did not move. He sat for an hour, which was just about the longest period of waking stillness he could manage. Oh, the effort to run down these females. Would it never end? Who was this woman? She had been a sensible, eager child. She had grown to a seductive and playful young woman. When he married her, Herbie had discovered his wife to be a romantic. She came with a trunk like an actress. She dressed for dinner and danced in front of the fire. She saw herself as if in a mirror, always. Why? What was she? Was she so uncertain that she had to put on the costume of the others? So empty, so unformed. Was this the consequence of losing all family when she was twelve? If it was, he couldn't blame her. He could only keep watching, trying to catch her. When he thought she was adapting, she was not: she was throwing herself into a role. Until suddenly the season was finished and she had to find another.

He sensed the season was finished. The glamorous devoted wife and mother living in a log cabin was done. She was moving on to another role. He tried to speak to her, but she lay vacant and unmoved. He loved her, he couldn't help it. She was like the nymph running him to death. He was running behind her, tiring, but she was not.

Gwen did not appear to notice when her husband left.

She slept for weeks, drugged by the doctor. When she staggered out of bed she was blank, absent, angry. She returned home and observed that her husband was stopped up with grief. She wondered who he grieved for. Was it for Isabel? Or for someone called Gwen, the precocious Quaker girl he'd married, who was living out of place, forever abandoned, forever betrayed? Or his daughter Iona, bewildered, clutching her father's leg?

Part Three

Chapter 30

THE SHAPE OF IT

Gateway, July 21, 2011

After another beautiful beginning, the day had gone off. This happened: some cloud got stuck on a peak, some system blew in through the gap. They could have gone walking on the boardwalk beside the fens. It was an easy place for Iona to push her walker. But it looked like rain.

"Feel like a spin in the cemetery, Mum?" said Ann.

"Yes, I do. A visit."

As Nancy, Ann and Lynn loaded Iona into the car she smiled gaily. "You are my runaway daughters. I tried to do the same. But now you are back. I wonder why. Is it because I am going to die?"

"Mum!" That was Ann.

It was just down at the end of Main Street, but they drove. And by the time they got the walker got out of the car, it was raining. Darkly, coldly, thoroughly.

In the shade of the big firs they unfolded the walker, hoisted Iona out of the passenger seat and pulled the walker into place so she could grasp the handles. She set off, her four wheels sticking and stopping on the uneven ground.

Nancy opened the gate. Lynn helped push the walker. Ann held two umbrellas, one high and one low, over herself and her mother as they walked up and down the little paths. Pulling her hood tighter, Nancy headed for the protection of the wide-branched Douglas firs in the oldest part of the cemetery. The others followed. The trees stood immense and dark, unmoved by the downpour. Underneath was a portion of shelter. Iona spun her walker around, and they stood looking out.

"I know a lot of people in this cemetery," said Iona. "But none of them—" She struggled to find a word, and then stopped.

"None of them . . . ?"

"What, Mum?" Lynn tucked Iona's raincoat tighter around the neck. They all fussed over her, three hens and one chicken.

"None of them— Oh, I don't know what I was going to say. None of them—"

She probably meant to say that none of them was living. But she had a superstition: she would not mention the end of life, or death for that matter. If you asked her, she said she supposed it had to come. Perhaps when she was "old."

She made the effort to finish her sentence: "I was going to say, none of them is alive anymore."

They began to laugh, and the laughter did what it used to, spilled over its own edges, becoming shapeless, out of control, then two-sided. They were laughing with and laughing at their mother, and that made the sisters nervous, which turned the laughter to unstoppable giggles. They had to walk in circles to contain it under the tree: the love, the pity, the tension.

Iona said, looking puzzled, "I used to like looking at graves. Always something new to see!"

That one was intentional, that joke. Not quite so funny.

"Though now it seems a little too close for comfort."

"Do you want to be buried here, Mum?"

"*Nancy*!" said Ann and Lynn simultaneously.

"Well?"

Ann shot her an outraged glance, and Lynn busied herself wiping the handlebars on the stroller.

Iona did not like references to her age. She could make them, but others could not. "I think that's a little rude," she said pertly.

Nancy lowered her voice so her mother couldn't hear, muttering about denial and why they all had to pretend that what was coming was not coming. Divided again: that felt normal.

She gazed at the figure of the old woman, deep in thought and fierce as she stooped over her walker. What was it like to approach the end the slow way, the achingly slow way? She was not sick. Dying of old age was what it was called. Nancy would not recommend it, though Iona didn't complain. She was just grateful to be here still. Terrible how grateful we all have to be in the end, thought Nancy.

They stood on, waiting for the worst of the downpour to end, peering through the rain at the nearest stones. There were British names, Polish and German and French. Many Italian. There were a few Chinese and one Japanese. No Stoney Indian, though all the best people around here had a touch of it. Scots, Ukrainian, Irish.

"Hard to believe they're all buried here together. As if they all lived the same lives. Or died the same death and got in line for the same afterlife."

"You don't think they did, Mum?"

"Absolutely not! The ones with money get better lodgings at the end." She peered through the rain. "Look, is that Mr. Foxx?"

The stone was hard to miss, six feet tall with a couple of angels standing guard. No doubt Mrs. Foxx's design.

"Now his wife, she had *ideas*," said Iona. Anyway, who could forget Foxx, with his name plastered on everything in town? The *Trumpet* had been his starting point, and then it spread everywhere. The Foxx Hotel, the Foxx Restaurant, the Foxx Trading Post. The monument was engraved in the same font as the newspaper's name.

"You know we never liked the Foxxes. Now I don't think he was so bad. If you were Herbie Wishart you had to have a rival. It could have been anyone."

They stood a little longer. Eventually the rain let up some.

"Shall we brave it?"

"We've got to do our visits," said Iona.

It was a kind of a lark. Catching up with the dead. Rehearsing the list. They hadn't done it for years.

"Where do we start?"

"Aunt Isabel. Let's go see her."

There was the modest grey stone. *Isabel Hodgson. Born Washington, D.C., 1888. Died in these mountains.*

"You know she's not there."

"There's no date."

"They never knew the date."

"They just wanted to put her by her sister."

The next stone read *Gwen Hodgson Wishart 1896–1962,* and simply, *Made these mountains her home.*

Iona stood there looking. Her lips moved, but she did not speak.

"You don't seem to have much to say to your mother."

"She doesn't have much to say to me," said Iona.

Were they supposed to laugh this time? No one knew.

Iona stared at the grave. "I loved her, though. Everybody loves their mother, don't they?" she said, looking around for affirmation. She straightened up and pushed her walker forward. Being in a family stricken by a celebrated tragedy forced you to straighten up. "People used to come and see her, as if she were a local monument."

"She was, I guess. A curiosity. Coming from the East—and all that," Lynn said.

"She wasn't the only one who came from society. There were lots of them." Nancy.

"No, but the rest of them brought their money. My mother was written off. Her family never forgave her."

"For what?" Indignant Ann.

"For coming here. Staying here. It must have seemed to them she took a side."

"They sound horrible."

"I doubt they were. They were just—proper." Iona smiled more gently on her mother. "I think all of that—the matchless butler, the dining table set for twenty, and the painted landscapes, the great swollen drapes, the social position they had—*that* wasn't so hard to lose."

"What *was* so hard to lose?" Nancy asked.

"Family. I wasn't enough, you see."

"How could you be, one little girl?" Nancy again.

"Family and 'Friends,' with a capital *F*. And you could say she lost her faith. What a lot of *F* words." Iona's mouth worked, lips closed.

"But not *the F*-word."

"No." Iona giggled. "She lost all the *F*-Friends. But she found more small-*f* friends in Gateway. And that's why we've got the Three Sisters Hotel!"

Now, all these years distant, eighty years, more—unthinkable it was—now, when her life was curving back to the beginning, Iona was flying above the landscape of her days. The more she tried to understand the geography of her making, the more she thought it strange. Both her parents found her too fine, too precious for their world. Her mother and her father had laboured to make a living in that inhospitable place, among others who laboured and yet judged their labour unfit. And both had decided their daughter would be above it.

Her mother didn't want her playing with miners' children, and her father wouldn't take her to the backcountry. They both thought she was better off by herself. How lonely she had been. Had they followed

Dr. Smallwood's order not to have another baby? Or had it simply not happened? Had they thought it was a mistake to have her? Did they think she was so frail, so breakable, so out of place?

"'In my father's house are many mansions,'" said Iona. "'If it were not so I would have told you.' My mother said that. I thought she was talking about the family home in Washington. 'I go to prepare a place for you.' I always thought she might abandon me."

"Shall we go see your father?" That was Lynn, always trying to wrap it up.

He was only a few steps away, but out in the open. No tree or shrub had been planted near him, and none had approached him either. Herbie Wishart. Run down at last. Outside, and unprotected. On the stone where there might have been a cross was a saddle made of soft stone, stirrups and all, and at its foot, a drowsing dog. Whoever buried him hadn't put the gun in.

But they didn't look at Herbie.

"Who knows if he's really there," said Iona.

Her daughters looked puzzled but said nothing. It wasn't the right moment to question Iona.

The rain was finally over, but they were soaked and cold. It was time to go home. Nancy pushed down the hood of her jacket. The wet needles of the fir trees gleamed as the sun came out.

As they turned toward the car Iona looked up.

"When did you last speak to this man?"

It was one of Iona's leaps, but Nancy knew what she was talking about. Kaz, the stranger who had telephoned, was coming to visit.

"A few weeks ago. You saw him too. The night we went to the Wolf Den. He phoned our table."

"I know what you're thinking," said Iona, turning on her daughter. She was suddenly cross. "You think I should know him. But I don't." She pushed at her walker; it was stuck on a ridge and would not move forward. "You think I'm losing my mind. But I can't be. I'm thinking all the time."

Nancy smiled at this. "Mum, I have no doubt you are."

"I am going over my life. It is very absorbing. I can see the shape of it."

Nancy laughed.

"Girls, I'm serious! I told you, when you get near the end it's like being in an airplane. That's how I feel. Like I'm somewhere above, watching an old woman struggle through her days."

Chapter 31
IONA

Gateway, 1930s

Before her muteness, Iona's mother was shimmery and light. The picture and the sounds returned to her even now: blue-green water murmuring under the mossy bank, herself being cheered on to walk, a form bent over with arms out and a sweet treble voice. "Thee can do it! Look at thee, look!" Purrs of approval when Iona reached the goal, the hard breastbone, the curved arms, the breath in her throat.

It was true: she could do it, walk on her own two feet. But she preferred to ride astride her mother's hip, held in place with two hands under her bottom, her cheek pressed against her mother's cheek in a permanent kiss. Her mother chucked her chin. She hid her face in her mother's shoulder. She could feel the slippery fabric, maybe a pearl button, and the tiny soft breast that was her very own possession.

She could put out her hand with its chubby palm and little spike fingers and touch whoever was looking at her, touch them in the mouth to see how those sounds were made. Then she was on her feet again. She knew herself to be small and crossing tricky ground, tree roots she could trip on, dead leaves, little sockets of water. It must have been in the fens. A ring of bystanders chiding, but her mother with the singsong voice and then a great swing upward into arms.

But that was long ago. It had ended. Iona did not know why. Others stepped in. There was a word for it: breakdown. The reason given? There was a secret, and her father didn't tell her mother. But someone did.

Their life began again after a fashion. Gwen tended to Iona in an automatic way. She moved efficiently through the house, face muscles slack. Herbie reached for Gwen, she passed him coldly; he held her, she pushed him away. Then Herbie retreated, bent and lifted up his daughter as a substitute, gave her a whisker rub.

Gwen's silence had begun in late summer. It went on for months. In winter she became distantly fond, patting people, putting her arm around her daughter, smiling but not holding anyone's gaze. At New Year's, as if by fiat, she began to say yes. Yes, yes, when she was addressed. On occasion she could be roused to say no. It was Dr. Smallwood's view that she had gone crazy with grief. This opinion was delivered to the couple in the doctor's study. Iona was included on the understanding that she was too young to take it in. But she remembered—the room, the small chair in which she sat, her father's pipe smoke, the dim light from the window, the finality of the judgment.

Gwen herself accepted the idea. If she was not crazy, she was at least a melancholic. But Herbie was not so sure. Sometimes she looked into his eyes, and he looked into his wife's eyes, and the knowledge passed between them that this was more complicated than insanity: it was rage.

Herbie told the doctor his wife had imprisoned herself in an iron-clad set of rules designed to punish her for being alive, and to punish those who loved her for their love. Her silence, he was convinced, was optional: she could speak; she could be ordinary and affectionate and laugh, if she allowed herself to. But she did not. She was the most stubborn creature on earth.

Herbie was a good talker. Iona felt the air move: the doctor was a little annoyed to have it explained to him. He begged to disagree. Dr. Smallwood said whatever the reason for this breakdown, this silence, this was delayed grief. The Wisharts should definitely not have a second child.

Herbie argued: she had lost her family. Shouldn't she replace it with more children?

No.

All this Iona remembered.

After they went home, Gwen began to speak again, in a measured way; he had called her bluff. Do you want toast? Drink your milk before you go. Iona and her father kept their hopes up. Her gaiety was gone, but there was that empty kindness. And she still wanted to dance. They put on the phonograph at night. Herbie put in a small floor of varnished wood where they made their turns to the windy music. After the dance they went into the bedroom and closed the door and went to sleep with their arms around each other. Iona saw. It allowed her to sleep too.

The days were ordinary: silent, but reliable. Gwen was at home and behaved like a mother. But at twilight she put on an Indian blanket and walked. She walked Main Street and the streets behind, over to Mineside, up to the springs, her head down, stopping when a neighbour hailed her. She turned up outside doors and waited without knocking. If invited in, she melted away. She was tolerated, known. In her ramblings she became the town's *memento mori*, an instance—and not the only one—of what the mountains could do. There was also the climber who'd broken his back, who was wheeled in a chair with a rug on his lap. There were miners' widows. She was not the only one, but she was the most otherworldly of these mascots. Housewives touched her arm and greeted her, gave her tea, tried to ease her confusion. "Time to go home, Gwen, it's getting cold." Storekeepers opened their doors for her. "Did you come for milk? Store's closed, but I'll get you some." They rallied around her and she became part of what made the town itself.

Another memory: Iona was in the Vienna Café with her father. "Your mother is a saint," Pappos said to Iona.

"Oh Jesus, Pappos, who wants a saint in the family?" said Herbie.

But he tapped her hand when he said it.

Iona loved the winters, when her dad was in town. The two of them were happy in their way. The café was a space to share, away from her mother's blank smiles. They drank tea and ate pie together, relieved of the burden of her. The pie was good. Pappos took their order and, before it came, picked up his mandolin to serenade them. Herbie got a slug of whisky in his tea, which made the mandolin tolerable.

Pappos's philosophical banter was part of the service. He liked to go on about the many nations that found their way to Gateway. He made no bones about who was best. "The Italians gave us laws. The Jews gave us our faith. Yes, they did, admit it—Christianity came from a Jew. But the Greeks—we gave you the truth."

"That right, Pappos?" Herbie said. "Maybe you could give me a little taste of it now, along with this pie."

"She's getting better, your wife is," Pappos would say. "I never believed what the doctor said, that she was crazy. She was just gone for a time."

Herbie grunted.

"You're in a tough spot. She's waiting for you to find her family, Herbie."

Iona was alarmed. Herbie gave Pappos a warning look. "That ship has sailed, I'm afraid. It was a long time ago."

"No, listen, Wishart. I tell you. Let her have hope. Hope is a mystery. We don't know what it is, but it fills our life. We hope from the moment we are born, and we die hoping."

"If you say so."

"Okay, Herbie, you don't want to talk about it. Let's not talk about it." He strummed his mandolin, tuned it and strummed again, the first few bars of "Shine On, Harvest Moon." "What about this slump? How will we get out of it?"

Maybe the whole world was in a depression, and Gateway was going downhill. But to Iona the town was full of excitement. Down by the river was Artists' Row; she could go there and watch Uncle Gus or Aunt Phoebe or any of the other artists painting in their gardens. On Main Street you could buy fudge or moccasins. There was a Chinese restaurant too, open twenty-four hours a day. When you went in you could see the staff playing mahjong for their earnings. You could skate on the river. On the radio you could pick up Salt Lake City and Denver. And there was a new ballroom. Every Saturday night a dance orchestra played: the musical mining Cassalis family contributed Frankie and a couple of other boys, and their sister Renalda sang.

If Herbie was in town, he and Gwen went to the dance. They were the best dancers. Iona knew the cha-cha with the chase in it. When the Latin beat started she would stand up from where she sat with the other kids and dance along.

"What have ya got booked for the summer?" Pappos rang in the cash so the drawer opened and shut it again without taking their money.

"Couple of small trips. That's it. If I get more I'd need a new man, and who would that be? The fellow I worked with last year got work from the CPR guarding the Chinese workers crossing the country under bond. I can't pay that kind of money. You can't compete with the government. At least when the tourists come back, we'll be ready. They're paying the prisoners seven-fifty a month to build the road up Mount Menace. Slave labour," Herbie said.

"It's the only way to build anything. Look at Rome," said Pappos.

Iona was afraid of those labourers, the unemployed, the *tramps*. The government let some of them live in tents and moved them around in trucks, in dull work clothes. Others came and went on the trains, inhabiting the edge of the forest, the margin between the town with its lit windows and the black, untracked wilderness, the black country. Her father knew it better than anyone. He ran on his snowshoes up and down slopes and over frozen rivers, but forbade her to follow: too dangerous.

The mountains were too big, too cold, too steep. They were the haunt of her mother's family, the lost and the dead. At night the headlights of cars moved across the ceiling of her bedroom: to Iona these were the ghostly family returning from years of frozen exile. She imagined her uncle and aunt, Maxwell and her grandfather—people she had never met—as grim, iced figures, faces wrapped in scarves, cheeks pitted with hail. She tried to change the picture and imagined they had settled into a farmhouse on the western slopes. She knew they were Quakers, but what was that? Maybe they were like the Hutterites she'd seen in summer markets, hair in nets, finding eggs under the chickens.

When that vision failed to bring comfort she went into her parents' bedroom. Gwen lay curled away from Herbie, who roared like a fire in his sleep. She got in bed between them.

Her mother told her to believe the family would come back alive. She tried. But belief was a kite and needed the right wind, needed to be tugged to stay up. On those nights her belief collapsed. The air went out of it. People did die: children climbing on logs at the river fell in and were swept to their death; men chopped a leg with an axe and bled to death. It was easy to see they were all dead. Had to be.

Then she wished she could live somewhere else, in one of the big cities her mother talked about, where the streets were lit all night long.

Iona had ridden one of the ponies past the station, across the tracks and into the fenlands. The end of August was harvest season in a mountain town, and her mother wanted vegetables from the Chinese garden. Where the willow ended and the path rose into trees, she came into sight of the mine, the houses built above it, and the little church with its steeple higher yet. She heard the mine whistle.

She pulled on the reins and stopped. There were always whistles, but this one was at a strange time of day and it went on and on, reverberating across the hillsides. Was there an accident underground? She remembered one: the whole town had stood at the log-framed portals to the dark tunnels that worked their way up inside the mountain, waiting for the bodies to be brought out. It was strange to think that a mine went up, but it did, because that's where the coal seam was. Had it happened again?

She looked down on the wide dirt street. The whistle kept blowing, and the street filled. Women came from the houses, babies in their arms or drying their hands on their apron fronts. Miners in groups ran out of the portal, soot-faced and goggled. The postman was stopped in front of the store with his horse and cart.

Iona clucked her own horse on until she came to the veranda of the Sacco Boarding House.

"Is there a flood in the mine?" said Mrs. Sacco. "Is somebody hurt? My dear," she said, "can you be my eyes and ears? Ride down and come back and tell me?"

Iona started down the track. When she reached the store, the postman was organizing search groups. One crying woman stood in the centre of the little crowd.

The woman was new in town. She had just got off the train. Her children were playing tag outside as she went to the shop. When she came back, they were gone. Two girls and a boy—ten, seven and three.

"Must've been no more than a minute, or we'd of seen them."

"I was setting up my account and arranging for milk," she defended. "I have their coats. The girls are in white dresses."

"Don't worry, ma'am. The whole town will look, and they'll find 'em."

Iona wasn't so sure. There were bears. Wolves. And sinkholes. Shafts you could fall down.

One team of miners went to do the houses and backyards, another to the paths around the mine buildings, another the trails above the town. The whistle still blew. The teacher had all the kids out in the yard and was shielding her eyes against the sun, peering up the mountain. The mother whimpered and dabbed her eyes. Then a three-year-old boy toddled out of the store. She seized him by the shoulders and shook him, trying to get him to say where his sisters were.

"Suppose they've wandered down to the slag. Could be they decided to go pull some carrots."

"How would they know there's carrots to be found?"

Two men set off running toward the pyramid of coal bits. Iona followed on her horse. When she arrived, the men had summoned Slippy, the only one of the Chinese workers who spoke English. The Chinese workers huddled and looked frightened while Slippy shouted in their language. They fanned slowly toward the edge of the forest.

It was sunny here on the bench above the river, but forest encircled the hamlet. It was pushed back but never far enough; the flanks of the mountain were treed and thick, and at the edge began little trails that petered out just a few yards in. You could feel the cold air at the entrance to the shaded undergrowth.

Iona rode back to the store. The women had taken the mother and child to sit on one of the verandas. But being comforted only seemed to make her more frantic, and now she was howling.

"The church," someone said. "Maybe they're in the church."

"That's not likely." A boy with a large head of springy blond hair said it, wryly, bringing humour to the panic. He was from the mine school, older than Iona by a couple of years but she knew him. Walter. He made deliveries from the butcher on her side of town. He was a friendly boy with natural authority. Everyone liked him but Iona's mother: he was the son of the man who had set the dynamite at the Hodgsons' quarry, so to her mind he was tainted with the tragedy.

She thought Walter was right. No kids would play in the church. Churches were cold and no fun. But the fenland was flat, with bottled-up, log-crossed streams all through it. The trees with their shallow roots fell in wide angles far over the banks. You could walk on them, hang off them, make forts under them.

"I'm going to look in the fens." She turned her pony around.

"Good idea. Can I ride with you?" said Walter.

She let him get on behind her and started out full of purpose. Then she faltered. She was afraid of the girls especially, like ghosts in their white dresses, as if they were already dead.

"I don't want to find them if they're drowned."

"They won't be drowned. They're just exploring."

"If they're alive, wouldn't they hear the whistle?"

"They just got off the train. They don't know about whistles. Or maybe they can't find the way."

He was a soothing, calm boy.

The air was silent. The whistle had finally stopped. There was no one left to summon. They were all out looking.

In the fens the air was warm. The sunlight was sweet on the slow water, the moss bright. She tied the horse, and then she and Walter wandered. They each took a little path; these tangled and came back upon each other. They ran, each trying to beat the other to the next joining. She ran a little farther each time he tagged her, and a little faster, and she half forgot their task. But Walter remembered and shouted, "Children!" and Iona shouted too. They'd forgotten to get their names. If they were alive they would have come. Iona would have seen a white dress.

"They must be dead," she said.

"You needn't be so afraid," said Walter. He reached for her shoulders. He put a hand on each and held them steady. He smiled into her eyes.

Then the whistle began to blow again. It meant either success or failure. Iona got on the pony, and Walter ran beside her.

Mrs. Sacco was on her veranda again. "Found!" she cried.

The girls were not hurt, and only the younger was even frightened.

They had followed a path up behind the church and got into thick forest. Walter was right: they heard the whistle blowing but didn't think it was for them. Then when they thought they should go back to their mother, they couldn't find the way.

Iona had to go on to get the vegetables. Her mother would be worrying. Walter waved goodbye, and she felt a touch of sadness; she doubted they would play together again. She would remember that game of tag in the fens, an idyll against fear.

Chapter 32

THE BAR AT THE THREE SISTERS HOTEL

Gateway, Spring, 1933

IONA WAS LONELY. They had no relatives in Gateway. Other families were large: uncles, aunts, brothers, sisters, grandparents grew thick on the trees. There was a music teacher to whom Iona went twice a week. She played piano first, and then she learned to sing. Gwen wouldn't let her go into the choir at the Catholic church, but the choir mistress gave her private lessons. The cowboys teased, and she had books.

But she was full of restless energy. Skating on the river and riding a pony around town did not use it up. Singing did not use it up: it gave her more. She knew she was stronger than she ever was able to prove. On the way home from school she climbed the railway bridge with the boys. In winter when there was fresh snow, the girls played pie, making a big circle with their footprints and cutting it into slices across, then chasing each other along the cuts. Sometimes she saw Walter Mariner doing deliveries. When the other girls went in, she hung around Main

Street and threw snowballs at windows. Once she went home she had to be quiet.

Her mother told her about life in Washington, her own experience growing up with a brother and sister. Theirs was a storybook family, Iona thought, with a big house and a butler and politicians who came to dinner. But in no storybooks did Iona see her own life, except maybe in *Heidi, A Girl's Life in the Alps*. She loved the part where Heidi had to put on all her clothes, layer after layer, to save carrying them on the steep climb up to her grandfather's house.

Of her mother's family, there was much to tell. Humphrey was unhappy, and his father was hard on him. He confided in Gwen that he wanted to be born in another time and place, another family. He was sulky and disapproving of all family activities. Isabel was much older, a distant nine years, a shimmering young lady, elegant and dreamy. She was the opposite of her brother, thrilled with life and ready for anything. Of course it was easy for her, Gwen said: she was beautiful.

Gwen, the youngest, had been practical. She tried to pull the rest together when her mother died. She followed her professor father's reasoning and knew to please him. You had to use clear grammatical sentences and show just enough, but not too much, spunk. Gwen had always known what to do: she was the real leader in the family, and she was angry when she was forbidden from going on the summer's expedition.

Instead she had gone to the Friends for the summer. She told Iona about the old stone meeting house, plain and rectangular, with two ranks of pews that faced each other, not forward. There was no priest, no pulpit. There were no sermons and no hymns; a worshipper could speak if God inspired him; otherwise, there was silence. That was the Quaker way: Friends joined together in silent worship. They followed their inner light.

Sometimes her mother spoke to God. She told him that she no longer believed in him. Oh, there was someone—an order-keeper or a puppet master; she knew there was someone, and that was the man she addressed herself to. You could not call it praying. It was pleading and scolding.

"How could you do this? How could you leave my sister and my brother alone in the mountains? What kind of god are you, anyway? You may think that I deserve it. I may be a sinner, but what have they done wrong?"

When she gave up blaming God, she tried to blame Maxwell. She discussed him with his maker, the great butler in the sky. Who was this man you sent to us, anyway? Maxwell was a member of the coloured race, much defended by the Quakers. He was a very smart man. He could have done anything at all: he could have been president, they all used to say.

Of course he couldn't have been president, she knew that; he couldn't even vote for president. But he should have been. Maxwell was infallible. He was devoted. It could not have been his fault.

Where did Maxwell come from? Iona asked. Gwen didn't remember. From nowhere, it seemed. And he had gone to nowhere, lost in the mountains, claimed by no family, noted in newspapers as "along with the family butler."

They discussed these matters when Herbie was away on the trail. Iona loved it when her mother showed what she called "spunk"; when she knocked the dishes around in the kitchen and shouted at God, and when they danced at night to the phonograph. But none of the fun lasted. It would drain away to sadness. When Iona sang, her mother chided her: music distracted and words mislead, she said. When Iona wanted a party, Gwen inveighed against ceremonies as empty forms. Though she did attend the Winter Festival on the grounds that it celebrated the cold, and she felt people should be happy with the everyday.

The Depression dragged on. Herbie didn't go out of town anymore. The pack-train business had all but dried up. Foxx had seen it first. He'd got out of horses and into cars and buses. Then he bought the hotel, figuring at least the bar brought in steady income. Why did Herbie not get a hedge against the hard times? Why didn't he see them coming, the man who could feel the presence of a bunch of rams half a mile away? The answer was that he did see change on its way. He sensed a way of life and travel in the Rockies collapsing, but he did not react. He was a hunting guide and he led pack trains—that's who he was.

Horse touring had always been expensive. Herbie's scale was flexible, depending on what he thought the trade would bear. But he'd never got above his top rate of $175 a week a man, all in, and that was in the twenties. Costs caught up to that. Touring was tough in the Canadian Rockies because nobody lived there. In India you could have tea on silver platters halfway up the peak for pennies, brought by the local inhabitants of the Himalayas. They would work for you, and feed you and your horses too. But in the Rockies there was no one; you had to carry in every teabag, and now—since Parks was disallowing grazing—the oats for your horses too. Sure, rich folk were his customers, always had been. Only now those rich folk weren't so rich.

It was a come-down for him to become manager of the Three Sisters Hotel. When Foxx offered him the job, it was either an insult or a kindness, most likely both, and both pissed him off.

"Wishart," he said, "you know the joint better than anyone." Meaning he spent a lot of time there. "Take it over, and you can still run your pack trips out of it, if you have any."

With a wife and child to support, Herbie had no choice. It had to be easier to make the grub list for meals for twenty boarders and a kitchen that stayed put than for a clutch of pesky dudes with cooking equipment that had to be packed and roped onto a horse's back, he said. And the place suited him; it was full of characters. There were the miners and the hockey players and the curlers and the few hard-core tourists still making the trip. They gave Herbie an audience, and he enjoyed it.

Iona was often sent there to give her father messages. Crossing the veranda was a test of her daring: often there would be six yapping sled dogs in harness tied up. That would mean Abe was inside. Abe toted provisions into the backcountry by dogsled and lived in a shack along the track outside of town. He always wanted to take his eight sled dogs into the bar with him. Herbie allowed him two.

At the bar she might come face to face with Constable Fury, who was asking why a certain miner had been found drunk on a bench at the station. Might have frozen to death, except alcohol didn't freeze. Her father, behind the bar, would not answer because he was holding forth.

"Oh sure! At some point a few years ago Ottawa gave all the rangers the task of writing daily activities in a log. The very first day, one of the rangers came in here and showed his entry: 'Shot a guy.' Not a word of a lie!" Herbie saw his daughter out of the corner of his eye, winked and kept on with the story. "Manager said he 'magined they were going to want more detail than that. So the ranger ordered another whisky and wrote, 'Raining like hell.'"

The tourists who'd been brought down from the Hot Springs Hotel for a bit of local colour laughed uproariously. Iona giggled. Even the fourth or fifth time it was funny.

"There's my favourite little girl," he'd say, pointing to a seat.

She stayed as long as she could.

How often had she heard the story about Juice Barstow? His real name was Bruce, but Juice was what they called him. He was another of these remittance men from England, lived across from the station in a respectable boarding house and came out looking like a perfect gentleman in a tweed coat with tie and vest every morning at ten thirty when the bar opened. He had the delirium tremens, and his hand rattled so bad when he tried to lift the glass that the whisky spilled out. So he wrapped his tie around the glass and then pulled it up his arm and around the back of his head and let it come down beside his left ear, where he grabbed it with his left hand and pulled—so he had a kind of pulley to lift the glass-holding hand up and down. He was the only guy who knew how to fix the boiler.

But then came the night he needed a drink very badly. It was a Sunday, so the bar and even the liquor store at the Sanatorium were closed. He was handy, even when thirsty, so he got into the engine, hijacked a train and drove back up the line to Laggan, got a few bottles, and drove back down. CPR was so mad they charged him with theft. But Juice got a smart lawyer from Calgary, who got him off. It was the wrong charge. The train was on the track the whole time. It never left CPR property.

But eventually Iona had to deliver the message and go back home. Her mother would be annoyed when she came back smelling of smoke and beer. "Those old drunks," sniffed Gwen, "like a plague on the place." When Herbie came home, they'd argue about it. "Not doing the girl any harm," he'd say. Why shouldn't Iona hear about the drunks and remittance men? The whole place was built by them; it was her history. There was no money in the West, was the problem. All the banks were in the East. Without their remittances there'd be nothing here at all.

Iona loved the stories.

Snuggles was another barfly. He got his name from the habit he had of kissing his horse. He drank in the Three Sisters most days. He didn't do much else, except every once in a while he would write to his parents in England to tell them he had so many acres east of Gateway in the foothills, so many head of cattle and a barn for the winter because the snow got too deep for the cattle to scratch it up with their hooves.

Her father talked about Snuggles whenever any dudes came in sightseeing. He relayed how the man was a fictionalizer of some genius; he wrote his parents how the sun came up at five in the morning, and he stood there looking south with the flat prairie to his left side and the rolling foothills to his right, all rose red, and how it set into the craggy jagged row of snow-clad peaks at the end of the day. In fact Snuggles wrote such stirring letters from the bar that a letter came back from his parents saying they were proud he'd done well, and they'd like to come out and have a look.

At that Snuggles didn't turn a hair, but sat down and wrote them back that he was overjoyed they would take an interest in his poor little venture. It was possible to get here by train, although the train cars were rough and served no food, so you had to buy bannock and pemmican from the Indians at the stations. But oh, how he cherished the idea that they might make these sacrifices just to see him, never mind the danger of Indian attack, mostly in the past now, though there'd been a recent battle in which a number of policemen had been killed, valiant police who were defending the settlers and especially their women, who the natives liked to drag off. The enslavement was apparently not all that bad, although when they slashed the Achilles tendon it did not heal and those who had been rescued after years of crawling on their knees were unlikely to walk again.

He laid it on and hopped off to the post office and came back for another whisky, saying confidently that he'd never see their faces again: the English hated to travel anywhere, despite what you might think when you looked at all that pink territory on the globe. Those occupiers had not travelled willingly; they were forced out, because there was no room in England, and anyway the Queen owned all the land.

But lo and behold, by return came the letter: they were arriving.

"Mother will take ill," said Snuggles, "or Father will have a big case before the court." Only when they cabled from Montreal did he bestir himself to make some plans. Fortunately most of the ranchers drank at the Three Sisters too. Before the afternoon was up he'd got himself a property on hire. It was on a hill looking west and had a thousand head of cattle and a small ranch house—nothing too showy because he had to convince his parents that more needed doing. He'd pay for the use of the ranch, the foreman, the cowboys and the housekeeper, the horses—the whole kit and caboodle—with what the parents gave him.

Herbie didn't see him for a while, but he could imagine how well he treated the folks—put them up in the single bedroom and had the neighbours in for dinner, in formal dress. The month went off without a hitch. Snuggles teared up at the station saying goodbye when they offered a hundred thousand pounds to build a proper house. Snuggles paid the rancher and had enough to keep drinking for two years after that.

"Snuggles, oh no. Snuggles is plain awful," Gwen insisted.

"No, he isn't," said Herbie. "He's pure genius."

But Snuggles gave Gwen her advantage.

When Herbie finally got a ten-day trip booked, he asked Snuggles to keep an eye on things while he was gone. Gwen insisted he'd done it just to make her mad. Maybe he had, but Herbie defended his choice. Snuggles clearly had management skills, and he was educated, could talk to anyone. Anyway, there wouldn't be much to worry about while Herbie was gone.

It was June, time of the big runoff as snow melted up high and came roaring down the Bow. The town flooded once in a while, in fact fairly regularly. It was floating at the best of times. That was because underground lay a huge pool of water stretching from the base of the mountains to halfway across the prairies. This water was warm; it had been held captive for geological eons.

The scientists knew all about it, and the miners, too, because they ran into it while tunnelling. This aquifer prevented rain from sinking in. If the spring runoff was too fast and rain came at the same time, water came up through the pavement and the drains that Ottawa had finally installed, and flowed across Main Street, turning the station waiting room into a wading pool, causing the waiters in the Vienna Café to put on their waders and everyone else to go down in their basements, if they had basements, with buckets.

A poor time to leave, said Gwen. But Herbie claimed he had no choice and went on the trip. And sure enough, it began to pour with rain. When he got back five days later he went straight to the bar. Gus had caught a glimpse of the horses heading in and alerted Gwen, who instantly sent Iona off.

"How'd it go?" Herbie said, cornering Snuggles with a whisky.

Iona slid onto a chair beside him. He gave her a pat.

"Well, it rained hard for a couple of days," said Snuggles. "Folks were bailing, and the bar patrons were a big help. Constable Fury called us outside to get shovels and widen the creekbed; we were putting sandbags on the shore."

"What about in the bar here?"

Snuggles allowed that he went down to the basement just out of curiosity and noticed that there was a foot or two of water in it. He assumed it had happened before.

"That all?"

No, the next day he looked down there around noon. The water was up about eight stairs: if he walked down it would be up around his chest. But the men were thirsty from manning the dikes. It was evening when he opened the basement door again, and the water was within a foot of the ceiling.

Interesting. The ceiling was the floor of the bar. Much higher and it would be around the drinkers' ankles.

"Jesus H. Christ, what did you do?"

"I took care of it, boss."

"How'd you do that?"

He had made a general announcement to the clientele, warning them. "I told them to breathe through their noses," he said. But before long he feared the water was rising and he'd have to pop out for a pump. "So I asked Gwen to come down and take charge. She was very helpful."

When Herbie and Iona got home, they found Gwen washing up. She gave Herbie one of her impassive hugs and started running the bath. Then she read him the riot act.

"*Quis custodiet ipso custodes?*" she said.

"What does that mean?"

"It is not good to have a drinker manage the drinkers."

"So you're going to speak Latin now," he said. "Good, good, whatever language you like. You went to finishing school. I sometimes forget that."

It wasn't fair: she hadn't. She'd gone to a Quaker school.

"You need to have a manager while you're gone," she said.

"What manager hires a manager?" Herbie said.

"The manager who's not at home."

"I can't afford to."

"Then I will do it."

"Over my dead body."

"If necessary."

"*Dad,*" said Iona, "Mum is better than Snuggles."

He had snorted. "Well, she might be, but no wife of mine is going to show her face in that place—"

"*Dad*, she already did."

When Gwen got feisty, Iona could be feisty too. She and her mother smiled at him, identically—untroubled, guileless.

"Gwen, you're not well."

"Perhaps I am," she said, beginning to circle the room. "Perhaps I am."

"If you are, that would be a grand thing. Simply grand. But even so I refuse you permission," he said. "That place is not for decent women."

He raised his voice; her mother raised her eyebrows.

"I do not need your permission. For that or anything else," she said.

They sent Iona to bed then, and the rest of the argument was carried on in whispers and hisses, with slamming doors and roaring. In the morning Herbie was gone, off to deal with the horses. Iona went to school, stopping on the bridge to see how far the water had gone down. She came home and had dinner. No Herbie, but then he wasn't usually there; he was at the bar. After they'd eaten, her mother got her Indian blanket and said she was going out for a walk. Iona saw her making her way along the river path, setting her small boots down firmly on the places where the mud had dried. She followed at a distance.

By the time Iona got to the hotel, her mother had replaced her father behind the counter in the bar and stood trying to pull on the handles for draft beer. Not tall enough to reach, she asked one of the waiters to get her a crate to stand on. Then she began to pull beer, giving her sweet smile each time she handed over a mug. She took the money and stepped off her crate, and went over to the cash register, at which point she looked up and saw Iona.

"Go home, Iona. I don't want you here."

"I thought you might need me."

"I don't. I'm perfectly fine." Her mother closed the drawer smartly. Then she picked up the telephone to call Ulla, who rushed in, in minutes flat, in high dudgeon, to take Iona home to bed.

The next morning Ulla appeared again at the family breakfast table.

"Gwen working in the bar? It's deplorable. What can you be thinking?"

"It was her idea," Herbie said.

"Leaving her child at home?" Ulla said.

"It's better than taking her along," said Herbie.

Tight lips. "Next time bring her to me. If there's a next time."

"Oh, there will be."

Iona's parents looked oddly serene, oddly unified.

After that, when Herbie was away, and even when he wasn't, Gwen went to work. At first Iona showed up to see if her mother was okay. But there was no need. Gwen presided behind the bar. The patrons sat at the round tables, each laid with a piece of orange towelling, separate but together in a kind of solidarity, slumping with fatigue after a day underground, talking about the union or the hockey. When voices got too loud or a fight broke out over a regular's table, she did the eyebrow thing and quietly chided.

"Watch that! There's a lady present," someone would say.

At closing she herded the customers out the door. The usual little clump of children or dogs would be waiting to accompany them on the treacherous trip down the street. Then she made sure the kitchen help washed the glasses and turned out the lights, wrapped herself in her blanket and walked home beside the river. She did this day after day, and within two weeks everyone simply accepted it, even her husband. There had been no trouble she couldn't handle. It was a tough place, but the men knew Gwen and they knew her story and they listened to her.

Gwen had entered another phase. Herbie and Iona could only watch. She said she was herself again. That alone was baffling. To her family Gwen had several selves: there was the one Herbie had first met, forbearing, regal, older than her years. There was another Iona recalled faintly, the young mother both tender and joyous. There was the silent madwoman. Now she had emerged as the hotel barkeep, which was apparently some combination of them all. Herbie said it was sudden, and he was suspicious of the change. But Iona had seen it coming, by minute degrees, through silence and time and prayers and rants and dancing on the polished wood. Maybe all her mother had needed was a job. Maybe all she had needed was another meeting house, and not finding it, she had decided to make do with the Three Sisters bar.

Gwen flourished in her job. She wore stern little day dresses with buttons up the bodice and puffed sleeves and skirts that went halfway down her calves: she looked like a cross between a child and a prison matron. She came to know the men and learned their shifts, their regular tables. She took an interest in their children. She knew their lives were hard. Under her keep the bar may not have got much better, but it didn't get any worse.

After she got the hang of it, she insisted Herbie get the licence in her name. It made better sense if he was going to be out of town. He did, and this development became a news item. She loved the attention that came with the story of a sheltered Quaker girl from Washington, D.C., becoming the first female bartender in all of Alberta.

It was Gwen's idea to start the music on Saturday nights. A couple of young men would load a piano onto a dray and take it around the front and into the bar. There was always a fiddler and an accordion, a bass and a drum eager to play. She convinced Foxx to take out a few tables to create a tiny dance floor. She even let Iona and the other teenagers sit in the beer cooler and peer around the corner so they could listen.

When school began in the fall, Iona began to do her homework in the Map Room. She liked spending her evenings there. The occasional uproar in the bar was a relief after the terrible quiet of home. The cook would make her a sandwich for dinner. Ulla clucked that Iona's life was peopled with drunks, but they were harmless. She came, like her father, to love the characters. There was one named Sammy who camped up in the Spray from spring until the snow fell. He didn't work; he hung around his tent and drank steadily. Constable Fury said there was nothing illegal in what he was doing. When he was out of bottles, he saddled up his horse and kicked him in the rear, and the riderless horse came down the road and into town and went straight for the Three Sisters bar for whisky. The horse was called Daisy. Iona was fond of Daisy.

The town was used to Sammy, but Gwen wasn't. The men watched to see what she would do when the clerk from the front desk came back and said Sammy Morris's horse was outside.

"I can accept that the man is destroying himself and that I can't stop him," she said. "What I can't accept is his treating Daisy so poorly." She was tender toward all animals, and horses especially. But she was the manager of a bar, God help her. She asked him for forgiveness and told the clerk to load the saddlebags with whisky. However, she drew the line at kicking a pony in the butt. They had to call a cowboy out of the bar for that. Gwen wrote down the number of bottles on Morris's account, and Daisy headed back up toward the Spray.

Chapter 33
THE STRANGER

Gateway, July 15, 1933

While she was in the Map Room, Iona would slide open the various great wide drawers and pull out the papers. They were grand and mysterious, finely inscribed with feathered wings and scallop shells and diagonal connectors.

Coming in one day with crates of eggs, Herbie found her there. She was startled by his appearance at the door.

"Dad! You scared me!"

He put his arm around her, unguarded for once. It was odd, but the hotel had become a home. They felt like a family in it.

She leaned against him, not taking her eyes off the map. She couldn't link the lines and swirls that indicated heights and valleys to trails she had ridden, because she had not ridden there. She saw them as pattern, a tapestry. Blue and black lines lay among the peaks like lizards with long bodies, legs outstretched and fine claws. She gazed at the thick caterpillar-shapes that were lakes, the black strings that were rivers and the lighter lines of streams joining them. The straight lines, angled at intervals with letters leaning along them: *CANADIAN PACIFIC RAILWAY.* The pockmarks, the wedged-in names: *PRESIDENT RANGE, WHALEBACK.* The other words set at angles: *MT. VECTOR, PAINTER RIVER, BONNET GLACIER. BOW RIVER, BATH CREEK, SUMMIT.*

The oldest map was simple, black on white, without a grid. The paper was dirty and broken at the folds. He pointed at the date: it went back only forty years. Iona had learned about Europe and Greece, mapped since ancient times.

"Before these, where were the maps of the Rockies?" she said.

"In the heads of the Stoney people," said Herbie. "I've seen them draw them out."

He flipped through the other maps, looking for one in particular.

Iona knew the date of the Hodgson expedition: it was 1911. In that year the maps first were set on a grid. Two years later there was a map with a scale. *One Inch Equals One Mile.* Recent maps were more elaborate, with squares of pastel—green, yellow, pink—and numbers alongside the peaks. *350,000.* Or *5.*

Her father explained to her that the closer the lines ran together, the steeper was the terrain. There were curious empty white spaces. She asked him: What happens in that place? Is nothing there? He laughed at that. There is no empty place. Don't be fooled. This makes it look easy, but it isn't. You go there, and find you've got to walk through two miles of muskeg or a burnt forest. No, no, no, these may be the sum of our knowledge, but they are not the sum of the place.

He put his finger to where the lines wound tightly into a dark spot. "The Watchers. I stood right here with Isabel and Humphrey."

He didn't mean to bring it up. He was off guard, he was happy, and the memory escaped. But he kept on talking. "Your aunt couldn't make head nor tail of a map. All she could see was embroidery, doilies and seashells. But Humphrey. Humphrey took to it. He could read a map like a book. I saw that. I showed him our route in. He memorized it; oh sure, he stared and he took it all in."

She stood a little straighter and blinked hard. The lines on the maps radiated, wavering.

"Why did you say that, Dad?"

She felt his fixation on the Hodgson party rise up between them. He could not get it right with his daughter. He ran hot and cold; he cared too little or too much. They were always out of step. At moments for each of them a fury of love came dangerously close to the surface. But when she seemed to read his mind, he grew secretive. He looked at Iona balefully. She knew what he was thinking, because he said it often enough: she was a strong character, too strong for a woman. Iona hated her father then. He just would not let it be. He had to be in control: why? Something about the Hodgson party. She knew it.

Why had he said it? Maybe he intended to share with her a simple moment that—despite the tragedy—made him smile in remembrance. Or was he stirring the embers, looking within himself for some buried clue? He hadn't wanted his words to fan hopes that were finally dying.

Herbie went out and picked up his egg crates again. Iona stared at the paper open on the table.

Gwen was behind the bar when the man appeared. He came in through the batwings, wearing a cowboy hat and a swagger, his grin as wide as the door. A stranger, but one expecting to make a splash. The place came to a stop; there was something electric where her eyes and his met. Gwen disconnected herself from his gaze, stared through him and pursed her lips, her most common greeting.

"Would you be looking for Herbie Wishart?" she said. Because most people were.

"I suppose so," he said, "but first I would like to give my sister a hug."

Gwen's chin pulled in and her eyes narrowed; she stiffened her back and seemed about to fall, but by an effort of will she did not. She made as if to step toward him but thought better of it and stayed on her box, holding on to one of the beer pulls.

"Can it be Humphrey?" she said in a low voice.

The din in the bar started up, folks who'd sensed something was up shushing folks who hadn't. He shouted over it.

"Yes, it's me. No word of a lie, little sister!"

He put one hand out and swung around the end of the bar, knocking off a foamy mug, took two long steps, put his arms around her ribs from behind and loosened her grip on the pump handles. He lifted her off her box and set her down on the floor.

There was a general clamour and outcry. "Watch what you're doing with our Mrs. Wishart!"

From the back came a jubilant voice: "The mountains have returned him!"

Gently, his hands on her waist, Humphrey turned her around and drew her face into his chest. She made smothering noises until he let her loose.

"I doubted thee. I doubted thee, Humphrey," she said, pounding his shirt with her fist. "For so many years I believed. I prayed for thy life. And then I doubted. I gave up. I am ashamed," she said.

"Ashamed? Whatever for? Aren't you happy? Aren't you glad to see me?"

Iona came out from the Map Room, pencil in hand, to see her mother in tears, chiding: "I'd not have known you. Not from near, not from far. You are so changed." As if he should not have been.

Snuggles stepped up. "How are you, stranger? So you're the brother? Mrs. Wishart, are you sure it's not just a bloke from out of town wanting a free drink?"

Gwen ran out of the room.

Humphrey stood receiving the amazed welcome of the drinkers, his long legs in cowboy boots and a wide-open smile. "I am the brother, indeed."

Gwen came back into the bar, an actress taking a curtain call. She covered her mouth and tears ran down her face. "Am I dreaming?" she asked the miners. "Have I gone mad?"

"No, ma'am. You were mad; now you are seeing right," said one.

She remembered Iona and pushed her forward. "My daughter."

Humphrey looked down at her.

"You look like your mother did when I last saw her," said Humphrey, smiling sadly.

Gwen kept asking him how he could have done it to her, why it had been so long, why he hadn't written. She asked about Isabel, their father, Maxwell. Iona didn't ask at all. It might be pressing their luck to test him on those subjects. What if he was not Humphrey? She wanted him in the family anyway.

By closing time the whole town knew about the miracle. Iona held her mother's hand when Gwen spoke to the crowd that appeared on the veranda.

"In my heart I knew he'd return. I always knew it!"

Answers came slowly over the next few days: Humphrey had been on a ranch in the interior of British Columbia. Herbie found it hard to believe he had missed it all, so he kept pushing. On the ranch, there was no electricity. He didn't get news; maybe he didn't want news.

Herbie pushed harder: what about the others?

Those long years before, in the quarry, Humphrey had wanted to escape. When he did, he assumed the family went home with their blessed fossils and released him to the Rockies without a backward glance. Only when he finally wanted to be in touch did he realize that he was presumed dead along with the rest of them.

He had decamped that morning, when the full moon still hung in the dawn sky, with some tack and his little sack of clothes. He was lucky: he had found his horse a little way from camp and got away silently. He was furious at being hounded by his father to be a *man*, distraught that he wasn't, in his own mind, a man, and excited about being a cowboy. He took the trail he'd seen Phoebe Dixon and her brother walk, southward over the ridge, and was out of sight before anyone stirred.

The maps he had memorized came to life before him: the rivers and their tributaries, the peaks and valleys. He hoped no one saw him arrive at Laggan—he was careful to wear not his hunting homburg but an old cowboy hat he'd picked up from the outfitter. He let the horse go and skulked at the edge of the crowd on the platform with his brim down and hopped on the noon train without buying a ticket. Over the Summits and a few stops past the western slopes he descended from the car, barely twenty-four hours after he'd left the camp and before anyone but his family knew he was missing. Ranchers came to the station looking for hired men. He was a tenderfoot, but he was young. He was hired that morning. He said his name was Cecil Green.

The disappearance of the Hodgson expedition was in the news within a week. Humphrey didn't hear. Humphrey didn't know he was lost. He didn't know that the whole family was lost. Not until the next spring, he said. By then he'd been working on the ranch and living in a bunkhouse with eight other guys for nearly ten months. No one knew that Cecil Green was related to the missing Hodgsons, if they thought about the missing Hodgsons at all.

But one day in town Cecil picked up a fellow. Yes, that's what he did then: he wanted them to know. He was coming clean—it was why he'd sought Gwen out. He went to the station and found those types fresh off the train with their wobbly eyeglasses and their tight collars and took them to the bar in town and then to a boarding house that turned a blind eye. This fellow had been reading a paper. It lay there in the boarding house on the floor. When he got up, Cecil nearly stepped on it. There was a picture of a man in a wide-brimmed hat standing behind a tripod with a camera's accordion nose pointing out at some mountain ranges. Nearly a year had passed by then, and some journalist had dug up a new theory, an interview with that woman—Phoebe Dixon—something about a storm, an avalanche, a failure to reach the rendezvous.

All lost. It was a staggering thought.

So that was why they weren't looking for him. He had put it down to the fact that he was worthless, and they had figured out his secret. He sat down and put his head in his hands. He'd had an easy exit, no storm, no landslide, enough money for a ticket and away he went. But they—how had they got out? Or rather, how had they failed to get out? All these disasters of weather and geology: had God conspired to detain them?

His young man pursued him to the veranda, where he paced, the heels of his boots smacking the hollow floor, the toes of them pointing like a ballet dancer's. The fellow was confused and frankly disbelieving, and they did not part on good terms.

Even then it was twenty years before he came back.

Herbie heard this tale with skepticism, Gwen with grief.

"Why?" said Gwen. "Did you not think of me?"

He had thought of her, yes. But there was shame, too, and guilt. If he had stayed, might he have saved them, with his internal compass, his level head? Yes, he grieved them, but he already had given them up, buried them. It was of Isabel he dreamt, usually. He had wanted to say goodbye to her. He had nearly gone to her tent that night, but he was afraid she would tell. And his little sister, Gwen, if she was truly orphaned, was she not better off in some Friends school in Washington, believing he was dead? "Don't you see?" he said to her. He wasn't ready to advertise who he was now, or where. He always knew someday he would write the relatives in Washington. When the time came, when she was grown up. But the time was long in coming. Because he liked being Cecil Green. His life as a cowboy suited him fine. Still, Humphrey Hodgson crept up on him: Humphrey gave him bad dreams.

He had settled, one brave day after the transcontinental phone lines went in, for a telephone call to Washington. He got someone. An aunt. He said who he was. She did not believe him. And then he asked about the others, and maybe she did believe him. Are you mad? How cruel! she cried. He asked about Gwen, but she would not discuss her. She had married out of Meeting.

And that was all, until he saw the article in the paper, and Gwen's picture: "First female bartender in the province of Alberta."

Iona did not have the words for what he was, but she could see it now. He was one of those girly men. She watched the light dawn on her mother's face. It all fit: the misery of home, the mockery of his father. Isabel must have known this; she had been Humphrey's protector since the beginning. Their father would have had him locked up. For once she was glad the professor was gone.

Gwen believed the man who said he was her brother, and she forgave him. He *was* her brother. She gave her daughter a solemn squeeze. As for the family that remained back east, his story confirmed that she was unforgiven. She and Humphrey both. But what about the higher authority, could he forgive? Was Humphrey's behaviour beyond God's compassion? The happiness that radiated from him could not be wrong. She was glad to have him home, but she would have to remonstrate with God. Again.

Chapter 34
THE OTHER SHOE

Ottawa, September 15, 1933

THE FIRST SHOE DROPPED ON A FRIDAY. Massive budget cuts to Parks. It was in all the papers. Helen and Mr. B hunkered down to see what they could rescue. They said they'd sleep on it for the weekend. On Monday the *Trumpet* crossed Helen's desk.

> *Prime Minister R.B. Bennett, our man from Calgary representing the Rocky Mountains Park, got up there in Parliament looking like a stuck pig in his gold lace and his white satin trousers and his cocked hat. One wonders how on earth he got himself inside that rig. He must have had help. With the same grim determination with which he raises the tariff & cuts down the civil service, he cut funds to Parks.*

On Tuesday the other shoe dropped. Mr. B sat her down in his office. He said he had been thinking overnight. He had decided to fire the secretaries: it was the only way they could continue to do their work in the parks, which now spread from east to west and would be the saviours of the nation. That was his response, his solution to the problem. Helen was flabbergasted. She took a long—very long—look at this man she so admired. Then she blew her stack. She gave a strong rant, winding up to "And you'll soon find out who did all the work around here!" Then, in a final salvo, she offered her resignation. She wasn't sure she meant to; it had become rhetorically necessary. Still, it was done.

She walked out of his office and across the room toward hers—she had her own now—and by the time she reached her door, everyone knew. What was she thinking?

"This entire career she's given everything for, she has just thrown away?" she heard one of the young women say, incredulously, as she sailed past.

"Maybe Miss Wagg was tired of passing that Birks store with all the diamond rings in the window to go up to the office every day," said another of them.

What thanks did she get? For these foolish hens she had given it all up? Helen fumed. But no, it was not for them, she countered. It was for the *principle* of the thing. Let the little bitches suffer tomorrow when they found out their jobs had been chopped. She didn't care. She cared about the idea of women's work, not the stupid fools who did it.

Five days later Helen's mother had a fall. Helen got the news on Sunday, when she was still sitting at her kitchen table with a pot of tea, trying to absorb the fact that she'd stomped out of her office on Sparks Street and did not have to go in tomorrow. By then she regretted her outburst, but—unfortunately—her remarks had been uttered and could not be unuttered. She was forty-five, ancient. They'd fired the support staff, and she was dead sure they were going to make a man the head of the publicity department. If she had stayed, she'd be back where she started, running errands. She would not see herself overleapt like a pawn on a chessboard.

She was terribly hurt, and personally disappointed in Mr. B especially, but when she took stock, she wasn't exactly sorry. She would do a great deal in the line of duty, but she would not move backwards. Full stop.

And there was more. If she really looked at it in her mind. There were decisions she had disagreed with. There were matters that did not reflect well on a department charged with the protection of nature and glories of the wild. There had been compromises, too many to name. They had put a bounty on wolves, and now there was one on coyotes. This was so the hunters could do their work in bringing down the caribou. Only now the caribou were declining. It appeared that once the branch began to mess with the numbers of a species there was no end to it. They were playing God, and they were not much good at it.

Another troubling issue was the Indians. It wasn't up to Parks, Mr. B said, to decide what happened to hunting grounds, but he tended to take instructions from the hunting guides. Which was like putting the fox in charge of the hen coops. They all blamed the Indians for the loss of wildlife, but Helen had seen too many mounted trophy heads to accept that. She had raised her feelings about the Stoneys at the Pity Plains, but she had not been heard. And the matter was not resolved.

But this was her sister on the telephone. Mother was in the hospital. She had climbed on a chair to fix a curtain, fallen off and broken her hip. There was to be an operation in the morning. Helen left her apartment in Ottawa and took the train to Lowell and arrived at the hospital by taxi. There was a cluster of people around the bed. Here she is, said someone, and the bodies parted. She looked into her mother's face. The old woman's eyes were shut, and it was not clear to Helen that she could understand. Maybe that made it easier. Helen took her hand.

"I quit my job," she confided. She squeezed her mother's hand to see if the message had gone in. But she could not tell.

The doctors were saying they could not do the operation. They said her mother was too frail: she couldn't take it.

At that, Mrs. Wagg opened her eyes, looked straight at Helen and said, "Help me."

"The doctors are helping you, Mum," said Helen. "We'll see that they do their job." She said it shortly, without grace, but her mother closed her eyes with something like relief. The oxygen mask was taken away, and in two hours she was gone.

Helen now had something to do, and a funnel for her feelings. The death of a parent—if not the loss of a job working for ingrates—was something to be sorry about. She moved into her mother's house in Lowell and began to sort out the contents. She started with the china cupboard. Place settings for twelve: When had the family been that big? When had it come together for a meal?

Mother was an old woman; yet, as Helen was discovering, even old women valued their lives. *She* might be an old woman to those secretaries, but she was not discardable, not yet. She thought about the help her mother had asked for. Asked *Helen* for, despite the clump of others, including her sister, waiting at the bedside. She had seen Helen as the competent one, as being able to handle the great matter of life and death. It was acknowledgement, of a sort. Had she longed for it? If so, she had it now.

There were so many china cups, each a different pattern—pink or yellow roses, burgundy leaves tumbling downward, gold rimmed or not. She liked a thin china cup against her lip; it was very true. None of that thick crockery that chipped. But so many fine cups: who would want all these cups? Her sister no doubt had dozens of her own. Helen used only one at a time. She had never had a tea party in her life, which made her an oddball. More than odd, if people only knew.

It was a shame that her mother had not died a few weeks earlier. Or later, so she could have heard the other shoe drop. Their last conversation had been the day before Helen quit. Helen had burbled on about the budget cuts and the secretaries without giving away her true concern: she would be demoted to cover the gap. Her mother had absorbed the upset but had not intuited why. This lack of intuition had always wounded Helen. She herself was attuned to others' feelings and was frustrated when this sense was absent. Her own mother did not understand. She was hurt! She was losing all she'd built! And she didn't see why she should have to spell it out.

The principle of equal work for women meant nothing to Mrs. Wagg, because work for women itself was to her unseemly. She had always said her daughter was an error in the grand plan. (And a further aberration for reasons that she suspected but could not countenance.) What she failed to grasp was that the job was Helen's *life*: a gift and a joy for thirty years. So when Helen said, peevishly, "I might just quit!" it raised no sympathy.

And now Helen was ambivalent, as she stacked the china cups in slippery, unstable piles of four and then five and then six, taking bigger and bigger chances that the little towers would fall. The familiar bitterness was there, but it was mitigated: in the end the old woman had looked to her for rescue. She was ashamed, for she had returned no compassion to the dying woman.

However. Her mother was gone now and not to be telephoned. She was picking up the bits of a broken twig-shaped cup handle when there was a knock on the door.

First she wiped her face with a cold washcloth, then she went to answer it. The postman was already back at the curb. He had brought a letter, addressed to her at her office, redirected here. How had they found her? Why had they bothered? It must have been Mr. B who forwarded the letter. All right, she couldn't hate the man. Of course he was a mother's boy and he couldn't write—and what had he done all those years? Only inspire others to do their best. Which, she had to admit, was enormous, and she did not for a moment undervalue him, though he must have undervalued her.

The letter, which she carried out into the sunshine and tore open while standing within the fragrant, bosomy protection of the caragana hedge so as not to be seen reading it (such a nosy town) was from Chief Buffalo Child Long Lance, typed on CPR stationery that he must have pinched from the company back when he worked for them. He was in the motion picture business now.

"I am going to star in a movie about the Stoney life—the authentic life," he wrote. "Come and write the titles."

Helen folded the single page. She looked out toward the unseen sunny street of human life. In her state of mind it was a shock that he or anyone was kind. But how welcome! Inside the house she shut the door. She confronted the china cabinet once again, more stacks of gleaming saucers and behind them more stacks of cups, each one tipped at a slightly different angle, its rim like a small changing orbit. An entire solar system was on those shelves. She began to hum.

Perhaps this was not an end to her writing career, but a new and thrilling debut in the film world.

Helen had already written for the movies. Parks had been producing its own films for years, the very first government films to be made in Canada. A couple of young men headed up the productions, decent fellows from the supplies department. The first film they made was about the photogenic Rocky Mountains Park—how could it have been otherwise? Needing a writer, they invited Helen to go out with them and title it. It was her second trip west.

Once she got to Gateway it was very simple. The boys went to a waterfall or attended a hayride and took pictures. She tagged along taking notes. Then the boys would splice their pictures together and run them through a projector. Helen might rearrange them to make a narrative. She took the slide of the mountain goat and put it after the slide of the bear snuffling in the raspberries, and took the original sixteenth slide—sunrise on the peaks—and made it first. Then she wrote a story connecting the pictures. In this way she had soon scripted a dozen documentaries.

Her favourite had been the feature on Indian Days. It was the most picturesque event in the park and the only time you saw the native people in their finery. At other times they had to get a pass to leave the Morley reserve. It was Herbie who talked her into recording the festivities. "It'll help us and help the Stoneys," he said. The Stoneys were hungry. They were paid to attend, but once there they had to rustle for themselves. Their food was mostly gophers and the like, said Herbie.

She had gone to Gateway for the filming. She remembered the wonderful smell of the smoke and all these little kids in bare feet. Every night they'd do their dances on the lawn at Hot Springs. At the end the tourists joined them in an Owl Dance. Helen too: "I'm better at this than the tango," she had said to Long Lance. He had been the obvious choice to write the captions. Once he finished them he came to Ottawa on his CPR pass. Together they put the reel in the office projector. The titles showed up on a card, typed in white. She sat down to watch it with him.

ONCE THE STONEYS WERE THE LORDS OF
THE VAST MOUNTAIN COUNTRY.

By that time there was motion picture. The shot opened on a hundred teepees set up by the buffalo paddock. Then came the parade, jerkily approaching the camera, the mile-long ride to the hotel single file, solemn and exotic—men on horseback with high, wide-brimmed hats and braids, wagons full of Indian women and children in checked dresses that fluttered in the wind. Down Main Street into Gateway they came and out the other end, over the bridge and into the forecourt of the Hot Springs Hotel. They all looked like chiefs in those headdresses, but they couldn't have been. They milled about on horseback in front of the cavernous great doors of the baronial hotel. The camera caught a waiter in a dinner jacket with a large circular silver tray balanced on his palm at shoulder level, offering canapés to the riders. One gloved hand reached toward the silver disc. Then the shot cut away.

Suddenly they were on the flat reservation land. Horses tore across the screen creating small explosions of dust, then tore away from the screen in an S-path, and more dust rose. It was beautiful to see. The riders were weightless and boneless and blended into the horses' backs. When one was tossed he ran to catch the horse and leapt on again.

... KEEP ALIVE THEIR OLD TRADITIONS IN RITUAL DANCE AND CHANT ...

The sun was very bright and the feathers and the buckskins of the natives, even their horses, seemed to be bathed in white, reflecting it. When a shawled woman went by on horseback, the horse pulling three poles with a bundle tied between them, the title read:

... THE ANCIENT TRAVOIS AS A PERAMBULATOR ...

"Clever, Lance." Privately, she felt the scene would have been more affecting without that lounge music. "What is the theme music exactly?"

"It's the Gateway dance band. They play every night at the ballroom in the Hot Springs Hotel. There's a drummer, a sax, a banjo. And listen to the trombone! Italian family, very musical."

Then came a couple of depressing clips of Indians in overalls holding pitchforks. One began to pitch hay up into a wagon. Half of it landed; the other half blew away. The men looked sheepish in their farm clothes. Even Helen could see that it was humiliating.

"Who got them to pose that way?"

"We paid them."

The last title read, *At the water hole*. Two Mounties rode up to where two Indians clad in full regalia stood at the edge of a pond, dismounted, and shook hands. They patted the noses of each other's horses.

> THEY CANNOT CONVERSE WITH EACH OTHER, BUT THE CHIEF ADMIRES THE MOUNTIE'S HORSE WHILE THE POLICEMAN RETURNS THE COMPLIMENT BY ADMIRING THE MEDALS ON YELLOW HORSE'S BREAST, GIVEN TO HIM AND HIS CHIEFTAIN FATHER BY THE PAST RULERS OF THE BRITISH EMPIRE.

Altogether it was a strange newsreel. Long Lance knew what he was talking about when it came to the Indians. Mostly. Though he was followed by a cloud of incident. Soon after he made the newsreel he got caught *in flagrante* with the wife of a hotel guest in Gateway and lost his CPR job.

But he was a good friend. The other eventuality had been dealt with back on the trail and had left them with a curious intimacy and no illusions. He hadn't desired her in the first place, she knew that. But she owed him a favour: her dislike of the act had opened her eyes to who she really was.

Truthfully, Helen thought, the cleanup of her mother's house was a bore. She took it on only because her sister was seeing to events at the church. Because it was anathema to her to leave a job unfinished, she went to find a brown paper bag—one that only weeks before had come to the door by way of a grocery store delivery boy, bulging with Mrs. Wagg's bacon, bread and cans of soup, with perhaps a roasting chicken wrapped in pink waxed paper and tied with string.

She held the bag just under the lip of the cupboard with her left hand and slid her right arm to the very back of the deep space, and then pulled it in a wide semicircle toward herself, bringing all the cups and saucers yet to be united with their matching piece to the edge and then over it, into the bag.

She picked up those that had fallen on the carpet—a few were broken, but not enough—and put them inside the bag. Then she folded the two sides of the open top together and rolled the fold over itself three times neatly, placed the bag on the ground at her foot and stamped all over it. Wonderful. Was that not a lucky sound, the sound of crockery breaking? Like a Jewish wedding.

Then Helen went to the telephone and sent Herbie Wishart one of her bristling telegrams.

> *All women under my management dismissed* STOP
> *Have fired self in sympathy* STOP *Arriving Gateway*
> *film job offer* STOP

Later that night her bravado failed. Lying in her childhood bed under a tufted chenille spread, she rewrote the telegram in her head. It should have said: *Out of sympathy with Parks. Chucking it all for a chance to work in moving pictures with Long Lance. Please tell me you think that's a good idea.*

It took a few days, but she got a night letter back. Herbie seemed to have read her subliminal message.

> *Terrible idea* STOP *Do not come here no tourists in town everyone*
> *broke* STOP *Do not hitch wagon to Long Lance* STOP
> *He is trouble* STOP

But she had already packed her trunk and bought her train ticket. She boarded at Union Station in Toronto as soon as her mother was buried.

She found Herbie Wishart in the Three Sisters bar. He was working behind the desk writing figures in a book. As a kind of signal, she carried the hat he'd chosen for her years before. She was no longer the foe in Ottawa, foisting her idea of the park on a subject population. She had changed teams. In her mind, at least. He walked her into the bar and called the bartender.

"Gwen! Can we get Miss Wagg a whisky? My wife," he explained as the petite woman who looked like a schoolmarm slid a filled glass along the bar to Helen.

"I thought she was fragile?"

"Not anymore."

Times changed people.

They sat.

"You quit your job?" he asked.

"I know I'll miss the ride. It's like with mosquitoes—on the trail all you do is swat and complain, but when the trip is over you realize you had a great time."

"You know what's happened now to your Long Lance? He's fallen out with the tribe over his claim of being a chief: apparently it was only honorary."

"He'll survive. He's a part of the place."

"I give you that. He's so fake he's a true Rocky Mountains original, like the souvenirs in the trading post."

The log room was dim. Woodsmoke made her eyes water. She was elated. She felt the stirrings of a free voice inside. Parks had had her loyalty for all those years, and now they—she could not bring herself to say "he" or "Mr. B," but who else could it have been?—had betrayed her. She could say what she wanted. She could do what she wanted. And she had a foot in the door of this motion picture business.

The director, a greying man whose cowboy hat was not a natural fit, was surrounded by a small cloud of nattering young people. Based on the novel *Land of the Western Peaks* by Mrs. Edythe Murcheson, his movie starred Alan Ladd and, opposite him, a brainless blonde whose name

Helen refused to recall. There were a half dozen chiselled young men playing Mounties and settlers, and the same number of Indians, plus a woman whose beauty destined her to be kidnapped. Long Lance, no longer young enough to be one of the braves, was a chief and carried his buckskins elegantly, though when she narrowed her eyes she could still see the dinner jacket and cummerbund and that cigarette held close to his chest. For about three days Helen was at a loss as to what her job *was* exactly, but she was so damned efficient that soon they could not do without her or her clipboard, and they did not even know why.

Authenticity was the aim of this film: it would record the "vanishing" lifestyle of the wild red man before the great eye in the sky blinked and Indians, teepees, horses were gone. The struggle of the people to live without the buffalo, that was the story. The handsome young lovers who married early in the film set out to farm, but the soil did not yield and the rain did not come. There was a store, and white people came through with alcohol . . . It was a weak story, in Helen's opinion. She knew how to improve it but would wait for her moment. Mrs. Edythe Murcheson was arriving on the set any day. Meanwhile they filmed the riverbanks and the unfolding blue hills at dusk and dawn.

But there was a problem. People drew into clusters to speak worriedly. Some issue about Long Lance's contract. Or his passport, she was not sure which. Lawyers were brought up from Calgary. It turned out he had not been born in Canada. But that didn't matter: Indians didn't acknowledge the border. He had been in the Canadian army, had he not? He was decorated, was he not? Did he not go to West Point, if only for a short time? Was he not Blackfoot? Oh, apparently not—but Cherokee?

Helen sat down with him. He could explain. And he did, endlessly—leading to another misunderstanding.

Stoney experts came to talk about the Sun Dance. The Sun Dance was sacred, and secret. Long Lance had written about it, an article that was widely published. The Stoney medicine man was unhappy about that. Long Lance's expertise was called into question. He claimed again he was raised a Blackfoot. But that version of his life story had already been dismissed. It was as if he forgot which one he was telling. Consternation spilled over onto the set, and grim-faced messengers came and went. Then the men with earphones like aviators shouted fruitlessly for Long Lance and eventually found him in his teepee, where he was drinking whisky and had cornered a maiden. Helen crowded into the doorway.

"Chief Buffalo Child, we have serious allegations against you."

Long Lance straightened his clothing and smiled engagingly.

"We've written. We've now got the records from North Carolina. You're not a full-blooded Indian. You're only half an Indian. The other half of you is a black man."

Long Lance unfolded his legs and stood, graceful as a cat. "Gentlemen, I can explain."

But even Helen could see from the doorway that he could not.

"I am not certain what that changes," said Helen blithely over the telephone to Roger, the man in Parks who now had her job—with a higher salary, no doubt. "If most of us were as much as half of what we said we were, I'd be amazed."

"He put himself about as one" came the reply. "He *said* he was a full-blooded Blackfoot. He *claimed* he was a chief. We have used him for park business. I'm not going to review for you the horrors this is bringing down on us. And it's not as if he's just some—regular person. He's a black man!"

"Well, that's not exactly true either. He's only half black. He's mixed-blood."

"And it's not that I mind—"

Yes, you do, Helen thought.

"It's the lying. Now he's got off another, saying he was adopted, that he's really a Cherokee. I can't keep up."

"He does speak some Cherokee."

Her successor growled.

"Just exactly what is it that you would like me to do?" she said.

"Helen, you know what Parks has put into his employment over the years."

"Surely I don't need to remind you that I don't work for Parks anymore."

"But you have our best interests uppermost."

She did not. There was an argument to be made for Long Lance, tainted though he was with his grandiose gestures and his lies. He carried the messages of one closed world into the other closed world. Like a spy, a double agent. She did not share this thought with the office. Why bother?

But as it happened, Mrs. Edythe Murcheson chose that day to arrive. Helen was upset. Edythe recognized a sensitive soul and took her elbow. They went to the Hot Springs Hotel for a drink and sat staring over the valley.

"In fact Parks loved him because he was conveniently worldly, yet he could bring us heroic tales from the teepee. It was actually *because* he was a phony."

Edythe was a regal widow, had been a beauty in her day.

"I knew it too. I knew he was *faux*. I wasn't sure in what way, but I took it on board long ago. I didn't mind. I knew he was full of bullshit."

Helen enjoyed saying *bullshit*! Edythe's eyes flickered with glee.

"He wasn't authentic, but he was genuine. If you see what I mean."

Edythe did see. What a relief. Nobody else would have, except perhaps Mr. B in his better days.

"From his point of view it was much better to be an Indian than a black man. The Indian is noble, and furthermore he's disappearing (apparently) and, hence, no threat."

"Mixed blood is a funny thing," said Edythe. "Where I come from he's not even a half-breed. He's half black. And when it comes to that, there is no half, as you know. If you are any bit black, you are *black*."

"He speaks up for the Indian. Does it really matter if he's one or not? That's my point." Helen sipped her cocktail.

"But the complication is that he spoke up for Indians who, it transpires, don't particularly *want* to be spoken up for, or not by him." Edythe had a quizzical look, a half-smile that seemed to say, *Haven't we met before?* It flustered Helen as much as it made her reveal herself.

"Well, yes, but they need spokesmen."

"Wasn't it they who uncovered his secret?"

"The old Stoney chief wanted to find out where he was born. It's not clear he intended to lose Long Lance for the cause. He just wanted him to come clean."

"I understand. I understand perfectly," said Edythe. "I think he's a fascinating man, and I believe he should be forgiven and people should just stop trying to define everyone." She smiled again in that engaging way, and Helen felt a warm thrill down her throat and into her abdomen, as if she were drinking honey and fire, not gin and tonic.

When she went home she was so buoyed up by her conversation with Edythe that she thought she'd try Roger at the Parks office again.

"The circumstances may be a bit queasy, but he does good work and it's what is needed, and I think you should stand behind him."

"Oh, Helen, you know better than to justify a lie!" Roger said he was surprised that Helen's grasp of the morality of this was so—well, slipshod.

Helen put down the telephone. What a nerve! He was ten years her junior. If she was slipshod, he was a prig. He saw everything in black and white. That's because he was one of the people who was rewarded by life and believed it to be because of his virtue, and not blind luck. He learned the rules, played by them well and felt justifiably superior. She felt a great splash of hate in her heart for the man and vowed never to speak to him again.

But she bled for poor Lance. If he wasn't an Indian chief, he should have been. Why this great intolerance for mixtures of things? He had moved forward finding gaps where he could fit—in the Canadian army, at the western newspaper, at the château in the Rockies, in the world of make-believe in the movies. All very well to pronounce piously that he could have just played himself. It wasn't true. He would not have been welcome, anywhere. Well, anywhere except perhaps Gateway.

"Parks can repudiate him," she said to Edythe, "but the movie will go on, surely. This is show business."

She went to bed in a fury. Let him who is without sin cast the first stone. Or words to that effect. If you see only in black and white, all people are false; all are not what they appear. Which of her own flaws would trip her up? Which would snare a foot as she ran, fleet as time, through the years of the rest of her life? She had not been a particularly good person. She was not a dutiful daughter. She did not volunteer to plant tree sprouts on Arbour Day or go to church except on Easter. She kept her curtains closed. She harboured unusual thoughts. At this moment, with the particular focus of Edythe, they thrilled her.

But in her defence you could say she was false but forced to be so by the dictates of a small-minded society. Was there forgiveness for this? Wasn't it like Long Lance? He chose to be Indian rather than black because his options were limited. All right, he was not a chief of the Blackfoot tribe. That had been overreaching.

Helen Wagg, as she liked to address herself when engaged in self-examination, was half man and half woman and pretended to be all woman. She undersold all that work she did, all the responsibility she took on. She propped up a man who did not function. And why was that? So he could be a screen for her. So she could get in the door. It had been easier to stand behind a man than be one.

She disliked being in Mr. B's shadow, so why had she not stepped out in front? Given him an elbow in the ribs and got on with it? Perhaps it was her mother. No, not really. Who, at the age of fifty, was afraid of her mother? Mr. B was, but never mind him. Why had she not got on with it? Because it was not possible: the world would not have allowed it.

Helen was someone other than who she appeared to be. That had made her, like Long Lance, a person without a refuge. She was not even a half-breed. She was one thing, the thing that lay at the bottom: a woman who loved women. She wondered how it was that no one had seen through her, how her predilections had not announced themselves with her bossiness, her pack of female friends, her lack of a husband, her lack of what they called sex appeal and her hatred of blondes.

Perhaps no one really cared. No one really *minded*, as one ought to say.

She had never liked Lance's lies. But she had allowed them; they were a curtain to be brushed through, a stage effect. His inventions had actually inclined her toward him. He was creative. Parks had needed him. He made them look good.

But here was the rub. The stories he had told of the Indians and the parks, the waterhole, the handshake, the legends on the breakfast menu—they were not true. The real story was hunger and banishment. It had not been told, not by him and not by her. Mr. B, she had felt, saw the wrong of what was done. But he, too, had become entangled in his own myths.

Land of the Western Peaks was too far along to change. Long Lance remained the chief and was charming to everyone. The producer and director were a bit frosty, but the Stoney seemed to prefer him now that he had been outed as a half-breed and a black man. Helen and Edythe invited Lance for a drink at the Hot Springs Hotel. Lance escorted one, then the other, for foxtrots, which was grand because no matter how clear Edythe and Helen were about their feelings, they were not brave enough to dance together.

"I can explain it, I told you," Long Lance whispered in Helen's ear.

"Don't, please." She tried to see a change in him, to spot shame or remorse, but he was like an unbroken line of rollers on a beach—one story came roaring in, and when it tumbled you just had to look up and there came another.

When the film wrapped, Helen Wagg told Herbie she'd be back, and when she was, they'd tell the real story of Gateway.

"That'll be good," said Herbie. "There's a few of them."

Right now, she was going to Hollywood. Edythe had dozens of other novels that could be adapted.

Chapter 35
IONA

Camp 88, Morley Flats, May 1941

It was spring—at last—the end of May. The cornflower-blue sky had blown clear; the sun was shrinking the scallops of icy snow on the riverbanks. Iona walked with her coat open and her hat in hand, cold and careless.

She had nothing to do. Her dad was taking some politicians hunting, pulling out all the stops: his plan was to take them by truck on the logging road to the trailhead and then ride into Ribbon Lake, where they'd camp overnight. He'd hired a bagpiper to play from an island in the middle of the lake.

"What's my job, Dad?" she'd said that morning.

"You're helping Potts deliver to the camp. Down at Kananaskis."

"That's it?" An alternative meaning for the word *camp* had entered the lexicon. It was no longer something you did around a fire; it was a prison. Herbie had work there, but nobody liked it.

"That's it."

"You don't want me going up to Ribbon? I could sing." Not to the bagpipes but with a guitar.

"No." He didn't even bother giving her one of his excuses: long way, weather playing havoc, important men talking. "They fish. It eases their minds."

"Alma's German," Gwen said. Alma was the new cook.

"You're not suggesting she's a spy?"

"No, but they might think so. They might want to lock her up."

"Don't be ridiculous." Herbie defending his bigwigs.

It happened: the Austrian guides were under threat.

"Look what they've done to the Japanese. None of them are spies either."

"Most of them were, I heard."

"Don't you be ridiculous now."

She turned away. Her parents would argue no matter what she did. She hated it, but sometimes it could be turned to her benefit.

"Potts doesn't need me for deliveries," she said. "I might go in to Calgary to sing with Frankie Cassalis and his band."

"We've talked about that. You're not."

"I'd get paid at least."

"She's got a point," said Gwen.

"I would just like to do something useful like everyone else in the world!" Iona shouted and stomped off the veranda.

But instead she found herself in the truck heading down the highway toward Camp 88 with Billy Potts. Everyone knew about the camp, but it was "secret." She supposed the government was ashamed of it. The first winter they had kept all the prisoners in tents by the river, where they nearly froze. A couple of them committed suicide. Now the government had improved the housing so it was little boxes in an ugly grid cut into the forest and surrounded by high fences.

Oh sure, camps appeared every time there was a war, said Pappos from his lunch-counter pulpit. Appeared and then disappeared, the inmates with them. Not pretty, but useful. The prisoners provided free labour, and the camp gave work to the locals. The outfitters were hired to supply meat and potatoes, welcome work as gas was rationed and tourists couldn't come.

She had jumped out of the truck at the wooden guardhouse while Potts waited to be inspected.

"Be back in one hour," he said. "Or I'm a dead man."

She loped down to the river.

The melt was on. Chunks of ice had detached themselves from the pack somewhere upstream. She watched as one sailed merrily with the current. It was shaped like a boat, like a battleship maybe, with a small upper deck that stood out of water. The larger, longer and pointed second deck was submerged and coolly blue. Another chunk twirled past her and out of sight, sinking as it went. In a few seconds another came along, then another. They were regularly spaced; there must be a mathematical rule about how they were released. She watched each one until it was carried out of sight or diminished or sunk. Then she turned to look upstream for another. That was when she saw the boy sitting in the bushes a little upstream from her and up the hill.

At first she thought he was an Indian. Stoney land was next door. She looked away. Then she looked back. He couldn't be. Black hair and amber skin but clumsy as he pushed himself up and stumbled backwards up the hillside, dislodging rocks and breaking branches. Chinese maybe. There were a few in Gateway. How Long now owned the grocery store and had produced an entire family from China. But this was not a boy she knew.

He had been trying to get out of sight, but now he went still. He sat folded up, his hands between his knees and his head down, as if waiting to be slapped on the back of his head.

She saw a boulder a few feet ahead and sat on it. She sat for long minutes. She was the last person to care if he was doing something wrong. Or if he had a job he didn't like and was skipping out. She was the rebel around here. She shook her head: don't hide, it's a free country.

She stared until his eyes turned to hers. She telegraphed: I'm harmless, just a girl sitting above the bank of a river watching the ice chunks drift downstream.

He began to move, putting his hands on the ground on either side of his thighs and pushing himself backwards inch by inch.

"Whatever you're doing it makes no difference to me. I'll just pretend I never saw you."

She scrambled to the edge of the river and started picking up stones. When she was sure he was long gone, she went back up to the camp. Billy Potts was waiting for her.

"Don't tell your dad I let you go for a walk," he said.

Potts dropped her at the hotel. Her mother was behind the bar. Iona sat on a stool in front of her. "I wish I could sing here." She'd been practising with the Cassalis family.

"Iona, you would try the patience of Job. Not with this rough crowd—you will not sing."

"You're a hypocrite. You work here yourself!"

"It's my job, Iona. Thee is too young."

Her *thee* came back now on occasion—when she felt pious, Iona supposed. It had been reborn with Uncle Humphrey.

"Boys I know are in uniform fighting."

"Is that what thee wants?" her mother said. "To be in uniform? To fight a war?" Horrified.

"No, I want to sing. I told you."

Silence. Stern, smug, closed lips. Iona could not stand it.

"You can't keep me here forever. Just because of this war."

"Well, when your dad gets back with his VIPs, why don't you let them know that their battles are upsetting your little world."

There was nothing to do, nothing at all. Iona slapped the counter and stood up; she walked to a window and looked out.

She asked idly, "Mum, who do they have in that prison camp? Do they have any Indians in there?"

"For heaven's sake, I hope not," said Gwen.

"Why would they send Germans all the way here?"

"Because this is far from everything. Too far for them to go back and rejoin the war against us. Or send their spy signals about where to attack."

"It seems kind of stupid."

"I agree with you, Iona," her mother said. It must have been the only time, ever. "Unfortunately we don't make the decisions."

"Mrs. Starchuk is working there."

"I know. So is Mrs. Mattson. The job is a blessing for that family."

In front of the station the girls were playing hopscotch in the long evening light. Mrs. Starchuk was sitting on the front porch in her full winter coat with fingerless gloves, embroidering a towel.

"Tired of running after boys?"

Iona had been known to skip out of the girls' club meetings, where the Finnish women came to share their skills with the needle.

"You remember that?" She stood on the top step.

"Everyone remembers, Iona. Come and sit with me."

Iona took the rocker. She felt awkward because she hadn't come to be friendly. "I saw Angie playing hopscotch," she said.

"She's a one," said her mother. "Wouldn't sit to her needlework either."

"How do you like working at the camp, Mrs. Starchuk?"

"Those poor men. That's my opinion. My thoughts aren't popular in town, but war is not kind to anyone. Last time it was Ukrainians they had up at Castle Mountain. Now we've got Germans. I ask you. We've got German neighbours. Right in town. Lucky they're working in the mine 'cause that's essential. Otherwise they'd be fired." She pulled her thread through her lips and snapped it on her eye tooth. "If you want a job there, I'll ask for you."

"I don't. But I could make a show to entertain them. If Dad would let me."

Mrs. Starchuk said nothing for a few minutes. Then, "He won't."

"Mrs. Starchuk, are there Japs in the camp?"

She continued to gaze unperturbedly at her embroidery. "Not real ones. Not from Japan. No. But there are some from Vancouver."

"What are they doing there?"

"People say they resisted."

"Resisted what?"

"You know, when they were rounded up. We were told that people went quietly. But these ones didn't."

Iona willed her to say more.

"We only came to this county ourselves twenty years ago, so I wouldn't want to criticize, but—"

More stitching.

"I never heard about that," said Iona.

"There's a lot you never hear about. Never hear about it and all of a sudden there's men in chains building a golf course." She snapped her embroidery hoops apart and held her work up to the street light. "Getting too dark."

"Did they fight?"

"I don't know what they did. All I know is there's a few of them in Camp 88. No more than boys." She reached for her little scissors and cut the bright yellow strand close to the eye of her needle.

One week later Iona was back in the cab of the truck with a displeased Billy Potts. "Signed on for trail rides, not prisons," he said, jerking the gearshift hard to the left. The gears snarled.

"It's a car. You can't just pull on the reins," said Iona. She was a good driver, not that anyone ever let her drive.

The sun was in their eyes that morning: he fixed a grimace on the road ahead. She pulled down the visor.

"You need a hat with a brow."

"Doesn't work with my hair."

"You dressing up for somebody?"

"Just looking my best for the war effort!"

He grunted. "Itching to get out of here, aren't you? Wonder how long your dad's going to be able to keep you home," he said.

"That's another war," said Iona. "Him against me. One of us has got to win."

Potts laughed soundlessly, shaking his shoulders. "If I were a betting man I'd lay my odds on you."

They turned onto the River Road; it was rutted and muddy. There were men standing along it. The camp was on the left.

"What are they doing?"

"Got them building a lake now, don't they?"

The men fanned out across the flat places. Some had shovels and picks. Others were loading stones in wagons. They smiled and waved at the truck. There were two observation towers, just one storey higher than the barracks-style homes.

Billy parked in front of the camp entrance. "You stay in the truck."

"How can I help if I stay in here?"

"My instructions."

It was hot. She put her feet up on the dash. The camp was pretty well deserted. Then she saw the Japanese boy. He had on an apron and was crossing to the washhouse—or maybe it was cookhouse—up a little hill.

She looked out the back of the cab. Billy had gone somewhere. The atmosphere was easy. The place didn't feel like a prison camp. She got out, shaking her hair.

"Hey," she shouted.

She could see the boy was no older than she was, and maybe younger. "Did you bring potatoes?" he said in perfect English.

"Are you from Vancouver?"

"Powell River. Up the coast."

"I saw you sitting on the riverbank last week."

He looked at the ground in the gesture she already recognized.

"They let you out?"

"I work in the kitchen. I have two free hours in the afternoon." His eyes took in the barrier of mountains, the wide flat corridor where the highway was. "Where would I go?"

They said in town that if a prisoner got away, all the guards had to do was set a guy by Whiteman's Gap and wait three days—he'd come staggering out. There was no other way.

She could see Billy going into the office. He couldn't tell she was talking to the boy because they were standing far apart. She turned sideways and put her hand over her brow, looking up the mountain. The men were cutting trees to make a road up there.

"I'm going down to that river," she said.

She walked on the sandy, stony bank. The water cut under the roots of the great fir trees until they leaned over toward the stream, farther and farther. A tree might stand at an excruciating angle, like a semaphore arm, for years. Then one day it would fall and lie on the water, or across a nearby bank, making a bridge to a small island.

That's what this one had done. Black and spiked, it lay like a drawbridge across the shallow flow. Its tip touched a sandbar in the wide eddy of the main stream. She wanted to get there. She crouched on top of the downed trunk and tried to walk, holding one branch after another. She got halfway to the island, but the spikes were closer together there and more fierce. Below her the water ran cold and high, freed of ice. She edged down so that she was sitting, one leg on either side of the tree.

She heard a soft whistle from the shore.

He was there, standing in the trees, not hiding this time.

She was embarrassed. She couldn't go forward, and she didn't want to turn around.

"What are you doing?"

"Going to the sandbar."

"You might fall in."

"I won't fall in. I live here," she said. It was a stupid thing to say.

"Want help?"

"No, of course not."

"Then come back in."

She didn't hurry about it. But she got back up onto her feet, squatting, and worked her way around half a circle so that she was facing back to the bank. She held on to a branch in each hand. Squatting, she swung one foot forward and then the other. Not ladylike. Tarzan-like.

He stood at the shattered base of the downed tree holding out a hand. But she didn't take it. She jumped off the log onto the bank.

"I have to go meet Billy."

"Who's he?"

"He works for my dad."

"Your dad works for the prison?"

"No, he's an outfitter. Hunting guide. This isn't normal."

The boy settled down on the bank. "They give me a fishing rod so I can catch fish for the officers. I am just watching now to see where the fish stay."

She dusted the bark and black moss off her trousers. "I might see you again here."

"I hear they're going to send us away. To the Slocan Valley. Where the others are." He meant others like him. "More Germans are coming."

She'd lived in this valley forever and now the world was funnelling in. "Well, good luck," she said. "I hope they let you out soon."

"Yeah," he said.

His face was closed, beautiful and strange. She felt a stirring. There was nothing forward about him. The words that came out of his mouth were few and sincere. She edged her way to the path and then looked back. A flicker in his eyes acknowledged her, but his lips were closed.

"Ruining the world as we know it" was what Gwen said about the Germans. The Poles were no better in her mind, nor the Italians. Still, she didn't want to see them incarcerated. The Finns were about the only ones she still had time for. And the French Canadians, because they didn't want to fight.

"They're not pacifists, Gwen," Herbie said. "They just don't want to be in Europe's battles."

"Perfectly sensible," said Gwen. "Everyone else has gone mad."

The usually convivial drinkers in the bar were now likely to get to their feet and promise to break each other's heads. The only way she could stop it was to get the band to play "God Save the King."

"Wars are like that," said her father, his pipe hissing and his feet white and ribbed where he'd taken off a pair of wet wool socks.

He'd been in the backcountry for a week. Hiding out, her mother called it. What did he know about wars? What did she? She had some idea, she said; she'd lived in Washington through the first one.

"No getting away from it," he said. "Handy to have those big rams to stand in for the enemy when you're too old or too rich or too important to fight."

Iona seethed at everything her father said. He was in her way. He was stopping her from living. All he gave were prohibitions. *You will not marry a miner. Or a cowboy. You will not go out on pack trips. Or sing in public.* What did he think she should do, anyway?

At least she got to sing in private with the Cassalis family. She loved to wander over there at night and pitch her voice to theirs. They swayed while they sang and sometimes danced too. Strange that Gwen had forsworn it, because she's the one who had taught Iona to love dancing. Did her mother think that the more pleasures she denied herself the greater chance she had of finding her other blessed relatives alive?

Humphrey's return—if it was Humphrey; sometimes she wondered—didn't settle her mother down. The cowboy was added to their life, but he didn't replace the lost Humphrey, really, not the brother for whom Gwen had got used to pining. Now she ran the bar and preached to the rest of them. Iona wondered if her mother remembered her glamorous dreams. Perhaps she had transferred those proscribed dreams—the satin dresses and peridot pendant, the foxtrot and rumba, even the singing lessons—to her daughter, the better to batter away at them.

"Iona, lass, what will we do with you?" said Herbie, cheerfully oblivious to her rage.

"It's music she wants." For once Gwen stood up for her.

"That's not practical."

"Were you practical when you came out on the train a wild nineteen-year-old?" said Gwen to her husband.

Grunt. "She can play the piano at the Legion."

"There's more drunks at the Legion than in all of Calgary, if you ask me." There was silence for a few minutes, and then they seemed to change sides.

"Now she says she's got a ride up to the Hot Springs Hotel on Saturday night. The Cassalis boys are playing," Gwen complained.

"Nothing wrong with that," said Herbie.

"She hasn't got a proper dress."

"Now who's giving her airs?"

At the Cassalises' everybody sang. "We sing through our troubles," they said. Frank Senior had come across Canada on the train from someplace in Italy with a name tag around his neck and went down in the mines at fourteen. He got into the miners' band though he never had a music lesson. Played the saxophone like an angel.

All five kids were the same. They never had lessons, but Tommy could pick up a violin and play by ear. Frankie Junior and Marcello had trumpets they'd played in the school orchestra. Renalda had a nice alto voice, but she was married now and didn't go out at night. That was what made room for Iona. They saved enough to buy a standup bass, and Luca was good on it. They were sheepish, mocking themselves when they played. Their mother called the music "that racket" and sent them out to the front porch.

She could hear the thrumming at night in the deep stillness of the valley. She'd go to the bridge and cross over to Mineside, where people had bigger gardens and cows and pigs were loose. The dogs yapped as she walked toward the saxophone's wail. She took her cue from the boys and stood quiet before letting her voice climb the scales with them and drop between. She kept her eyes on the shadowy face of Frankie Junior, and now and then he'd give an appreciative nod. No one asked her to come or said they might meet again. When it got too cold one of them would say, "My fingers are stiff. Maybe that's it for tonight?"

Iona would shift her feet and pick up her shawl.

"Walk you home?" Frankie would say to Iona.

"No. It's okay," she'd say.

But he did anyway. He was a lot older, Frankie. Older than any brother could have been. But younger than her father. More like an uncle. Which is what she called him. He wore a white shirt and a white scarf over his jacket; you could see it in the darkness. No one wore white around here.

They would go silently past the front yards: the Finns had a sauna, the Matsons cows. That family had a pet elk they'd raised since it was a colt, and a living room lined with grizzly pelts. There was a woman at a well. Frankie had a cigarette in his right hand, and the red ember on the tip of it waved back and forth at his side like a nib with something to write.

"I like your voice," he said once as he dropped her off.

They must've been practising for a year when Frankie dropped by the house to give her a message. She went to Mineside that night. They were playing inside the house, which signalled a promotion. The band had work. Could she join them? She would have to talk her dad into it, but she said she was sure she could. The point about playing at the Hot Springs Hotel was that there was a chain of those big railway hotels all across the country. If they could get on there, maybe the band could hop along the string of hotels, eastward to where all of life was.

Chapter 36
JUN

Calgary, July 1941

I KNOW YOU, SHE SAID, looking into the eyes of the bellhop at the Palliser Hotel. He wore a blue uniform and a pillbox hat with a wide chinstrap. He was lean and a little taller than she was. He bent from the hips to pick up her case. His ears, pushed out by the tight white band of the hat, were red. He walked away ahead.

She paused in the lobby and looked through the bar to the dining room. It was grand with elaborate plaster flowers over the doorways and a high ceiling. She took off her hat and shook out her hair, conscious that it was chestnut, that it shone, that the curls she had put in overnight bounced. She looked all through the bar and the lobby, scanning, as if for someone she knew: there was nobody; she was miles and miles—seventy-five, to be precise—away from home.

The bar was full of men. Ranchers in their Stetsons, soldiers from Currie Barracks, salesmen and travellers too old to be in uniform. A scattering of women stood in the foyer in high heels and tight little jackets with skirts that fluted around their knees. It was a clean, bright crowd, and for a minute her confidence collapsed. They looked prosperous. The women intimidated her. But she hadn't met the man she couldn't please. She turned back to the bellhop, who had called the elevator and was standing at its open door. She looked at him again and knew who he was and why he had not spoken.

The elevator doors—brass, gleaming—churned to be off. She removed her coat, folding it carefully over her arm. She signalled that she would wait for the next one. She looked back across the lobby to the doorway, where sunlight fired the revolving doors. The bellhop looked resolutely at his feet.

When they were alone inside she said, "Five." Then she added, flatly—a statement, not a question: "You're the boy from the camp."

Boy seemed right because she felt older. But she regretted the word *camp*, which left a cold feeling.

"You disappeared. That's what they said. You were going to be sent to southern Alberta."

He looked at the row of numbers spread in an arc over the door. The pointing hand moved from *1* to *2* to *3*.

"It's okay, you don't need to answer. And I won't tell. I don't have anyone to tell in the first place. Anyway it's legal to work as a bellhop at the Palliser. Isn't it?"

She stepped off. He lifted out her suitcase.

"I'm singing here tonight. If you get a chance, put your head into the ballroom and have a listen. My uncle's band. He just got the booking, and they don't have a singer. That's the only reason I got to come," she confided in a rush.

He let the elevator door shut. She walked silently in the long carpeted hall with shut doors on each side, no sign of life.

She stood in a yellow pool of light. She bent her head and tossed her hair. Before she sang she let her eyes alight warmly on face after face, people sitting at the tables—men mostly, some cowboys, but men in suits, women with hair swept up, men and women with their heads together. This was elegant. The smell of alcohol was sweeter than in Gateway. She liked the smell, but she rarely had a drink. The laughter was silky. She was warm, very warm in the lights. She was excited, and a little warble came into her voice at the end of a phrase.

The Cassalises were all inward smiles and nods, counting on each other without looking, only occasionally sending a half-lidded look her way. Frankie announced the songs, and she sang them. Between times she turned her back and licked her lips and ran her fingers up beside her temples, feeling their dampness.

At the end of the first set she thought she saw the blue uniform of the bellhop at the entrance to the bar. She wondered if he could hear her from the lobby. Suddenly the evening was over and they were pushing her to get her coat.

"We all have to work at seven." Frankie would be in the office; the others would be taking the mantrip down into the mine.

"I don't. I'm going to stay overnight in the hotel room."

"I promised your father to take you home."

"What's the point in my going home? To drive all that way and then turn around and come back?"

She moved back and away from the doors so he had to move in or speak more loudly. He wouldn't because he didn't want people looking at them.

"Bye, Uncle Frank. I'll be waiting for you when you get here tomorrow." Iona thought, What can he do? What can my parents do? I'm not asking anymore. I'm telling. They can't stop me. I'm just going to do what I want. They'll give up. That's what they'll do.

"What will you do all day?"

"Maybe look for a job. Maybe sign up."

Tommy came to the door and waved. The truck was there.

"I can't leave a young woman alone in the city."

"Come on, it's the war; everything's different, don't you know?"

Uncle Frank. He gave her one last look: he was worried, quizzical, sympathetic, but hands off, not taking a side. He knew her parents and their cautions, but he didn't control her. This had to come. He knew that the singing had started it. He felt it while she was with the band, nudging, nudging herself into the unknown. He said he hoped for only small damages, and said good night with resignation.

She'd taken a few drinks then, which she was not supposed to do. The Japanese fellow was standing in the foyer.

She waited until everyone else had left the bar. Then she went out to the foyer.

"How did you get out of there?" She tugged at the elbow of his uniform. "Did they let you go?"

"Don't!"

"I guess they finally realized you weren't a spy?" But she doubted they would realize anything that sensible. She shouldn't have said it; maybe she was drunk. She went to the elevator.

Up in the hotel room the snare drums took up the space between the bed and the bathroom. But there were white tiles and thick wooden windowsills and heavy pleated curtains with a rod to pull them by. She could hardly get around the standup bass to get to the cupboard. She thought seriously of calling a bellhop to help, but then she might get *him*, and if she didn't she'd have to tip and she didn't know how much.

She hung her dress in the closet. She turned down the bed, shifting men's jackets and cases of sheet music to the other side of it. The sheets felt smooth and cool as water. What did they do to sheets at the hotel to make them this smooth? They didn't dry them on the clothesline, that was for sure. She lay on her back, hardly moving. It was her first night away from home. She was jubilant. Sleep came and went, chased away by the dazzling spotlight, the narrow eyes of the pianist, the strange agitation.

She'd never belonged in that place in the river valley, where the mountains marched on either side higher and colder, blacker in summer, whiter in winter, than anywhere on earth. She was away from it now. She feasted on small parts of the evening—that instant in the elevator when she recognized the boy from the camp. His profile under the white pillbox with the chinstrap. Long eyelashes, wide bones, eyes almost black and tight-lidded. A Japanese fisher-boy is what he was.

The next day she found him idle near the front doors after breakfast. He was on his break. "Will you tell me now how you got away?" she said.

They went out into the street together.

The pacifists were the lepers of the camp, they and the Japanese Canadians, who were anything but pacifists, having been arrested out of their martial arts group in Ocean Falls. But those were the men with whom Jun made friends. One was a slim and pale boy named Oscar, from a religious community in the south of the province. The two played many silent, vicious games of ping-pong, which Jun won. It kept his reflexes sharp, which was good because he could not practise his karate. He hoped that Oscar's general helplessness would lead people to assume Jun was helpless too.

The two were assigned to the kitchen.

The camp was curiously relaxed. There were guards in the wooden towers, which were not towers but raised boxes about fifteen feet above the ground, and there was not much to look out for except coyotes in the bush. Prisoners climbed Mount Baldy for sport. The knives were sharp. The doors were unlocked. Oscar washed potatoes; Jun peeled and chopped. It was better than cutting down trees. They were kids, and the officers were planning to move them on. The other Japanese had already been sent to another camp in the interior.

The cook thought Jun was from the tropics. He didn't know that Japan was full of mountains and that the snow was deep on the western side. Jun's English was good, and the camp made it better. He learned words like *borscht* and *stew*.

When the ice broke on the river Jun said he could catch fish. He watched the water move for two days, and on the third he came back with half a dozen small bass, which the officers ate. After that, they sent him out several days a week to supplement the diet. While he watched the water find its way around the rocks he lost his anger, which was a good thing. Then he could think straight.

Every week he saw the Chinese laundry truck come from Calgary. The men unloaded crates of clean uniforms and bed linen, and carried off barrels of dirty stuff. The prisoners washed their own clothes and hung them on a clothesline, where they turned stiff as boards. But the guards and officers had the laundry service. Jun began to time his visits to the wash shed with the arrival of the truck—always Tuesday. He came forward to help the camp clerk roll out the barrels. When they got to the truck, he helped the men lift them.

He did this a few weeks in a row without being asked, and the truck drivers started to think it was his job. He held back the next week, standing in the shade of the shed. He noticed that the clerk looked around for him. He was expecting the help. Good. Out Jun came. Now it was established that this was part of his job.

"Some of these are really heavy," he said to the men from the laundry.

"People stuff them too full."

"I'll even them up."

Every Tuesday he went into the shed before the truck was to come and redistributed the soiled linens in the barrels to make them all a manageable weight.

The Chinese were ambivalent about him, he could see. On the one hand they hated the Japanese. Most people did. On the other hand they were Asians too.

"Thanks, boy" was his reward one day.

And the next week: "Why you in here?"

"Resisting arrest. My *sensei* said we should fight the arrests."

"Your *sen-see*?" The men laughed.

"Teacher."

"You like Japan?"

"I like Canada. Been here since I'm a baby. My country."

The Chinese grunted. "We just come. No papers."

After Jun helped load the barrels he got them to play a few games of ping-pong.

"Today you win?"

"No, today I win!"

The younger Chinese guy was pretty good. When they finished they shook hands. Then Jun walked back around the front to see if there was any more loading to do.

Then one week he didn't appear.

"Where's that Jap boy? Gotta move out those barrels."

Oscar was there. "He went fishing."

"Doesn't he know it's Tuesday?"

"Cook wants fish because officials coming to dinner."

"You better help, then."

Oscar went into the shed and, with the clerk, put his shoulders down to the first barrel to tip it on one edge and roll it.

"Heavy."

"Too full! Those morons always overfill. Jesus H. Christ."

They rolled it on one edge to the truck. The Chinese helped them lift it. Three men. One barrel, up on the back of the truck. Then six more barrels. Those ones weren't so heavy.

In Calgary the men stopped the truck behind the back of the laundry and stood by the door talking. Jun couldn't understand them, but from what happened after, he figured that one of them said, "I'm hungry." And the other one said, "We need to unload that so the girls can start washing." Then the first one said, "Eat first, then unload," and he was more convincing, so the other one agreed.

They walked away. Jun heard their feet on gravel. He waited a few seconds and was about to start rocking the barrel when he heard the footsteps coming back. The young one had left his hat on the seat. He put his head inside the door just as the barrel tumbled.

Jun was halfway out, his hands and one foot on the ground, the other foot caught up in the sheets. He contorted his face, begging the boy—it was his ping-pong opponent—to be quiet. The boy's face was knotted with anger. He watched Jun disentangle his foot, but he did not call the alarm.

"No good you do this to me. They'll blame me. I need job!"

"Are you going to turn me in?"

"You lucky old man gone."

"Because I can turn you in too. You have no papers."

"Maybe soldiers come looking?"

But Jun told him the soldiers would not come looking. He'd taken care of it. They thought he'd gone west on the highway. Oscar would swear to it. Then Jun ran down the alley. But not before asking where the Japanese people were.

"Stockyard," said the Chinese, pointing.

Jun found the Japanese. In this province they didn't have to go into a camp; all they had to do was sign into the office. He found a family whose one son had gone back to Nippon before the war and not returned. He went to the office with them and signed in his place.

In the little cluster of Japanese families there were some fellows who worked for Massey Harris. Another guy was a gravedigger. Jun tried that but hated it. Then he got a job at the Palliser.

"Lucky," said Jun.

"Lucky," agreed Iona, and they parted, he going back to work as his break was over, and Iona heading down Ninth Avenue on foot.

Iona found a respectable boarding house where she could pay her way by cooking—until five o'clock on days when she sang with the band, when she ran out the door and down three blocks to the hotel. And on Sundays she went back to Gateway. It was a solution, for a while. The Japanese boy named Jun had disappeared. She asked the other bellhops. He'd been let go.

When she finished the breakfast dishes at the boarding house she went down along the tracks and found Third Avenue. There was a corner store that sold bread. She walked in and asked if any Japanese people lived around there.

"Any's who did is long gone," said the short woman behind the cash. "Can't say I miss 'em either." She looked at Iona balefully.

"No, ma'am," said Iona. "I am sure you don't." Her mother's barkeeper's way with strangers—the art of pretending to agree and keeping your thoughts to yourself—was useful. "Guess there's still some around, though," she said. "I myself can't tell a Chinese from a Jap from an Indian even."

"Oh, the Chinese and the Japs they just fighting all the time, that's how you know. They hate each other."

"Do they?"

"Indians don't come around here much; they stay out in Montgomery by the river."

She liked Third Avenue. The tracks, the roughly dressed and surly customers in the hotel bar she passed—it was an adventure to be searching for Jun among them. A thrill, maybe; a disobedient act, certainly; and a way to be herself, not the young woman her parents thought they had raised.

Puzzled, and a little bit sorry, Iona returned to work. She went on singing in her white satin until one night she saw Jun, dressed in normal clothes—rather poor clothes, they looked to be—in the splendour of the Palliser, talking to the other bellhops.

"How come you're here?"

"There's no law against it."

His face had changed; now it was hurt and defiant.

"They like me here. They just can't hire me, that's all, because people complain. The boss even asks me out for a beer."

The band was starting a new set, so she went back, stepping into her spotlight, Cinderella to her carriage. She looked toward the door and saw him turn and go. She drank one glass of gin. Then she held the microphone in front of her throat and the voice poured out. Her dress shifted around her hips. She loved nothing more than this.

Part Four

Chapter 37
HELEN'S FILM

Hollywood and Gateway, Summer 1958

It all started when Mr. B wrote to Helen. She and Edythe were living comfortably, if carefully, in the Hollywood Hills. They didn't have much work. But they had a house with a swimming pool they could use all year round. *Land of the Western Peaks* had flopped at the box office, despite Long Lance's moody charisma. There was film interest in the Rockies, but Helen and Edythe could not get in on it. The studios wanted male directors, stories about men; it was very discouraging.

When the letter arrived Helen took it out to her lounge and flopped down beside Edythe. "Mr. B," she said, waving it. Their friendship was restored. Because in the end he, too, was pushed out. He was writing a book, he said. In it he would wax mystical about the parks system in Canada. People said they just followed the Americans, but that wasn't true. They had Yellowstone, but Canada was the first to have a whole parks system. Mr. B had often been invited to Washington to talk about it. Now he was going to get the whole story on paper.

Helen wrote him back, an encouraging letter: You do that! It needs to be told.

After that, his missives came thick and fast. Helen read them seated poolside.

His thesis was "Parks: Genesis and Destruction." Concerning their beginnings, he was modest. He said the time had come, and he was merely the instrument. But now he had become disillusioned. The people in charge were devoid of inspiration. That was his point. He said there was no hope in Canada for "our aims" and that the country's greatest resource would be squandered. People were becoming overcivilized. "All the good people, all the *believers* in good, are gone. The people in power worship the tourist dollar and kneel at the foot of development," Mr. B charged. "But it's the wrong kind of development. We knew all about development. We were developing upstanding citizens." He wanted every Canadian to devote time to his senses, to what came in through ear, eye, nose and fingertips.

"It sounds as if it will be wonderful," Helen wrote back. She could feel him trying to draw her into the project, and resisted.

It was true that writing never came easily to him. She used to say she was no more than a Girl Friday. She got over that. Then she said she was an administrator. But that wasn't true either. In fact she was the writer. She wrote the guidebooks. She wrote the speeches. She wrote the reports. She had to. As she explained to Edythe, seated in the matching and adjacent lounge chair, there was a domestic situation. Mr. B had been married. Had the wife died? She wasn't sure. Now he supported his mother. He adored his mother, of course. He was like a man trapped in amber. He was that attached.

"In today's parlance you'd call it a *complex*," said Helen.

But she wasn't going to write his book, and somehow, without her, it seemed the project was jinxed. He made half a dozen starts and threw out the drafts. Then at last he got going on one that pleased him. Shortly after, there came a setback. He had finished nine chapters and was on the tenth when the manuscript disappeared. Apparently a servant got it mixed up with some old papers. Or perhaps it fell off the desk and got into the wastebasket, he said.

"I don't buy it," said Edythe.

He was discouraged, but he did start again. And then that manuscript, too, mysteriously disappeared. It also was thrown in the garbage.

"Okay, that beggars disbelief. I am sorry."

Helen could see it was sabotage. Someone had a hand in it. The wife, if living. No, the adored mother. Poor man! Of course her friendship with Mr. B was through business and was always carried out with complete discretion, she told Edythe, but she felt for him. She wrote again.

And he replied, confiding in a circumspect way. "Lately conditions have not been favourable to my making any progress, though I jolt and spurt with ideas. Remember long ago I warned you. The task of completing is yours."

"Yep," said Edythe. "You've flushed him out in the open. Wants you to do it."

She did not reply to that letter.

Then she heard, through an Ottawa friend, a woman from her bridge club, that he was ill. She wrote, but the letter came back.

It must have crossed with his last note.

He was sending his personal papers to her. By the time they arrived, he was gone.

It was sad for Helen. Like receiving an urn of ashes. A box of scrap paper, just something from a wastebasket, worse than Carlyle's famous ragbag in *Sartor Resartus*. When she read the obituary in the newspaper she noticed the upcoming book was mentioned.

The task was hers. And she did try. If she had not been so used to framing up sentences from whatever came out of his mouth she wouldn't have been able to make head nor tail of the notes. But here was the gist: too much of the conception of Parks, and of the execution as well, had been about money. They had struck a great deal for the country at first. It seemed a miracle. The investment was small compared to the enormous profit. That was perhaps, he said in hindsight, and she agreed, where a mistake was made. This idea of likening the parks to a kind of stock market venture. Because it stuck. And it wasn't their true motive. It was only a way of explaining to others who didn't have the conviction, a way of putting it in language the non-believers could understand.

Because this was Canada, they had to use the economic argument. Sir John A. himself had to use it to invent the country in the first place. He always got the credit for Parks too, which was ridiculous. He was fond of saying that the parks might recuperate Canadians wearied by urban life, but his real hope was that they would also recuperate the treasuries. Well, the treasuries would have to get along by themselves now. The wilderness had gone from making money to costing money.

But after that, the notes become incoherent. Helen was not a religious person. Nor was Mr. B, at least not in a traditional way. But he had been in touch with the Creator. A spirit, the Great White Bear, that Snowshoe Walker they sometimes spoke about, call it what you wish—he had been in touch.

"How," said Helen to Edythe, "am I going to make a book out of that?"

Edythe got up and dabbled her toe in the chemically blue water. "I don't think you can. The book is doomed. It died with him."

"Yes, it did," said Helen. "The real task to complete is my own work. I just have to decide what that is."

It felt momentous to say that. She got up and poured them both a gin. When she came back she was thoughtful.

"You know what it is. You always did. It's the other side of the story."

"You mean my film about Gateway and the Rocky Mountains Park and the Indians and the outfitters and the tourists?"

"*What*, exactly, about them? That's not a film. That's a dissertation."

Helen went to the poolside and flicked water on her friend's face. "Such a wet blanket, you are."

"I'm serious. Take one storyline, not twelve."

"All right, the biggest story to ever come out of there was the disappearance of the Hodgson expedition."

"Then that's your story. Go out and get it."

"Don't you think I'm a little past it?"

"You're fresh as a daisy, Helen."

It was June when they turned up in Gateway. Officially they were checking out locations. They were also considering actors. Helen's idea was Herbie, playing himself. They brought a camera and told him they were doing research. Helen said she was going to tell the real story of the Rocky Mountains Park.

"Take one," said the voice off-camera. "Herbie Wishart. The Outfitter."

"Ah, Helen, no."

They were old friends now, and they were old too. Old old, by ordinary count. Though Herbie dodged and weaved as he always did.

"Come on, Herbie, you're famous and you promised."

"Promised, did I? Only one time I thought maybe I was famous and that was the day a stranger walked in here, came up to the bar and said, 'Do you know where I can find the outfitter Herbie Wishart?' It was a rare day when I was in town.

"'How the devil did you hear of that reprobate?' I said.

"'I've heard his name mentioned in high places. Over the years. Savoy Hotel. In London, England,' said the stranger."

Out came the falsetto laugh.

"Oh, sure! The fellow was like you, Helen—he had a goddamn microphone. I put him off. 'Now Sam Gallant,' I said, 'he goes back further. *He* knows where the bodies are buried.'"

"Wait a minute," said Helen. "Bodies are buried?"

"Figure of speech! Figure of speech! Jesus, woman. Do you want to hear this or not?"

"Sorry, Herbie. Go on. Tell your story."

"Well, the fellow wasn't having any of it. 'Truth to tell, it was the Marquis of Exeter mentioned your name, Mr. Wishart.' Oh my. The Marquis of Exeter. I can tell you in confidence, I used to poach his estate. Before I left England. But that was, hell, nearly sixty years ago. Fancy him remembering. Or his heir, must have been—maybe a grandchild, even. Trying to track me down. I refused him, Helen. Just like I'm going to refuse you." He pulled a pipe out of his vest pocket and some tobacco out of the pouch in his trouser pocket and began to pack the bowl. Once it was lit, he seemed to reconsider.

"Maybe I made a name for myself. Maybe. Folks come looking. That I won't deny. But it's all for the wrong reasons."

"Who comes looking?"

"There was the American ambassador . . . or was it the CIA? I told them they had the wrong man. Gallant's the one. He was the guy showed Major Rogers the way through the mountains for the railroad. Sure he did. He always said Rogers made it by killing the trees on either side of him by spitting out tobacco. I was a latecomer."

"You can't fob me off on Sam Gallant. What are the wrong reasons, Herbie?"

He wasn't stopping for questions.

"You don't want to know what happened to him? You do. Sam walked Main Street for many a year; the railway hired him as a tourist attraction. Local colour. He finally went into delirium tremens and was taken to hospital. Where he died. So you're out of luck there. But I tell you, in the early days strange things happened. You heard of the gold rush? Well, sure. That's what it was like here. But there wasn't any gold. Just hot water."

And he clamped his teeth firmly down on his pipe.

"CUT! CUT!"

"He's perfect, Helen," pealed a voice.

"Edythe, I know! Don't give him a swollen head."

The light on the camera went out. A couple of chairs fell over, and there was the sound of cursing. Helen in her element.

"Bring that camera in, bring it in on his face. Skip the bottle and the glasses, we just want the old man. Sorry, Herbie. How old are you? Seventy-eight, that's what I said. Not much older than me. When the red light goes on I want you to tell us about the hot water."

"Don't patronize me, Helen."

"You promised. Remember, you're talking to that." She pointed at the camera. "About the hot water."

The light came on.

"The Stoneys already knew about the hot springs before the white man came. Oh sure! They would go there in winter with their old and their sick for healing. Immerse them in the steaming waters, and the old would come out without pain, and the sick would come back from the edge of death. There's those who say that even a big old grizzly used to bathe there, ease his bones.

"And so it went for a long time until this railroad business. Couple of squatters it was who noticed the steam coming out. Found the trail and clambered to the edge. It was a sinkhole, brimmed all inside with fallen timbers, hazardous and vile smelling. Boiling, it was, with a green algae carpet all around and rimming that a giant fern forest of horsetail. Oh yeah! And around it grew orchids. And in it were salamanders and tropical fish. I tell you the straight truth. But to these squatters it was just green. Green like money.

"Mind you, everyone was a squatter then. You had to be. You built your shack. Then you filed your claim. You couldn't buy the land if you tried. So these blokes and the railroad and even the government wanted to make money from the springs whether they were sacred or not. Probably they were, and that's why it backfired. But anyway, they all got into a fight about who owned it. Of course the government was the government, and so it won. They turned the whole place into a natural park."

"CUT!"

"*National* park."

Herbie Wishart opened his palms, shrugged. "I'm telling you what I know."

"You're giving me another of your tall tales," said Helen. "But that's okay." She put up her right hand and stepped back. "Okay, okay."

"Those days the Indians were still hunting up in here. Oh yeah! They used to go early in spring up to the gulleys to look for stray buffalo. But by the time I'm talking about, the buffalo were already gone. Missionaries were here. Living with the Indians like little gods. They thought Christianity would help those wild people adjust to their new lives. And it did not. But the famous ones got mountains named after them. Right out here, there's Rundle, isn't it? And a fine man he was. Did not understand the red man, but nor did any of them. The Indians themselves were hungry because the land the government gave them was good for nothing.

"Like I said, the Indians trapped in the high plains. The white men followed through that gap right up there." He gestured out the window, and his eyes followed, lingered. They were eyes with a lifetime of skyline-searching behind them; baby blue, sharp as vinegar, and though weary now, they still set the crumpled, beaked face ablaze.

"I used to come upon their traps, when I was out checking mine. I used to camp next to 'em; they knew all the best ways. All the explorers did the same. They only went to places the Indians already knew about. Then they discovered them."

He laughed and mopped his brow with a clean white handkerchief.

"One old Stoney said there was a mammoth up there, beyond the Summits. Mastodon of some sort. Well, I suppose there was at one time. White men tried to convince them to show them the way up, but that particular secret the Indians weren't giving away. We call it the Inaccessible. You can't get in with horses, you can't get in on foot. Oh, Erwin said he got in somehow, but he's long dead. Tell you the truth, I kinda believed there was somethin' up there too. A creature."

Herbie got out his handkerchief and wiped his brow again.

"Damn hot, Helen. Don't know why I said I'd do this. If you don't mind my saying, you're a bit long in the tooth to be making movies—"

"I've waited all my life to do this."

"That's what I mean."

"Don't you want to get your side of the story out there?"

With that she'd said too much.

"My *side*?" He eyed her, suspicious.

"Your version?" she amended. "Of the story of the place, you know."

"So it's you too, is it, Helen? Trying to get the truth out of the rascal who misplaced the scientists? The damn fool guide whose party went missing fifty years ago? You too, Helen?"

And he clamped his teeth on his pipe. Interview concluded.

Chapter 38
KAZ

Gateway, June 25, 2012

THE PHONE STARTED RINGING as soon as the painters went up the ladders.

"Is Walter there?"

"No, I'm sorry, he's gone out."

"That's okay," said the voice. "I'll talk to you, then. What do you think you're doing to the Three Sisters Hotel? Looks like you're changing it."

"We got a little tired of the green and yellow. We thought we'd go for the heritage red. Only above the logs, where the siding is."

"I don't like it. It's always been green."

"Well, did you like how we cleaned the logs?"

"They sure needed it."

She put down the telephone, and it rang again. A man this time. "Appreciate you're cleaning up the hotel. Is that a primer you're putting on? You aren't seriously thinking of red?"

Nancy put down the phone again. She could hear someone outside talking to her sisters. It was not an elderly person. This was a guy of about thirty.

"Hey, what're you doing with that paint?"

Anyone who'd been in Gateway long felt no hesitation in speaking out. Don't change it! That's our hotel. We like to walk by. It turned out that the Mariners had bought it, but they didn't own it. The town did. People knew where the hitching posts were, and they knew that every miner in town had had his own round wooden table with the orange terry towel on it. They knew that some trapper had carried a lynx into the bar and that the packers had annual balls. They didn't come drinking here, though. These townsfolk weren't patrons. The patrons were bikers going through; they were construction workers only around for the length of their contracts. There were no more miners and virtually no packers. The native people didn't come here anymore either: they went east from the reserve to drink in Cochrane. But it was a fixture.

The phone kept ringing until Walter came home from the seniors centre and called off the painters: Quit the red, fellows, we're going to go back and paint over with the same cream and the dark green. Then he sat out on the veranda on the bench still labelled THIS BENCH IS FOR THE COMFORT OF OUR SENIORS and accepted thanks. Iona sat beside him with her walker in front of her.

When the next man came by and began to reminisce about the time the hotel manager was shot at his doorway, Walter invited him up. The sisters brought out chairs.

"Did he die? That manager lived in a suite around back, yes, that's right. No, the Wisharts had their own house. They never lived here—did you, Iona?"

"Mother wouldn't have heard of it!"

They were still sitting on the veranda facing the sun when Kaz Otaka walked up the street. Walter, Iona and their three daughters: Lynn, Nancy and Ann. Kaz stopped below the stairs.

"Well, the whole family! Back at the old Three Sisters Hotel. Can I take a picture?"

He raised his camera.

"Just a minute," said Walter. "Who are you?"

"He's a friend," said Nancy.

It seemed to her today that Kaz's first call had been a long time ago. But it was no time at all, only a matter of weeks. And just in time. Iona was more confused now, less present. There had been conversations—with Kaz, among the sisters, with their father. She had known from the day he called their table from the door of the Wolf Den. He was so sure, so gentle in delivering his facts. Her sisters called him spooky; he wasn't. Just careful. It had been a shock. And they were concerned for Iona's health.

Now she welcomed him up the steps and into the lounge. Iona came behind on her walker.

"I'll leave you two and get some tea."

Iona took her favourite chair where the light fell over her left shoulder. Kaz reminded her that he was Jun's son.

"But that is so strange because I have just been thinking about Jun."

For long years she had not, of course; she had put him out of her mind, and no one had said his name. She had put him so far out of her mind that for all that time, he did not exist. She regretted that. She needed to bring him back. This was her time for summing up.

She told her daughters: This is the advantage of age; you have these marvellous minutes and hours when you are up above with a perfect view. Her mode of travel was one of those old biplanes from the war years. The ones with the open top that could roll over. She was flying over her life in one of those. It meant she could suddenly and magically call up an entirely trivial memory: who was in the passenger seat that time she was stopped by the RCMP for drunk driving? When she came up with the name—it was Dora Minkowicz—it was a triumph.

She took a roll, and now the young man Jun appeared on the landscape, in all his youth and with his dark eyes lined with thick, dark lashes, wearing some sort of uniform—not for the army, what was it? He was a bellhop. He had been important. Before Walter. After, her husband dominated the landscape, the years of marriage and child raising and ever since, stretching to this improbable length. But he did not dominate her. Or the girls. She got her way, when she had to. But with Jun it was different.

Years before, when she sang and shimmered. That was where Jun appeared, Jun as a young man, whom this other young man—who was not young at all, at least sixty—was talking about. When she pushed through the revolving brass doors of the big hotel. She struggled hard to listen. She didn't want to miss any part of his tale. The revolving doors turned, flashing in the low lines of sun. Jun was at the Palliser Hotel. Before that, Jun was in the camp.

"He lost his job," Iona said. "Why? He must have got all mixed up with the Germans."

The visitor laughed. "No, that wasn't it."

"Of course not." Iona hated her failures of memory. "I'm so stupid."

"You are not stupid. Shall I tell you?"

As the war went on, it was harder and harder to make a living. The family left Calgary and moved to a farm north of Edmonton. There were Ukrainians nearby, and these people taught them how to farm. Jun went to live there, he said.

Iona could hardly hear the young man because at that moment a dream returned, a dream she often had. She was in her own house, the house in Gateway where she had raised her children. She went down to the basement. Gateway basements were never much good because the water table was so high. They often flooded, and the sewers backed up—once they *got* sewers—and the walls were musty. But this basement, in this dream, was different—high and dry.

She opened a door, and there was a room, empty of life and full of matching furniture, a blue-and-white-dotted quilt on the bed, a closet she did not dare open: in doing so she would be disturbing the privacy of a lost person, someone who was loved but had been ill or absent. Did it belong to the sister or brother she never had? No, that was the wrong generation. This was now, and the knowledge of this room and the person who lived in it was new. It was frightening. In her own house.

She started awake: she was not in her house but in the Three Sisters Hotel. Think how many unknown rooms there were in this hotel—the establishment that her father had run his trips from, where her mother had managed the bar, and which now her husband had bought! Those people had imprisoned her. They had kept her here. With the stories inside the room. How terrifying. In her dream, she went out and shut the door on the room.

But when the door was behind her she felt pulled back toward it and coaxed inside. She looked with anger on the visitor, who was talking, though she couldn't hear him—anger and pity. It was his fault she had fallen into that time. The time of Mrs. Wallister's boarding house. Because now she knew: that was where the dream room was. She was a prisoner not in the hotel but in the boarding house; she had chosen that herself.

Yes—she flushed—it was her own room. She had brought him upstairs. There had been such urgency to it. She had thought she would faint. Is it possible to faint from desire? She remembered being up against a wall, standing between the bed and the tiny nook with the sink and cupboard. There she had stood with her back pressing hard against a foot-wide bit of wall. She had to do that to keep her knees from giving out.

He was always whispering, but what did he say? She had no idea if he wanted her as much as she wanted him. She thought this was what sex was like. How could she have understood that this was the only man with whom she would ever feel that? All of it—the music, the war, his darkness, that he was a fisher-boy—all of that was part of the excitement. But the rest, the way her pelvis licked at him, and the force in her arms, her aggressiveness, the things she said to him, the way she wanted it, wanted it: oh, she was crazed! What was wrong with her? Was she sick? She blamed her parents: she had been too protected.

Kaz, the young man who was not so young, kept talking. He must have known, and he showed no signs of disgust with her for it. How embarrassing it was to recall this now, in front of a stranger. She hoped he wouldn't tell. She was a lady. She had always been a lady, after that.

She and Jun learned how to do the thing and kept on doing it. There was no caution in either of them. He was free and so was she. There were other couples, men with Japanese women, women with Japanese men. She and Jun saw them sometimes, when they walked by the railway tracks, in the eastern part of the city past the stockyards. Nothing would stop her organizing her life around this. When the singing ended she stayed at the boarding house, washed dishes there and saw him at night.

Her freedom was beautiful but so short. She tried to get back the joy of it. Jun had to get work somewhere, that was it; he went north with other Japanese people. He came back, they quarrelled; he was desperate, she was lonely. She took a course in stenography. She was no good at it; it was all tidiness, which she abhorred. She thought of moving farther away, to Winnipeg.

Jun came back. They spoke of marrying. Then—what happened? He didn't know who she was, really. What did he know? Only that she sang in a band and lived in a boarding house. He thought she was cheap. But it was he who cheapened her. She tried to tell him, but she could only tell him about her father and her mother, the scientists and the hunters and guides, the Three Sisters Hotel. He did not seem to grasp it.

It was painful to speak with him. He was just a boy, younger than she was, separated from his family, a registered alien. He needed food and money; he was proud and would not take from her. Not that she had much to give. She earned her keep at the boarding house, or almost. Somehow she thought he could too, but he could not—not in that city, where even the Japanese market gardeners with the stall near city hall had packed up and gone because no one would buy from them. He was angry at the war, and she was exhilarated to have escaped her parents' clutches.

"You look different. I don't know what you're doing all week there in Calgary," her mother complained.

"Washing dishes and learning shorthand. It is *work*, you know."

"There's something a bit fancy about you. I don't like it. My father would be turning over in his grave."

"If he had one."

"What was that?"

"Nothing. I didn't say anything."

Her father was jolly now that he'd given up the struggle.

"Everyone runs away at nineteen. I did. You did, Gwen. This is a family of runaways. Iona did, but maybe she didn't run far enough," he said, looking at her keenly.

There were months, or was it years? Did she take a job as a stenographer and sometimes go on muddy roads to a place in the country, to visit him, on weekends? Yes, that was it, and then a terrible scene and the feeling of her heart breaking. No, be honest, it wasn't her heart breaking. It was like an addiction she had to fight, like Snuggles with his drink: she had to force herself away from him. Because Gwen knew. She had guessed, and she had come after Iona, cornering her.

"You are with child," she charged, apprehending her at five o'clock in the afternoon outside the brass revolving door, as Iona was about to enter.

Iona had another gig with the Cassalis brothers, handy because she'd been fired from the boarding house. "Your sins shall find ye out," said her mother. But she often said that, over matters more trivial, like when she had hidden her Brussels sprouts in her apron pocket so she didn't have to eat them, and they began to smell, days later.

Gwen took her by train to the old grey house in Edmonton overlooking the North Saskatchewan River valley, a tall, sombre house with a walled garden, like an old nunnery, where there were unwed mothers. Her mother got her settled, almost kindly, and went back home. Iona was flippant and mocked the nurses. She was a singer in a band, and here she was being treated like a child! She did want to escape, but she was lethargic too, and it was easy there—no more dishes to wash and a piano to play and various kind older women coming by with knitted booties. That had been another room, in another house.

Iona smiled on the young man who was not young, Kaz. She had known this room for a long time but had not spoken of it. That had been a lost time, but now she reclaimed it. She had been so caged at home that even the shame of it was exciting. She had not been humble. She took a certain pleasure in Gwen's pain. Jun did not write, but that was considered normal, even desirable.

And then the child. A gruesome birth full of screaming and blood. It had made the next three, the later three—the births of her daughters—seem easy.

She could feel him in her arms. She had held him against her breasts and felt his warm breath on her shoulder. His head had been large for his long spine, and it wobbled. She had wondered if there was something broken in the child.

She did not remember much apart from the tender smell of his head. Mostly she was furious that she could not sing. Perhaps that was the explanation: she had been in mourning. Singing was her job. Singing was her career, her glory. Had she lost it forever?

And where did the baby go? Gwen wanted it. Gwen would raise it. "He is a child of God." Then Herbie got involved. Forbidding it. They would not have that child in their home, shaming Iona for the rest of her life.

Iona thought perhaps she should tell the man Kaz this. Tell him that, as usual, she had been making her parents fight. She went and found Jun, and she gave him the boy.

Chapter 39
AFTER THE WAR

Gateway, October 1945

Before she knew it she was back in Gateway. What a dump. She was back because she had no place else to go. She had come home to show her parents how miserable she was. Twelve hundred people and one industry. Miles from everything. Everyone who could leave town had left town. She, Iona, was the one they had picked for getting away, but now here she was again! She didn't know what people thought. She didn't care if people knew about that convent.

Frankie Cassalis knew. He was sorry for her and not quite as shocked as her mother. This happened, you know, men met women and they made love and babies got started. Such was life—what are you going to do? He kept in touch.

The war was over, and women were losing their jobs. She worried that her looks had been affected and spent a lot of time looking in the bathroom mirror. The light was so strong: it revealed a sallowness she'd never had before. She began taking long walks up the mountainside.

Even in her misery Iona had a sense of this thing called motherhood. She pitied her mother, who was grief-stricken. Gwen had so little family. But her new empathy did not prevent explosions on the front porch as Iona came and went, ate a bowl of soup and disappeared into her room. Herbie was out on the trail whenever possible. His daughter had got herself in trouble, was how he put it. He'd always known she might go wild, that one. He played poker and curled in the league. Time crawled. Later it would not stop for anything. That was when she was happy. But not back then, when she was at home, twenty, with nothing to do.

The war was over, and tourists reappeared, a few at a time. The power company began to build a dam on the Bow and rented rooms at the Three Sisters Hotel for office space; a thousand workers were housed in the same camps that once had held German soldiers. There was still no other bar in town, and the Hot Springs Hotel had not reopened yet. The Three Sisters now had live music every night except Sunday. With Foxx's permission, Herbie took out a few more tables and widened the dance floor. There were lineups on the veranda every night. Her father always said he should have got a cut of the beer sales. Iona wasn't allowed to go there, not even to help her mother. "Especially now," said Gwen. Iona was a fallen woman who might fall again.

Slowly, life returned. If she could find a friend with a car she could get to the dances in Calgary on a Saturday night. She saw Frankie Cassalis there, and he said that the Hot Springs was reopening, they were hiring. His younger brothers had got work: twenty-six dollars a month, plus board and room. The manager told them that Italians were good for two things: being waiters and being crooks. "Which are you?"

"We're musicians," they said.

He hired them to work the tables. But within weeks there were problems with the band, and he promoted them from busboys to band members in white tie. Before long the Cassalis brothers took over the gig. Frankie invited her on a Saturday night, to sit at the band's table. They had another singer.

One day Iona came into the house, arms full of half-frozen sheets from the clothesline, to see two men, her father and the Safeway manager.

"Iona. Come and speak to us."

Herbie was grinning like a monkey. He'd never wanted her to appear before men who were drinking, and now he'd found her the perfect opportunity, singing in the aisles of a grocery store, where no self-respecting man ventured. Safeway had come to Gateway, in a building with plate-glass windows and a parking lot. But it was a chain store, and people didn't like that. They were used to their own local businesses. Safeway had to work to attract customers, and it was while talking to Herbie Wishart that the manager got the idea of hiring a singer to go up and down the aisles serenading the customers.

"How can you even think this is possible?" Iona said. It was beneath her.

Her dad chose that minute to say they wanted her to pay rent.

Iona stood at the intersection of Cleaning Products and Canned Goods. Over in the produce aisle, which was self-service, a new thing, she could see people squeezing the peaches even as she began to tap her toe and snap her finger. Music, she had said to the manager. What was she going to do about music? You're the music, he said. No, no, no, I need some kind of music. A tape recording. She wished she could get Frankie Cassalis to play with her, something, a little drum, piano, to attract attention, but no.

"You sang over all that noise at the Palliser in Calgary," her father said. "The Safeway will be quieter."

The Safeway was not quiet. It had a high ceiling and was full of glass. The surfaces were all hard, and the excited voices of women exposed for the first time ever to fresh produce out of season bounced off the walls. The meat locker gave out a freezing blast of air when the butcher went in and out. She moved farther down the aisle, opened her mouth and began. People she knew were there, the mothers of girls she'd gone to school with. Of course the girls were all gone away, married now, living elsewhere mostly. She hated it.

"*I don't want to set the world on fire.*"

She walked down past the cans of instant coffee.

"*I just want to start . . .*"

It occurred to her she could make it funny by coordinating the lyrics to the products—

"*. . . a flame in your heart.*"

Where were the matches?

Mrs. Cornwallis smiled at her. Hello, dear. She wanted to talk. But you couldn't talk while serenading. Here was a tourist woman with a couple of kids who wanted Raisin Bran, while the mother wanted porridge: looked like it was going to be a fight. Iona skirted them. She found her way to the paper products and planted herself by the Kleenex for the next song.

"*I'm laughing on the outside. Crying on the inside.*"

She kept a plastic smile on her face and let her eyes rove, seeming to connect but not connecting with people she knew. She was tempted to drop her chin and sing to the packed shelf of spice jars, but she didn't; she was an entertainer. She tried "I'll Be with You in Apple Blossom Time" over the fresh fruit and "Ole Buttermilk Sky" at the dairy section. Unfortunately most of the songs were about love and marriage. She didn't like them, but the shoppers did.

The smile was still there, and the *I'm here but not really* look, when he stopped in front of her in his topcoat and felt hat. He was dressed for business and she didn't recognize him. He waited until she finished singing.

"It is Iona Wishart, if I am not mistaken!" He took off his hat. He sized her up in a respectful way, and she felt a little something bloom in her that had been wilted this past year. "Nice song. Last I heard you were making music in Calgary."

So he didn't know.

"I'm back but just until I get another job singing," she said, to make it perfectly clear that she had left this place as she'd always pledged she would.

She sized him up too, remembering Walter as a boy, skating on the river with the rest of them, hard at work even in his leisure, patrolling the edges of the group, telling them where to go and where not to go, because the ice got thin.

"I thought you were at university in Edmonton."

"I finished. Then I got a letter saying, 'We have an opening for a mining engineer at three hundred dollars a month and a house.'" He shrugged. "I never thought I'd come back, but here I am. And glad to be. Especially when I see you."

It was a corny compliment but sincere. He asked her if she would go out with him one night. She had her evenings free and nowhere to go.

She did her hair before leaving home, rolling it smoothly up across the nape of her neck, fixing the wave above her forehead. But she met Walter on the street: she didn't want her parents to see him. "Just going to see the Cassalises about some music," she lied.

It was a spring night and not dark. They walked along the river on the footpath everyone took home from school fifteen years earlier. They talked about the girls who'd got married and the boys who were killed overseas. She said she was saving her money to leave. There were ducks upended in the creek, and the sun was metallic on the surface. From the wild roses all along the banks came a light perfume that mixed with the vanilla smell of wolf willow.

"Don't you see," he said, "there's nowhere as lovely. I've looked."

"Where have you looked?" Scoffing.

"France, England."

"That was during the war."

"I know, but I could tell." He sounded very certain.

"Oh, please don't say that!" The world that beckoned her was available no more; this was the best place. It was what her father was always saying and not what she wanted to hear. Walter went quiet. At least he knew enough to do that. Nobody could tell her anything; that's what they said. She would not listen; that was what her mother said. She was a time bomb, an itchy, unhappy, excitable young woman.

Walter just smiled and squeezed her arm with his. And suddenly she laughed. God, it was lovely. Lovely to be with a man on a beautiful night in the mountains.

"You were a smart boy," said Iona, "and now you've grown into a smart man."

Through summer and fall they kept company. Walter made up little picnics for them to eat at Grotto Lake above the town. He took her to the dances on Saturday night at the Hot Springs Hotel; she listened to the Cassalis brothers play, but she didn't get up to sing with them. They didn't invite her. Besides, it didn't seem quite proper when she was with Walter. The Safeway gig ended: one day the manager came past and turned off her tape player. "That's enough of that," he said, as if she had been annoying him.

It was winter by then, with months to come of short days and long black nights. Everyone told her Walter was a catch, a good man who would be a good provider.

Chapter 40
A REGULAR VISITOR

Gateway, Summer 2011

Kaz told Iona about his life. The Japanese family had worked and saved and made their way across the Rockies to the lower, worn ranges to the south and west by the time he was ten. They found cheap land in the dense bush and started over. There were nine children, three of them adopted. The town nearby had grown up during a gold rush. A huge brick hotel a city block long was still standing. In the war, one thousand Japanese Canadians had lived in it.

"So many?" said Iona.

Those prisoners had left the area when they were released: their memories drove them away. But it meant that the locals were used to people like them and even liked them. Kaz's family grew vegetables and sold them in the market.

Education was the way out of it, out of what had happened—education and silence. Jun visited when he came home from university; he was studying to become a teacher. The aunt and uncle—that is what they called themselves—were stern disciplinarians. Kaz laboured over his schoolwork at the kitchen table. The cane was nearby if his page didn't look perfect. He did his mathematics on an abacus. They wanted him to be a scholar, perhaps to go to medical school, but there was something wrong with his brain, Kaz said.

Iona said she had always felt that way about her own brain. It wouldn't stick to a task.

"Mine," he said, "sticks too hard to a task and can't move past it."

They laughed softly together about their miscreant brains.

What Kaz learned intuitively was the bush. He walked along rivers holding on to alders, pulling himself. He went on snowshoes in the deep powder of winter, and on foot in summer. He could snare rabbits, and stalk birds and get their eggs. Anyone could get them when the eggs were in nests in the grass; the hard part was when you had to climb trees. He wasn't afraid of shinnying up a tree, the way the other kids were. He was light and could hang by his hands. He came to be in charge of getting food for the big family.

Iona was listening intently. Sometimes her lips moved. When he said that about climbing the trees, she said, "I'm not surprised." Her voice was so small you couldn't hear.

Kaz said his uncle used to take him into the dense bush. His uncle who was not his uncle knew how to cut down a tree with an antler. Yes, it was possible.

"How did he know that?" said Iona.

Kaz took a deep breath. "He learned it in the camp. In the camp they didn't have tools; they found antlers in the forests, and they used them. At the house where I grew up we didn't have tools either, but it was because we were poor."

"And hungry," said Iona. She remembered that.

"Yes, we were hungry," said Kaz.

So he and this uncle would go into the woods together and up over mountain passes. These were some of Kaz's favourite memories, tracking deer in the woods with the man called Jun when he came to visit. The not-uncle turned out to be his father, said Kaz.

"Yes," said Iona. "I guessed that."

Jun taught him to look for hog's backs, where the land went up in a hump and came down again, and terraces, which were dry edges over a drop, because there the trees didn't grow so thickly. He reasoned that the old Indian trails would have been there because it was easier to walk, and they could see down into the valley so they could spot wildlife. He knew certain things, like that the forest is always more dense on the north side and less dense on the south side. Kaz looked forward to visits from his father because together the two would go out hunting. Winter was better for travel always; they went on snowshoes.

He went to university in Calgary and took up Nordic skiing. There was to be an Olympics in Japan. He trained to get on the team. He decided to go to Japan to see what the trails were like. He knew almost nothing about the country. He ended up in Nagano, a snowy region, working at a cross-country ski resort where the Japanese team trained. He observed. The coaches were bullies who yelled at the skiers and derided them. The skiers suffered pain and injuries. What for? he thought. Medals were not of interest to him.

"No, no," said Iona.

Her eyes kept closing, and it seemed she might be asleep. But he found if he kept on talking, in a few minutes she would open her eyes again.

But there was an old man he noticed. A retired farmer. This man used to arrive in the middle of the worst blizzards. He would appear out of the dark, swirling maelstrom with a shovel and an axe. He never seemed to have any trouble finding his way. He was the man who tended the trails.

"I thought, This is a job I would like to do."

So he followed the old man and learned by copying. The old man accepted him; they understood each other, even with the simple Japanese

Kaz had. They used to play Go in the evenings. Those were two happy years. And when he came back to Canada he became what the old man had been, a trail-maker.

Her eyes were firmly closed now.

"Are you doing all right, Mum?" said Nancy, spinning through the room. "Would you like some more tea?"

Iona woke up. "I am enjoying this story," she said, looking across at Kaz. "It's a good story."

"It's not a story; it's my life."

"I know, dear, I know. You know I'm very proud of you."

Kaz stood up and approached Iona, looking as if he might hug her or kiss her. She lifted her hand toward him, an elegant hand—all knuckles, purple veins, liver spots and protruding moles, her diamond and engagement rings loose on the finger, but elegant nonetheless. He took it and bowed over it, pressing his lips to it.

"Goodbye, my dear. I do hope you come again."

Chapter 41
IONA AND GWEN

Gateway, Fall 1958

Iona was at home with her children when the call came. Her mother had fainted, at work. She never forgot the date, September 25. But the year was vague. It must have been in the late 1950s, because she packed the girls into the back seat of the Buick Special and drove down Main Street with the horn blaring: there were no traffic lights. Where was Herbie? Out on the trail, she supposed. And where was Walter?

She pulled up to the veranda and leapt up the stairs leaving the girls to follow, Nancy on her heels and Lynn in charge of Ann, who was still a toddler. She halted at the entrance to the lounge: it was dark, as it always was—darker, even—and it took a minute for her eyes to adjust. Smoke coiled through the slashes of sunlight that came in the small windows. Gwen was laid out on the floor. She was still girlish and laced into the strict daytime dresses she favoured to preside over the theatre of the town.

The drinkers were gathered around and a dust-covered construction worker knelt behind her head. The room was very still. The only movement was the man's deliberate rocking—forward onto his hands to press down on her chest and then backwards, lifting her elbows up and away, as if he were loosening her wings. They made a tableau: Juliet in her tomb, Christ taken down from the cross, any of those Renaissance paintings her mother had never seen, because there had been no European tour for her, as there had been for her brother and sister, no, this was in red towelling and knotty pine, with golden glasses of beer and winking brass hardware.

She went to her mother's side. The man applying artificial respiration was sweating, and dirt streaked his face. "She's not coming around."

"What happened?" She bent to pinch her mother's nose and breathe into her mouth and thought how rarely they had kissed.

Gwen had fallen off the box she stood on at the beer pumps. It raised her a foot so she could work the handles. It was the same overturned wooden crate she'd used since her first day, with worn hand holes on the sides. She had stepped back or lost her balance, no one knew for sure, and had tried to catch herself but had failed. She had gone down hard, hitting the mirror and then the countertop, and was unconscious—or perhaps she'd fainted first and that was why she fell: perhaps she'd had a heart attack.

It wasn't working, the man said. But it was: suddenly Gwen was panting, she was speaking. Cries of relief in the crowd, and hope. Then it turned to confusion because Gwen was distressed. Her words came fast but not in a language anyone understood. She clasped Iona's hand and shut her eyes, and her lips went still. She returned to some other struggle.

"Everyone is here," Iona said. "We're sending you love."

And they were. Everyone but Herbie. Herbie was not present. Iona felt a thrill of rage and squeezed her mother's hand again.

But Gwen's breathing had stopped.

Voices rose. We have to do something else. Take her to the hospital. Someone had propped the door open; Iona's daughters were grouped inside it, shivering. She'd forgotten them. It was winter, but there was no snow. Perhaps Gwen had broken her neck; don't move her. The men made a stretcher out of the darts scoreboard and gently nudged her onto it. Four of them carried her out, one on each corner, but it hardly needed so many.

Someone had a truck—Iona's Buick wouldn't do—and they put her in the back. Iona got a car robe from her trunk and covered her. The driver set off for the hospital, built on the grounds of the Sanatorium and slightly more scientific in approach. Then she and the girls piled back into the Buick and followed. Word had travelled; there were spectators.

Then they were all in the emergency room with her.

It was too late. Iona knew, already, from the expression of finality, of summation, on her mother's lips.

The doctor pressed his fingers into the side of her neck to find a pulse. "She's gone," he said.

There was that moment of astonishment. Just a moment. A change of state, momentous and barely noticeable.

The nursing sisters—yes, they were nuns—faded backwards. It seemed faintly indecent to assume the spirit was gone so quickly. Iona was indignant. Then she wondered why. Was she protecting her mother? And what from? The miners and the construction workers, the patrons of the bar, were still waiting outside. Someone took the girls away and no doubt delivered the news to Walter. Iona asked if she could sit alone with Gwen.

She pulled up a chair to the bedside. That cooling form was her mother, mysteriously rendered helpless and delivered into her hands. What had she been trying to say in those last panicked speeches? If she was gone, or going, what was the destination? Although she was religious she never spoke of heaven. She had said only that what lay beyond death must be "for our own good." How unappetizing. Iona hoped it was better than that.

She thought of the days they had danced together to music on the phonograph. They had marched to Sousa, they had swayed to torch songs: it was strange to remember now. Her mother had such gaiety. But later it was silenced by a mysterious, unshared faith. She remembered long ago, as a small child, she had had "meetings" face to face with her mother.

Shall we sit together and worship? Gwen would say. Who was that young woman? She had been an unknown child from afar when fate handed her to Gateway. She had kept faith with that event, her defining act at nineteen being to marry the guide who last saw her family. Gwen had seemed at first incapable of living up to that choice. As a Quaker she was charged with making her days a reward and a worship in themselves. But in the end she had done so, hadn't she, in an entirely original way, as those men outside would attest. She had triumphed.

Iona touched her mother's cheek. It was waxen, already. A kind of radiance was developing. She watched as the light grew. There it was. Her inner light. It grew, under her waxing skin, shone for her daughter. Iona wept. Then the light began to dim.

Such a short life: her mother wasn't even sixty. A life held together by will. In each decade she had revisited and reframed her enormous losses. She had thrown her life into all she had been taught to abhor: the killing of God's creatures; music and drinking too. Noise and celebration, and rough justice. All of it—and she had held her outpost.

A word her mother was fond of was *waiting*. She had waited, all her adult years, for God to show his hand. She had kept vigil, and with some reward—Humphrey was returned to her. She had been dutiful. But what about love? Did she love her husband or was he simply that to which she was wedded? And her daughter? Had she loved Iona? Had Iona loved her? The answer was—almost. But not entirely. She tried, she sometimes succeeded, but there was an obstacle. That was the truth of it.

When Herbie came back, they planned the memorial. There would be no funeral, no *empty forms*, as Gwen would say, no priest, no choir. Humphrey arrived. Ulla was in New York. There were no other close friends. The patrons of the Three Sisters bar turned up at the Union

Hall. Herbie was the greeter. Neither he nor Iona spoke. But the miners came forward, and their wives, one after another, to praise Mrs. Wishart.

"She had us wrapped around her little finger, she did, I don't know how," said one.

"I knew when I went to the hotel at ten o'clock that Mrs. Wishart would have him bundled and out the door."

"A kind heart and a fierce temper. We were all afraid of her."

"That little woman was a saint."

At the wake at the Three Sisters, beer was on the house. Humphrey tended bar. Iona and her father sat by the fire, stunned.

"Does this seem an indelicate way to send her off, dear girl?"

"There was no other possible way."

This was the trajectory of her mother's life: born in Washington with a silver spoon in her mouth, died in Gateway with a draft pump handle in her fist. There was a grandeur to it.

"She was a handful," said Herbie.

"Is that all you can say?"

"I left you with it, dear girl, didn't I?"

"Often."

"Did you mind?" Genuine bewilderment. "I thought you girls were happier with me gone."

I only work here. Walter said that too. It was just men wanting attention, wasn't it?

"Oh, for Christ's sake, Dad." Iona had the urge to punish him, even though he was suffering, even though he had declared himself devastated by the loss. "Don't pretend you don't remember. You were always off hunting, off on a pack trip, on your trapline—you were always out there. We could never reach you. And when you came home, we had to tiptoe around . . ."

His face took on a stubborn look of innocence. "Iona, if you knew."

"If I knew? I knew a lot. I was more married to her than you were."

"Now you're being foolish. I need another whisky."

But she wasn't letting go. "What should I have known?"

"She knew what it meant to marry a mountain guide. That was our bargain."

"You might have let her go on the trail. You might have stayed around sometimes. You just went off and did what you wanted."

Someone handed Herbie a whisky.

Herbie stared at it. He stared at his daughter.

"Did I now? If I could explain," he said.

Iona's eyes filled with sullen tears. "Dad," she said, "it's a little late."

"No, it's not. It's just the right time. If you would listen."

Iona was ashamed. Her tears were not for her mother. Those would come later. They were for herself, for the years, the entrapment of family. *Family*: the very word was a cage. The perfect union of man and woman and child. Contained within that space and preserved, behaving according to God and the institution. Meek and mild and acting according to plan. It was a little like a park: preserved in wild state, a contradiction in terms. Each of them had tried to escape. But the enclosure was still there—and three people were never fully themselves when inside it.

"You said I wasn't ever at home and that I was out hunting. And I don't argue, lass. I don't disagree." He threw back the whisky.

Iona wasn't going to help her father. She said nothing.

"I don't like to admit defeat," he said. "I don't like to give up. But perhaps it's time."

He was trying to explain something. Iona wiped her face.

"I've been looking, don't you see? I never stopped looking."

"For what?" she said stupidly. That was pretending in the same way he had pretended innocence.

He gave her a tired smile. "I don't need to tell you."

"Why don't you?"

"You're a hard lass."

Iona turned away. "It's not the time to speak of this," she said.

"Do you not know, lass? Do you not know what I've been looking for out there? Is it necessary to spell it out to you?"

Not that old story.

"I suppose I should have let it go. That family, that innocent young lady. How could they have disappeared? It drove me, that. Can you understand? I'm not saying every day I searched for traces. I'm not saying that. But it put me in the habit, didn't it? I was scouring the place. I went on with it, and it became what I did. Search."

She looked at him. Of course. It was why he was gone, he was saying. The Hodgson family was the real reason for his physical absence, not just the need to be on the trail. "That innocent young lady" was the root of his obsession, and something more: she was the cause of the curious near miss of his emotions. She saw it then.

"For Isabel, you mean. It was Isabel all the time."

Herbie raised one hand as if to tell her to stop. But he didn't argue.

They sat in silence. Another whisky, another few greetings, accepting the condolences; they sat on.

"One time," he said.

"Do *not* tell me about the violins."

"No, lass, this was another time. Just before freeze-up. I was by the river hunting upstream. There was an eddy, offside and moving more slowly. And it had frozen over, while the main current had not, because it was moving faster. So here was a full circle of ice, sitting on the water like a plate, slowly turning, gleaming, edges smooth, perfect, like it was drawn with a compass. I looked at it and thought it was me, that ice circle stuck turning and turning, on its own, getting nowhere, and the river rushing by."

"I've never seen such a thing."

"I knew then it was time to give up the hunt. I'm not going to find her."

And Herbie cried.

But Iona did not give up. "Did you tell Mum?"

"She knew."

Iona's anger only rose. "You had it over her. You had Isabel. You had the wild. You had the country."

"No, lass, they all got away."

"Not your wife."

"Oh yes, she did."

Chapter 42
HELEN'S TAPE

Gateway, Summer 1970

HELEN WAS IN TOWN GATHERING MATERIAL.

"My god, Helen, what brings you back again?" said the old man. "It's been a long time. You've been in Hollywood. Or is it France?"

"I meant to come sooner. Events got in the way. Edythe's not made of money, you know." She'd been trying to raise the funds for the film for years.

She talked to Herbie again, this time without the camera. She had a reel-to-reel tape recorder. Said it was easier to get at the truth without a camera. He had been beginning to look forward to this movie. He wanted to talk about the wars and the Germans; he thought that would spice up the plot. Make it a spy movie.

"No, Herbie, I want the real stories."

"I'm telling you, we had spies. Both wars. And before and after. You wouldn't believe what went on here in the backcountry. Why not? Huge place, nobody here, keep it all secret. We had the fellow who was the model for James Bond living at Lake Minnewanka. We had atomic scientists meeting up at Lake Assiniboine. Secret meetings. They decided right here to drop the atomic bomb on Japan. You didn't know? Sure!"

Herbie had the truth in his head, but he wasn't going to tell it to Helen.

After Gwen, other people started dying. Herbie liked to say how he and his wife had never had a cross word—well, except that one time when he had painted the kitchen floor without sweeping it first. When he did that, the old-timers guffawed on their veranda bench. I can't see you sweeping floors, they said, and we could hear you two fighting over the back fence.

First it was Phoebe Dixon, but not before she finally got her book of wildflowers published and was praised to the heavens. Made a lovely book, if you could afford it. 'Cause you didn't see the flowers so much anymore.

Then it was Ulla.

At the end of the thirties the Nazis tried to persuade Gus to go back to Germany, where he could hunt on the royal reserves. Herbie reminded him of learning to draw the kaiser's pigs and cows. Hey, your status must be going up if they are going to let you at the royal stags! Sure it had: he was famous and blond where he still had hair, and he represented all that wonderful Aryan stuff. Gus told the Nazis he was going nowhere because he had the run of thousands of square miles in the Rockies. Of course, then he had Ulla too.

After she died, Gus stayed winters in New York, where he could visit his paintings in the outdoorsmen's clubs, but came to Gateway in spring. He kept working in the studio on River Street, behind garden walls he and Ulla had erected to keep the deer from ripping up those delphiniums she babied into enormous blooms. All of them went wild in the end, and Ulla's flowers were all over town. Purists called them invaders.

Herbie would drop by and point out when a buck's hind end didn't look right, and poor Gus would go into paroxysms of revision. The place smelled of paint and flesh gone bad, of musk and whisky, of formaldehyde—or maybe that was Gus's breath. The setting sun would come in on the window side of the studio, sneaking around the Fist the way it did to give the river and the cabins one long yellow slant of gold. The stag's dark brown eyes would light up, and it was as if the dead were alive.

"Jesus Christ, have a look at all these animals," he'd say to Gus. "You got more in here than I've seen in a year on the trail. You know it's slim out there. You heard the caribou are gone? Pretty much. And we got no wolf—not except for that one people saw down by the highway last year. There are no grouse at all. You never see a lynx now."

Okay, maybe that was the sort of thing he'd tell Helen for her film.

"Getting old is a hell of a thing and here's why: you outlive your folly. Tell you the truth, I was wondering why it had seemed so essential to catch them, to remove them from their pinnacle and their fens, to serve meals of their flesh. I could feel the itch still: I always had the instinct. Remember, I'm a throwback to primitive man. Or so they said. I knew where an animal was even if it was passing half a mile away. But what I wonder now is why I had to shoot it."

It was strange, but by then Gwen's way of thinking had invaded him. She used to say that the wages of sin was death. Well, he guessed he knew what their sins were, and Gus's wages—his wages were to be forever making changes to those big canvases. You couldn't even say he had gone out of his mind, because he'd always been that way. Herbie'd have to pry the palette out of his miserable claws. Tell him whatever he was working on was perfect.

Herbie had been wary of Gus for a long time, but after Gwen was gone even that wore off. They were the last ones left; if they didn't have to like each other, they at least had to keep company. They'd sit in Gus's overrun garden and reminisce. Oh, there were stories! He'd known Gus a long time. He remembered their first hunt together. Sure! First hunt. Must have been before the Great War.

They went over Sawback Ridge. Herbie saw a large bear disappearing behind a little hill about half a mile ahead the outfit. He called a halt and said, Okay, Gus she's all yours; now get going. Gus pulled the rifle off the saddle and started in her general direction. He walked and walked. Herbie followed until he knew they were close—he saw a gopher watching and then he saw a black fox stalking the gopher, but the gopher was only watching this other spot, which is where he figured the bear would be. Sure enough. She was behind a bunch of rocks and trees about fifty feet away. She wasn't watching any of them. She was digging a hole. Must have come upon some good grubs.

Herbie could feel the bond. He said, Gus, she's yours. But Gus stepped sideways to let him have the shot.

He got her through the shoulder. The force of it threw her onto her back and into the hole. Then she sat upright, grabbing her hind legs with her front paws and biting them. Like there was some kind of pain and she couldn't bite her shoulder, so she bit the thing she could get in her mouth. Very human.

Gus went closer; she was no danger then. Herbie'd seen bears rise on their hind legs, taller than a house, and look you over just as they were about to go down. It was a kind of salute, he judged, one creature to another; he'd seen them acknowledge the better hunter. But this one was down. Why hadn't Gus taken the shot?

Though he'd hunted for fifty years, Gus was not the better hunter. He choked.

"Last time I went out on a pack I shot a grizzly, remember? At seventy-nine."

"Who was seventy-nine—you or the bear?"

"You're a mean son of a gun, aren't you, Herbie Wishart?"

Herbie remembered another bear, a great big sow. This one had come close enough that her stench was making them gag. And Gus froze. *Froze.* So Herbie finished it. What else?

Yes, Gus choked. Or he missed. Many a time. And he talked such a big story. It was what Herbie couldn't stand about the man. Sure, he had the goods on Herbie—or Herbie feared he did—about the Hodgson expedition, but it wasn't that Gus dangled that in front of him, or even that he smirked with Gwen about how sophisticated the two of them were. No, Herbie didn't like him because Gus was a bad shot.

But all this thinking reminded him of a story for Helen's tape, and he started to laugh.

"When the outfit caught up, one of the packers came running even before we had her gutted. Gus liked to gut 'em right away and stuff newspaper inside so he could draw the position, right? Well, I'd just got out the knife and this guy runs up. He had a little bottle, which he unscrewed the top of, and he squeezed himself right up beside the she-bear and started combing through her pelt. Gus says, 'That's my bear! What d'ya think you're doing? I gotta get her cleaned fast and draw ze claws before they've relaxed!' But no, the packer is picking and pinching and going, 'Oh yes, ah! Got it!' Pleased as could be. You know what he was doing? He was gathering fleas. He had an order from a British collector who was paying him twenty cents per."

He laughed on, the falsetto rising. "We had so much fun I break out laughing just thinking about it. What can I say? It was a real place then."

Helen said the holdup on the film was money. To be precise, Edythe had run out of it.

"Really," said Helen, "it's all in the voices. Film is so cumbersome. I still want to tell the story. So I'm making a radio documentary."

"Oh-oh."

"No, it's good. That's what the material wants to be. I can't get in the way of its becoming."

"Oh, hogwash, woman. I've known you a long time, and you are no *artiste*. You are nothing but a government hack."

"And you, Herbie, are nothing but a poacher."

"Too true," he said. "So your film is going to become a radio program? Or is it just that you're too old for it, Helen?"

"If I am, you are."

"I am," he said. "I don't mind admitting it. Too old. The old-timers are all gone and only I'm left."

"Yes, and that's why I'm here," said Helen. "You've got the stories, Herbie. Always did. Let's get 'em in the can."

Herbie pulled down on his pipe and thought about it. The temptations of preserving it, so that when he was gone people could still laugh at the adventures. The temptation of paying his wages. Yup, the wages of his sin.

"So no camera?"

"Why, are you that vain?"

"Hell no! I love radio. No need for that pesky camera. Or the bright lights. You can scare people half to death like Orson Welles and that end-of-the-world stuff."

He paused and puffed on the pipe. Okay, he thought, here goes.

"I was talking about Gus. You know he finally went?"

"I don't know why you keep talking about Gus, but sure, I'm listening."

"I was just saying, about Gus and his studio and all the taxidermy. Talk about the last days . . ."

He brooded. Imagine Herbie Wishart brooding. It didn't last; he brightened into a rant. "Oh, it was a real place then."

"And what is it now?"

"Now? Overrun with hippies and back-to-the-landers. Oh, sure! We have streakers. Did you know? Right down Main Street. Come out of the bar and take it all off and run to the bridge. Knackers turned to brass. We got longhairs toking up on the riverbank.

"An art school, built opposite the Hot Springs Hotel, looking down on us; all manner of privileged young folk come to play their violins and act in plays in the fresh air. Sorry, that's *plein air*."

"You were telling me about Gus."

"Oh, Gus would have been fine if he'd kept his mouth shut. But he never, ever could do that, as I learned to my peril. He wasn't a Nazi, the way they said. His politics went back way further than that. 'Hunting is ze sport of kings,' he'd tell his classes. Not a word of a lie. This is how he'd go on. Aristocrats, the rich. 'Democracy does not favour my art, the art of wildlife painters. Artists who painted kings and the splendid animals they pursued had *status*. They were highly respected. Nature was their subject, and they were its faithful servants.'

"You see the problem with Gus? Sure, he brought fame with him to Gateway; art magazines came to write about him. Gus enjoyed that fame a great deal, but he had the misfortune to outlive it. Nobody cared what he'd done. He was out of style. He never liked the idea of people slathering their feelings all over a mountain lake. Thought modern art was just an excuse for bad technique. 'As if you and your own miserable thoughts matter!' he'd say to the students. They didn't like that. They called him Mooses and Spruces."

Helen cackled.

"But Gus claimed that if his mooses had been people, he'd have been Rembrandt."

Helen was very glad the tape was running.

"Gus went in a hard way. Okay, you think it's just deserts—a fellow whose manhood was based on bringing down some magnificent, unarmed thousand-pound creature should get shaky in the end, along with his shooting arm. Now I sound like Gwen, God rest her soul! What could she know? I never let her out of Gateway. We couldn't have any more deaths in this family. Then, too, I didn't want her spoiling my fun.

"But she wasn't wrong, was she? If you manage like I did to miss out on all those big diseases and the godawful accidents, you get this thing called wisdom. It causes you to realize how wrong you've been for so long. Helluva thing. Wouldn't wish it on anyone.

"That last summer, Gus was working day and night beside a pile of antlers that reached up to the crossbeams of his log cabin studio. I'd spot him when I walked by. One day I knocked, and when he didn't answer I banged. Finally he opened the door. He had a huge stag wired up in a frame, head lifted, feet together, trussed over the horns and around the belly. The heavy rump didn't look very stable.

"'Stag from over ze Brazeau will not come out right and I'm going to haf to do it over, so don't count on me for dinner!'

"He thought I was his wife! I said, 'For Chrissake, Gus, Ulla was gone years ago. Died!' I had to shout it at him. 'What ze hell?!' He looked so stricken I was sorry I brought it up.

"Well, the poor man was addled, wasn't he? I went over to the Vienna Café and came out with one of the cowboys. We tried to get back in the door, but Gus had locked it. I saw through the window that he was standing there with a pistol.

"'Jesus, Gus, you got a licence for that thing?'

"'How many meals of elk haf you enjoyed courtesy of me and zis gun? How many? Christ, without me you would haf starfed to death.'

"Maybe it was tough to aim while drinking from the hip flask. We broke the door. The stag was shaking in its frame. And Gus was down.

"Jesus H. Christ, the place was eerie. All those trophies going mothy! The antler pile was ten feet high, right to the ceiling. Elk, caribou, sheep, moose—all tangled together. A mounted bison head stretched four feet into the room. A trio of sheep crowded into the corner. Wolf tails on a shelf. Bones lay around—hip bones, pelvises, jaws. Gus was careful about anatomy. Owls. A hawk. What was in those glass boxes? Butterflies." There was a pause here before he started again. He cleared his throat. "*Nothing*—there was nothing he didn't kill and keep."

Helen kept one eye on the tape, grateful it was still running.

"But worse than the studio was Gus. He was down, but he'd missed the shot and made a mess of his head. I finished it. What else?"

There was silence. The sound of wheels softly turning, a brushing sound of the old, dry tape on its spindle.

They had begun again.

"Take me back to where we were," said Herbie. "I'm okay. Let's do it."

"So nothing escaped Gus, you were saying. His desire to kill the animals. But not much escaped his razor-sharp eyes either. I remember when he spotted Hodgson's camera on the trail. Whatever became of that?" She thought she had waited a respectful time. She thought she was subtle. But careful tending of an interview subject had never been her talent. "It makes you wonder—did he also know where the bodies were buried?" said Helen.

He erupted.

"Oh, I know you, you crafty old broad!" Herbie roared. "Come here skulking around. Is that what you're after? You came around here asking about the Hodgson expedition? You think you can fool an old man like me? No, we won't be dredging that up. No. And no, I didn't mean Gus had anything to do with Isabel Hodgson. He acted like he knew something, but he just did that to get me mad. He wanted to have it over me. Anyway, Helen, that's enough. No more."

Helen said something, but it was obscured by scuffle and clatter.

"Not going to dig that up again," said Herbie. "If that's what you're after, not a chance, lady."

"Herbie, I'm truly not. I just want to know about the last days of the outfitters." The sound improved again: she must have put the mike back on the stand. Then more roaring and Helen lost her temper too.

"Okay, maybe I *am* asking about the Hodgson expedition. You and your buddies were always hiding something. Don't think I didn't know!"

"I don't feel like talking."

His pout was nearly visible. Then, "Gus didn't know about any bodies. It was only the camera. He found the camera. And we didn't know—

neither of us knew—what the camera would show. We were not going to have it discussed in public. Didn't want the Mounties and the CIA all over it. Trouble was, I never trusted him and he never trusted me. That was it. That was all, Helen. I don't feel like talking."

"You never don't feel like talking. Sorry, Herbie. Sorry. I didn't mean that. Don't let me interrupt. You were going to say—"

"No."

"Please."

"Nothin'. There's no secret in this. I'm not talking."

"Herbie. Look. We're two old people fighting. What are we fighting for? There's nothing to protect, and no one. You want to take it with you? Don't. Just talk."

He was weakening.

"Herbie, I blew it at the last minute. Just like Gus. I don't have the instinct, see? You're the one. Finish it. Please."

Chapter 43
THE TRAIL-MAKER

Gateway, June 2012

KAZ CONTINUED TO VISIT IONA the next summer. She called him her young man. She wanted to hear about making trails. "Look how long it's taken before anyone would tell me," she said, waving gaily from the room as Nancy or Walter went past.

When Iona's eyes closed, he stopped talking. She opened them again.

"You were telling me about Japan, before," she said. "But I don't remember hearing about when you came back."

"When I came back to Canada I started working for some of the resorts. Some of the backcountry lodges. I got a job with landscape architects, but mainly I worked on my own. I still had the impulse to do great things. And I did things. They may not have been great, but they were daring. I took risks. I pushed myself. Once I snowshoed from Calgary to Sechelt. I snowshoed across the Summits. I wanted to go to Disneyland; it seemed like the Mecca of our culture."

He and Iona chuckled about this.

He was so gentle with her. Nancy watched and marvelled. He was a patient man. A kind man. He told his mother who he was, about his life, indirectly. And Iona understood.

"I want to ask you a question," Iona said. "There was a place, they used to call it the Inaccessible. Is it still there?" she said. "No, it can't be. It was so long ago. I'm so stupid."

"You're not stupid. Far from it," said Kaz.

"No, I'm not," she agreed. "What I mean is, of course it's there. Places don't go away. But how you get there changes."

"Very true."

"What do they call it that?"

"No place is really inaccessible now," Kaz said. "Humans are very determined about getting places. It wasn't quite inaccessible then, and it isn't now. Helicopters buzz over it bringing skiers in winter and climate scientists in summer."

She looked disappointed.

So he thought about it for a while, and then he said, "Unless it was straight up a rock wall, but even then. Maybe if it was in a valley with overhangs."

"You said there are roads high up in the mountains."

"The explorers called them roads. I read their books, and I see it. They never went anywhere the Indians didn't go first. You can read about it. The explorers complained sometimes—the road ended, they'd say. They actually had to break trail." He laughed. "There were no roads! Only trails."

"Do you think there is a lost or forgotten pass up there?"

She seemed to want there to be one.

"Noooo. No. Well, maybe. There was one that was abandoned. It was called Pass in the Clouds. I went on it once. It was used by Blackfoot and Kootenay for raids. It was really high up, well over the treeline, and quite technical. But it was a well-beaten trail."

Chapter 44
FOG

Camp below the Quarry, August 28, 1911

When Doctor Professor Hodgson stuck his head out of the tent in the morning he knew something was odd. The horses were still and nearby, waiting to be loaded, as if they knew it was time to go.

And Humphrey was nowhere to be seen.

Maxwell sat quietly, staring into the embers of last night's fire. "Good morning, sir."

How Long had his back turned.

"Where is Humphrey?"

"I don't know, sir." Maxwell looked up gravely. "He's gone."

An early morning ride seemed preposterous given what was to come.

"Do you know something about this, How Long?"

The cook shook his head. The professor took some coffee and looked petulant. It was extremely inconsiderate of Humphrey to have disappeared. It would delay their departure.

"What is the meaning of this, Maxwell?"

"The boy was restless."

How could he have the impertinence to be restless when they were engaged in such groundbreaking—no pun intended—work? When Isabel had not got up to join them for breakfast, Maxwell scratched on the canvas door of her tent. That was when he discovered that Isabel was not there either. They should have checked on her in the night; she'd had that bump on her head.

Hodgson became even more angry at Humphrey.

"So he's taken his sister off on a little adventure?"

But only one of the horses was gone, his.

"They're riding together, then. Or they're walking, and brought one horse in case she tires."

They had done this before. Got up early to climb to the top of the peaks where the light hit. Could they be climbing up to the Watchers? Could be the ridges on the other side of the Snow Bowl. But would they not have left a note, a sign?

"There is a difference," Maxwell pointed out. "There is a difference in the way in which they are not here. Humphrey has taken his things." Humphrey's tent was empty, his pack gone. "Isabel, on the other hand, has left everything." What could they do but wait? They did that, all the day. At night Hodgson swore they'd leave in the morning. But of course they could not—not without his children.

"Maxwell, are you sure they didn't leave a note that you somehow mislaid?"

"It's possible, sir. It may have blown away."

On the third morning the professor's impatience came to the boil. He insisted that they begin to load the ponies with the slabs of rock that were prepared. The cowboys were mostly silent as they worked, except to protest when they thought one beast was overloaded or the load unbalanced. Neither Isabel nor Humphrey returned that day either.

"Pardon me for saying, sir, but I do not think your son will return," said How Long, holding out a note. He'd found it under the coffee tin, where he kept his kitchen things. "Seems like he thinks we see it first thing that morning."

The note said that Humphrey was leaving to find himself a new life, that they should not worry or follow him and that he wished them well.

"He'll be long gone on the train," said Maxwell.

And that left Isabel. Humphrey hadn't mentioned her. She must have followed her brother. And maybe he didn't know, or wouldn't admit he was taking her away? Still, it seemed odd. Had she wandered off in a stupor? Cast herself in the lake in a fit of misery? But she had been much happier.

The far walls of the mountains seemed to give back a greater silence. Hodgson brooded all night, only speaking to repeat, "I cannot comprehend it."

The butler managed to convince Hodgson to wait another day for Isabel. The cowboys were told to search for her, but they just rode out of sight and waited. Maxwell and the professor unloaded the ponies.

On the fourth day the little encampment woke in a fuzz of fog. Everything around them had disappeared. Below had disappeared. Above had disappeared. There were no peaks and no valleys, and only a half dozen nearby scraps of trees. Even the mountain sheep were confused: two rams butted in to where How Long was relighting the fire. The season had changed. The butler and his master argued. Maxwell did not want to leave. They could not abandon the girl. But suddenly Hodgson was in a terrible hurry. They should have been on the trail. Perhaps they would have found his children. They had tarried here too long. They had to get back. They had to get back—but they could not go without this enormous load of fossils.

"These rocks will change history," said Hodgson. "They will change prehistory." He paced and waved his hands as if he were addressing an auditorium, not an empty bowl in the mountains. "Of all the cruel dilemmas, I have been selected for this."

His tragedy was positively Grecian, he said. "How can we measure the worth of one lost daughter against the story of life? If we can know how life began, shall we not try? If we lose our daughter in the struggle, how shall we be judged?"

And even the lives he saw in front of him—How Long, Maxwell, the cowboys, his own—did they not merit consideration? They could be caught on the mountainside. Wishart often said it: winter could arrive in an hour in the midst of a summer day. They could not travel well in snow with the immense weight of the rock. Probably she had jumped on the back of her brother's pony. Or run off with Herbie Wishart in the night. Perhaps she was with Phoebe Dixon at the Railway Hotel. There was no possible way for them to find out while they sat here, and there would be no one riding in to give news of the lost members of the party, not in this weather.

But neither could they move out in the fog. How Long said it would burn off, but it did not. Billows and billows of it came from the west, over the Great Divide, all day. In the morning, once again, they awoke to see it had plugged the atmosphere all around them like cotton batting, like a muzzle pressed over their mouths and noses to hold them still.

On the fifth morning a stiff, cold wind began to blow from the north, and they made themselves ready to go. The professor had not wanted to take the straightforward route to the station at Laggan, but now, when that way seemed to offer the only possible hope of finding his children, he agreed.

But the fog was not so much gone as on the move. It hurried ahead of them, at one minute revealing a granite mountainside, the next sliding that vista closed like a Japanese shoji screen. It played a merry game with them, sometimes hugging them so tightly that the ponies stopped walking, and the last tinkle of their bells echoed away into some unseen gulf. They stood for an hour, and then the fog moved again, revealing them on a trail up against a rock wall, wide enough, but opening to a scree slope below.

The cowboys sulked. The trail was not good. Who made it? Did the horses know it? Of course they did. Well, why had the pack train now arrived at this place, which surely was just around the mountainside from the campground? Could the horses be leading them in a circle, back to the camp?

Chapter 45
THE OLD TRAILS

Gateway, June 2012

"The old trails are the best," said Kaz to Iona. "They're smoother because their roots have rotted. They're better because each succeeding generation improves on a trail."

"Do they really?" said Iona. "I'd like to think that."

If a man is walking he sees a better way to go, a few steps above or below. Moving a loose rock. Passing a stubborn root. And the next man after him sees it and takes that slightly changed way. Maybe the whole camp is walking behind him. Or maybe another man or woman, the third down the line, decides differently and stays on the first path. And after that, every second person takes one or the other, and the space between the two sets of foot tracks gets worn and the path is wider now, where it had been a little precarious.

"And gradually the children of the trail-makers figure out shortcuts."

"So the Indian trails are still the best?"

"Indians use a bulldozer now," he said. "But you can see by the evidence on the ground how a trail gets made. A trail that was made over thousands of years is different from one of those cross-country trails outside of town." A long-term trail—that was what he called it—could date from the ice age. That was before the horse. Such a trail simply followed the openings.

Iona said, "What openings?" Did he mean gaps like Whiteman's?

"The openings in the forest. Small-scale openings in the forest," he said. "The biggest impediment is a burnt forest. Also a river. The early visitors with no horses would be looking for ways of crossing rivers. The first people would have to go up and down to find a place to cross."

"Did they have boats?" Iona said. She remembered her father having to ford the rivers. The pack train swimming against the current. Every now and then a horse being swept downstream. The pack lost. The horse found hours later, having scrambled onto shore. Losing them the better part of a day. He would be telling her mother by the fire, drinking whisky, home late.

"They may have had primitive bull boats—willows bent into a shape like a huge kettle drum and covered with hide. They might even carry it for a ways. Framed hide boats probably date back ten thousand years. But no canoes. This wasn't really a watery country."

"During runoff it's watery."

"Of course they'd be knowledgeable about the melt. And they'd stay away from bogs. They'd look for hog's backs; they might be old eskers because they are drier. You know what I mean by a hog's back? I mean a steep ridge, like a spine. They're created when some strata is tilted steeply up and then the edges erode." He used his hands, describing it for her. She watched his hands moving; they reminded her of something, something very old and stirring to her heart.

"They'd follow the edge of a terrace because it's dry there. There won't be any trees along the edge. Those are the oldest trails. The best example near here is up across on the terrace by the hoodoos on Lady MacDonald."

"How do you know these things?"

"I've been in the bush all my life. I've studied. And I've walked them. I've found flakes. Debitage, they call it. It's the waste from where people sat making their stone tools. The flakes of rock. On shores where lakes have gone up and down you can find flakes. I've found knife blades three or four inches long on the south-facing slopes. Did you know that? The south-facing slopes were the better places to camp, because they melt and the forest doesn't grow as thick."

"There was a network," said Kaz. "There were junctions. When you read the explorers' accounts—"

"I never did."

"Oh, you should! It's very interesting. There were trails. Not very wide, sometimes only wide enough for horses. But most of them were footpaths. And that's what they were following. The Indian trails. Everywhere the white man went, he went on these paths. The Indians showed him the way. Guided him."

Iona marvelled that they shared their trails so freely.

"They traded goods with the whites. And of course, the whites paid them. We're all for sale, in the end," said Kaz.

"Were there any trails they didn't share?"

"There was the Pass in the Clouds. I told you I went on it once. High up, very technical. I don't think they ever shared it. There was some fear around it. Used to be a legend—something was up there, maybe a mastodon, some huge creature, remembered from after the ice age. Certain trappers did know about it. You used to hear tales about it. It was way beyond the divide, very high; it went over and down to the other side. Very tough. I don't know how I survived it."

Chapter 46
THE WAY BACK

On the Trail, August 30, 1911

THE FOG SETTLED AGAIN, warmly, and then cooled, as if to cushion and hold them. Then the rain fell, straight down, heavy, grey. They stood on. The ponies were reluctant to move. Not reluctant, that wasn't the word for it: they refused. The cowboys wouldn't force them. "They'll take us down." He jerked his head into the cauldron below, where fog and rain obscured the grey bottom. "They'll take themselves down." The cowboys said they should unload the rocks.

"They are fossils! You are very ignorant," said the professor.

They stood on, inundated, cold, unable to move. When the fog shifted, when it breezed past them and up and then down again, they glimpsed their situation. It wasn't so bad. They could spread out. Not stand in a line. But there was no shelter. They stood, shifted ground a little and stood on.

And one of the Tree brothers said to the other, "You suppose Wishart made off with the girl?"

The other said nothing.

The first then said, "Mebbe he's on his way back."

His brother Tree spat into the wet. "And we'll meet him?"

"We're not going to meet him."

The professor consoled himself while standing there by thinking about the great advance in scientific knowledge that would come about through his bringing back the fossils. Maxwell for his part said little, only adjusting his position from time to time to try to make the professor comfortable as he leaned against his horse, then against Maxwell himself.

At some later hour the fog began to shred, the lower regions of it moving to the west, the upper hanging firmly above. There was green forest below; there were rocky crevices, open bare patches. And there was a way forward. Whether it was the right way forward nobody seemed to know, and the ponies were not telling anyone.

"We're going back," said one of the Tree brothers. "You'd better come."

"We won't," said Maxwell.

Somehow it was easier to break up a party that had already been broken up.

"Wishart will be pissed if we don't bring the pack train." The other Tree.

There was a small standoff. But the cowboys couldn't wrest the ponies away—how could they?—from the party who rented them. After a few minutes they kicked their horses and headed back, while Maxwell and the doctor professor set out forward the way they had been going, with their saddle horses and four burdened packponies, determined to make the most of the light allowed them.

They walked and led the ponies until they came to a place that was flat and wide, where they undid the ropes and put down the stones. The ponies cantered loose; Maxwell suggested they hobble them, but the professor had learned from the guide: he said no, they wouldn't run away.

"I would, if I were that pony," said Maxwell.

But he couldn't make the doctor laugh.

Hodgson limped around in a circle with one hand on the small of his back. It was a gloomy party that sat around the campfire, ate sparingly and drank the whisky. The doctor wanted to believe that the state they were in was the fault of one of his underlings—Maxwell, possibly, or How Long. The cowboys were beneath blame, and anyway they were gone.

Overnight the temperature dropped, and in the morning things looked cold but better. However, once they had, with difficulty, mimicked the diamond hitch and got the rocks tied on the backs of the ponies and set out on their way, it began to hail. Hard balls of ice the size of marbles came hurtling around them, bounding off their hats, the horses' necks, rattling on the stones, stinging the face and hands.

"He's throwing everything at us," said Maxwell, looking upward and meaning, of course, God.

"I have begun to wonder," said Hodgson, "if he really wants this secret to be revealed. If he wants us to reach the station. First he has taken my son and now my daughter."

"We could remove the fossils, leave them for next year. We can find our way back. We did it last year."

There was a definite lift of spirits at this prospect, as if the stones were the reason for their being lost.

Because they *were* lost. And hungry. They might as well say it. They had got turned around in the fog. Even with all the standing they should have been at the tablelands by then; nothing looked familiar, and they would know where they were if they were where they were supposed to be. And Wishart—they felt sure he would have been heading their way: they'd have met him face on. Met someone. They were going the wrong way. By this point they'd lost How Long, too, and half expected him to appear, jolly and provisioned.

It was a trail. That was what fooled them. It was very definitely a trail—worn bare, and the roots rotted out where they'd been exposed, softened. Anyone could tell by getting down to look that it had been travelled before and often. But it was not the trail they intended to be on.

They soldiered on. Their diamond hitches were not correct: the burden slid and unbalanced the ponies, had to be retied, with the two of them arguing as they threw the ropes back and forth across the ponies' backs. When they moved, they seemed to be climbing more than they were descending, but it was hard to tell, the terrain bucked and rolled so; what they'd crossed was soon behind them and forgotten. It would be two more days before Doctor Professor Hodgson would hear of leaving the fossils by the trail. And by then he had been reduced to a tearful old man bewailing his fate to the heavens. Raving, really. Maxwell stayed calm even when Hodgson turned on him. "I am beginning to think, Maxwell, that you were sent here to lead us astray!"

They did leave the camera and film. They set it down in a protected place among some rocks and off the trail, but near a junction, and the professor bade it a solemn farewell.

They had no grain for the horses and little food for themselves. Maxwell tried his tricks of finding fish and game, but he seemed to have lost the knack. However, he shot a goat, and warmed them with large servings of goat soup.

They continued on for two days after that, now more convinced than ever that they were on the wrong trail. They were both in a strange mental state now, disoriented, half starved, and they began to turn on each other. They reached a glacier and began to cross it, an exercise that shredded the ponies' legs and tried their energies to the limit, as their feet kept sinking into calf-deep snow and ice. On the glacier the trail disappeared. But they made it to the other side, and this time two goats found their way into the kettle.

The professor was not himself, as Maxwell observed. To march had become a way of living, of carrying on; it had become what they did each day. It had ceased to be about getting anywhere because they didn't know where they were aiming. At the campfire he suggested that they would come out of it farther along the railway line, on the other side of the Summits. In retaliation the professor began to suggest they turn back. With the weather better it might take only a few days. They could leave the fossils there, he now agreed. They could rest and feed, he explained, then come back for them. Maxwell was grateful for the thoughts, he said. They would discuss it that night and come to an agreement.

But overnight another blizzard came in.

Chapter 47
WALTER

Gateway, June 28, 2012

A YEAR HAD GONE BY. The hotel was restored. It was late June, and the family had come back to enjoy their work. It was raining. It had been raining up high, too, after a record snowfall year. The runoff had begun. The river was high.

It could last forever, this funny building with the hip roof that recalled old France. The logs were now a woody orange, and looked brand new, but they weren't; they had been washed and re-chinked and sanded and sealed. The veranda, too, was sanded, though the handrails with their hitching rings remained. There had been arguments over the hanging baskets of flowers; Nancy thought they were unnatural. If God had wanted flowers to swing in the air he'd have made them grow in baskets with a chain, she said. Ann countered that there were many places in the world where flowers did dangle from heights. But not here; this is not the rainforest, said Nancy. In the end, because Iona wanted colour, they compromised on big bushel baskets that sat on the newly painted wooden veranda floor.

The lobby had new flagstone on the floor, but the old windows were still in place; you could see the ripples in the glass. Walter grumbled about new wine in old bottles, but he was pleased. The bar itself was Rundlestone: what else? The lights were iron and yellow glass, and they looked handmade but had been bought at Costco in Calgary. The old chairs made of stumps and the burls of trees had been re-glued and given new legs. The signs saying Do Not Sit had been removed. Photographs were reframed, and there was light on them so you could see the old faces, even under the brims of the old hats. The dozen small bedrooms upstairs had been made into five big ones with bathrooms. The third floor, which had once been the packers' dormitory that doubled as a dance floor, then had slept the construction workers who built the dam, was bare and empty and waiting for ideas.

The three sisters had done their inspection. Walter cornered them and took a picture on the iPad they'd given him for his birthday. The camera function was his favourite: for the rest, he had trouble with the swipe motion. His fingers would not touch so lightly. But Nancy had been walking away.

"Hold on, I'll take another."

They complained. He complained back. Family of women. Don't mind me, I only work here.

Then he sat in what had been the Map Room and was now a little office, and gazed at the better photo.

These were his daughters. He was glad he'd had three of them. Herbie used to say the curse was on him, but Walter never minded. Despite what he said, he knew how lucky he was. You needed as many as you could get when you got on in years.

What a trio.

The one on the left held a bouquet, the one in the centre looked wary and the third was still walking away, although she had turned her head to smile back at the camera. Lynn, the eldest, was the one with flowers. Ann, the youngest, was in the centre. She lived in Ottawa, but she came out more often now and stayed longer these days. Nancy, smiling over her shoulder, was the one they all said was the image of her grandmother Gwen, dead these fifty years but remembered as the manager of this hotel. Nancy had been the devil to raise. Herbie had spotted it in her right from the start: changeable, wild. Wilful. But she would keep it going, the hotel, the story. Nancy was the one who was interested—she had found something in the basement, she said. All tied up in plastic and hung from a ceiling rafter in a dark corner, probably to keep it from getting wet. Some reel-to-reel tapes. She had gone to find a tape player.

He studied the image, rotating the tablet to the left, to the right. There was something in the women: even they admitted it. If you asked him, which no one did, it came from that same orphaned girl, his wife's mother, who was fearsome. She never liked him much, though he got her daughter out of a jam, didn't he, by marrying her: poor Iona wasn't so happy stuck back here in Gateway and going nowhere. Otherwise he'd never have had a chance with her. The love of his life, she was. Gwen had greater things in mind for the girl, was that it? Cried up in her bedroom the whole of their wedding day. She had not wanted photographs taken. She had a phobia about cameras. A difficult woman but held out locally to be a saint. No, it was not hard to credit that she was the grandmother of the three sisters whose image he held in his hand—and also of the man Kaz, which he now understood, though his wife did not seem to, not fully.

You see, there had been a reason for coming back. He would give her that and be glad of it. A son after all these daughters. You could even see a touch of Hodgson in the Japanese man.

Gwen would like to know, he supposed, that her face lived on. They all had it in slightly different forms. It was comical, really.

Lynn's flowers were not for her; somehow flowers were never for her. They were for her mother and would go on the long table being prepared for dinner. Ann looked like a businesswoman, but she was not; she was a professional troublemaker and rabble-rouser. Her arms were folded as if she were trying to hold herself together. She looked resigned to her fate, unhappy but not likely to escape.

Unlike Nancy. Over fifty with a perpetual bubble of laughter in her throat. Her plucked eyebrows were high, as if she were astonished, her upturned lips stretched wide and her hair pulled back with a band that could have made her look severe, but didn't because of the thick waves that sprang out from it and rested on her shoulders. Once, her mother would have said she was too old to have long hair, but Iona no longer said things like that. She had become all sweetness and appreciation, and said only that she was so proud of them all.

Nancy had something up her sleeve with those tapes, no doubt about it.

The girls were in their prime. Before long they would show signs of age. Already there had been a cancer scare; there had been divorces. He wanted to remember them this way. He didn't want to see much more of their aging, of what life was going to do with them.

They were strong, he gave them that. Of course it was as much about this place they came from. A beautiful and a hard place. Women who came here had to leave their fear at the door. Oh yes, that had been the way in the old times. Fear of what, you say? Hard work. Bears. Cold. Long, dark winters. Freaks of weather. Rough men. Bloody accidents. Not knowing where your living would come from one day to the next. The fear of insignificance and maybe the acceptance of it, coming to understand how little your life meant in the grand scheme of nature. Most of all you needed the strength to invent yourself against this enormous backdrop. No comfort in the landscape, except on a rare day by a stream in a meadow. Very little was given; you got nothing for nothing, as Herbie Wishart used to say. If they were up to it, the rewards were grand: starry nights and deep waters and tiny blossoms you could only see if you bent over them, and best of all, an escape from the parlour.

If they were not up to it, well, that was different. He'd seen it. They were beaten down or beat themselves down. There were women he could point to who drank themselves stupid every night, or who fled back east, went crazy, had a fatal accident. There were the leavers and the stayers.

The women in his family—before these three—had been stayers. Had stood on in the grip of terror. His mother and grandmother watched their sons go down into the mine, year after dark year, and be spit out again at the end. His mother-in-law, Gwen, gaped in horror whenever she thought of where her sister's bones might rest, to her dying day. She had God, they said, but no one knew much about her God and if he was of any assistance. A Quaker. Well, there had been Quakers around here. It was because they could come in the summers and have a grand time in the mountains and pretend it was work. They didn't allow themselves leisure, you see. Everything had to be for knowledge or the greater good. Bit of a killjoy, Gwen was, although they said she'd been a romantic girl. She did love her husband, Herbie Wishart, and lived her life out in honour of that feeling. Did she believe that he would find her father? Or just that he would *be* her father, her brother and her sister? And when he wasn't, what then? Walter never even knew if she loved Iona, and neither did Iona. But he'd seen that same gape of horror on his wife's face when there was a mine accident or an avalanche, skiers lost, as if it were a hand-me-down.

The issue with these women, he thought, was that it was a man's world. So to speak. For the most part. He knew the girls would get on his back for saying that, but truthfully it was. Only a few went out into the forests and the peaks, made friends with the place. Now maybe it was different, with the athletes you saw stroking up the hills on their mini-skis with wheels. But not then. Not for Gwen. Herbie, her husband, had the magnificent wild, the place that truly held his heart. He had the music at Sawback Ridge. He loved to tell that story of the ghost violins in the sky. She had the town, the kids, the gossip, the meddling neighbours, the bar at the Three Sisters Hotel. It divided them. Iona got the message that she should make her father and mother one again. It was an impossible task. Marked her for life. He, Walter, ought to know.

Marriage did not come naturally. Iona had no idea what it was all about. But they had done well, and besides they had a lot of fun. He was proud of that. She was a passionate woman—that helped. Did a great job with the girls. And he had given her her head, just the way you did with the ponies in the mine. Give them their head, and they found a way.

She had another life, he knew that. Had known it when he saw her singing in the grocery store. The music told him. That was okay. Iona sang her way out, and she sang her way back in again. Their daughters studied and married and left and now had a chance to come back. And once they were in school, he let her sing again, occasionally, with the Cassalis boys. Weddings and the like.

The rain continued. He went out on the veranda. A few of the old-timers were on the bench.

"River's rising. It's going to flood."

It never flooded the way it used to, now that they had the dam and the berms. Each generation a step ahead. He had done what he intended, given them back this place. Let them do with it what they wanted.

Chapter 48
CANADA DAY

Gateway, July 1, 2012

THE TOWN WAS OUT IN FORCE, lined up along Main Street waiting for the parade. It was Canada Day. There had been a flood on the other side of the highway. Creeks had overflowed; culverts were washed out. But the river had stayed within its banks. Water came up from underground and got into the basements, but downtown Gateway was intact, though soggy. It only made people more determined to get out there and wave their flags.

All the kids and most of the adults were dressed in white with red balloons, or in red-and-white-striped bloomers, or in red and white cowboy hats, pompoms, bike shorts, top hats, clown shoes. Some had bobbled red antennae on their heads. Lynn, Nancy and Ann stood behind their parents, who as old-timers—a word they hated—had been presented with small aluminum folding chairs and tiny flags on thin wooden sticks.

Who was in the parade?

The Red Deer Royals had big French horns in the back row and a lot of snappy percussion. Their drum majorettes wore long red sarongs tied around their waists and twirled white wooden guns.

Snowy Owl dog teams in harness, pulling sleds. They were panting (it was warm) and their tongues hung down near the pavement.

Then came the Larkspur Flower Shop van, bedecked with orange paradise plants; this was one of the local businesses started by a hippy and embraced by the town. The staff skipped alongside, wearing rhododendron-leaf hats studded with rosebuds. The owner had his arms full of long-stemmed orange-red roses, and he threw one after another into the crowd.

Then followed the Czech masseuses from On Your Face Aesthetics, pushing prams. Goodwrench Motors had a 1925 Cadillac tow truck on a float. It was totally rust covered, as if it had been winched up out of the river. Andalusian horses. The Bar None Dude Ranch with its lone white buffalo. One solitary, smiling Stoney, solemnly receiving wave after wave of applause. He wore a fringed, beaded jacket in soft suede and his feather headdress rose from his crown and dropped to behind his knees.

Jump Start, a kids' program turned into a marching band. The kids were twirling lawn chairs and hockey sticks. The Two Brothers taxi company. Canadian Pacific with the Puffer Belly Express blowing bubbles. The hockey team on a huge flatbed truck shooting piles of candies into the crowds of kids on the street.

Olympic athletes-in-training on their wheeled mini-skis, Canadian flags waving from their poles. More marching bands, one in blue from Calgary, its members twirling their batons. The bands from Texas and Ontario had cancelled because of the flooding. Never mind. There was the Stampede Queen. The Indian Princess.

Mountain Rescue.

Bagpipers in kilts and with a giant drum.

A big contingent of miners in hard hats, lights on.

Fire trucks loaded with handsome firefighters bringing up the rear and spraying everyone with water.

People collecting money so that Gateway could have a parade next year too.

And very last, an organic ice cream bike with a trolley.

*

Ann and Nancy and Lynn sat at the newly installed dining table in the Three Sisters Hotel with their parents, Lynn's husband, her daughter and grandchildren. And Kaz. Who had been welcomed but not named. But at least Walter had stopped saying, "Who is he?" and "What is he doing here?"

Outside the window lay Main Street, bathed in a cool grey light. It was ten o'clock at night. These were the white nights; you could be on the peak above until ten thirty and still see your way down. The flood-swept wild roses were reasserting themselves all over the banks of the creeks; you could smell them, mixed with the vanilla scent of wolf willow.

With his wine glass Walter saluted Big Sister, Middle Sister and Little Sister. "When the tourists come, you have to tell them which one is which." You could be mistaken, because they were ranked in mountain fashion: Big Sis was small and thin but her peak hit the highest altitude. Middle Sister was the most balanced and well shaped. And Little Sister was in front, massive and lopsided. You also had to tell tourists that they were named not for regular sisters but for nuns. And show them how, hooded, draped with snow, they looked like they were wearing habits.

It had been a golden day, and now it was a perfect night, completely still with a crescent moon rising in the darkening sky over Whiteman's Gap.

"Did you read in the paper that eighty-nine percent of Canadians believe this is the best country in the world?" said Lynn.

"That is discounting the oil sands pollution, the water shortage and the disappearing wilderness." That was Ann.

"And the bunnies. Don't forget the bunnies."

The bunnies were testing the moral fibre of the town. They attracted coyotes, which in turn threatened dogs and small children. They ate up people's gardens. On any given evening, from any spot in town, you could see half a dozen of them. People sat in the dark taking potshots.

"It's a plague. It's biblical," said Iona. "We're being punished."

"What do you mean, Mum?"

But no one was listening.

"Nature, red in tooth and claw," said Iona.

Lobby groups—twenty-seven of them in all, representing every possible political stripe—had so far prevented the town council from removing the rabbits. Gassing was too cruel, sterilizing too time-consuming; shipping them to a sanctuary was expensive and a bit sanctimonious for a town founded on hunting. An offer had come from the Falconry Club of Calgary to bring their birds to town to take care of them naturally. The town council was unlikely to vote in favour.

How had Gateway become so well-meaning?

How had it become so tame?

"It's a hard place. People need to be as tough as the place, your dad used to say," said Walter to Iona.

"Bunnies or not, let's face it," Lynn's husband said, "we are extremely lucky to be here. God's country."

"It was more than luck, it was hard work. We have people to be grateful to—our own grandparents, for a start," said Lynn.

"Here's a toast. To Herbie Wishart. And Gwen Hodgson." That was Nancy.

"He dealt in death," Iona said. "He dealt it out to so many. The mounted heads of the creatures carried off to stately homes and the arrowheads to museums."

"Mum! You're our philosopher."

"I always was," she said. "But no one was listening."

"Don't forget Joe Mariner. Grandpa Joe." Nancy again.

"Dad sometimes talked about that day when Herbie Wishart took him up to the Hodgson quarry to set dynamite," said Walter. "He always felt guilty, as if it might have been his fault they disappeared."

This was new information. Walter never spoke about such things.

"It wasn't his fault," said Iona.

His wife and daughters watched him, waiting for more. But he had said all he wanted to say. After the silence, with the conversation seeming to have broken, people turned to their neighbours and mentioned hardships and how it used to be colder and there was more snow and the miners never saw daylight all winter. Then they stopped speaking because Kaz was talking.

"Still, those guys were the lucky ones," he said. "They had the run of the place. Mountains in three directions, nobody there. All you had to do was get a couple of horses and go. Set up a tent wherever you felt like, shoot anything you wanted. We got here a hundred years too late."

"No, you didn't. I can assure you," said Iona. "You did not."

"They ruined the place," said Ann shortly.

"They didn't think it would ever end; they didn't know the animals would be diminished by what they did. You've got to judge them by their own time." That was Nancy.

And Lynn took issue, as always, with her sisters. "How do you do that? Judge people by their own time? We can't. We are not in their time. No matter how much we look at history, there are things we will never know about any past."

"How do we judge them, then?"

"Judge not, that ye be not judged," said Iona.

"But we must, if we want to move forward," said Ann to her mother. And to her sister she said, "We should judge them by the standards of our own time, is that what you're saying?"

"Don't put words in my mouth."

There was a collective breathing in; hostility between the sisters always made people nervous. Iona's back was so rounded that her chin hovered near the tablecloth. But her voice rang out in the gap.

"But what is our own time, and can we even know that? A time is not defined until it's all over and done with. And besides, we live in many times—as children, as parents, as old people."

"I agree," said Ann. "We need years to see what 'our time' is. Anyone who says he can know it now, who thinks he does, is shallow. Or blind."

"Well, I guess you're talking about yourself, Ann," said Lynn, goading. "There you are in Ottawa, fighting the good fight. You must know all about just what we are living in and where we are supposed to be going."

Ann looked horrified. "Oh no, *Ottawa* is what's out of step. People trying to stay elected . . ."

"I hope we're all a little out of step too," said Iona gaily. "What's wrong with that?"

"Nothing, Mum! Most people are just trying to make money. Most people live in big cities. Nobody feels the way you do anymore. When I say 'you,' I mean this family. The attachment to this place. The need to carry it on, which is what Dad's managed to talk us into!"

Everyone laughed. Ann's eyes filled with tears. They were picking on her. Always did. She kept on. "What we're talking about is legacy."

"So here's a question," said Nancy. "Is it worthwhile to go against your time, go *against* the common attitudes?"

"It can make your life miserable," said Lynn. "You won't get the rewards that others do, and you'll see your enemies prosper."

"But maybe you have principles!" Ann.

"Maybe you'd rather be remembered." Lynn.

"Is this a worthy aim?" said Walter. "Your grandfathers didn't expect to be remembered."

"Or your grandmothers," said Iona.

Ann winked at her mother and raised her glass in her direction. "So who cares what happens when you're gone? You're not going to be here."

"Your family does, I guess, if it's a personal legacy. You want them to think well of you." That was Nancy.

"Why? You're gone."

"It's like leaving a mess for the next person. You don't want to leave a mess. You don't want what you did to hurt them."

"Most people close their eyes to that."

"Not most people!" said Lynn.

"Many." Ann again, who could never be consoled.

"I have something to say."

"Quiet, everyone. Mum wants to talk."

Kaz helped Iona to stand. She got to her feet, placed her hands on the table and straightened. She loved speeches. She had given many a good one over the years—at birthdays, at wedding anniversaries. She had in her mind exactly what she was going to say. And she said it. She was glad they were all together. It was what she had lived for, this family, to have them together.

Not so! Not the mother I remember, thought Nancy. Iona was a rebel, unhappy; she wanted to sing and she wanted to get out of Gateway, and she wanted them to get out of Gateway too. Had she forgotten? Or had she convinced herself otherwise? Nancy had liked her mother's unreconciled self. She was left to ponder whether this was the wisdom of age or the final capitulation. One or the other.

Tonight Iona was proud of everyone. Everyone. "I made the right choice." She praised her husband. "He supported me. He held me in his arms every single night." Her four children. Everyone applauded, and she sat down.

Nancy turned to smile at Kaz. "You can speak," she said. He was shy. She didn't blame him.

He stood.

"Thank you for including me. I have wanted to meet you all for a long time. Especially you, Iona." He squeezed her hand.

It was good they had done it—adopted him, thought Nancy. But the strangeness of it had not faded. There were four of them now, and one was a brother. Four who called Herbie grandfather. What did it mean to be descended from someone, to be the child of his child, the child of anyone's child? Were they supposed to notice resemblances?

Oh, please, she thought. Not.

That blood ran in her veins too. What did it mean, exactly? We learn lessons because we observe our elders' lives; we practise what they practise, sometimes. We see the personalities from the inside, and we bend to fit the space left to us. But do we inherit a likeness? In absentia? She could not accept that there were genes devoted to whether you choose to eat meat or risk getting parking tickets. Whether you can make trail, maybe.

The salmon was delicious. So was the wild rice, the asparagus.

"You couldn't get this food here when we lived here," Iona said.

"That's nonsense," said Walter reflexively. "There were fresh—"

"What do you know? I'm the one who sang in the Safeway."

Her daughters laughed and Walter piped down, as he had told "the girls" to do so often.

"God, Mum is tenacious," said Nancy to Lynn. "Not to mention that she has a great appetite."

It was true; she tucked into her food with zeal.

"Is it my imagination or has she come out from under Dad's rule?"

"She has. Now she's the matriarch. That's what you get when you hang in to the bitter end."

Why must ends be bitter, as beginnings were humble? Iona wasn't bitter, and she wasn't humble. She had never been conquered, had she? She had let them run riot over her, but she had prevailed. Nancy gazed at the old woman, fierce as she bent over the table, her chin nearly touching her plate. What was it like to approach the end the slow way? Dying of old age, it was called. Nancy would not recommend it, though Iona didn't complain. She was just grateful to be here still. Terrible how grateful we all have to be in the end.

"Do you think you might stay?" said Kaz to Nancy.

"I'll see," she said lightly. "It would certainly be a change." Elk grazing in the backyard and radio announcements of bear sightings. Possibly it would soon be the only place in North America where a person could breathe.

"What about the hotel?"

"An innkeeper has to be a personality." That was Walter, at the other end of the table. "Nancy can handle that part."

"I will not be the innkeeper."

"Bet you will."

"This place is too big. And a bit haunted."

"You could run it as a B & B."

"I'll come to visit, as long as it's possible," Iona said.

"Good, Mum. I hope so."

Kaz spoke to the table. "They're not replacing most of those bridges that washed out, did you know? So some of those old trails will be closed. And they'll grow over. Certain places will be wilder than they were even when Herbie Wishart came."

No one took it up.

"We need two more bottles of wine."

It was ten thirty and the sky was now the colour of steel, grey with a blue sheen.

They pushed back their chairs and went out the veranda door, crossed the street and then fanned out. Some climbed up the children's slide in the park; Lynn sat on a swing, Ann stood on the boulders. Kaz and Walter carried Iona up the side of the little hill in her walker, like an empress in her palanquin. They set her on top of the little rise, from which she waved daintily to everyone. The neighbours were coming out of their houses; kids were already sitting on the hillside in the grass, in their pyjamas and dressing gowns. The sky still had a little light in it, in the west. But it was time.

Nancy stood beside Iona. From this vantage point she could see down Main Street to the base of the Three Sisters. A subdivision was beribboned with streets; the mined ground, wormed with tunnels, had become backyards that sometimes collapsed. If you leaned sideways you could see behind the false fronts of the original buildings that still stood on Main; where you thought there was a building was only air.

The explosions echoed against the rock walls north and south, and the river gleamed in reflected colour between them. Against the black of the mountainside, showers of light erupted—a dahlia, a twister, a run of green lights turning and dropping into a white shower. The sound arrived a second later, the slow pounding, the easy little whistle of the next one coming. The valley contained them.

"Best bear banger there is."

Blue balls shot to the heavens and finally turned into white drops. The red was piercing, so red, a fire, and it transited from black mountainside into bluish-black sky. Huge hovering high things, they banged and burst and then seemed to linger in the night, not only above the town but above the hills. The valley was reduced to certain avenues of white light—unambitious and tentative, wobbling off into the dark green trees, which seemed to own the place still, and especially at night, after the daylight had fooled you into thinking it was yours.

The trees spread an absorbent darkness out of which no light came, not a sliver. Then came another burst. When you looked at the town in those few seconds, you could see: it wasn't up to much, this settlement. It was just a little place, celebrating itself—boastful, but half lost in landscape.

The coloured fire leapt out from a dot, spilling back down fountain-style. There were firecrackers that burst into rings and still others that were seekers, little missiles whistling on their way. Rings lined up one above and one below, and then there were popcorn-style white sprinkles low in the sky all over town. The colours erupted in front of the grey Miners' Wall, the dead rock, and left their puffs of smoke trailing. The sound bounced like balls against the mountains: every elk, deer, coyote, every rabbit and bear in the valley lifted its head.

In the flashes of light, in the intakes of breath, in the wait for the next one, Nancy tried to fix the town in place. But she couldn't: when the flash was gone and the light was out, Gateway vanished time and again. No, it can't, she thought. Why can't I see it? There are lights in the houses, in the bars, on the streets. In the tunnels beneath—now that is darkness, what you get in there. But all this is on the surface, under the sky. Why are we so faint?

Chapter 49
HELEN'S TAPE DISCOVERED

Gateway, July 2, 2012

NANCY GOT THE REEL-TO-REEL PLAYER from someone at the seniors' home. And she put the reels in place and turned it on. The voice was gravelly but weirdly alive, as if it came from the next room.

> Don't rush me, woman, this is my confession! Helen, you've pinned me down. I guess it's about time. I'm going to tell it. This is for Gwen, who didn't live to know. Though I think she always suspected. And for Iona, who deserves to know.

"Yes," said Iona. "For me."

> Most of them were gone, and he was living on. Sure! Me and my damned long life. You wouldn't want it, but on the other hand you wouldn't give it away. Couldn't. The times he should've died out there! He'd gone through them all and worked it out: it wasn't because he was extra smart, because he had been very stupid at

times. And was he lucky? Yes. But even luck wasn't enough to keep you alive when it was twenty below and your eyes were freezing shut and you couldn't light a fire.

No, it must be because he was doomed. To live forever.

The valley was lonely once, but not now. He missed the loneliness of the old days. His harmonica—good company when you're on the trapline. It's not lonely now, this place: it's chock full of shades. Oh, yes. They grow and shrink, with the sun's angles. They rise and fall through the burnt timber like Mary's white butterflies. Sure! The runaway aristocrats and the miners, religious zealots and artists of note, dauntless Swiss guides who never lost a climber, scientists set to discover an ice worm or a secret of the beginning of life. Everyone came chasing something, whether it was a living wage or some wider version of himself. Or herself. Don't forget the women.

"Get to it, Herbie. Don't spin me any more tales." Another voice, female, strong and sardonic.

He always said that night after Isabel hit her head was the last time he saw them. Right? You know he said that. That they must have wandered off. Or got into a rock slide. They'd been putting dynamite around. He blamed Maxwell, who thought he knew everything but didn't know the mountains. Sometimes he even thought Maxwell had done it on purpose to make sure those fossils would never be unearthed, because after all we should not know the secret of life. What would we do with it if we did?

Gwen always suspected he knew something more.

The truth was, he did.

Okay, Helen, you better make sure you're getting this.

"I'm getting it, don't you worry."

*

The truth was, he had seen Isabel. That night he and his party had not left, although they said they were leaving. They jingled down through the bowl and up the other side, and stopped at the entrance to the first pass. He loosed the ponies. Francis Erwin made dinner. They lay down beside the campfire. It was a full moon, and Herbie never slept on a night the moon was full. He got up silently: it was probably three in the morning, and the moon, which had come up in the east and travelled across the sky, disappearing behind one of the peaks to the south, now emerged in the west, where they had come from.

With his boots in his hands he stepped away from the fire. It was cold: fall was coming. Several of his ponies were in sight. As if he knew silence were a necessity, Timbo took a few steps and pressed his nose into Herbie's chest.

Herbie whispered and pushed the nuzzle away. He stepped back over the ridge and looked across at the darkened campground beneath the quarry. He had his binoculars with him. There were rams grazing near; he could see them. But he was searching for something else. His sense of game told him there was movement. He scanned the site: nothing. But then he saw, heading down the path that he and his ponies had taken, a figure. Thin, wavering a little, but proceeding all on her own, on foot. He knew it.

He set out in his snowshoe pace, loping, hardly bending his knees. He was fast. He lost sight of her for the first part of his run. But he had to believe she was still moving toward him. He counted one thousand steps and started over. He came to a place where the slope of the trail allowed him to look ahead to where she should be. At first he didn't see her. Then he did. She was still moving, slowly among the last of the summer flowers, cool blue in the bright moonlight, deep in concentration. Perhaps she was sleepwalking.

He counted another thousand steps and another. He came upon her in the middle of the Snow Bowl. She did not see him coming; she was looking at her feet. She frightened him, but he did not frighten her. She showed no signs of emotion but accepted his hands on her shoulders.

Where are you going, Isabel?

No answer.

Were you following me? What do you want? Is it me you want?

Remember how young he was. Barely thirty. And impetuous. A wild man who seldom saw a woman like this, so white-skinned despite her summer on the mountainside. There was nowhere to hide in the bowl. The flowers were finished, they had gone to seed, but they made a soft carpet.

He put his arms around her and drew her in. Her thin form sought his warmth. He was always warm, never wore much of a coat. Her throat was the most beautiful thing he had ever seen, columned, like marble with the tendons stretched. He placed his mouth on it. She whimpered. He was kissing her lips then, kissing and kissing, kneeling and falling. He covered her against the cold, put his arms around and under her: she was so slender that each went around her so she was bound against him as if by ropes.

There was nothing you could say against what they did. It was perfect, it was needed, in the dying scent of the flowers and the dew that came later while they slept. The way she laughed and opened her eyes for the first time that morning, dazed at being with him. There was nothing wrong. He knew that.

His mistake was to let her go. Standing up and pulling her wraps around her just before dawn, busy, distracted. She picked up the bridle from the ground, fussing with it, Caruso's bridle—why had she brought it? Had she been trying to find the loose pony? He took the bridle, hung it on her shoulder and wrapped the rein around her palm, folding her fingers around it. Don't lose it, he said. Worried that the family would be getting up, that they would miss her, discover her gone. His chivalry came back from his schooldays. He would escort her.

No, don't come. You mustn't come, she said.

He said he wanted to walk with her back to the camp, see her safe in bed. They had time. The moon was gone behind something. The light would come, but not soon.

But she would not listen. And away she went.

She never made it back to the camp. That is what he came to understand. But only after many, many years. She had not been there in the morning. They waited, and she didn't come. At first he thought she had found and ridden off on Caruso. Or gone with Humphrey. When Humphrey reappeared after so many years he came to believe she had lain down in the Snow Bowl somewhere along the narrow little foot track, tired, overcome, maybe not right in herself because of the explosion. She must have lain down and been hidden in the flowers and the hummocks of moss and the streams of water that ran through, and never got up. That is what he had come to believe. What Sam Gallant knew, and Gus guessed, was that it was her bones washed up in the Pity Plains a decade later. Not the horse. Her bones, her "carcass," and the bridle she had been holding. The horse was not there. That was the truth of it.

That was what Sam meant to say. Herbie got it, and he never told anyone.

Because how do you tell something like that?

Over the years he gleaned that the Hodgson party, what remained of it—the doctor professor and his man, Maxwell—had got onto the high pass that went toward the Pity Plains. They could have found help if they had made it there, but the Stoneys swore they never did. The camera, sitting in the snow where the trail met the cutoff to the pass, was proof.

So there you have it. The end of the Hodgson expedition: Isabel lying in the flowers; two men fleeing on snowshoes; everything else stripped away—the horses, the cowboys, the cook, the rocks, the young man, the camera.

Two guys on snowshoes. Do you know how hard it is to track a man on snowshoes? He can walk straight over the undergrowth whether it's willows or fire ruin. He can walk straight up a slope if he does it right. And he doesn't leave a trail. No one will see the footprints because when the wind blows, they are gone.

And Isabel. Many's the time he had an image of her, wandering, in her foolish tea party hat, tattered and ripped from its weeks living in the branches of a tree. Humming and talking to herself, stopping to pick a flower, twirling it, dropping it again. Oh, if he could cross the spaces as he once did, twenty miles in a day, sinking, sweating—the snow slumping in the sunny patches, turned to ice in the shady patches—running where he could, he might have reached her. But he came to know she was not out ahead of him. She was in a different season altogether.

There was a lot of snow up high. If that rain joined it and it all came rushing off the peaks, into the rills and valleys, it might just lift up those bones from wherever they were, shift them to some shelf where mud collected, a sudden wall of mud, stopping and containing them and pressing them down under a ton of wet clay. Or maybe they were not bones at all but the whole creature, many-celled, vertebrate, complex, caught in one instant of exquisite existence, preserved in perfect delicate detail, legs and fingers and digestive system, fossils for some set of scientists when this place has retreated back to a shallow sea, another five hundred million years hence.

ACKNOWLEDGEMENTS

In reading these pages for the final pass, I recall how many people I have spoken to, how many experts have been generous with their time and how many archives and museums have showed me their treasures. Who said writing fiction was a lonely job?

I am grateful to the Access Copyright Foundation for a research grant, and to the A.O. Wheeler Heritage House Foundation for an artist grant. I put both to good use among the rich resources of the Whyte Museum of the Canadian Rockies in Banff and the Glenbow Museum Archives in Calgary. Special thanks to Reference Archivist Lena Goon at the former.

I have consulted the website MB: Living and Writing the Early Years of Parks Canada (mbwilliams.academic-news.org), a digital archive made available by Dr. Alan MacEachern of Western University.

Jean-Bernard Caron, Curator of Invertebrate Palaeontology at the Royal Ontario Museum in Toronto, generously gave his time and allowed me to look at the museum's holdings.

I am most indebted to Professor Donald Smith, formerly of the University of Calgary, for his boundless enthusiasm, matched only by his knowledge of western Canadian history. His aforementioned biography of Long Lance informed my ideas of that character, and it was thanks to Donald's extensive files that I was able to see the CPR menus Long Lance wrote.

I would also like to thank, among my friends in the Bow Valley, Mary-Beth Laviolette, Douglas Maclean, the late Ralphine Locke, Dave Rencz and Nancy Townshend for conversations and insights. Don Gardner generously shared his knowledge of trails, old and new, and Chic Scott read the manuscript with the eyes of an expert climber and mountain writer.

I am grateful to the whole team at HarperCollins Canada, particularly Iris Tupholme and Lorissa Sengara for their editorial insights, and to the dauntless managing editor Noelle Zitzer. Alex Hurley of Inkwell Management has been unfailingly suportive. Thank you, all.

And finally, my love and thanks go to Nick for everything from coming along on hiking trips to glaciers to offering glasses of wine and careful reads.